Dream Chasers

An Inspector Green Mystery

BARBARA FRADKIN

Rende

D1410158

Cover art: Chris Chuckry

Le Conseil des Arts
du Canada
DEPUIS 1957

The Canada Council
for the Arts
SINCE 1957

Canada

We acknowledge the support of the Canada Council for the Arts
for our publishing program. We acknowledge the financial support of the
Government of Canada through the Book Publishing Industry Development
Program (BPIDP) for our publishing activities.

RENDEZVOUS CRIME
an imprint of Napoleon & Company

2nd printing 2008
Printed in Canada

13 12 11 10 09 08   5 4 3 2

Library and Archives Canada Cataloguing in Publication

Fradkin, Barbara Fraser, date-
          Dream chasers / Barbara Fradkin.

(An Inspector Green mystery)
ISBN 978-1-894917-58-2

          I. Title. II. Series: Fradkin, Barbara Fraser, date-
Inspector Green mystery.
PS8561.R233D74 2007   C813'.6   C2007-903844-1

The Inspector Green Mysteries

Do or Die
Once Upon a Time
Mist Walker
Fifth Son
Honour Among Men
Dream Chasers

One

Lea Kovacev's pen hovered over the scrap of paper on the kitchen table. What should she write? She hated misleading her mother, or worse, lying to her, but there would be no peace in the household if she told the truth. It was twelve years since they had escaped from Bosnia, but her mother still acted as if they were under siege, and all men were brutes out to rape them. Lea could barely remember those months, which had been harrowing by her mother's account, but in her own fragments of memory just hot, dusty walks and tedious waits. Now she tried to understand, to be patient and reassuring, but she had her own life to lead here in Canada. She was seventeen, with dreams to explore, freedom to taste...

And love to embrace.

All men were not brutes. There was one, so tall that she had to stand on tiptoes just to reach her arms around his neck, so strong that he could sweep her off her feet with one arm, yet so gentle that his hands upon her were like feathers ruffling in the wind. He was her dark-eyed, curly-haired Romeo, and she was his flaxen-haired Juliet.

Their love had to remain secret because their motives would be maligned and their passion misunderstood by others who staked a claim to him. But she knew it was all jealousy and fear. Fear of the intensity of their love and its power to influence him. To soften and distract him, to blunt the killer

1

edge the others saw as the key to his success.

But the secrecy only added to the thrill, and today no one would keep them apart. It was a hot, hazy afternoon promising one of those sultry, moonlit evenings in June when it was already warm enough to lie out on the grass under the pine trees, away from the clamour of beach volleyball and rock music that filled most of the park. She was wearing a white sequined tank top that barely skimmed her belly button and a low-slung denim mini-skirt. Beneath the skirt, a brand-new, very special, black satin thong.

She smiled as she flicked her blonde hair over her shoulders. Juliet for the modern world.

From the depths of her backpack, her cell phone rang. She hefted the bag onto the table and rummaged under her towel and bikini until she captured her tiny phone. Glancing at the display, she frowned. "Crystal calling..." This was the third time since noon that she'd tried to call. She would want to know where Lea was going and what she was going to do with him, but her curiosity was getting a little too personal for Lea's liking. Maybe she'd been wrong to let Crystal in on the secret. The girl had her uses, but the price was getting too high.

Lea slipped the phone back into her bag unanswered and returned to the dilemma of the note. Her mother was working both jobs today, so she wouldn't be home until after nine. For what Lea had planned tonight, she figured the excuse would have to cover her until at least midnight, preferably until morning. Best to tell her mother she was working on a play at a friend's house with a group of other Pleasant Park High School students, and it might be too late by the time the rehearsal ended to catch the last bus home. Lea's mother always freaked out when she was out on the streets late anyway.

She toyed with the idea of writing the note in verse, which

always lifted her mother's spirits, but her mind was too scattered to concentrate on rhymes. Instead, she scribbled the note, wording it as vaguely as possible and ending with a promise to call at nine to let her know if she was going to sleep over. Signing off, she added a flourish of xxox's, banished the twinge of guilt from her mind and slung her backpack over her shoulder. After one last quick trip to the bathroom to touch up her lip gloss and straighten the silver cross that nestled in her cleavage, she headed out the door.

The street, as always, was dead quiet. Tall trees loomed over the modest bungalows, and beneath their canopy, the air hung dank and still. A songbird warbled in the maple tree on their lawn, and a couple of honeybees darted among the rose bushes. Her mother's idea of heaven. No landmines, no drunken militiamen. Every square inch of this little garden was like a gift from God to her, even though her fifteen-hour workday left her no time to enjoy it. Sundays, her day off, were spent weeding, pruning and coaxing a rainbow of blooms from beds that circled the house.

Lea felt another twinge of guilt. She had her job at McDonalds, and during the summer she would collect as many hours as she could, but it still didn't amount to half the hours her mother worked, and the pay was a mere pittance in their monthly budget. Lea knew she should probably take on other work, even babysitting or tutoring, to help out, but instead she was going to spend the evening lying on the grass by the river, enjoying the feather-light touch of the most perfect boy in the world.

Mother had been young once, she thought. She had been in love too, before Dad died. Surely in time, she would understand.

*   *   *

The aging bedsprings creaked as Inspector Michael Green rolled over and opened one eye. Pre-dawn light bathed the unfamiliar room in pale grey. What the hell was that godforsaken racket? It sounded as if an entire army of angry fishwives was camped outside the window. What had happened to the idyllic country morn Sharon had promised? What had happened to sleeping till all hours with no alarm clocks, no radios, no early morning briefings at the station? Not even Tony, their energizer bunny toddler, was up yet, for God's sake.

Green lay in bed, trying to ignore the spring that poked into his back. Crows, he realized. Flapping and screeching in the pines overhead. They were soon joined by the warbling and chirping of other birds and the scolding chatter of a squirrel.

At the sound of the squirrel, Modo, their Lab-Rottweiler mix who weighed in at over a hundred pounds but thought she was a Chihuahua, began to crawl out from under the bed, where she had hidden when they first arrived at the cottage the night before. Being a Humane Society refugee, Modo did not handle change well, and the pitch darkness filled with alien smells and sounds had sent her into a panic. She had not even emerged for dinner, and all night long at every creak and thump in the cottage, her pathetic whimper had emanated from beneath the bed.

It had not been a restful night. But squirrel chatter was a sound Modo recognized, and since in the city it was her job to chase every one of them away from Sharon's bird feeder and up into the trees, she struggled out from under the bed to report for duty. Green slipped out of bed and padded to the cottage door. Modo bolted outside, stopped to relieve herself on the nearest patch of weeds, then looked back at him expectantly. All around her, nature was waking up, and she obviously figured it was high time he was too. Besides, there

4

was no way she was staying outside by herself.

After feeding her, Green hunted through their food bags for the Bridgehead French Roast he had packed, unearthed a battered aluminum kettle in their supposedly fully equipped housekeeping cottage, and brewed up a full pot of coffee. By the time it had dripped through, a salmon pink glow filtered through the trees in the east. Curious to see the place by the light of day, he threw on some clothes, took his coffee and, with Modo glued to his heels, slithered down the steep, overgrown path to the lake.

Sharon had found the cottage on the internet after a particularly long and exhausting week at Rideau Psychiatric Hospital, when she had thought she couldn't survive another day without a respite. "This will be a chance to catch our breath, read, take lazy walks and teach Tony to swim," she'd promised, with a dreamy glow in her eyes that he could not refuse. So far, the ancient beds, battered kitchenware and screaming crows did not seem worth the eight hundred dollars she had shelled out for the week of summer paradise, but then the price of paradise was high in the Rideau Lakes area, which was less than two hours drive from Ottawa.

He stepped onto the rickety dock and contemplated the surroundings. There were cottages on either side, pressed uncomfortably close but still empty this early in the season, with blue tarps over their boats and plywood over the windows. Weeds choked the shoreline and poked up through the rotting planks on the dock.

He perched on the edge of the dock, sipped his coffee and eyed the lake. It was glassy calm in the pink light of dawn. Wisps of mist drifted over its surface, and in the distance he could see the silent hulls of small boats. The serenity was almost scary.

Green knew nothing about the country. The summer holidays of his youth had been spent running up and down the back alleys of Ottawa's Lowertown, playing marbles in the dusty yards and tossing balls back and forth between parked cars. He was approaching his quarter century mark with the Ottawa Police, most of it in the gruesome trenches of Major Crimes, but before his marriage to Sharon, his summer holidays could be counted on one hand. Occasionally in a misguided spirit of pity, colleagues and friends had invited him up to their cottages for weekends. He had tried to enjoy the fishing, the camaraderie and the simplicity of country life, but inwardly he had chafed. No radio, no TV news, no take-out deli sandwiches at midnight, no wail of sirens or crackling of radios...

I'm a crime junkie, he thought, as he gazed out over the peaceful lake. A whiff of breeze rustled the trees, and far out, the plaintive trill of some bird echoed over the water. Sharon's right, he thought, I have to learn to relax, to appreciate silence, nature and the simple pleasures of my family's company. Maybe here, in this rosy magic dawn, I'll make a start.

That optimism lasted all of two minutes, before the first mosquito whined in his ear. At first he tried to ignore it, but then its friends arrived. Swatting and brandishing his arms in vain, he sloshed half his coffee down his crotch.

"Fuck this," he muttered and headed back up to the cottage. The swarm of mosquitoes escorted him. Inside, miraculously, Sharon and Tony were still sleeping. After changing his pants and replenishing his coffee, he sneaked up to the car with Modo at his heels again. She leaped in ahead of him and settled in her favourite spot next to Tony's car seat. Green turned the key to activate the radio, then fiddled with the buttons until he found an Ottawa station with a strong enough signal to reach this rural backwater. The cheery patter of the morning DJ filled the car.

6

Cradling his coffee, Green sank back in the passenger seat with a sigh of delight. Just in time for the six o'clock news.

He listened through the thumbnail reports of suicide bombings in Israel, tornadoes in Kansas and a minor earthquake in Indonesia before the local news came on.

"Ottawa Police have stepped up their search for a local teenager first reported missing early yesterday morning. Seventeen-year-old Lea Kovacev told her mother she was getting together with friends Monday evening, but when she failed to contact her mother or return home by midnight, her mother became concerned. Police do not suspect foul play but ask anyone with any knowledge of her whereabouts to call them."

Green's instincts stirred. Just over thirty hours had passed since the girl's disappearance. By her own account, she was getting together with friends. Seventeen-year-old girls dropped out of sight temporarily for all sorts of reasons. An impromptu trip, excessive partying, an undesirable boyfriend, or just the impulse to shake off the parental bonds for a while.

What was different about this case? What had caused the police concern, despite their official denial of foul play?

He reached for his cell phone, then hesitated with it in his hand. As the head of Crimes Against Persons, Missing Persons fell under his command, but a missing teenager was routine, even if the police had stepped up their efforts. There was an entire Missing Persons' squad with the power to ask for extra resources or support should the case merit it. They didn't need his meddling. He was on holiday.

He pictured the mother sitting frantically by the phone, waiting for the police or her daughter—anyone—to call. He thought about the other young women who had disappeared in Ottawa in recent years, about the desperate searches and ultimate heartbreaking discoveries. Was that why the police were concerned? Were there signs too eerily similar to those earlier cases?

Then he thought of his own daughter, so defiantly confident and invincible. A little shiver ran through him. Hannah was also seventeen, and because school wasn't quite finished, she was staying in the house alone for the first time since she'd come to live with them a year ago. Green had been reluctant to go without her, but in truth more out of distrust of her motives than fear for her safety or desire for her company. When Hannah had challenged him on it, Sharon had sided with her. Distrust her, and she'll make you pay, Sharon said. Trust her, and she'll try to live up to it.

Easy for you to say, Green thought now as he toyed with his phone, fighting the urge to call her and satisfy the ridiculous fear that had threaded through him at the news of the missing teen. Was Hannah safely at home, or was she out at one of those starlight parties she loved so much? He didn't delude himself. She had arrived on his doorstep at sixteen, defiantly trying to be thirty. He knew she smoked dope, slept around and probably flirted with the wrong side of the law. But did she know where to draw the line? Did she know how to heed her instincts for danger and keep herself safe?

In the end, he settled on a third alternative. He phoned Brian Sullivan. Sullivan was back as acting staff sergeant of Major Crimes now that Gaetan Laroque had gone off on stress leave. Sullivan would have no direct knowledge of a routine missing persons investigation, but if the police feared something worse, then the Major Crimes detectives would be working the case too, at least on the sidelines. Sullivan was Green's oldest friend on the force and could be trusted to understand his reasons for calling. There were not too many cops Green felt he could lean on, but Sullivan was the first in line. Besides, he had a teenage daughter of his own.

Sullivan answered his cell phone on the fourth ring, and to Green's surprise, he didn't even bother to tease him for checking in on his first day of vacation. "I was hoping you hadn't heard," he said.

"Why?"

"Because I want you to enjoy your holiday, you turkey. Your wife and son deserve that, even if you don't."

Green digested the implications. An early morning chill hung in the air, and he shivered. Hugging his fleece around him, he curled deeper into the seat. "It's that bad?"

Sullivan paused. "It doesn't look good. This is a nice girl, a good student just finishing Grade Twelve at Pleasant Park High School in Alta Vista. Never gave her mother any trouble, and she hasn't been heard from in thirty-six hours."

"Shit," Green muttered. Sullivan didn't need to say more. Alta Vista was the neighbourhood Sullivan lived in, Pleasant Park the school his own daughter attended. It was a dignified family neighbourhood of leafy old trees and sprawling split-levels, not some crime centre of the city. Green knew Sullivan was thinking of the other young women from similar neighbourhoods whose deaths they had investigated together in recent years. In too many cases, their only crime had been to be young, attractive and alone.

"Officially we're calling it a simple disappearance," Sullivan said, "and we haven't ruled that out. The mother is the overprotective type, so the kid may have just run off with some boy, and she'll get in touch with her mother when she comes up for air."

Green could hear the roar of traffic in the background and the sound of Sullivan drinking, probably his morning coffee. He'd caught his friend on his way to work. "You don't sound convinced."

9

"Well, her friends say she's not the type to let her mother worry like this. We know she lied to her mother about where she was going, said she had a play to rehearse, but there was no such thing. So she may have gone to meet someone secretly instead."

"That still leaves all of yesterday unaccounted for."

"Yeah. That's the worrisome thing."

"Any lead on a boyfriend?"

"Not yet."

Green heard the suspicion in Sullivan's tone. Neither needed reminding that when a woman meets with foul play, her male partner is the most likely culprit.

"That's why the media blitz," Sullivan added. "So if it is a case of innocent lovers running off, we're hoping one or both of them will come forward."

"Who's lead?"

"Ron Leclair took it over."

Green winced. Leclair was the sergeant in charge of the missing persons unit. In Green's opinion, he had his eyes too firmly fixed on the next rung of the ladder to watch what he was stepping in. However, if this became a high profile case, it could make his career. Provided the girl was found alive. Which meant Ron Leclair would pull out all the stops in his power to ensure she was.

"Have you got enough men assigned?"

Sullivan chuckled. "The guys back here do know how to wipe their asses without you, Mike. I'll tell them you've okayed whatever we need. But for now, it's MisPers' call."

"For now." Before Green could say more, the car door opened, and Sharon peered in. She didn't say a word, but the reproach in her dark eyes spoke volumes.

10

Two

Jenna Zukowski thought she'd made very good time, but when she arrived at Pleasant Park High School, she found the parking lot almost full and police everywhere. The media vans and cameras were being held at bay across the street by a cordon of determined police officers. One, a hulking bruiser with a Hitler mustache, stood at the entrance to the lot, snapping out orders to his minions. He stopped her as she tried to turn into the drive and leaned in her window, his eyes flicking over the car's interior. She felt her face burn with embarrassment at the jumble of fast food wrappers and coffee cups scattered everywhere, but beneath the peak of his black cap, the cop's face remained expressionless.

"I'm Sergeant Gates. What's your business here, ma'am?"

Jenna felt the familiar flush spread further up her cheeks. Her body's betrayal added fuel to her indignation. What were all these police doing here, intimidating innocent people, when they should be out looking for the monster who preyed on women in the streets? For she had no doubt Lea Kovacev was dead. The police were lying to the public in order to prevent panic, and probably to cover up their own incompetence, because they would never have called in this three-ringed circus if they thought Lea was a simple runaway. God knows, Jenna had never been able to get them interested in any of the cases she'd dealt with.

"I'm the school board social worker assigned to this school," she replied stiffly. "The principal called me early this morning and requested my help with the students."

The police officer's eyes remained expressionless. "What kind of help?"

The flush deepened, and she clutched the steering wheel to hide her shaking. "Supportive counselling, answering questions the students might have. When an event like this occurs, the whole student body tends to get upset, particularly those who knew the girl well."

"Our own officers will be conducting interviews throughout the day, ma'am. I advise you not to discuss any particulars with the students that might influence their statements, and if any of them have information pertinent to the case, no matter how trivial it appears, please direct them to one of our officers."

She inclined her head slightly, not trusting herself to speak through her outrage. Who's going to speak to me at all if they know I'm going to turn them over to the cops, she thought as he waved her through. Ever hear of client confidentiality, officer?

Inside the school, the secretary directed her to the staff room, where the principal, Mr. Prusec, had called a meeting. When Jenna entered, she was greeted by a sea of tense faces. She saw her own pessimism reflected in them.

"Above all," the principal was saying in his nasal singsong, "the schedule for classes and exams should carry on. The students need routine and a sense of normalcy, and even if they're upset, their exams will distract them and give them something to focus on other than their worries."

This announcement drew grim nods from some teachers and exclamations of disbelief from others. "What if they can't concentrate!" a young woman said. "It won't be fair to them."

"Then we'll take that into account when assigning their marks. And anyone too visibly upset to work should be quietly sent to the guidance office. We'll have all our guidance staff,"

Mr. Prusec paused to gesture offhandedly at Jenna, "plus our board social worker here, available to provide assistance. But we don't want a stampede."

"There are media and cops all over the place," said another teacher, whom Jenna recognized as Mrs. Lucas. Jenna had never dealt with her directly before, but she had a reputation as a tough, no-nonsense veteran. One of those fossils who'd been teaching since before Jenna was born. "The kids will have questions."

"I'll make a short announcement over the PA just before classes start, telling them what we know, which is essentially nothing at this point—" he stared hard at them in warning, "and informing them that if they have relevant information, they should let their teacher know, so that an interview can be scheduled with the police."

Jenna pictured the chaos that would ensue from that request. Breathless with apprehension, she jumped in. "I think teachers should just steer everyone to the guidance office and let us decide if the police should be brought in. Otherwise, if students have to approach the teacher in front of their peers, there will be all kinds of rumours, questions and pressure."

Mrs. Lucas fixed her with a withering stare. "I think we know how to speak to a student privately."

Jenna felt another flush building and fought it in vain. It was her Achilles' heel, betraying her self-doubt and undermining her attempts at professionalism at the very worst times. She was twenty years younger than most of the teachers in the room, and despite her MSW and her clinical training, few of them thought she knew a damn thing about human nature.

To add to her humiliation, it was the principal who rescued her. The perfect incarnation of white, male, middle-class domination. "Jenna has a good point. Direct all students with any kind of involvement to the guidance office. The police will be starting with routine interviews of all the students in Lea's classes, so exams in those classes will have to be postponed. Assign the students a study period." He paused. "And for the love of Pete, don't let them start talking about it!"

As the teachers filed out of the room, Jenna fell in step beside one of the guidance counsellors, an attractive young man with a goatee and a single piercing on his left ear. She knew he was married, with a baby adopted from China, but that didn't stop the tingle of pleasure she felt at his closeness. Of all the staff, she felt he understood the world as she did. No macho posturing there.

"It's difficult to operate in the dark," she murmured. "Do you know anything about Lea Kovacev?"

The man chuckled. "Well, you know how it is, we seldom see the well-adjusted ones. I think she worked with the newcomers' club in school."

"What does that do?"

"It's mostly for new immigrants, although kids new to the city can go there too. Basically it's to help kids make friends."

"Have the police condescended to tell us anything, even off the record?"

"Not much. They spent most of yesterday talking to her friends and trying to track her movements. So far we just know she went home after school and then went out again around four in the afternoon, with her backpack, a cell phone and a beach towel—"

"Beach towel! That's a clue, surely!"

The guidance counsellor paused in his doorway with an indulgent smile. "I'm sure they're following up on it. But there are a lot of beaches and pools in the city, and maybe she just planned to sunbathe in the park."

Jenna considered the implications. It was true that in the affluent neighbourhood of Alta Vista alone, there were probably dozens of backyard pools, but if Lea had gone instead to a public park or one of the city's beaches, there were always perverts lurking around hoping to satisfy their sick fantasies with the unsuspecting young girls who played there. A shiver passed through her. Girls had so little knowledge of—or control over—what they stirred up.

*   *   *

Green managed to wait until ten a.m. before he finally caved. Even in the likely event that Hannah was still asleep, ten o'clock was a perfectly reasonable hour for a parental phone call. There had been no further news releases about the missing girl, but Sullivan had assured him he'd call if anything developed. No phone call meant they were still slogging along, tracking down everyone Lea had ever talked to, following every lead and probably combing every public park within a five kilometre radius of her home. A huge task, but as time passed, hope was surely dimming among all concerned.

To his surprise, Hannah didn't even answer the phone. When the answering machine kicked in, he dialled again, thinking she might have been slow to wake up. Still no answer. He dialled her cell phone. Voice mail announced the caller was unavailable. He scowled. Hannah carried the phone around on her belt as if it were a lifeline and never turned it off.

He debated whether to leave a message. He and Hannah had been virtual strangers a year ago when, in a fit of pique at her mother, she'd come to live with him. Every seemingly simple decision took on layers of unspoken meaning in the complex dance of feelings between them. Accusations of interference and mistrust would fly, and the closer he inched to intimacy, the more prickly she became.

15

"Oh, just leave a message!" Sharon exclaimed in exasperation after fifteen minutes of listening to him dither. "Whether she gives you hell or not, she's going to know you care."

So in the end he left her a chatty message about their arrival and the news of the missing girl, signing off with a casual request that she give him a ring just to let him know everything was okay.

He took his phone with him down to the dock, where Sharon, in a valiant attempt to make a swimming area for Tony, was clearing weeds from the patch of muddy shoreline that had been billed as a beach. For two hours, he forced himself to build a sandcastle with his son, complete with moat and coloured stones to reinforce the walls. It was a hot, sunny day, and the lake was filled with the roar of speedboats and the high-pitched squeal of small children towed behind on tubes. So much for peace and quiet.

By noon, Tony's enthusiasm for coloured stones had waned, and a temper tantrum was brewing over the sandcastle that refused to stay standing. What do I know about sandcastles, Green thought irritably as the walls caved into the moat yet again. His parents had come from a small village in Poland, and from their limited immigrant perspective, beaches and water were dangers to be avoided. They had confined family holidays to picnics on the Rideau River in Strathcona Park, where they had all watched the ducks from the safe embrace of a distant shade tree.

With a cheerful announcement about lunch, Sharon scooped Tony into her arms and headed up to the cottage. Green picked up his phone and checked its battery, which was still fine. He dialled home. Voice mail. Hannah's cell phone. Voice mail. Finally he gave up and phoned Sullivan. To his credit, the man didn't utter a single gripe about interference.

"No breakthrough yet," he said, "but we're narrowing our search down to the most likely spots. Lea works at McDonald's, and she told a co-worker on Monday that she hoped the weather would stay warm, because she was planning to go to the beach. So we're focussing on area beaches."

Green did a quick mental inventory. Ottawa was located at the convergence of three large rivers, all of which had swimming areas. As well, the wilderness playground of Gatineau Park, with beaches on its three lakes, was only a short drive across the Ottawa River into Quebec. He visualized the city map. Alta Vista was bordered on the west by the Rideau River, with its magnificent beach at Mooney's Bay. He pointed that out to Sullivan.

"Yeah, and Mooney's Bay has the most parkland, so it's the best for parties. We're concentrating there, but according to her friends, she didn't like the crowds and noise there, so she preferred to go somewhere more private."

"Like where?"

"Anywhere in the park, as long as it was by the water."

Which doesn't narrow it down much, thought Green. Almost all the waterfront in Ottawa was parkland. "Did she have access to a vehicle?"

"Her mother doesn't own a car, so that leaves out the beaches in the Gatineau Park."

"Unless someone else had a car. If she has a secret boyfriend, they may have been looking for privacy."

Sullivan paused. "I'll ask Ron Leclair to alert the Sûreté du Québec and the RCMP, since strictly speaking, Gatineau Park is in the RCMP's jurisdiction. Meanwhile, we've got guys combing the beaches at Britannia and Westboro for her too. We've also got officers at her school trying to shake loose a clue about a possible secret boyfriend, but you know how teenagers are. Misplaced loyalties and all that."

Despite the blazing noon sun, Green felt a chill as he hung

up. Misplaced loyalties, conspiracies of silence, a pack mentality of us against them. How little he knew about Hannah's friends and the places she hung out. But he did know that, coming from Vancouver, she loved beach parties, and Westboro beach on the Ottawa River was a mere stone's throw from their house in Highland Park.

It seemed irrational to fear that there was a connection, but why the hell wasn't she answering her phone?

*　　*　　*

Jenna accompanied the anxious student from her office and glanced out into the main guidance room. Students, mostly girls, still filled every seat in the waiting area, and the guidance secretary was busy on the phone, fielding calls from parents. Despite the admonition not to talk to each other, the girls were excitedly sharing the rumours they'd heard and the tidbits of knowledge they possessed about Lea's life. None of them looked too stressed, she noted with relief, but then teenagers could hide a mountain of feelings beneath a flighty façade.

One girl sat apart, staring at her hands and twisting her many rings round and round her fingers. She looked harder than the others, her skin disfigured by acne despite a heavy layer of make-up, and her body stuffed into the trashy clothes that young girls thought they had to wear to gain the attention of boys. The school dress code had been circumvented by a loose-fitting, virtually transparent white overshirt, beneath which was visible a lacy tank top stretched over size D breasts and an expanse of tanned stomach accented by a silver ring through her belly button. Her blonde hair escaped her ponytail in a cascade of ringlets that framed her face. She'd be a very pretty girl if not for the acne, the ton of smoky eye make-up she didn't need, and the sulky frown.

Jenna walked over to introduce herself.

"Crystal Adams," the girl responded, accepting Jenna's hand in her moist, limp grip. Jenna ushered her into the little office the school had provided her. The door had a glass insert which prevented privacy, and the space inside was overtaken by a desk and computer, but she squeezed Crystal into the guest chair and contrived to look as welcoming as she could.

Crystal twisted her rings. Seven, Jenna noted with interest. Some were discreet bands of silver, others gaudy clusters of cheap stones.

"What brings you here, Crystal?" Jenna prompted eventually.

Crystal shrugged. "Have they found her? Do they know what happened?"

Jenna shook her head. "Did you know her?"

"Oh, yeah, we were friends. Kind of."

Jenna waited, not sure what to ask. Then she remembered her Rogerian training: when in doubt, reflect. "Kind of?"

"No, we were. But like, we weren't in classes together or anything, but we sometimes hung out. Like at parties and stuff."

"Are you worried about her?"

"Well...I guess."

"Any reason in particular?

"Well, you know, just that she's missing, and that she..." Crystal trailed off and twisted her ring savagely. "I'm wondering if I should go to the police. I mean, I don't want to get people in trouble."

"Do you know something about what's happened to her?"

In answer, Crystal sneaked a glance through the glass panel in the door and slouched lower in her chair, as if to hide herself from the students outside. "This is confidential, right? You can't tell anybody...?"

Jenna nodded and was just trying to formulate the limits of confidentiality when Crystal leaned forward. "I think she was going to meet someone. I mean, not that I'm saying it was him! He'd never do anything like that. But I think she might have thought there was more going on with him than there was. She was—like—obsessed with him."

"And he didn't feel that way about her?"

"It was just a fling to him, you know. That's the way him and his friends are. She's pretty, and she's sexy, and what guy wouldn't go for her? But he could have any girl he wanted, and he wasn't going to drop his whole life for her, you know what I mean?"

Jenna knew only too well. How many men had drooled over her own size D breasts and promised the moon just for a chance to get their hands on them? But women were just objects to them, one well-shaped body as good as the next. She'd told them all to go to hell.

"So what do you think happened?" she asked the girl.

"I don't know what happened. I phoned her cell a bunch of times the day she disappeared, because I wanted to tell her not to push it. But she never answered. Never returned my calls either." Crystal looked up, squinting through her eyeliner. "Do you think I should tell the police that?"

Jenna weighed the information the girl had provided. Beyond her speculation, she had very few facts. "Do you know the boy's name?"

Crystal stiffened. "It wasn't him. He had nothing to do with it."

"But then..."

"That's what I'm trying to say. If she didn't get her way with him, she'd have freaked out. She thought she could get any guy she wanted—she usually did—but this one was different. That's the point I'm not sure of. I don't know what she'd do if she got upset."

Jenna tried to make sense of her. "Then you're worried she's done something bad? What?"

"I don't know!" Crystal burst out. "You're the social worker. Run away? Killed herself?"

"Wait a minute. You think Lea might have killed herself?"

"Well, tried, you know? Taken a bunch of pills just to get his attention." Crystal squinted at her again. "It happens, right? I mean, my mother once—"

"Has Lea ever talked about killing herself?"

"No, but then she thought this guy was over the moon for her. Romeo and Juliet, she said they were. And those two killed themselves, right? I saw the movie."

Jenna sat forward in her chair, preparing to rise. "Crystal, I think you probably should talk to the police about this."

"But I don't really know anything."

"Maybe not, but if it helps find Lea..."

"They'll want to know the boyfriend's name, right? He's got a great future ahead of him. He doesn't need his name dragged in just because she's a drama queen." She shoved her chair back and groped for the doorknob. "I feel better. I don't think she'd kill herself. She's too full of herself for that. Even if she swallowed a bunch of pills, she'd be sure to end up on his front doorstep so he'd know what he'd done to her."

She yanked open the door. "Wait!" Jenna dived to intercept her and laid a restraining hand on her arm.

"She's going to turn up all innocent surprise once she gives him a good scare. You wait and see," Crystal said.

With that, she tore herself loose and flounced out the door.

*   *   *

Jenna spent the rest of the morning calming the fears of Lea's friends and classmates, but she found her mind wandering back to what Crystal had said. Not about Lea's tendency to play drama queen nor her possible histrionic suicide attempt, but about the boy she'd been involved with. A boy who had a great future ahead of him, who could have any girl he wanted, and who might view Lea's demands as a mere inconvenience. Perhaps even more, as an obstacle to his pursuit of utter sexual abandon. The more she thought about it, the more she worried.

At noon, she headed down to the staff room to join the clusters of teachers opening their Tupperware lunches. Lea's disappearance and the heavy-footed presence of the police were the talk of the room. She joined a table of three, including the scary Mrs. Lucas. No one paid her any attention, as a young man, clearly shaken, was voicing his outrage.

"The cops interviewed me three times. Three times! Once yesterday and twice today, the last time calling me out of the room in front of my entire class! That's how rumours start, I tell you. I just teach the girl. I hardly know a thing about her, but because I'm a man—"

"And cute," interjected a very pregnant, thirty-something woman. "Let's face it, Nigel, half the girls are in love with you."

"That's hardly my fault," Nigel exclaimed. "But apparently Lea told some of her friends she had a crush on me, and they told the cops. I'm telling you, I don't even dare smile at a girl."

Jenna rolled her eyes but kept her impatience to herself. Men always thought they had it so tough. Instead, she steered the conversation to her own concerns. "Does anyone know if she has a boyfriend?"

"Lea's had lots of boyfriends," Mrs. Lucas said. "She's a pretty girl, but it hasn't gone to her head. She still takes the time to be nice to everyone."

"That's refreshing," the younger teacher said. "So many girls won't give each other the time of day once they figure out the pecking order."

22

Jenna tried to picture pretty, outgoing Lea in the middle of a group. Would people look up to her or ridicule her for talking to so-called losers? The distant pain of her own high school tinged her thoughts. Along with another memory of a boy even more inept than she was, who had followed her around like a lovesick puppy because she had been nice to him. He had turned up at the end of her laneway, outside her window in the dead of night, and finally on the shortcut through the woods from school to her house.

Her pulse quickened. "Sometimes it's the quiet ones who adore from a distance that are the most dangerous."

Heads swivelled towards her around the table. Eyes narrowed. "You're talking as if something bad has happened to her," Nigel said.

"Well, aren't we all?" Mrs. Lucas countered. "I know Lea. I've taught her English for two years. She'd never leave her mother without a word. They were extremely close. She wrote me a journal piece once about how they escaped from Bosnia together on foot through the mountains after her father was killed by the Serbs. Lea felt a huge obligation to her mother, for all that she'd lost and given up so that Lea could be safe. She'd never cut off ties of her own free will. I agree with Jenna, she's been abducted...or worse."

That silenced the threesome for a moment. As the unspoken words "by whom?" hung in the air, Jenna's thoughts returned to the boyfriend Crystal had described. The police should be looking for this boy. They should be dragging him down to the station—preferably over hot coals, she thought, indulging a private fantasy about all the sleazeballs she'd known—and they should be forcing him to confess to the part he'd played in her disappearance.

"Does anyone know who she's going out with right now?" she asked.

Mrs. Lucas grunted. "I gave up trying to keep up with today's kids long ago. They seem to hang out in groups and try each other out as casually as I change clothes."

The pregnant teacher laughed. "That's not saying much, Pat! How many outfits do you have? A sweat suit for winter and a white T-shirt for summer?"

But Mrs. Lucas merely shrugged and brushed imaginary lint from her white T-shirt. "But you know what I mean? Sometimes it's hard to tell if they're dating or just friends."

"And sometimes it's not, the way they hang on each other," the pregnant one said. "I remember hearing she was dating one of the theatre students. But then again, actors and relationships...here today, gone tomorrow."

"But seriously," Jenna said, "if we could figure out who her boyfriend is—"

Mrs. Lucas's eyes narrowed. "You seem awfully focussed on a boyfriend. Do you know something we don't?"

Jenna felt her face burn. Damn! Just when she was beginning to feel more confident with the woman, her stare reduced Jenna to a small child again. "No, no! I just think...you know how boyfriends can be. Jealous, possessive. He could be the culprit."

Looking unconvinced, Mrs. Lucas snapped her tupperware shut and carried her coffee mug to the sink. "Well, it's a stretch. Much more likely that some pervert got her. The jail sentences they get, and the way these girls dress, it's a disaster waiting to happen."

The bell rang, and a collective groan rose from the tables as teachers pushed back their chairs, picked up their papers and filed out the door as if heading out to battle. Jenna sat alone with her thoughts. Mrs. Lucas could be right. Certainly there were enough perverts on the prowl for vulnerable prey. But if Crystal was right, Lea had been going to meet her boyfriend, who did not share her passion for the relationship. He was a successful boy with a great future ahead of him that was not to be derailed by the demands of a clingy, overly possessive girl. Within this school alone, how many boys would fit that bill?

Pleasant Park High School was a large, prestigious school with special programs for the artistically gifted, and among its students were the future authors, musicians, painters and actors of the country. Some never pursued their talents beyond high school, but others went on to headline on Broadway or write a Governor General's Award winning novel. Talent, promise—and massive egos—abounded at Pleasant Park. What if Lea's boyfriend had been among that elite crowd? She had been dating an actor who would certainly fit the bill.

Jenna lingered in the now empty staff room. It was really up to the police to track down Lea's boyfriend, but they were probably narrow-minded jerks with no imagination to see beyond the obvious. No kid would confide in them in a million years. But if she told them what she knew, they would demand to know her source, and her social work standards of practice were clear. Client confidentiality could not be broken just to spread a vague rumour. In fact, she could not even mention Crystal's name. But that wouldn't stop them from bullying her to get it out of her. Cops didn't give a damn about sensitivities or confidentiality, only about results.

She needed an outside source. If she could discover the name of Lea's boyfriend on her own, she could hand him over to the police without having to mention Crystal's name. Crystal would be protected, the boyfriend exposed, and perhaps, just perhaps, Lea would be rescued before he could do her any serious harm.

A woman had to do something, Jenna thought as she marched off in the direction of the drama room.

Three

Two o'clock that afternoon found Green inside the car again, hunched over the radio. The news on the missing girl was brief. Dozens of officers and volunteers had been dispatched to search the wooded areas along Ottawa's waterways, and a photo of the girl had been released to the public with an appeal for anyone with any information to contact the police. Superintendent Barbara Devine, the head of CID, had even secured a ten-second sound bite which she used to assure the public, with a ferocity and confidence she couldn't possibly feel, that the police had made the girl's safe return their number one priority. No expenses spared, no resources untapped.

Quite the attitude reversal for Devine, for whom purse strings, bottom lines and promotional prospects were usually the top priorities, Green thought. She must have been pressured by the higher-ups in the food chain, who were ever mindful of public image and positive press. After all, beautiful, blonde, innocent schoolgirls should be safe in their own communities.

All schoolgirls should be safe in their own communities, even blue-haired ones, Green thought as he dialled home once more. Still no answer. He was just leaving another message on Hannah's cell when Sharon opened the car door and slipped in beside him. This time she looked neither annoyed nor reproachful. Her gentle fingers caressed his arm.

"Why don't you drive into the city and check on her?"

He looked at her in surprise. Was she as worried as he? Was she saying his anxiety was more than the paranoia of a police officer who'd seen too much of the depraved side of human nature?

"It's only an hour and a half drive," she added. "You can be back before suppertime."

"But this was supposed to be our family time."

"I know." She flashed him a wry smile. "But Tony's having a nap, and he'll hardly notice you're gone. And Hannah is family too. You have to take care of this."

He hugged her, buried his face in her dark curls. "Thank you."

She held him. "Bring her back with you, okay? Kicking and screaming, if need be."

Taking nothing but his wallet, keys and cell phone, Green drove at breakneck speed up the busy, twisting Highway 15, grateful that his little Subaru had all-wheel-drive, but wishing it was equipped with lights and siren too. Eighty-six minutes later, he was weaving through the narrow, leafy streets of his west end neighbourhood. The house looked empty and undisturbed. Today's *Ottawa Citizen* still sat in the middle of the front porch where the delivery boy had tossed it, and the mail bulged from the box.

Green unlocked the front door and stepped into the hall. It echoed eerily, as if it had been abandoned for a week instead of a mere day. A shout to Hannah elicited no response, and a rapid search of the premises yielded no trace of her. He tried not to panic. This was the same girl who had climbed onto a plane in Vancouver on a whim when she was barely sixteen years old and had flown east to visit the father she had never known. The same girl who, upon arrival, had hung out on the streets of Ottawa for days without a word to either parent before fate had delivered her into Green's hands. She was no stranger to the grand gesture of liberation. But she was still an innocent girl, albeit blue-haired

27

instead of blonde, and now finishing her first year at an alternative high school, a far cry from your model student.

He debated phoning his father, who lived in a small senior's residence in Sandy Hill. Hannah had adored her gentle, old-world grandfather ever since their first meeting, and she showed him a sensitivity and affection she never shared with her father. But Sid Green was eighty-five, frail and partially deaf. Scars from the Holocaust had left him with a weak heart and a penchant for paranoia that no amount of security on Canadian soil could ever quite counter. Even a casual question about Hannah's whereabouts would send him spinning into panic. Until Green had exhausted all other avenues, he would not put his father through that.

He stood in the middle of her bedroom, looking for clues. Its severe black decor—Sharon called it eggplant, but it looked black to him—reflected a goth influence but she had recently added some brightly coloured posters of music groups other than Three Inches of Blood and Avenged Sevenfold. The clothing strewn across the floor was red, turquoise and even pink. Progress.

He looked for her school bag. It wasn't there. Nor was her cell phone or her school agenda book, despite a detailed search under the piles of books and papers that littered every surface. He did, however, turn up her little black purse and her wallet, complete with credit card, bus pass and student ID. Also in the wallet, he noted with resignation, was a fake ID with her photo and name, but a date of birth four years earlier that her real one. It bore a Vancouver address, leading him to wonder how long she'd owned it.

So she had taken her cell phone and her school bag, but not her credit card, bus pass or IDs, fake or otherwise. He tried not to imagine the worst. Perhaps she had just gone to stay at a nearby friend's house, where she would not need money or ID.

Perhaps they were using a friend's car. He realized with a pang how little he knew of her social circle. She rarely brought friends home, and when she did, it was only a quick stop between one party and another. Introductions, if they were given at all, were a perfunctory flick of her hand in his direction.

"Deedee, this is Mike," she'd mutter. Not father, not Dad. Even after a full year, he had not yet earned that privilege.

Hannah was an extrovert who ranged far afield in her pursuit of new thrills. The names and numbers of her many friends would be on her cell phone or in her agenda, both of which were nowhere to be found. But her high school was as good a place as any to start his search.

Norman Bethune Alternate School was a rambling Victorian brick blockhouse on a side street in Old Ottawa South. There was very little about the ivy-covered exterior to suggest that it was a school, which was probably intentional, and Green had to bang on the dark, heavy door several times before a woman opened it a crack to peer out at him. She looked like an aging hippie, with her grey hair tucked into a frizzy braid and ropes of beads cascading over her braless chest.

He introduced himself and held up his badge for good measure. She frowned and did not budge to open the door. "All the students are gone, Mr. Green. I'm just locking up."

Green stood on the doorstep feeling like a supplicant as he explained his inability to contact Hannah and his concerns in light of the missing girl. The woman looked unmoved.

"I'm sure she's just taking advantage of your absence to stay with friends," she replied, edging out the door. "Students here are quite independent, and we find it works best to allow them freedom of choice."

He wanted to strangle her with the beads that drooped over her scrawny chest, but he behaved himself. Politely he asked her name and made a point of jotting it down. Eleanor Hicks, guidance counsellor.

"Can you at least tell me if she came to school today?"

"She did not."

The woman spoke without a hint of concern, and Green forced himself to remain polite. "Is that usual for her?"

"For Hannah, yes." Hicks pulled the door firmly shut behind her and headed down the front walk. "You have to understand, Independent Learning Credits are just that, Mr. Green. Hannah directs her own pace and quantity, and she gains credit as she fulfills the assignments. I can tell you she's doing very well with that freedom. Independence suits her."

With Hannah, there is no other choice, he thought to himself. "I know that, believe me. I was like that too," he added, hoping to breach the barricade of her mistrust. Why do people always equate police with authoritarian control? "I'm not going to force her into anything, but I do want to know she's safe. I'm scared. Surely you can understand that."

"I'm sure she's safe. She has a good head on her shoulders."

"No one said Lea Kovacev didn't," he countered. She had reached her bicycle and was fastening her helmet. "Please tell me the name and address of at least one of her friends."

Her lips drew tight. "Student records are confidential."

"One friend. Off the record. I won't say where it came from."

Perhaps the anxiety in his tone finally touched her, for her disapproving scowl softened. "I can't give it to you, but I will speak to some of her classmates tomorrow when I see them—"

"Tomorrow! That leaves a whole night when she could be in trouble!"

She sighed. "All right, give me your phone number. I'll speak to one or two of the girls tonight when I get home and tell them you're worried. It will be up to them to call you if they want."

Green bit back his frustration and scribbled his cell number on his card. The wait was going to drive him crazy, but it was probably the best he could hope for without dragging in subpoenas, justices of the peace and the rest of the heavy artillery of the state, for which he had not a whit of justification.

*   *   *

By five o'clock in the afternoon, the Ottawa Police headquarters on Elgin Street was normally winding down, the day shift and administrative staff heading home and the evening shift already out on the streets. Today, however, as Green came off the elevator from the parking garage, a crackling energy gripped the second floor, where the major crimes squad was housed. Every desk was occupied, and several detectives were clustered around the corner conference table, hunched over their laptops. They looked up as he passed by, but no one registered surprise at his presence there during his supposed holiday. After almost fifteen years in CID, I guess I'm a fixture, he thought. For the fifth time since leaving Hannah's school, he checked his cell phone for messages, on the remote chance he had failed to hear its ring through the rush hour noise. Nothing.

Brian Sullivan was not at his desk, but Green spotted Bob Gibbs in the corner. The lanky young detective sat with his phone jammed between his ear and his shoulder, while his slender fingers raced over his keyboard. His fine brown hair stood in harried tufts, and his eyes were red-rimmed with fatigue. Gibbs was a committed, meticulous detective who would sleep at his computer if it helped solve the case faster. If anyone besides Sullivan knew the latest details about the missing girl, he would.

Green was just heading over towards him when the door to the stairwell flew open and Superintendent Barbara Devine swept in. She was dressed today in a surprisingly conservative navy suit, her flair for drama limited to a red silk scarf at her throat to match her crimson nails. Her eyes raked the squad room like a hawk searching for prey until they lit on Green. She skewered the air with a manicured nail.

"Mike! Just the man I need!"

A muffled snigger drifted across the room from an unknown source. Green turned toward her in dismay. "I'm just in here checking..." He hesitated. Devine didn't need to know about his domestic tribulations. As her subordinate, he operated on the principle that the less she knew, the better. "Something in my office, Barbara. I'm on vacation, remember?"

She waved a dismissive hand. "This will only take half an hour. Mrs. Kovacev is camped outside my office, demanding an update on her daughter's case. I don't have time. I'm late for an appointment already." She glanced at the elegant gold watch on her wrist as if to drive home the point, then her eyes took in his jeans and rumpled Bagelshop golf shirt. Her arched eyebrows shot higher. "Good God, Mike. I need a senior officer, but what kind of impression—"

"I'm on vacation," he repeated. "Besides, I don't know the case. Staff Sergeant Sullivan is the man to see."

She barely glanced around. "But he's not here, is he?"

"Then Detective Gibbs—"

"Gibbs!" She snorted. "I don't have to tell you the media is all over this case, Mike. We need a respectable profile. We can't have Mrs. Kovacev and all the other tearful mothers of teenage darlings filling up airtime on the six o'clock news. Which I guarantee will happen if she walks out of this station dissatisfied. You don't have to actually know anything, Mike. Just hold her hand awhile. You've done that so often, you can do it in your sleep."

Green ignored the hidden innuendo, choosing to assume she meant his kindness and not his seductive prowess. Even so, practice hardly made perfect when it came to his hand-holding skills. Faced with the tears and anguish of relatives, he always felt clumsy and inadequate. There was nothing he could do to ease their pain, except go out and catch the perpetrator responsible.

But before he could rally further protest, Devine pivoted on her stiletto heel and stalked back down the hall. "Get a tie on and wait by the elevator. I'll send her down."

Green did keep a tangle of well-worn ties in his desk drawer for surprises like this, but even a tie wouldn't salvage the golf shirt. Besides, he had more important worries at the moment. He dashed over to Gibbs, who'd witnessed the exchange, along with half the squad. Gibbs's lips twitched in a faint smile, which he quickly brought under control.

"Any breaks in the Kovacev case?" Green demanded urgently.

Gibbs shook his head. "Neighbours saw her leave the house around four in the afternoon, and a bus driver on the #149 bus recalls picking her up at the corner of Pleasant Park and Haig. According to the bus schedule, that would have been 4:15. He thinks she got off at St. Laurent and Walkley, probably to transfer buses, but we have no further sightings of her. We checked—"

Hearing the hum of the elevator, Green jumped in. "How many officers do we have on the case?"

"Between Uniform, General Assignment and our squad, thirty. Plus volunteers. The whole neighbourhood and several schools in the area are pitching in. If she's still in the city, we'll find her."

The door to the elevator slid open, and Green hurried over to greet the frantic mother. Whatever picture of grief and desperation he was expecting, his first reaction was one of surprise. Lea Kovacev's mother stepped off the elevator with her broad shoulders squared and her blue eyes clear. Even before he could speak, she extended her hand. "Inspector Green? I'm Marija Kovacev."

She was a tall, regal woman with silvery blonde hair swept into a bun at the nape of her neck and high, sculpted cheekbones that hinted at Slavic blood. Even devoid of make-up, her skin was porcelain-smooth, and only a faint charcoal bruising beneath her eyes betrayed her recent ordeal. If the daughter had inherited even half her mother's looks, Green thought, she'd arouse the fantasies of just about every red-blooded male who crossed her path. Under the circumstances, not a comforting thought.

Her handshake was firm and her stride unfaltering as she accompanied him back to his little alcove office. He unlocked the door, trying to remember how clean he had left it. Inside, his phone message light was blinking furiously, and a dozen memos spilled over his desk. Only two days away, he noted wryly, and already a week's worth of paperwork had piled up. He swept the memos into a stack and gestured her to the small chair that was squeezed between his desk and the door. She perched on the edge and propped her purse on her knees as if preparing to do battle.

"Mrs. Kovacev, I can imagine how worried—"

"My daughter Lea is a good girl."

The woman had a soft, lilting, Eastern European accent that reminded him of his own parents. He nodded. "I know. I want to assure you we're doing everything we can—"

"You asked if she took drugs, or if she has a boyfriend. You think she ran off with him because I am too strict. This is impossible."

He wondered how blunt Ron Leclair had been. It was the obvious theory for police to operate under, and more often than not, it would be true. But Marija Kovacev was in no mood to hear it, so he held up a soothing hand. "We don't know anything, Mrs. Kovacev. I know how scary this is, but when a teenager goes missing, we look at all possible explanations. It doesn't mean we believe them, but we don't want to rule out anything that might help us find her. We have dozens of officers out looking for her. We've been tracing the bus route she took, tracking down her friends—"

"I left Bosnia so that she would be safe. I have a degree in mathematics from the University of Sarajevo, but I work in a home for old people, and I clean bedpans so my daughter will be safe. If you don't find her..." her voice faded, and for the first time emotion quivered on her lips, "my life will be nothing."

"We will find her," he replied, feeling hollow. "I know it's hard to be patient, but in almost all cases, missing teenagers turn up safe and sound by the end of the week. We don't have any reason to think that anything bad has happened to her. No witnesses have reported trouble, no evidence has been found..."

She raised her eyes to his. Now, looking into their depths, he saw the panic she strove so hard to keep at bay. "Do you have a daughter, Inspector Green?"

He nodded, his answer stuck in his throat.

"And if a policeman told you about all the statistics and all the police who work on the case, would you be patient?"

He thought of the silent cell phone in his pocket, of his own desperate plea to the guidance counsellor at Hannah's school. "No."

A grim flicker of triumph lit her eyes. "Good. You are a better man than Sergeant Leclair. Because you know that when it's your daughter, and you have not heard from her since two days, and you know what I know about the savage nature of men, to be patient, to trust...this is impossible."

He had no answers for her, no hope beyond platitudes, but he handed her his card as a gesture of understanding, and

Marija Kovacev left his office seemingly lighter of heart for having shared her burden with him. Green, however, felt profoundly shaken, as if the enormity of her fear had only just hit home. He returned to the squad room to find it suddenly crackling with tension. Brian Sullivan was bent over his desk, talking on his cell phone and jotting in his notebook. His massive linebacker frame was rigid, and a deep frown furrowed his brow. The other detectives had stopped what they were doing, and all eyes were fixed on him expectantly.

After a brief conversation, Sullivan signed off, flipped his notebook shut and looked at the others. His face was grim.

"They found her backpack."

"Where?" a half dozen detectives asked in unison.

"Shoved under a park bench at Hog's Back Falls."

Green froze in the doorway. "Anything else?"

Sullivan shook his head. "One of the high school students found it. We've secured the scene, Ident's been called, and Uniform is focussing its search on the vicinity. I'm on my way out there." He looked around at the tense faces. "It could be good news, I suppose. The terrain is rough and isolated around there. She could have fallen, gotten hurt." He grabbed his jacket. "At least we know where to look."

Green stepped forward to intercept him. "I'm coming with you."

Sullivan frowned, as if surprised to see him. Green tried for a casual shrug. "To see what develops. I've been talking to the mother, and I promised to keep her informed."

Sullivan's eyes narrowed, and a slight smile crept across his face. "Enjoying your vacation in the country, Mike?"

Four

Sullivan flicked on the emergency lights, but even so, half a dozen police cruisers and the Ident van had arrived before them and lined the curb of Hog's Back Road just east of the bridge. Sullivan passed the official vehicles and pulled the Malibu into the parking lot near the edge of the falls. Already they could hear the roar of tons of white water plunging through the gorge.

Green climbed out and glanced around the park. The late afternoon sun glared harshly through the trees and glinted off the shiny silver roof of the fast food pagoda nearby. In all directions he could see meandering paths, grassy knolls and copses of trees. Hog's Back was much tamer than it had been in his youth, when the sheltered nooks had provided the perfect cover and ambiance for young lovers, and where the high rocks along the gorge beckoned to the daredevil divers seeking thrills in the churning water below. Now the paths were paved, the lawns manicured, and a three-foot ornamental iron fence ran all the way along the top of the gorge to keep the divers out. Knowing the determination and ingenuity of youth, he wondered how successful it was.

Hog's Back Falls Park was just one section of the ribbon of green spaces that ran along the banks of the Rideau River all the way from the heart of Lowertown to the sandy expanse of Mooney's Bay. Beaches, picnic areas, woodlands, ball fields and bike paths flowed one into the next, creating an outdoorsman's paradise but a patrolman's nightmare. Green considered the sheltering trees and hidden nooks, the dips and turns in the landscape. There were a thousand places for an injured girl to get lost, a thousand places for a killer to hide a body.

"We should seal off all of Hog's Back Road at both ends," he said. "And call in K-9."

With a brief nod, Sullivan set off in search of the duty inspector, who was in charge of deploying resources. Green watched a phalanx of officers from the Public Order Unit methodically combing the grounds in huge boots and grey coveralls, sweeping aside shrubbery with long probes and peering into the shadows beneath the trees. Green realized from their attention to detail that they were looking for physical evidence. This area had already been searched for the girl herself.

A uniformed officer directed him along the riverside path towards the bench beneath which her backpack had been found, about a hundred yards from the pagoda and framed by a semi-circle of tall pines that screened it from casual view. The backpack had been placed in a plastic evidence bin sitting in the path. Ron Leclair, the lead investigator from Missing Persons, squatted by the bin, flipping through a student notebook with a latex-gloved hand.

The bag's contents were spread out in the bin beside it—a wallet, a folded towel, sandals and three neatly folded articles of clothing, including a green cardigan, a white tank top and a denim skirt. Did that mean she was wearing nothing but panties when she disappeared? Green wondered. Or had she changed into a bathing suit? The folded clothes suggested they had been slowly and deliberately removed rather than ripped from her body in a moment of passion. Or rage.

The entire fifty-foot circle around the bench was cordoned

off, and a solitary officer dressed from head to toe in a white jumpsuit stood inside the enclosure, methodically dusting white powder on the painted wooden slats of the bench. Green recognized Sergeant Lyle Cunningham from the Ident Unit, and he breathed a sigh of relief. Ron Leclair was doing this by the book every step of the way, knowing that if this ever became a crime scene, or worse a homicide scene, they would need all the forensics they could get to nail the killer.

At the moment, though, it looked anything but. There were no signs of disturbance, no broken branches or gouged turf to suggest a struggle. The bench sat all alone on the bluff near the end of the gorge, overlooking the white water and the sun silhouetting the high-rises across the river. It was a perfect spot for a romantic tryst, with the backpack tucked safely out of sight in the tall grass beneath. It was also a leisurely ten-minute stroll across Hog's Back Road from the bustle and crowds of Mooney's Bay beach. What better place to escape for a moment alone?

The problem was that the romantic tryst had been two days ago. What had happened in the interval, and why in all that time would she not at least have put her clothes back on?

The obvious answer send a sliver of dread down his spine. The black ornamental fence was intended to prevent the public from diving off the bluff into the water, but when he peered over the fence, he spotted a well-worn path meandering along the rocky bluff on the other side, suggesting that many had already breached the barrier in order to get closer to the thrill. The roar of the white water masked the voices of the officers nearby, but from their gestures Green suspected their speculations were much like his. Had she gone over the fence and fallen? Dived? Been pushed?

He followed the fence to its end point downstream, rounded the end and clambered back up the path on the outer side to reach the rocky outcrop. Below him the water tumbled down in foamy chaos. Spray landed cool and slick on his skin, and up close, the roar of the falls thundered in his ears. Suddenly he realized how far the drop was. He clutched the rock face and shut his eyes as dizziness washed over him. Why hadn't he remembered his fear of heights before embarking on this excursion? Now the safety of the fence was some twenty feet away, and the eyes of half a dozen police officers were fixed on him.

He forced his eyes open and willed them down to study the rough grey rock at his feet. There were no telltale scuffs or drag marks to suggest someone had slipped or been pushed over the edge. Loose bits of gravel and broken glass lay undisturbed. Studying each square centimetre of the ground, he picked his way out over the rock until he was directly opposite the bench. Nothing. If Lea had met with tragedy, there was no sign of it here.

What then? Had she simply run off with a boyfriend? Been carried away by the romance of the moment and lost all track of time? Had they got so drunk or high that her judgment and memory went out the window? But later on, when the drink and the drugs wore off, surely she'd realize she'd forgotten her backpack and return for it. Surely she'd phone her mother.

What girl would leave her mother frantic with worry for two whole days?

Don't even go there, Green chided himself, acutely conscious of the heavy, silent presence of his cell phone in his pocket. Of course she might, because teenagers are idiots, whose parents' existence are barely even on their radar. Hours are suddenly days. How time flies when...

"Mike, what the hell are you doing out there!"

Sullivan's voice crashed through his thoughts. He tore his eyes from the ground in front of him to see Sullivan peering down over the fence. Sullivan was one of the few who knew

Green was terrified of heights, and his eyes were wide with astonishment.

To Green's relief, he sized up the situation immediately. "You want a hand over there?"

Green nodded. Sullivan vaulted over the fence and slithered down the slope, grasping at shrubs to slow his pace. Out on the clifftop, he made his way over to Green with sure, nimble strides that belied his bulky frame.

"It doesn't look as if she fell or was pushed over," Green shouted, more loudly than he needed, even with the roar of the falls. "There are no marks on the ground."

Sullivan squinted down into the foam. "There wouldn't be if she jumped, though. All her clothes were neatly folded like she'd taken them off to go in the water."

Green shuddered at the thought. "Suicide?"

"Probably just misadventure. We'll have to ask her mother if she was a good swimmer and liked to dive. The mother should know if her bathing suit is missing too. That will tell us if she set off with a swim in mind."

Green nodded, but a small inconsistency nagged at the corner of his mind. If she had been wearing a bathing suit, why hadn't her panties been found among her clothes? "Can we carry on this discussion back up there on flat land?"

Sullivan chuckled. "Sure. Want a hand?"

"No! Just walk behind me." No point in giving the guys more to laugh about. Green knew that, as a Jew with two university degrees and an aversion to blood and guns, he was an oddity in the locker room as it was. His knees were wobbling when he clambered back over the fence, but he feigned nonchalance. He glanced questioningly towards Ron Leclair, who was just closing the student notebook.

"Not much useful stuff in here that I can see," Leclair was

saying. "It's her English notebook, seems to be mostly class notes, doodling and lots of stuff that looks like Shakespeare."

One of the officers guffawed. "Oh, like you'd recognize Shakespeare if he bit you in the ass, Ron."

Leclair grinned. "Well, it's not Don Cherry, is all I'm saying."

"Any names, contacts, phone numbers hidden among the Shakespeare?" Green interrupted.

Leclair sobered as if only just remembering his inspector was here. "Not that I could tell. But maybe you should take a look, sir."

Green ignored the jibe. He doubted Leclair was aware of the hint of mockery in his tone. Plenty of police officers had university degrees nowadays, and even Green's masters degree in criminology was not unusual. Unlike Green though, for many it was less about knowledge than about gaining a toehold up the promotional ladder. Leclair himself was ambitious enough that he'd probably go home and read a Shakespeare play that night, so that he could sound better informed in the morning.

Green nodded distractedly. "I want Ident to give everything a thorough going over first," he said.

Lyle Cunningham looked up from his camera. He had identified one useable print on the left side of the bench where the paint was still fairly new and glossy, and he was focussing his lens for the shot before he lifted it. "I'll get to it tomorrow. I've still got lots to do at the scene here tonight. When it gets dark, I want to check the vicinity for semen and blood."

Green rifled through his memory quickly. It hadn't rained since Sunday, which was one blessing, although dozens of lovers and hikers could have trekked through the scene in the last three days. Finding and matching any bodily fluids was a long shot, but all avenues had to be followed up. He was grateful that Cunningham and his partner had been on call.

The Ident officer was an obsessive, infuriatingly meticulous pain in the ass, but the evidence he collected and the case he built would be beyond reproach.

"Thanks, Lyle." Green glanced back at the MisPers sergeant. "Anything useful in her wallet?"

"The kid is a packrat and a doodler. There must be three dozen receipts from her local ATM and Mac's Milk stuffed into it. It'll take me awhile to sort through it."

"Has there been any activity on her bank card in the last two days?"

Leclair shook his head. "The first thing we checked after her known friends. She had a VISA and a TD debit card. Neither has been touched. In fact, her bank account hasn't been touched since Saturday, and even then there was no big single withdrawal like she was planning to do a bunk. She has a nice couple of grand in there which could have financed a decent trip somewhere, but her mother insists she is saving it for college."

Green's heart grew heavy. Their missing girl was looking more and more like everyone's perfect daughter. Phoned her mother like clockwork, studied Shakespeare and saved her money for college. Despite the romantic setting here by the falls, despite the absence of a struggle, he had a horrible premonition about her fate. Along with a pretty good idea of who had sealed it. Next to finding the girl herself, they needed to nail down the existence of any special boy in her life.

*　　*　　*

Jenna Zukowski let herself into her apartment and tossed her keys and mail on the bookcase just inside the door. They teetered precariously on the pile already there before tumbling onto the floor. An obese ginger cat who was ambling over to say hello shot back behind the sofa with surprising speed. Jenna picked them up and plunked them in the corner of the kitchen counter, where a secondary pile was already forming. Who had the time for this? When you worked all day and had to find time for yoga, shopping, cooking and friends in the precious hours left, who had time to vacuum and keep the junk at bay? It wasn't as if anyone ever saw the place. She met her friends at movies or in pubs. This was her private space, and if it was a pigsty, who was to care?

She was feeling particularly annoyed after her futile afternoon. No one else at the high school seemed to want to confide in her or to speculate on the identity of Lea's boyfriend. When she hinted that he might be one of the school's acting students, they clammed up even more. Even the female teachers, from whom she'd expected a little solidarity. No one wanted to imagine that one of their perfect boys next door might have a dark side.

The drama teacher turned out to be Nigel, the handsome young teacher who'd been offended by the cops' suspicions earlier in the day. No way he was going to give the cops any other innocent victims to go after, he said. Jenna stayed around to watch the rehearsal of the musical *West Side Story*, which was being staged that weekend by his senior students. She noticed that the three leading boys were not only handsome but talented. They belted out their songs with a clarity and power that might take them as far as Broadway some day.

She wrote their names carefully on her list of suspects. After the rehearsal, she hung around the main door of the school, hoping to see what they did afterwards. None of them acted at all guilty, at least as she imagined guilty people should act. No agitation or preoccupation, no shifty eyes or furtive gait. They laughed with friends, talked about acting ideas, hugged each other and headed off to bus stops. Two of them linked up with girlfriends who were waiting outside the door and went off with arms entwined. Unless my Romeo is not just a killer but a cheat, I can scratch them off my list, she thought.

That left Justin Wakefield, who played Tony, the doomed lover in the story. He had a voice like honey-coated chocolate and dark liquid eyes to match. Not that Jenna was obsessed with chocolate, although over the years, many more of her pleasures had been derived from the luscious confection than from men. Justin had emerged from the stage door with his knapsack over his shoulder and his head bowed in a sulky scowl. He had barely acknowledged the hugs and the encouragement from the others in the cast and had slumped to the bus stop alone.

As if he'd lost his best friend.

Jenna had scurried back inside the auditorium, anxious to catch Nigel before he left. Even if the drama teacher denied it, she should be able to tell from his expression whether Justin was Lea's boyfriend. Nigel had not had too many kind words about Justin's performance throughout the rehearsal, which he called worse than a braying donkey, so she hoped he would not be too protective.

Her hopes were soon deflated on that score. Nigel was talking to the musical conductor and paused only long enough to glare at her. When she finally seized a break in the conversation to pose her question, he exploded.

"You are playing a very dangerous game," he snapped. "It's no business of yours who Lea's boyfriend is. If the cops want to know, they will ask. But I will tell you this, in the hope you'll take your nose out of it. Lea is not Justin's girlfriend. Plenty of girls would like to be, and I'm sure one of them is, but it's not Lea."

"Does she hang around with the acting crowd?" Jenna pressed. "Maybe one of them will know more."

He took a deep breath, as if trying to make up for his initial rudeness. "She hung around here, yes. Sometimes. She liked the story and wanted to understand how each character felt."

"Anyone in particular she hung around with?"

"I've already told the police all of this." He picked up his thick black binder and turned towards the door. "Look, the students are upset enough as it is. Let's just leave it alone and let the police do their job."

I would do that, she thought, if they knew what they were looking for. But who else besides her knew about the secret lover, the Romeo to her Juliet. In fact, wasn't *West Side Story* a modern-day version of the play, and wasn't the character of Tony the same as Romeo? How was that for a coincidence?

By the time she left the auditorium again, it was after five thirty, and the rest of the school was deserted. There was no chance to follow up on Justin or to inquire about other school leaders who might fit the bill. Musicians, artists, maybe even exotic poets. Tomorrow she would have limited time to poke around, because she was booked at another school in the afternoon, so at this rate she might solve very little of the mystery unless another student came forward to confide.

As was her habit upon arriving home, she grabbed a Diet Coke and flicked on the television in the background as she sat down with her laptop. Google was her best friend. It had an answer for everything, from techniques for dealing with cross-dressing twelve-year-olds, which they'd never taught her in social work school, to the real scoop on the latest man she'd met at yoga. She navigated its quirks with ease and typed in the words "Justin Wakefield Pleasant Park Ottawa". Those few specific terms should be enough to catch anything there was on the net about the boy.

There were some newspaper reviews of shows he'd been in and an article about a recent Ottawa fringe show, but best of all, the very first hit was Justin Wakefield's own web page. How easy was that? She clicked on the link and found a gold mine. Blazoned across his home page was the announcement of his acceptance into the National Theatre School in the fall. A quick check revealed the school to be the most prestigious drama school in Canada, with an impressive roster of alumni including Sandra Oh, Michael Riley and Colm Feore.

Justin's web page provided a list of previous acting credits, which to her untrained eye seemed astonishingly long for a boy barely eighteen. There was also an effusive bio which thanked his devoted parents for recognizing his talent early and making the move to Ottawa from the town of Prescott so that he could pursue his dance, singing and drama lessons. Jenna had passed through Prescott once when she took a wrong turn off the 401 from Toronto, and she knew it was minuscule. Justin Wakefield, poised on the brink of future stardom, had come a long way indeed.

Some testimonials from directors and acting coaches described the sophistication and charisma that shone through, despite his simple beginnings. His confidence and work ethic were a rare treat among today's spoiled and insecure stars, they said. Jenna recalled the scowl on his face earlier in the day when the director Nigel had criticized his focus and lack of energy. "Where are you today?" Nigel had said.

With the opening night of the show less than a week away, could it be that mentally he was somewhere else, Jenna wondered? Reliving the last moments of his girlfriend's life?

Lea Kovacev's name intruded into her hearing, and she glanced up to see the six o'clock news just beginning. The camera panned over a scene of rolling parkland, police cars and yellow tape before zeroing in on a group of officers in dark grey coveralls with POLICE in large white letters across their backs. They were poking at the underbrush with long poles.

Jenna froze, dread crawling down her spine.

"We have yet to receive official confirmation," the local reporter was saying. "However, an anonymous source within the police services here told CTV News that a backpack has been found somewhere within the Hog's Back Park, and although police are waiting for formal identification, it seems likely from the description that it belongs to the missing teenager Lea Kovacev. She was reported to be going with friends to a beach, and just across the road, a few hundred yards away is Mooney's Bay Beach—" the camera cut away from the reporter's face to a broad, crowded expanse of beach, "a popular gathering spot for teens. Numerous sports such as tennis, ultimate frisbee and beach volleyball are played there, and close friends describe Lea as an athlete active in several high school sports. There is no word yet on the whereabouts of Lea herself, but police are optimistic that this discovery will narrow down the search."

Jenna shut her laptop in a trance. She had just had an epiphany. Sports! That was another field in which a young person could go far. Scholarships to university, berths on the Olympic team... For a young athlete on the rise, the sky was the limit in money and in fame. Jenna was going to have a very busy morning tomorrow, not only following up on the disconsolate Justin Wakefield but also ferreting out the star athletes who might have turned Lea's head.

*   *   *

Once the media broke the news about the backpack, Green realized someone had to get to Lea's mother before the woman came racing over to Hog's Back in a full-blown panic. The news leak had caused a small crisis in the police ranks, and Ron Leclair was frantically trying to stifle its source while still fielding directives about the search. In any case, Mrs. Kovacev's panic was unlikely to be soothed by the sight of the Missing Persons squad leader on her doorstep. The only other ranking officer, Brian Sullivan, was busy coordinating assignments with the duty inspector. Green considered sending him. Sullivan had an almost magically soothing effect on distraught victims, especially female ones. His very bulk inspired confidence, and his large square hands could be remarkably gentle.

Yet Marija Kovacev had not met Sullivan, and the sight of a large, official-looking stranger appearing at her door would be sure to frighten her. Besides, no matter how inept he was at support and sympathy, it was Green himself that she trusted.

Since Alta Vista was only a short drive away, he commandeered one of the patrol cars and drove to the Kovacev house. For a brief moment he sat in the cruiser, studying the neat facade and gathering his thoughts. Long evening shadows shrouded the street, blurring the details, but Green could discern a brick bungalow identical to hundreds across the city, built in the early fifties to accommodate the vets returning from the Second World War. But Marija Kovacev had made the most of the tiny box. A shaft of sunlight illuminated fresh white trim and lush, colourful flower beds that would have made Sharon green with envy as she wrestled their unruly, overgrown perennial weed patch into some semblance of style. It was a house tended with extraordinary care, by a woman grateful to be here, he thought. Sadly he picked up the evidence bin and got out.

When he rang the bell, the door flew open as if Marija Kovacev had been standing just inside. Her eyes widened, and she pressed her fists to her chest. Hastily, he held up his free hand in a reassuring gesture.

"We haven't found her," he said. "But we've found what we believe to be her backpack."

"Where?"

"By a bench at Hog's Back Falls."

"Oh! A favourite place!" She drew herself tall and sucked breath into her lungs noisily, as if struggling for calm. "But what about Lea? Where's Lea? Are you looking...?"

"Yes, we're looking." Spotting a media van headed down the street towards them, he took her by the elbow with his free hand. "Let's go inside. I'd like you to look at the items in the bag, to see if you can identify them."

Inside the door, she turned to him. "Your shoes—" She checked herself with an impatient shake of her head. "Ach! What does it matter?"

A half dozen shoes were aligned in a neat row on a mat inside the door. Understanding her force of habit, he kicked off his sneakers and padded in his stocking feet across the immaculate although somewhat worn cream carpet. For an absurd moment, he was grateful that for once his socks had no holes in the toes. The living room had the same immaculate but worn look, with mended floral slipcovers and an ornate wooden crucifix over the sofa. He placed the bin on the coffee table and pried off the lid to reveal the contents, all now safely encased in plastic evidence bags.

Marija peered into the bin. Clutching her hand to her throat, she sank onto the sofa beside it. "What happened to her?"

"All the clothes were neatly folded." As you taught her, he thought to himself. "There were no signs of trouble or struggling, nothing to suggest she was hurt or taken by force. We think she left there voluntarily."

"But why? Where did she go?"

"We don't know yet. But we've got every available officer searching the beach, the park and all along the shoreline. We've brought in our canine unit too. As soon as anyone learns anything, I'll let you know." He paused and gestured to the bin. "But you can help us figure out what she might have been doing. Are all these items of clothing hers?"

She nodded vigorously.

"Is there anything missing? Except a white tank top, which we retained for the canine unit. And a notebook, which we took down to the station for analysis."

She fingered the bags and rooted around between them. "Her...ah, bra and panties."

Green recalled the skimpy white tank top. No nubile seventeen-year-old girl would even consider wearing a bra underneath, even if it could fit. But he sensed Marija was uncomfortable enough as it was. "What kind of bra and panties did she wear?"

"White. I always buy her white. Perhaps she is wearing them?" She shook her head almost angrily, as if rejecting the evidence of her senses. "No. Lea would not leave her clothes and go away only with bra and panties."

"What about a bathing suit? Did she own one?"

"She has three bathing suits. She loves swimming."

"Can we look at them? See if any are missing?"

She seemed to recover some composure at the possibility her daughter was not running around half-naked. Rising, she led the way down the narrow hall to a tiny bedroom at the back. It was freshly painted in Wedgwood blue, with matching blue flowered curtains and duvet—a marked contrast to Hannah's "eggplant"—and to Green's amazement, her clothing was all neatly folded in her drawers. The girl was abnormal!

Marija emptied the contents of the top drawer on the bed and began to sort through the lingerie, all of it delicate but a practical white. She set aside first a red Speedo then a shapely black one-piece with virtually no back. She frowned.

"Her new bikini," she exclaimed in dismay. "It's not here. I don't like it, and I tell her that, but..." She shrugged in resignation. "Recently she wants to dress like all the other girls."

Green made a mental note. Romantic setting, warm summer evening, sexy bikini... This was all fitting together. "What colour is it?"

"Yellow and black. It's very little, only covers..." Her voice faded awkwardly. "Lea says it is not good for swimming."

I don't think swimming was foremost on her mind, Green thought. Marija had obviously made the same deduction, for she flushed as she busied herself folding the items back into the drawer.

"Is she a good swimmer?" he asked.

She nodded. "She is good at many things. She took lessons in the public pool."

"Diving too?"

Marija looked up from her folding, startled. "What?"

"Does she like to dive from the high diving board?"

Marija frowned, and Green could see her trying to make sense of his question. Suddenly, fear raced across her face. "The falls? You think..."

"I don't think anything. I'm just looking at possibilities."

Marija pressed her hand to her mouth. The stark panic in her eyes gradually died as she wrestled her emotions under control. Reason crept back in, and she shook her head. "No. Lea loves to swim, but she's careful. She's a lifeguard, and she knows the dangers of water. Never."

Unless she was so drunk or high she threw caution to the wind, Green thought grimly. Teenagers did foolhardy things all the time, believing in their utter invincibility, when in fact the human body is very fragile indeed. Before Marija Kovacev could make the same observation, he focussed her on practical details.

"Is there anything else missing that may give us a clue?

Even something fairly ordinary?"

She had moved from the lingerie drawer to straightening the knickknacks on the top of the dresser. A photo of a man in a silver filigree frame, her father perhaps, two hand-painted ceramic dolls, a Swiss cuckoo clock, a carved wooden jewellery box and an assortment of creams and make-up containers. She ran her hand lovingly over the jewellery box as she considered his question.

"Sergeant Leclair asked me the same question, and police searched all through this room yesterday, looking for clues. They even took her cell phone bill to check her records." She broke off with a sharp intake of breath. "Her cell phone! It should have been in that bag! She carries it everywhere. Possibly she took it with her where she went?"

"Does the bikini have a pocket?"

The brief flare of hope died in Marija's eyes. "No, there is not cloth for that."

Then where would she carry it? Green thought. She had left all her clothes and even her wallet with all her bank cards. Clearly she had not planned to go very far or stay away very long. Moreover, if she had gone for a swim, she would certainly not have taken her phone into the water. Not with the cost of the latest little gadgets. A further thought struck him.

"Does her cell phone have a camera or a video?"

Marija nodded. "I bought it for her birthday in April. The salesman said it had all the best technology. I can't understand how to operate it, but Lea was thrilled. She took pictures of everything."

She smiled faintly at the memory, obviously failing to see the sinister connection between pictures, panties and the missing cell phone. But Green spotted it, and his sense of foreboding grew.

Five

At six thirty the next morning, Ruth Mendelsohn left her house in Old Ottawa South with her Nova Scotia duck tolling retriever. She crossed Billings Bridge, which spanned the Rideau River about four kilometres north of Hog's Back Falls. By the time the river reached the bridge, it slowed to a languid pace as it meandered through marshy bays along the shore. From the bridge, Ruth spotted an official-looking Zodiac in the middle of the main channel. Not giving it much thought, she walked her dog up the bike path beside the river, relishing her early morning coffee and the chirping of the songbirds in the trees. This was her favourite time of day, before the roar of cars blocked out the birds and the breakneck blur of commuter cyclists transformed the bike path into a Tour de France circuit. Once they were far enough from the traffic, she glanced around and surreptitiously slipped off her dog's leash. He bounded off across the grass towards the shore. Ducks quacked and flapped angrily out of reach, but for once Digby had no interest in them. Instead, after snuffling excitedly along the shore for a moment, he disappeared behind an overgrown alder and began to bark furiously. Ruth recognized his high-alert, alien-invasion bark.

Shouting at him in vain, Ruth hurried towards the shore, swearing as the coffee sloshed out of her cup and spilled down her shorts. When she rounded the bush, she saw him in the shallow water at the river's edge, barking at the police team out on the river. Ruth's first reaction was guilt, for dogs were not allowed off-lead in this park, let alone in the water. She tried to grab his collar, but he danced further out of reach. Her sandals sank into the wet mud.

Her second reaction, once she'd absorbed the diving gear and the waterproof yellow clothes, was that this was about the missing girl. They were dragging the river for her body. Although they hadn't acknowledged Digby's presence, the ear-splitting barking could hardly be improving their focus.

Digby, however, was not to be reassured, forcing her to wade ankle deep in muck to secure his collar. As she leaned forward to snap on his leash, trying not to think about the turtles and mud-dwelling creatures that might be tempted by her toes, she caught sight of a yellow and black object coiled around a reed. At first she thought it was some exotic snake, and she recoiled with a small shriek. On closer inspection, she realized it was cloth, and when she fished it out of the water, she saw it was the skimpiest bikini bottom she'd ever seen. She pictured it stretched over her own expansive tush, and the unflattering image made her chuckle.

Don't suppose anyone even missed this, she thought. Then she raised her head to consider the men combing the river bottom just off shore. What were the odds, she wondered? The bikini wasn't remotely like the description of the girl's clothes reported in the media, yet it looked almost brand new and showed no signs of fading or rot from being in the water for long.

"Hey!" she shouted to the men in the water, brandishing the sodden bikini. "This was in the water. Could it be important?"

The driver of the boat looked over at her with an annoyed frown that vanished the instant he saw her find. He got on the radio, and within seconds he gestured to her urgently. "Stay in the water exactly where you found it, ma'am, and wait there. An officer will be right there."

Ruth stared at the slip of clothing in dismay. The police reaction told it all. They believed the girl had drowned wearing this bikini. Only now, when they found her body, the poor girl would be nearly naked.

The police responded very efficiently from that point, taking her statement and her contact information before sending her firmly on her way. Police in dark coveralls swarmed the marshy area by the alders, and others fanned out along the water's edge up towards Hog's Back. She could see similar activity on the north bank of the river, and she shuddered. She'd lived in her old brick house by the Rideau River almost thirty years. It was a tame river, at least within the city, since its force had been blunted by dams and canals. Small children frolicked in its waters, along with the frogs and ducks. She couldn't remember the last time someone had drowned in the Rideau, unlike its larger and wilder sisters, the Ottawa and the Gatineau. It seemed impossible that a girl in her prime, especially a strong swimmer as the papers reported, could have died here.

* * *

Sullivan phoned Green with the news at seven thirty. Green had managed a fitful night's sleep and had been up since dawn, preparing to do battle once again with Hannah's school. The news hit him like a sledgehammer in the chest.

"We've set up a command post in the parking lot by Billings Bridge," Sullivan said, "and the dive team are now concentrating their search on the stretch of the river downstream of the falls. We've got a local expert on the topography and currents of the river coming to meet with us at the CP. MacPhail's also coming to check water temperature and perform his magic calculations on the buoyancy of the body...stuff like that."

Green absorbed the news about the forensic pathologist's involvement grimly. "Has anything been released to the media?"

"Not yet."

"Good. Hold off until we have something." Green didn't bother with the qualifier "if". Lea Kovacev was at the bottom of the river, and it was a matter of time before the divers found her, or her body bloated enough to float to the surface. "I need to inform the mother, so make sure nothing leaks."

"Nothing will, unless the woman who found the bikini talks. But the press are circling like vultures."

After he hung up, Green glanced at his watch. Hannah's school started at nine o'clock. He still had an hour in which to check out the latest news from the search scene and speak to Lea's mother before he could intercept his daughter at school. Fortunately, her school was located in Old Ottawa South, a mere five minutes drive from Billings Bridge.

Although the challenge of coordinating the different teams on the case—the Ident unit, the ground and water search teams, K-9—fell to the duty inspector, the investigative aspects were still technically in the hands of the lead investigator, Ron Leclair. The case would not officially become a major crimes case until a body was found and the coroner ruled death to be suspicious. But Leclair was astute enough to recognize the potential for disaster in any misstep on his part and seemed genuinely grateful when Green turned up to check out the situation.

Green realized why once he'd waded through all the media trucks in the Billings Bridge parking lot and caught sight of not only Superintendent Barbara Devine, decked out in a photogenic lime green pantsuit, but also the police chief himself in full dress uniform. They stood before a phalanx of reporters. Lea Kovacev's plight had caught the imagination of the city. Green swore under his breath. Not only would every Tom, Dick, and Harry flock to the river's edge in the hope of finding the next clue—the bikini top, perhaps—but Marija Kovacev was going to learn the worst possible news as a chatty, late-breaking news byte on some local TV morning show.

He barely had time to check out the specialty teams and confer with the duty inspector before his fears were confirmed. A cab pulled into the parking lot, and Marija Kovacev leaped out, hurling some money in her wake. She raced wide-eyed through the crowd, accosting everyone in uniform before her eyes settled on Green. He drew her hastily out of earshot of the media.

"We haven't found her," he said before she could draw breath. "There's still hope, but I think you should be prepared."

She tore free of his grasp. "No! She's a good swimmer! That bathing suit—it falls off at the first jump."

"We're looking everywhere, and we have an ambulance standing by if we need it. But meanwhile, is there someone I can call for you? A family member?"

She was shaking her head vigorously. "No family."

"A friend then? I know how hard it is to be alone, just waiting for the word."

"I am not waiting. I look all night. I phone every person who is her friend, I went to her work and I walk on all the streets. Today I will go to her school. I will look through her locker—"

"The police did that."

"But they don't know what they look for. Names, pictures, poems. Lea's mind is always going. Imagining, creating. She write little poems—just pretty words about her thoughts— but I know somewhere in them are some..." Marija waved her hand impatiently. "What is the word? Clues? Where she would go, if she has a secret boyfriend..." Her chin quivered.

"Maybe your Sergeant Leclair is right. I pray to God that he is right. I was too strict, I keep her too close to me, and she can't tell me about her new boy. I pray she is away with him."

Green vaguely registered her new-found conversion to hope and recognized the desperate denial that fuelled it. His mind was caught up in her earlier words about Lea's creative bent. Of all the school books Lea could have taken to her romantic tryst, she had taken her English notebook, complete with doodles, notes on Shakespeare and poems. That notebook was now awaiting forensic examination by Lyle Cunningham. Lyle would be looking for fingerprints and bodily fluids. It would never in a million years cross his meticulous mind to look for hidden clues in a verse of poetry. Clues to her dreams and plans.

Clues to a secret lover, perhaps?

*　　*　　*

Jenna Zukowski drained the dregs of her Tim Hortons double-double and tossed the cup onto the back seat just as she turned into the Pleasant Park parking lot. She was still only half awake, seven thirty being an insanely early hour to be arriving at work, but she wanted to catch the school athletic practices to see if there were any likely candidates for her suspects list. Sports had never been her forte; beyond the obligatory high school gym classes and a woman's self-defence course at university, she'd always given physical exertion a wide berth. She could not grasp the appeal of whacking some stupid ball around a court or field, and the thought of sitting through several hours watching someone else do it held even less appeal. Yet to judge from the hockey madness that had gripped the whole city in the last month of the Stanley Cup playoffs, perfectly reasonable people went nuts over it, and a talented sports superstar could make more in a season than she could ever hope to make in a lifetime of humanitarian service.

She parked the car and headed towards the sports field, where she could see a clump of boys running around the track. They wore thin nylon shorts and sleeveless shirts and kept up a long, steady stride. Even at a distance she could see the sweat soaking through their shirts. Already at this hour, the sun packed some punch, threatening another humid day.

She veered over towards two middle-aged men who were sitting in the bleachers, baseball caps pulled low over their eyes against the sun. One was watching through binoculars and yelling at someone in the group to "pick up your fucking feet!" The other had a clipboard in his hand and a whistle dangling from his mouth. The official coach, she decided. His gaze remained on the track as she approached, but the other man lowered his binoculars and swivelled to watch her. She could see his eyes travel the length of her body before settling on her chest. She felt her cheeks burn. "Moron," she muttered, instinctively tensing up.

She had formulated an admittedly lame opening question about how the sports students were coping, but the more the man leered, the more tangled her tongue became. When she began climbing the bleacher stairs, the lecher punched the coach lightly on the arm and smiled broadly, showing a crooked row of nicotine-stained teeth.

"Hey Ken, this may be your lucky day."

The coach pulled his eyes from the track and turned to her with a distracted frown. On closer inspection, she saw that he was not much older than she was, perhaps thirty at the most, but years of overeating and inaction had given his flesh a doughy look. In contrast, the older man's stubby body rippled with muscles, each one proudly defined by the soft lines of his black silk shirt. A bodybuilder, she thought with disgust. The guy gets better all the time.

The coach removed his whistle from his lips. "Can I help you?"

"And if he can't, maybe I can," black shirt said.

"Put a sock in it, Vic." The coach rolled his eyes. "Don't mind him."

"I'm looking for the gym teacher," Jenna said, suddenly hoping neither of them fit the bill.

"Your lucky day too, sweetheart," Vic said. "You found him."

"One of them, at least," the coach amended. "I'm Ken Taylor."

Jenna introduced herself, and before she could get out the first word of her speech, Vic folded her hand into a hearty grip. His thumb stroked her hand. "Pleased to meet you, Jenna Zukowski. Social worker, eh? Don't mind me saying so, but you hardly look old enough to be out of high school."

She felt the red extend from her toes to the roots of her hair. She yanked her hand free. Ken smiled at her sympathetically. "Ignore him. You have something to discuss with me?"

"Yes, but...well..." She struggled to untangle her tongue. "It's about Lea Kovacev."

"Oh, is there news?"

"No. At least not that I know of. But I'm concerned about her friends and how they're coping, whether they need support..." She trailed off.

"As far as I know, all her friends have been taken care of. Guidance made a big push yesterday to touch base with them."

"Yes, I was helping with that. But it struck me that it was mostly girls who came down to see us. Girls have an easier time talking about things, expressing feelings, asking for help."

Ken smiled drily. "Whereas boys go out and punch someone? That's what you mean?"

"Well, no. I mean, not punch someone, but bottle it up. Pretend everything's cool and under control." Vic muttered something under his breath. Sensing a hint of mockery, she turned to glare at him. "Suicide statistics among young men back me up on that."

"You're right, you're absolutely right," Ken interjected. "But I've been monitoring the boys in my classes to make sure that if I see any hint of trouble, I speak to them. They may not go down to Guidance, but they talk to me privately."

"And were there any? I mean, boys that you were worried about?"

Ken frowned at her thoughtfully for a moment. "Not unduly," he said eventually. Then he glanced at his watch in dismay and shoved his whistle in his mouth. Waving his arms, he blew three blasts that left Jenna's ears ringing. Through gritted teeth, she persevered with her script.

"Do you know if any of the boys were especially close to her? Boyfriends or ex-boyfriends? Those will be the ones in the most distress."

Ken continued to wave as he started down the stairs. "I don't pay attention to that."

Jenna followed him, aware of Vic uncomfortably close behind her. "She must have had boyfriends. She was a pretty girl."

Ken stopped abruptly and swung on her. "Was? Are you suggesting she's dead?"

"No, no! Of course not! But I mean, it's worrisome, don't you think?"

"I don't think anything," Ken retorted. "And don't you go putting that kind of thought into the kids' minds either!"

"Whoa Kenny, easy now," Vic said. "I think Jenna's just saying what we're all thinking. Right? Just preparing ourselves. In case. In the sports business, it's always good to be prepared. Anticipate that bodycheck before it slams you into the boards."

"Oh, fuck off, Vic," Ken said as he strode off across the field.

*   *   *

By nine o'clock in the morning, the heat had already draped a soggy blanket over the streets. Behind the smoggy haze, the sun shone blurry white in the eastern sky, and not the slightest puff of breeze stirred the leaves in the wilting trees. As Green approached Norman Bethune Alternate School, he saw a group of students clustered in the shade of a massive old tree, fanning themselves with notebooks as they bent over their work. Green scanned the crowd anxiously for a familiar blue head, but to no avail.

He approached the group. It was like looking at a dozen Hannahs. Shredded clothes, body piercings and tattoos were everywhere, and hair styles ranged from tiger-striped mohawks to gothic black sheets. The students eyed him with suspicion, no doubt bemused by his Bagelshop T-shirt and jeans, but their eyes grew dark when he introduced himself. A lanky, skeletal girl in a long, multicoloured kaftan wagged her head back and forth. Her every move seemed to be in slow motion.

"Hannah never told us you were a cop."

I'm sure she didn't, he thought. He doubted Hannah even wasted breath on her boring old dad. "Do you know where she is? She's not answering her cell."

"Well, that's Hannah. She comes and goes. Smart though. When she's here, she gets more work done in half a day than the rest of us do in three."

"So it's normal for her not to be at school?"

"Oh, yeah. Especially now. It's so nice out, we'd all be at the beach if we didn't have stuff to finish up."

"Do you know where she'd hang out?"

The lanky girl's eyes shuttered. She shrugged her bony shoulders. "Hannah never likes the same thing twice. Drugs, boys, hang-outs, it's always got to be something new."

Green's heart chilled at the mention of drugs. He'd been in Major Crimes too long to be cavalier about it. Drugs meant dealers, and dealers meant trouble. "Any guesses?"

"Well—" The younger girl in the striped hair began, but the lanky girl shot her a scowl that silenced her in mid-word. Green wanted to throttle her but forced himself to be nonchalant. Throttling never worked with Hannah either. Instead, he dredged up a rueful smile.

"Look, I'm a dad. I worry. And because I'm a cop, I worry even more. Like right now, with this teenage girl missing, I'm imagining all sorts of crazy things. So please, if you know anything, tell me."

"We don't know anything," the tiger-haired girl said. "Not really."

"Can you at least tell me if she's all right?"

"I'm sure." The lanky girl bobbed her head. Her black hair swung in ropes. "The guy—the people—she's with are cool."

Green gritted his teeth to keep from screaming at her. "If you can reach her, or you hear from her, tell her to call me. Please!"

They exchanged glances, and to a person twitched their shoulders in a doubtful shrug. It was not a comforting response, but there was nothing more he could do beyond attaching electrodes to unspeakable parts. He headed back to the car, seriously debating the wisdom of filing a missing persons report. Hannah might never forgive him if he did, but if something was really wrong, or something had happened to her, he would never forgive himself if he didn't.

As he was nosing his way into the impossible traffic on Bank Street en route to the Elgin Street Police Headquarters, a police cruiser streaked by towards Billings Bridge, its lights flashing and siren blaring. Green's blood ran cold. At that very moment his phone rang, and he grabbed it, praying it was Hannah.

It was Brian Sullivan.

Six

Lea Kovacev had travelled a mere hundred metres from where she'd probably entered the water, and had come to rest on the rocky point of a small island just below the falls. The Rideau River, having picked up speed on its plunge through the gorge, raced white and angry over the rocks below the falls and split to encircle the tiny island in its path. Only five metres of water separated the island from the eastern shore, and it was easily crossed by a person wearing rubber boots.

She was still face down in the shallow water when Green arrived, her bloated body rocking gently in the reeds and rocks that marked the shore. MacPhail was completing his examination, and Lyle Cunningham was photographing the scene. Green splashed out to join Brian Sullivan, who stood knee-deep in the river a safe distance away. The rest of the officers clustered on the eastern shore of the mainland opposite. The roar of the falls rushed in to fill the human silence that had descended on the scene.

"Likely caught underwater on a lip of rock in the gorge and only dislodged when the body began to bloat," MacPhail intoned, showing none of the glee that usually accompanied even the grisliest of deaths. His mood was reflected in the faces of all the police officers on the scene. They had known the odds and read the danger signals, but they had hoped against all reason that they would find her alive. Dejection radiated from their slumping shoulders and their listless search of the grounds. There was no urgency now, no race against time. There never had been.

On his way to the scene, Green had pushed through the media, who were pinned back in the park above, mercifully out of sight. They were suitably sombre, waxing poetic as they spun the sparse information they'd been given into full-bodied stories of Lea's ill-fated end. Green knew that within minutes, the news would be on all the airwaves, reaching her school, her friends, and her mother. Someone needed to get to the woman first.

He eyed the body, which appeared to be naked. Lea's mother had said the bikini came off easily, and Green wondered whether the river had torn it free, or some human hand.

"Has MacPhail said anything about sexual assault?" he asked Sullivan.

Sullivan shook his head. "So far he's observed no signs of trauma, except some tearing of the skin on her shoulders and hips. Post mortem, he said, likely caused by the rocks in the river."

"Thank God for that small mercy. It might be a comfort to her mother, if anything could be. She needs to be informed before she catches the whole discovery on TV."

Sullivan nodded. "I sent Bob Gibbs and a woman from Victim Support over to give her the news. They'll bring her to the morgue for the ID when MacPhail gives us the word."

The two detectives watched in silence as MacPhail prowled around the body with his powerful flashlight, probing every inch and frequently signalling Cunningham to photograph a particular detail. Cunningham's partner could be seen stalking through the trees on the island, marking every broken beer bottle, used condom and cigarette butt to be photographed and collected. On this picturesque little island a stone's throw from Carleton University campus, there were sure to be plenty of all three.

It felt like an eternity before MacPhail straightened up, nodded to Cunningham and headed back towards Green and Sullivan. He strode through the water, oblivious as it engulfed his hiking boots.

"I came prepared for dirt and trees, not water," he announced in his booming Scottish brogue. Dr. Alexander MacPhail hadn't been near the Highlands in the last thirty of his sixty-odd years, but managed to sound more Scottish with each passing year. The joke in the police force was that he was drinking up Scotland shot by shot. It did not appear to diminish his acumen one bit, however.

He snapped off his latex gloves and crushed Green's hand in his powerful grip. "I thought you were on holidays, laddie."

Green stifled a grimace at the thought of where the hand had just been. "I am. Just dropping by."

"Oh, aye." MacPhail shot him a knowing smile. "HRH will be calling you back in, mark my words. Any time the press is going to shine a spotlight, she likes all her boys lined up neatly in a row. In their Sunday best as well," he added, arching one eyebrow at Green's T-shirt.

Green was wondering himself when Superintendent Devine would call. No doubt when the news of the body reached her ears. God forbid she should actually oversee the case all by herself. After ten years as Ottawa's chief forensic pathologist, MacPhail had her pegged to a T.

"Before she calls, I'd like some facts to feed her," Green replied. "What can you tell us?"

"Well, from the degree of putrefaction and the absence of rigor, I'd say she's been dead about two to three days, so she likely died sometime the night she disappeared. We know she only surfaced in the past twelve hours, since your lads searched this entire area yesterday evening, but with the water still so cold, it's difficult to estimate how long she was under beforehand."

"Cause of death? Drowning?"

MacPhail hesitated. "Impossible to tell at this point, till I get a peek inside. There are no signs of obvious trauma, such as a gunshot wound or crushed skull. There's water in her lungs, but that is inconclusive after three days submerged. There is some water debris in her nasal and oral passages which could also be consistent with drowning, but the debris could have been washed in post mortem."

"Debris? Like sand?"

"And algae. But I'll need microscopic analysis of her blood and bone marrow in order to confirm whether she was still alive when she hit the water."

"Any other points? Sexual activity?"

"I can't see anything forced. No bruising or tearing around the genitals. But as for consensual sex, that's impossible to tell, given the amount of edema. She was a sexually active girl, I can tell that, and with any luck the river won't have washed away all the semen if she had intercourse before she died."

With any luck, Green thought. Semen would go a long way towards pinpointing who she'd been with the night she died, and perhaps unravelling the mystery of how she'd ended up in the water without any clothes. Even if her ultimate death proved to be drowning by misadventure, that mystery lover had a lot to answer for.

"However," MacPhail was saying, and the twinkle in his blue eyes stirred Green's interest, "there is *one* thing, difficult to detect with the edema and the discoloration. I'll know more when I can get her on the table this afternoon, so I may have a more definitive answer for you then."

Green's eyes narrowed. "What thing?"

"Ach, it's naught but a wee tiny detail. Better lighting or a close look at the tissue will do the trick."

"What wee tiny detail?"

MacPhail swept his hand in invitation towards the body, grinning. "Shall we take a look?"

Green grimaced. He knew he should be taking a close look at the body, but the words edema and discoloration were deterrent enough. "Just tell me."

MacPhail laughed then lunged forward to grip Green by the upper arms. Green jumped back reflexively, thinking he meant to drag him over to the body, but in the next instant the doctor softened his grip and struck a didactic pose. "She's got these very small dark spots on her arms that could be bruises. Just like someone's thumbs were holding her very hard. Mind you, with the degree of putrefaction and the time in the water..."

"So you're saying it's possible she didn't drown accidentally?"

"I'm not saying that. Odds are she did. All I'm saying is that you shouldn't be packing away your interview forms and your evidence kits just yet."

Before Green could even digest the implications, a high-pitched scream echoed down the river bank, and all three men spun around to see a commotion in the woods by the shoreline.

A woman was shrieking, part rage and part anguish. "Take your hands off me, you fucking Nazis!"

Green recognized Marija Kovacev's voice, and he sprinted across the water to the shore just in time to see her tear loose from the half-dozen officers restraining her. She plunged down the embankment towards the water, slithering over rocks and clutching at branches to slow her descent. Her hair had come free from its neat bun and flew about her face in wild disarray, and her eyes were huge with panic.

Green caught her arm as she reached the shoreline. "Marija, wait."

She fought against his grip, staring through him as if he didn't exist as she strained for a glimpse of the body in the water. Sullivan and MacPhail moved to block her view.

"I have to see her!"

"Not here. Not like this," Green murmured, trying to sound calm. On the bluff above, he could see the media cameras clicking and caught a glimpse of Watts, one of Major Crimes' lesser lights, cosying up to them, as if hoping to get his picture in the paper.

"You promised you'd help me..." she gulped, "you'd tell me—"

"I'll take you to the morgue, where you can see her properly."

"Properly?"

Gibbs appeared at her side, accompanied by a defiant-looking young woman with a tag from Victim Support. Gibbs looked distressed. "Sorry, sir, I couldn't s-stop her."

"After what this woman has been through in her life," the victim counsellor retorted, "I thought she had a right to see her daughter. She wouldn't calm down otherwise."

"She wouldn't calm down anyway!" Green hissed, furious.

Marija slapped his face. "Don't talk like I'm not here! I am here. And I will see Lea!"

Green's face stung where the blow had landed. He gaped at her in shock, and for the first time saw not just the panic but the fierce determination in the woman's eyes. Silent seconds ticked by as they stared each other down. Around them, a small group of officers held their breath.

Green relaxed his grip on her arm marginally. "She's not injured, Marija, but after two days in the water, she doesn't look very good."

"Do you think I care?"

"But do you want this to be your last memory of her? Your last picture?"

"I have a picture of her forever in my heart. A thousand pictures. I must have this final one. To know the truth, to touch her one last time."

Green looked up at Sullivan reluctantly. "Have we got paramedics standing by? Some sedatives?"

Her eyes glittered, and for a moment Green feared she was going to lash out again. He steeled himself, but instead she simply gripped her hand over his. "In Bosnia, I picked up the pieces of my husband's body, and I held him together in my arms. To say goodbye and to know that he had my comfort on his journey. Lea..." Her voice snagged, and she sucked in her breath. "Lea needs that too."

Green was speechless. It went against all crime scene procedures and next of kin protocols, but when he looked over at the island, he saw that Cunningham had finished with his photographs and had moved on to the physical evidence. Lea's hands were bagged, and the coroner's staff was standing by with a stretcher, waiting for the word to remove the body.

"Get rid of the goddamn press," he muttered to Sullivan. Then he took Marija's hand and guided her towards the water. Without a word, the others parted to let them pass.

*   *   *

The lunch bell had just rung, and Jenna dismissed her final student of the morning with an undisguised sigh of relief. There had been a virtual avalanche of hysterical students following the announcement that Lea's body had been found. The principal had convened an emergency mid-morning meeting, and as a group they had hammered out a crisis response plan. The police had released few details, other than that the body had been recovered below the falls and that there were no signs of foul play, leaving the principal to conclude that she had been swimming in the falls against regulations and had drowned. Mr. Prusec had used the tragic occasion to warn students over the PA to take all precautions around water this summer.

Jenna was furious, not only at the principal's open broadcast of the tragic news but also at his implicit blaming of Lea for her own misfortune. What about the other possibilities? An unintentional fall, or a very intentional push? Where was the boyfriend in this scenario? Had he ignored her plight? Left her to die? Dared her to dive? Plied her with alcohol and drugs? One thing was certain; he had not come forward to shed light on the tragedy. He was hiding behind his anonymity, like the guilty coward he surely was.

Jenna had hoped Crystal would draw the same conclusions and come forward to discuss it further, but when noon arrived with no sign of her, Jenna decided she'd have to go on the offensive. She had to work at another school that afternoon, so she had no time to waste. She was just heading out of her office in search of Crystal when she spotted the gym teacher, Ken Taylor, talking to the Guidance secretary across the room. He straightened when he saw her and gave her a tentative, collegial nod, but he had the same dazed look in his eyes that she'd seen on the students earlier.

Well, well, she thought, is this the first staff member to admit they need someone to talk to? Mr. Macho men-only-talk-to-men himself?

He smiled a little sheepishly as she approached. "Can we take a walk?" he said. "I need to eat lunch, but I'd like to get out of here for awhile."

He offered her half his sandwich—peanut butter and jam

on white bread—and she suppressed a grimace as she declined. He led the way out the side door towards the tree-lined residential street next to the school. Resisting the urge to babble to cover her nervousness, she waited for him to speak.

"I want to apologize for my behaviour this morning," he said eventually. "I nearly snapped your head off, but the truth is I was harbouring the same secret fear myself that she was dead. I just didn't like you saying it out loud."

"Did you know Lea?"

He'd stuffed half the sandwich into his mouth, and he nodded vigorously in response. Bread crumbs scattered as he tried to talk. "She's in my Outdoor Ed class. And I'm the teacher advisor to the Newcomers' Club, which she is—was—very active on. She was a very nice girl. Private, kept her thoughts to herself, but very friendly."

"Was she the daredevil kind, as the principal implied?"

"She liked adventure, and she liked to challenge herself, but I can't see her doing anything as stupid as diving off Hog's Back."

"Did she do drugs?"

He shrugged. "Who knows? She had a lot of respect for her body, and she wanted it to perform at its best, so I doubt it."

He pulled out a Coke can and punched his empty lunch bag into a ball, his melancholy gaze fixed on a distant point ahead. Looking at him now, she saw that despite the unappealing extra chin and the wisps of fine brown hair combed carefully over his bald spot, he had gentle grey eyes and a pair of impish dimples when he smiled. Not too bad to look at after all, she decided, and sneaked a peek at his left hand. No ring. And a peanut butter sandwich for lunch. Both signs of bachelorhood.

Feeling a blush coming on, she brought her thoughts firmly back on topic. "She might have experimented though,

73

if a very special boy asked her to. A sweet-talking boy can get a girl to do many things just to please him."

He shifted his grey eyes to her pensively. "And vice versa, I might add. The power of attraction can be blinding."

"At that age, yes," she hastened to say as the blush reddened her cheeks. "Do you know if she had a boyfriend?"

He resumed walking at a brisk pace, leaving her scurrying to keep up. "You've really got a thing about Lea's love life, don't you?"

"Well, it's just that I heard she had a secret boyfriend, and I'm wondering why he hasn't come forward. He's supposed to be a big star at the school. Actor, musician, athlete..."

"That covers a lot of territory. Who's to say he's even from this school?"

"That's just what I heard. I could be wrong, but there are a lot of talented kids at this school. The arts students, for example. Would they have been her type?"

He cracked open the Coke and slurped noisily. "I didn't know her that well, but I think she'd be hard to please."

"What makes you say that?"

"She was a pretty girl and friendly to everyone, up to a point. But she guarded her privacy and didn't let people get that close."

"You mean there might be lots of guys mooning over her who wouldn't have a chance?"

"I didn't say that. Only that it would take a very special guy for her to let them in. A lot of these artsy types are pretty self-absorbed."

"What about an athlete? You said she liked the outdoors and adventure. You probably know most of the top athletes in the school. Would any of them be her type?"

He didn't reply for a moment while he dug into his pocket for a chocolate bar. Mars Bar. Nothing lo-cal for this guy. "I'm not sure all this speculating gets us anywhere. Lea's dead. That's the whole tragedy. Dragging in other people just makes it worse."

"If it helps us understand why, or prevents another tragedy, it would be worth it."

He cast her a sidelong glance. She kept her eyes straight ahead and hoped her red face didn't show. She was way out on a limb here, going where no one else seemed willing to go.

"You don't watch much hockey, do you?"

She tensed in bewilderment at his abrupt change of topic. To admit a dislike for hockey in Ottawa this spring was to risk being run out of town. "No, why?"

"If you did, you'd know that by far the biggest name in sports at this school this year is Vic's whizz kid, Riley O'Shaughnessy."

"Vic?"

"Vic McIntyre. The guy you met with me this morning."

"Oh, that asshole."

He chuckled. "Yeah, he's in-your-face. But he's also an up-and-coming player's agent, and right now Riley is one of his hot new finds."

"In hockey?" she asked dubiously.

He nodded. "Riley O'Shaughnessy is a forward for the Ottawa 67's, and he's shaping up to be a first round pick in the NHL entry draft at the end of the month."

"That's Greek to me, Ken. What does that mean?"

"It means he's damn good. And potentially worth millions."

Seven

Marija Kovacev spent fifteen minutes with her daughter, praying over her, weeping over her, and ultimately sitting in stricken silence as the morgue staff loaded Lea onto the stretcher. Afterwards, Green drove her home but made no attempt to intrude on the woman's private, unimaginable grief. Neighbours were waiting outside her home, and he handed her over with gratitude.

It was past one o'clock by the time he got to his office. He felt shell shocked. Please don't let there be any more crises, he thought. His message light was blinking wildly, and when he checked it, he found half a dozen calls from Barbara Devine. With a groan, he forced himself to punch in her number. She wasted no time on formalities.

"Who are you assigning to the Kovacev case?"

"It's Brian Sullivan's call," he pointed out irritably. "And he's handling it himself for now, pending the findings of MacPhail's PM."

"I caught the news footage of the mother charging the crime scene. Thank God you were there."

Green counted to five. It was either that or hang up on the woman, and the latter would be unwise, even if he didn't value his career. "Losing a child is a very traumatic thing," he said when he could trust himself to behave.

"I'm not an idiot, Mike. I know how hard it must be on

her. I'm just saying you handled it well."

Green said nothing, waiting for the other shoe to drop. It took all of three seconds.

"If it's murder, this could be very tricky. I want you on media and overseeing the different teams involved. Personally."

He didn't waste time pointing out that the police force had an entire department dedicated to media relations. "I'm on vacation."

"And the sooner this is wrapped up, the sooner you can get back to it. We all have to make sacrifices, Mike. I've set up a press conference for five o'clock, to lead on the six o'clock news. Prepare something appropriate. And for God's sake, get dressed!"

Green managed to hang up before unleashing a string of profanities at his closed office door. He dialled his home phone number and Hannah's cell, both of which went unanswered. When he phoned Sharon's cell to explain the situation, he could hear Tony babbling in the background, and he wanted nothing more than to rush back out to the country, sweep his son into his arms, and hold him safe and close forever.

Sharon must have heard the despair in his voice, for she put up no argument. "The poor woman. I can't even imagine. Barbara Devine may be a pain in the ass with her eye only on the Deputy Chief's job, but in this case she's right. Of course you have to stay."

He sighed. "I know. Anyway, there's still no sign of Hannah. I'm almost ready to put out a missing persons bulletin on her myself."

"Do you want us to come home?"

He thought of how desperately she had wanted—needed—this week in the country. "Not yet. I have a couple of other leads to follow and a few places to look before I totally hit the panic button. And if I find her, once I've strangled her, she's coming out to the cottage with me, even if I have to tie her up and kidnap her."

"I'll have a double scotch waiting. For you, not for her." She forced a chuckle, but there was no humour in her voice. Perhaps like him, she feared the worst.

*　　*　　*

He spent an hour working on the press release and dealing with urgent reports that had accumulated in his absence before casting everything aside in frustration and heading out. In the middle of this steamy summer day, the streets would be teeming with youth. Somewhere out there, someone had to know about Hannah.

A wall of heat hit him the instant he walked outside. The haze had thickened, and a hot wind buffeted the trees, portending a thunderstorm that would wreak chaos with the crime scene on the Rideau River. His shirt was glued to his back, and his hair hung in sodden strings by the time he was halfway up Elgin Street. At the height of the afternoon, its pubs and trendy shops were crowded, and languid clusters of young people hung out in shaded alleyways and under trees in the parks. Mournful jazz wafted from the bistros as he passed. Ottawa Senators banners still hung in the windows and bits of faded flags and costumes still clogged the gutters, the only reminders of the Stanley Cup madness that had transformed the strip into a screaming, horn-honking frenzy earlier in the month.

There was no sign of a tiny, blue-haired, pixie-faced girl. He passed the sprawling white courthouse and city hall complex and struck out across Confederation Square, dodging the traffic that raced around it from all sides.

The National War Memorial formed the imposing stone centrepiece of the square, but his destination was the desultory group of semi-clad teens who sat on its granite steps, smoking and fanning themselves. As he drew closer, he could see that Hannah wasn't among them, but he asked about her anyway. He hoped that in his T-shirt and jeans, he didn't look too much like a cop, but his inquiry was greeted by wary head shakes all around.

He headed across the Wellington Street Bridge, scanning the buskers along the way, then descended the steps to the pedestrian underpass, which was a popular hang-out. On this hot day, its concrete corridor was packed with street youth, sleeping, lounging, talking and smoking. These teens were poorer than their counterparts at the alternate school. Their hair hung in dirty, uncombed hanks and their clothing was flimsy, torn and ill-fitting. Tattoos, studs and body piercings highlighted every bit of visible skin. Displays of homemade jewellery, crafts and cheap accessories, probably stolen, lined the walls, and the sweet smell of marijuana clung to the humid air.

Still no sign of Hannah. He headed for the Rideau Centre and merciful air conditioning, then back out to prowl the tattoo parlours, jewellery shops and record stores of Rideau Street and the Byward Market. The Market had been his playground when he was growing up in Lowertown, but today's raucous mix of street stalls, bistros and trendy shops was a far cry from the farmers' stalls, flophouses and seedy taverns of his youth.

It was nearing four o'clock under billowing black clouds when he finally had to admit defeat. He had only one avenue left to pursue, and he could avoid it no longer. Reluctantly he walked up the six short blocks to his father's retirement residence. The squat brick building sat on a side street in Sandy Hill, only a kilometre from the crumbling lowertown tenement where Sid Green had settled fifty years earlier. His whole world was within a short walking distance, including the Rideau Bakery and Nate's Delicatessen. Nowadays, Sid rarely made the walk, which left him breathless and unsteady, but instead waited for his son to chauffeur him around. This time Green was on foot and pressed for time, so he stopped en route to pick up cheese blintzes, Nate's smoked meat, and a Rideau Bakery rye, hoping that perhaps his father's favourite foods would distract him from the gravity of the visit.

Green could hear the television even before he entered the room. Stifling heat and the stench of stale sweat assailed his nostrils. As usual, the windows were closed, and the drapes were drawn—an old habit originally intended to keep prying eyes out—but this time his father was not sitting in his old brown corduroy chair where he spent most of his waking hours. A *Seinfeld* re-run was blaring away in the empty room. With momentary alarm, Green hurried through the narrow kitchenette and glanced into the bathroom before entering the bedroom. His father lay on his back on the bed with the comforter drawn up to his chin despite the heat. His eyes were shut, but his mouth hung open.

Green rushed to his side, relief flooding in as he saw the rise and fall of his chest. For twenty years, ever since his mother's death had sucked the hope from his father's life, Green had lived in fear of walking in to find his father dead. He picked up his father's wrist, and Sid's eyes flew open in alarm. The next instant he scowled as he jerked his wrist away.

"I'm only sleeping. Can't an old man sleep?"

"You usually nap in your chair." Green studied his colour closely. In the dim light, Sid's pale, watery eyes seemed to glitter. Fever? He laid a hand on his forehead. Warm, but not burning.

Sid shrugged. "So I have a cold. It's not a crime. What do you want?"

Green held out the grocery bags. "I brought blintzes. You eaten today?"

Sid struggled to prop himself up on his elbows. "What's wrong?"

"Why should something be wrong?"

"Because my son is here in the middle of the day. And... what happened to the vacation?"

"Work came up." Green went to the kitchen and returned with a glass of ginger ale and some crackers, which he placed on the bedside table. He propped his father up with a pillow. "Plus, I thought I should come back to check on Hannah. We left her here by herself. I don't suppose..." he paused, choosing his words and his tone, "she dropped in or called you, the way she promised to?"

Sid raised his glass to his lips in tremulous hands. Two drops fell on his chin, but he seemed oblivious. A smile played across his face. "My little Hannushka. Never forgets her *zaydeh*."

Green's hopes leaped. "So she did come? When?"

"Yesterday? The day before? Who keeps track? What day is it?"

"Thursday. Was it yesterday?"

Sid shrugged. "She didn't stay long. Always in a rush, that little girl. Just like her father."

"Did she say where she was going?"

"With a friend. She didn't say, but I think it was a young man." Sid stopped, and the smile faded from his lips. His rheumy eyes fixed on Green accusingly. "Mishka, don't make her go away."

Green was startled. A quick denial rose to his tongue, but something in his father's tone gave him pause. Goose bumps broke out on his back despite the heat in the room. "Why, Pop? Did she say something to you about going away?"

"She's like you. Who talks? But she seemed upset. *Fermisht.* All the time she was here, she didn't sit still one minute. It was

81

Zaydeh, do you want a drink? *Zaydeh*, do you get lonely? *Zaydeh*, do your friends ever visit? When you're eighty-six years old, I said to her, who has friends?"

Green groped to connect the cryptic allusions. Sweat trickled down his back. "You said she seemed upset. Was it about friends?"

"Maybe, but not down inside." He tapped his bony, gnarled fist to his chest. When he picked up his glass again, this time his hand trembled too much for him to take a sip. He set it down. "I know you, Mishka. Your mind, it's always off somewhere else." He smacked his head for emphasis. "Don't make her go, like she doesn't belong here."

Green suppressed his exasperation. It was an old refrain between them. His father had always blamed Green for losing Hannah in the first place, and he lived in fear of losing her again. Green couldn't tell from his father's riddles whether Hannah had actually said anything about leaving, or whether his old paranoia was reading threats into innocuous words. He tried for a concrete lead. "Did she mention the name of this boyfriend?"

"No. You don't know him?"

Green shook his head. "Did she mention any friends' names?"

"No. She just said sometimes friends weren't friends after all, like my friends in Poland. I told her such stories are not for her ears." He sighed and lay back on his pillows, suddenly looking so frail that Green felt a twinge of fear. Even after sixty-five years, the betrayal of the Polish villagers he'd considered friends still ate at his soul.

"Has the nurse been in to see you, Pops?"

Sid waved his hand in dismissal. "They came, they listened—" he gestured to his chest. "They brought soup, and they said get lots of rest. Like I was thinking maybe to run the marathon."

Green smiled. As long as his father could joke, surely he wasn't dying. He stayed a few minutes longer to make sure his father was comfortably settled, then ducked out of the apartment, leaving *Seinfeld* on full blast for company. On his way out, he stopped by the main office to ask the nurse to check on his father later.

Once he made it back outside, he checked his watch in dismay. He was glad he'd visited his father, not only for the old man's sake but also for the news on Hannah. As of either Tuesday or Wednesday, she had been fine, although troubled about something. Perhaps she would show up home once she'd worked it out. It was a hope he could hang on to, anyway, while he coped with more immediate demands.

Barbara Devine's press conference was due in twenty minutes, and until he had Sullivan's report on the autopsy, he still hadn't a clue what he was going to say. His clothes were sticky with the sweat and grime of the streets, his feet ached, and his throat screamed for water. He caught a cab back to the police station to find Brian Sullivan waiting for him at his desk. The look on the big man's face was unreadable.

Green jerked his head to signal Sullivan to follow him and headed straight to the men's room, where he splashed cold water on his face and drank deeply. Once he felt half human again, he turned his attention to Sullivan.

"Bad news?"

Sullivan checked under all the stalls, then returned to lean against the wall. "What would be good news in this scenario, Mike? That she drowned, accidentally or on purpose?"

"It wouldn't be on purpose. No way was this girl suicidal. No, I mean—do we have a killer on our hands?"

"Who knows? MacPhail can't say. He knows how she died—cardiac arrest—but he doesn't know why."

"Cardiac arrest! She was a healthy, fit, young woman!"

Sullivan shrugged. "It happens. MacPhail found no diatoms

in either her bloodstream or her bone marrow. He thinks she was dead when she hit the water."

Green stared at him. He knew all about the microscopic organisms that lived in rivers and lakes. Diatoms were so small that if the heart was still beating when a victim entered the water, they would be pumped throughout the circulatory system. It was one of the hallmarks of death by drowning, although as a definitive test, Green knew it remained controversial. "Dead people don't throw themselves in the water. So is he saying someone else was there to help her along?"

Sullivan nodded grimly.

"Shit." Green turned the revelation over in his mind, remembering the faint abrasions MacPhail had mentioned at the scene. "Did he find any signs of trauma or a struggle?"

"What looks like two thumb impressions on her upper arms, like someone held her with enough force to cause bruising before she died. There are also post mortem abrasions consistent with falling on the rocks in the river. And her hip was broken, again post mortem. Probably some time after death, MacPhail thinks, based on the absence of bleeding into the tissue."

Green propped himself against the sink and gazed absently at the tiles on the floor. They formed a nice geometric pattern of browns and creams, nothing like the crazy jigsaw of this case. "So she struggles with someone, goes into cardiac arrest and then someone—maybe that same person—instead of calling 911, waits a bit and then tosses her off the rocks into the falls?"

"Well, he might not have known she was dead right away. Maybe they were both asleep, and when he woke up, he realized..."

"It's still a crazy reaction, Brian. If I found my girlfriend dead, I wouldn't toss her over the falls unless I had something to hide. Could he have raped her? Any sign of sexual activity?"

"Inconclusive," Sullivan said. "There were no obvious vaginal abrasions, but the tissue edema was too great to be certain, and the river could have washed away any traces of semen."

"Or our man could have used a condom."

Sullivan nodded. "There are still a lot of questions. MacPhail's ordered a full tox screen. He's put a rush on it, but he's treating the death as suspicious."

"At the very least it's interference with a body," Green replied. "But meanwhile we treat it as a homicide. We open a Major Case file on it."

"Already started. I'll keep the lead myself until we hear from MacPhail about the toxicology results."

Green nodded, and a ghost of an idea brightened his thoughts. "I'll sic Barbara Devine on the lab. She'll have the Commissioner of the RCMP himself ordering the rush. Did MacPhail see any signs of drug use?"

Sullivan shook his head. "Like you said, the girl was healthy and fit. Took care of herself, didn't even smoke much pot, from the condition of her lungs."

"So has he any idea what caused the cardiac arrest? A congenital abnormality?"

"Not that he could see. Her heart was healthy and properly formed. She had nothing much in her stomach other than what MacPhail thinks may have been a sports drink and walnut ice cream."

"Not even one beer or cooler?"

"Not judging by the smell. Of course, he'll do a full analysis and let us know."

Green's eyes narrowed in thought. "Did MacPhail say what could cause a perfectly normal seventeen-year-old heart to stop?"

"Besides drugs? He said it was highly unlikely, but extreme

emotion—terror or fury—or extreme exertion."

"You mean as in fighting for her life? Running away, probably terrified to boot?"

Sullivan shrugged. "It's as good a guess as any right now. Two things we know for sure. She wasn't alone the night she died, she struggled with someone, and someone hefted her body over the fence and threw it into the water."

"I'd say we're talking a strong young man here."

Sullivan nodded. "A hell of a strong young man."

* * *

Jenna Zukowski staggered through her apartment door, dropped her briefcase on the floor and sucked in a deep breath of cool, dry air. Thank God for air conditioning. Even her cat didn't budge, but merely greeted her with a flick of his tail. She tossed her keys and mail on the kitchen counter, peeled off her linen pantsuit and wilted into the armchair in her living room. It was a full five minutes before she rallied the energy to fetch a Diet Coke and fire up her laptop.

"Riley O'Shaughnessy hockey" yielded an astounding 634 hits on Google. For a boy not even out of high school, he certainly was generating a lot of news. She scanned the first page for a promising website that profiled his career. Wading through the alien world of hockey culture, she found herself utterly baffled. Junior A, Major Junior, Minors, scoring forwards, wingers, prospects, draft picks... She was able to glean that Riley had been born in Gananoque and had moved to Ottawa two years ago to play for the Ottawa 67's—which was called a Ontario Hockey League Major Junior team, whatever that was. Because of his scoring skill, he'd almost single-handedly brought the team to the Memorial Cup final this spring. The

Memorial Cup was not the Stanley Cup, which even she knew was the big hockey prize, but it was obviously important.

A couple of articles hinted at a recent fall-off in his game but suggested it was a temporary loss of focus that should not affect his future. Everywhere the articles trumpeted his statistics as one might the measurements of a contestant in a beauty pageant. Most of the numbers were meaningless to her, except for two. Height six-foot-three, weight two hundred pounds. She studied the photo of Riley dressed in full hockey regalia, leaning pensively on his hockey stick. Bulked up by the shoulder pads, he looked like an Adonis, but it was his face that caught her attention. Deep-set brown eyes, a mop of dark curls, and a shy, dimpled smile that could charm the pants off any girl.

Had he been Lea's secret love? How could she, Jenna, ever find out? It wasn't as if she could ask him outright, or even pump that obnoxious creep Vic for information on his golden boy. Maybe if she could see the boy for herself, she'd be able to tell. Surely his demeanour or the expression in those beautiful puppy dog eyes would betray the torment and guilt that he felt.

She glanced at her watch and saw with dismay that she'd missed the first few minutes of the six o'clock news. She turned her television on in time to see a panoramic vista of river and trees overrun with yellow tape and police officers. A reporter voice-over was announcing.

"...discovered by police searchers around nine thirty this morning on an isolated section of the Rideau River just south of the Heron Road Bridge. Police confirmed the body to be that of seventeen-year-old Lea Kovacev, who had been missing since Monday evening."

The scene switched to a close-up of a plainclothes police inspector who looked as if he'd slept several days in the suit he was wearing. "Obviously this outcome is deeply upsetting to all of us in the police and in the community, and our sympathies go out to her family and friends. The body appears to have been in the water two to three days. She was discovered not far from where her backpack was found in Hog's Back Park yesterday. The investigation is still in its early stages, and we don't know exactly what happened. We'll be conducting interviews and examining evidence; however, there is currently no evidence to suggest she was attacked, and so there does not appear to be any ongoing risk to the public at large. Hog's Back is a dangerous waterfall that in the past has been used by divers. We ask anyone who might have knowledge of her activities at the park to please call the Major Crimes Unit at the number on the screen."

Jenna listened to the police inspector with growing impatience. So the official cop line was going to be that Lea drowned accidentally while diving. Jenna watched as the broadcast went on to other news. Students at Pleasant Park were interviewed as they left the school. Shock and tears were etched on their faces, and Jenna cursed the principal's stupidity for not having called for her help in dealing with the media invasion.

When one of the students mentioned Lea's adventuresome spirit and her love of swimming, Jenna's annoyance grew. They were buying the cop's story that she had died swimming in the dangerous waters of Hog's Back and had thus been the agent of her own misfortune. This was nonsense! The police needed to know about her secret lover and her responsible approach to sport. Riley O'Shaughnessy was just a shot in the dark, but now that Lea's body had been discovered, even a glimpse of him might be enough to reveal the truth.

It was worth a try.

*   *   *

The rain was pelting down by the time Green reached home. He made a mad dash from the car to the porch and shoved his key in the lock. The front door swung open, unlocked. Adrenaline spiked through him as he slipped inside. A faint humming, off key but cheerful, emanated from somewhere at the back. Hope and fear swept him as he dashed through into the kitchen.

Hannah swung around in surprise, her mouth open and her hand frozen on the fridge door. She found her voice first. "Mike!"

He rushed to embrace her, his breath deserting him. Ignoring her resistance, he planted three kisses on her spiky head.

"What the fuck...?" she demanded, flushing with confusion. A half-smile hovered on her lips as she wrenched herself free.

"Where the hell have you been!"

"What do you mean? I've been out."

"I've been calling you for two days. I left messages, I went to your school—"

"Yeah, thanks for that. The gang got a good laugh."

Anger boiled in as his relief receded. "Well, *I* didn't! I've been worried sick."

"I was with a friend. You guys were away, so I stayed over at a friend's. What's the big deal?"

"The big deal is that I didn't know what had happened to you. A girl's been murd—a girl's body was discovered today, and I thought..."

"You thought I was dead? Sorry to disappoint you."

"How can you say that! You're my daughter."

"Oh. Yeah." She turned back to the fridge and pretended to be studying its contents. He stood in the middle of the kitchen, every muscle clenched, fighting too many feelings to trust himself to speak.

"Look, I'm a big girl, and you don't need to breathe down my neck, okay? That was Mom's specialty."

He gritted his teeth, battling an irrational rage that surprised him. "Wanting to know you're okay is not breathing down your neck. You're seventeen."

"I'm here, aren't I? Not a scratch on me."

"Would it have killed you to answer your messages?"

"I was at a friend's, and my cell phone was dead."

"What friend?"

"Nobody you know."

"I don't know any of your friends, that's the problem!"

"So you want to censor my friends now?"

"No! I just want to know who they are!" He wrestled his voice down a few decibels. "In case something happens."

"What's going to happen?"

"You don't know. That's the point. We could have been in an accident. Or I'm a cop, I could get shot—"

She rolled her eyes and fished out a tub of strawberry yogurt. "You work behind a desk, Mike."

This time he didn't rise to the bait, but waited her out. With a dramatic sigh, she sat down at the table and pried off the lid. "I was with a guy I know. That okay with you?"

"What's his name?"

"No one important. He's just a fuck buddy."

"Just a what?"

"A fuck buddy."

He stared at her in wilful disbelief. "What the hell is a fuck buddy?"

"Come on, Mike, what does it sound like?"

Again he waited.

"We fuck. That's all. Whenever we feel like a good fuck, no strings attached, we call each other up."

For a moment, he couldn't speak. In his job, he'd encountered nearly every sexual practice invented by men. Why did this simple statement of fact reduce him to incoherence? Her detachment, perhaps? "Is that all sex is to you?"

She gave a careless shrug as she dug her spoon in. "It's nicer if you're really into the guy, but this way, when you're in a dry spell, at least you get it off."

"Sex isn't just getting it off—"

"Oh, isn't it? You should know all about it. That's what you had with Mom."

Green stared at her. "What are you talking about?"

"You were young and horny, Mom was blonde and beautiful, and you couldn't get enough of her. But don't tell me there was anything but the sex for you."

"Is that what your mother told you?"

She licked her spoon, acting bored. "She said you were ready to hump anything that moved. But I've got eyes, Mike. Mom's pretty, but she's a complete ditz. She doesn't have a brain in her head to interest you, but that didn't matter when you were getting the hottest sex of your life. Too bad I came along to ruin your fun."

He'd been scrambling for a safer topic, and her comment caught him completely off guard. "What!"

Hannah stood up abruptly, snatched the yogurt tub and flounced past him towards the kitchen door.

He seized her arm angrily. "Wait a minute!"

She struggled. "I don't want to talk about you and Mom. It's ancient history."

"Obviously not. There's a lot you don't know—"

"And I don't want to know." To his astonishment, her voice clogged with tears. In one last defiant act, she threw the tub of yogurt in his face. Blinded and shocked, he released his grip, and she fled down the hall and out the front door, slamming it so hard the whole house rattled.

She slipped back through the front door two hours later. Green had showered and cleaned up the kitchen, and now he sat in the growing darkness in the living room, too drained to move. The rain had softened to a gentle patter that was barely audible on the roof. He heard her tiptoe down the hallway, heard her stifled breathing as she hesitated in the doorway, felt her eyes upon him.

"Hannah, come in here."

Instead, he heard the stairs creak as she began to climb.

"Hannah."

"I'm going to pack."

He couldn't detect a trace of defiance in her tone, merely resignation. What the hell does that mean, he wondered, for the tenth time wishing Sharon were here to interpret the adolescent female psyche and tell him how to react. He waited a few minutes, during which he could hear her shuffling around in her bedroom overhead. He hated the thought of the scene to come if he faced her head on, but the alternative— her departure—was worse.

Finally, he went into the kitchen to fix them both a cup of tea, half strength the way they both liked it, with lemon rather than milk. He could still remember Hannah's reaction when she'd first noticed they shared the same taste in tea despite there being sixteen years and two thousand kilometres of separation. She'd been puzzled, almost cowed. As he headed up the stairs with the tea, he hoped it would voice the yearning too difficult for him to put into words.

There was no response to his call, but when he nudged the door with his toe, he found it unlatched. Symbolic, perhaps? She was sitting cross-legged on the bed, sorting her CDs. Her hair hung in sodden strings, and her wet tank top clung to her tiny frame.

"I'll leave you all the ones you gave me," she muttered, not looking up.

As he took the tea to her, he found he was trembling so hard, he could barely keep the mugs steady. She accepted the mug with a fleeting smile of thanks. "There's an eleven p.m. flight to Vancouver, if you're free to drive me."

Part of him wanted to smile, part to weep, for she sounded exactly like his long-dead mother whom she had never known. Despite Hannah's almost total lack of exposure to her Jewish roots, Jewish martyrdom, like the tea, must be in the genes.

He could have parried her comment and continued to skirt along the edges of the emotions that seethed between them. They'd managed a whole year avoiding them and had built the beginnings of a tentative relationship that left them both at a safe distance. But the truce had been shattered, and he knew he had to get to the bottom of it.

"Do you think you were unwanted?"

She shot him a look of rebuke from under her long black lashes. He had violated the rules between them. Finally, she shrugged. "Of course I was unwanted. You only married Mom because she was pregnant. Three months after I was born—pouf, gone."

"Your mother left me."

"But you were glad of it."

"About her leaving, yes. But not about losing you."

"You don't have to say that, you know. I have Fred."

The barb deflected harmlessly. Green knew Ashley's second husband had tried his best to be a good stepfather to this wild, prickly girl, but she had fought him every inch of the way. "Fred is not your father. I am."

She rolled her eyes and edged away from him on the bed. "Look, thanks for the tea, but I have to get packing if I want to make that flight."

He stared into his mug, willing himself to tread further.

"When I first saw you in the hospital, all six pounds, ten ounces of you, I admit I was terrified. I'd never known any brothers or sisters or cousins—*Zaydeh*'s first family all died in the Holocaust—so I didn't know if I had it in me to care for someone so small and needy. It was a lifetime commitment that scared the hell out of me."

She didn't say anything, but he noticed she had not taken a sip of her tea, which she clutched as if two hands were needed to keep it steady. He breathed a little more easily.

"I wasn't very good at it," he said. "Your mother was right to leave me. I spent long hours at work, I left her alone with you all the time, but in those first three months I did begin to know you. I remember your first smile, I remember you holding my baby finger in your fist and staring up at me like you were wondering 'who is this guy?' And when your mother took you away, I was devastated."

This time she gave a small grunt. It may have been disbelief, or perhaps contempt.

"I know you're angry at me for dropping out of your life for sixteen years, and you have every right to be."

"Gee, thanks."

He ploughed doggedly ahead. "But I'm really glad you came back into my life. That took a lot of courage, Hannah. More courage than I had, and I thank you for it."

"Yeah. Well, all good things come to an end." She set down the tea and moved to slide off the bed.

He grabbed her arm. "What do you want me to say? I'm sorry? Would that be enough?"

She yanked herself free. "I don't want you to say anything. We're done! Go back to your perfect little world, with your perfect wife and perfect son—"

"You're not in the way! You're part of it!"

"I'm trouble, I know it. I'm trouble wherever I go. But at least Mom's had a year's break from me."

"Have you spoken to her?"

"Not yet. She'd just drive me crazy asking what went wrong."

He heard the defeat in her voice, and his throat ached. "What did go wrong, honey?"

She jerked open her dresser and began tossing clothes on the bed. "It's no big deal. I just get bored."

"I don't buy that. You were enjoying school, and I thought...I thought you really liked Tony and Sharon."

"And Modo. Yeah, it's been fun."

He sensed her slipping from his grasp, and he had no idea what might stop her. "What did I do wrong?"

She shrugged, still folding clothes on the bed. "I just don't like parents, and like you said, Mike, we're strangers."

"We're not strangers. You're that little girl who grabbed my finger, you're my mother all over again, you're my stubbornness and restlessness... And I don't want to lose all that."

She headed for her closet and dragged her backpack out of the corner. For a moment she contemplated the tiny bag and the massive pile of clothes on the bed. In that moment's hesitation, he made the only move he dared. He rose, placed his hands on her shoulders, and turned her to face him. She stared at his chest as he kissed her head. His heart pounded, and he waited until he could trust his voice.

"Will you at least wait until the school year is over, honey? Get your course credits, and then if you still want to go..." *I won't stop you,* he was going to add, but he found the words would not come.

Eight

Green arrived at his office Friday morning to find a copy of the *Ottawa Sun* planted in the middle of his cluttered desk. The front page was devoted to a huge picture of Marija straining against the restraints of three police officers by the edge of the Rideau River crime scene. Visible in the background was a cluster of Ident officers bent over an object in the water. The headline said "DISTRAUGHT MOTHER DEFIES 'NAZI' POLICE".

Green seized the paper to see who had written it. The photo was credited to someone he'd never heard of, but the story on the inside page bore a familiar name. Frank Corelli, long-time crime reporter for the *Sun*, who had somehow managed to capture Marija's shriek about Nazis and reported it with glee.

"Corelli, you *putz!*" Green shouted at no one in particular. He was just about to phone the *Sun* to ream the reporter out when another thought struck him. Who had planted this paper on his desk, and why? His question was answered within seconds by the Major Crimes clerk, who knocked warily on his door to inform him that Superintendent Devine wanted to see him as soon as he came in.

Barbara Devine had her own copy of the *Sun*, which she brandished when he walked into her office. "Mike, is this your idea of managing the media?"

He put on a suitably doleful face. "Barbara, it's news, and

like it or not, it's a hot story. We did everything we could to support the victim's mother, including giving her a moment with her daughter to say goodbye. It's unfortunate that the reporter chose to capture her worst moment."

Devine's crimson lips grew tight. "Unfortunate is not the word, Green. We look like a bunch of Keystone Kops, and I'm not authorizing thousands in overtime to support a circus act. What are your men doing downstairs?"

She was still a dangerous shade of purple, and Green wasn't sure whether that was an accusation or a genuine request for an update, but he launched into one anyway, in the hopes of diverting her attention from the PR disasters of her division. At this very moment, he said, Brian Sullivan was briefing the day staff, collating reports and setting out the assignments for the morning. All night, the graveyard shift had been out on the streets, pursuing inquiries. The local known sex offenders had been questioned, and their whereabouts on the night of Lea's disappearance were being systematically verified. Officers had also spent the night showing Lea's photo around at Hog's Back Park again in the hope of finding someone who'd seen her and her companion that night.

Her colour gradually returned to normal as she listened, and at the mention of a secret companion, she stabbed the air triumphantly with a manicured nail. "That's the place to focus your efforts, Mike. The boyfriend. Short and sweet and wrapped up before anyone else gets hurt."

"Gee, I would never have thought of that," Green muttered under his breath afterwards as he hurried back downstairs to the incident room, where Sullivan's morning briefing was in full swing. Ident photographs, reports, and jot notes of key facts lined the walls, and every chair was occupied around the conference table. Expressions were grave and eyes were fixed on Bob Gibbs, the department's technical wizard, who already had the case up on the screen. He was filling in bubbles with questions and assignments while Sullivan stood by the screen with a laser pointer in his hand. At this point there were three big bubbles unassigned—Boyfriend, Ice cream and Ident.

Green slid unobtrusively into a seat at the back and watched as Sullivan targeted the first bubble. "We now know she wasn't alone, so we need to nail down her companion. So let's reinterview all her friends and classmates at Pleasant Park High School. Put some pressure on them. Someone has to know who she was seeing. I have a teenage daughter. Keeping track of who's dating who is a top priority for them. Gibbs, why don't you and Luc take that? You can take a couple of guys from General Assignment to help you."

Gibbs nodded without enthusiasm. His eyes were red-rimmed, and his suit wrinkled, as if he could barely summon the interest for work. His regular partner, Sue Peters, had been severely injured during a murder inquiry a couple of months earlier, and Sullivan had tried unsuccessfully to find a replacement who suited Gibbs' meticulous style. Before Sue's injury, he had just begun to gain confidence and take on a more senior role, but without her brash, charging-rhino style—and the testosterone she seemed to stir up in him—much of the fight had been taken out of him.

Green suspected that his heart and his thoughts were elsewhere, wrapped up in Sue's battle to regain the mental and physical powers she had once taken for granted. Her progress was slow, and her doctors were making no promises about a full recovery. Sue was a fighter, and Green still doubted that a broken skull and a few hundred stitches could keep her down, but Gibbs was the one who sat with her day after day, witnessing her struggle.

Sue Peters would not have taken "I don't know" for an answer from any of Lea's classmates or friends. She would have pummelled them with the question in a dozen different ways, offering up possibilities and accusations until someone let a single name slip. Green could only hope that Gibbs' gentler, more diffident style would sneak behind the kids' defences and achieve the same result. With the finality of Lea's death, surely some of them would feel the need to unburden themselves.

Sullivan pointed the laser at the second bubble. "Ice cream. She had ice cream the night she died. The pagoda at Hog's Back sells it, so start with the staff who were on duty that night. But if necessary, check all the convenience stores and shops in the vicinity, especially along the route between her home and the park."

"It could have been a street vendor," one of the detectives said.

"Good point, Wallington. Check if there were any around the park. You and Jones follow up on the ice cream."

The door to the situation room opened, and Lyle Cunningham walked in carrying a sheaf of papers. Sullivan grinned. "Good timing, Lyle. I was just going to assign someone to bug you."

The Ident officer didn't even crack a smile. "It wouldn't have done you much good. We don't have much useful at this point. The fingerprint on the park bench turned out to be Lea's, so that confirms she was there but doesn't give us any lead on who else was. Luminol and fluorescence revealed no traces of semen or blood on her backpack or clothing, or on the bench or grass in the vicinity—"

"He might have used a condom," Green interrupted.

"Yeah, well, that doesn't help us much then, does it?"

"Has anyone searched the nearby trash cans in the park for a discarded condom?"

Watts snorted with derision. "Probably dozens of condoms in them. It's been three days."

Green fixed the detective with a deadpan stare. Watts had never impressed him with his intelligence nor his commitment. "It's still a lead that has to be followed up, even if we have to eliminate a hundred condoms from our inquiry. A girl is dead."

Watts shrugged. "All I'm saying is—"

"Sounds like a good job for you, Watts," Sullivan said briskly. "Should keep you busy till tomorrow."

Watts retreated into sullen silence, and Sullivan gestured to the Ident officer to continue. "I've sent the bikini to the lab to see if they can pull any trace fibres or fluids from it, but it's a long shot. We've got forty-two exhibits from the island where the body was recovered—including six used condoms," he added, glancing at Watts, and for the first time sneaking a ghost of a smile, "and we're still processing them, but on the face of it I don't think they'll give us anything. Her body came from somewhere else, and there's no reason to assume she or her companion were even on the island beforehand."

Green nodded. He knew it would take weeks to process all the evidence in what was likely an exercise in futility, but Cunningham could always be trusted to track down every lead, no matter how minuscule. Lea deserved no less.

"We've also recovered twenty-one pieces of physical evidence from the area around the park bench—all the fairly recent trash, including four cigarette butts, wrappers from a Mars Bar, a Snickers, two Skor Bars, an ice cream sandwich—"

Green pounced. "Ice cream sandwich? How recent?"

"Pretty recent. It hadn't been rained on, and according to Environment Canada, it rained in that area on Sunday night. Luckily we got all this stuff gathered before the downpour last night."

"That ice cream wrapper is worth a special effort, because she ate ice cream the night she died. Expedite that to the lab."

Cunningham gave Green a terse nod of acknowledgement before returning to his list. "We also found six marijuana roaches, an empty Advil bottle, three plastic Loeb bags, three Tim Hortons cups, a few shreds of wrappers from Subway, and a bunch of pieces of shredded tissue paper. The lab will try to pull DNA off the roaches." He paused to look hard at Green. "I've prioritized all the stuff that looks like it was deposited there after the rain on Sunday."

Green smiled broadly. "I never doubted you would, Lyle, but you know me. Mr. Interference himself. How's it going with the evidence search further afield?"

"The search team has turned up nothing remarkable. They've found hundreds of pieces of crap—after all, there's a sports field, a bike path and a picnic grounds in the area—but all we're doing is bagging it and cataloguing it. We won't bother to process it unless we get a good reason. Most of it is probably from Stanley Cup parties. The city should pay us extra for doing their cleanup for them."

Green glanced at Sullivan, who'd been watching the interchange with a patient smile. After twenty years of working with Green, he knew better than to protest or interrupt. He picked up the thread now. "Bottom line, Lyle?"

Cunningham scowled, a man not comfortable stating bottom lines one day into a homicide investigation. "So far, not a lot to help you out," he said, then held up the notebook in his hand. Green recognized it as the English notebook in Lea's backpack. "We were up half the night going through this—not a trace of semen or blood, and the only prints I could find were Lea's. She sure liked her Shakespeare."

"Let me see it." Green reached out, and Cunningham passed

over the book. Green flipped through it rapidly. Lea wrote with a feminine but confident hand, without any of the hearts and curlicues that were popular with teenage girls. He scanned the notes and short essays, recognizing quotes from Shakespeare and, in amazing contrast, *The Catcher in the Rye*. The whole back section of the book was filled with sonnets. Some were in Old English, others clearly in the style of the romantic poets. But were they all copies, or were some of them written by Lea herself? It would take time to tell which was which, and even more time to distill from the flowery language any hidden clues.

While all the field detectives were running around in the heat tracking down ice cream vendors and used condoms, this was a task he could easily take on himself.

*　　*　　*

Green's Shakespeare was very rusty. Throughout the requisite Shakespearean plays in high school, he'd been an indifferent student, rarely paying attention in class and even more rarely actually reading the plays that were assigned. He was more likely to know a Monty Python take-off on the great soliloquies than he was to have memorized the real thing.

In university, he'd avoided English wherever possible, preferring not to spend entire weeks dissecting the symbolism of some dead poet's impenetrable verse. Fortunately, psychology and criminology caught his attention and steered his urge to fix the world in a tangible direction.

He flipped through the sonnets at the back of the notebook, wondering whose practised eye he could enlist in separating original from invented. He noticed that over half of them sang praises of one fair maiden or another, some unattainable and others already caught in the author's charms.

There were only six sonnets that referred to a male beloved, which made his search much easier. How many female poets were there, and could he tell from the style whether one of them was a modern schoolgirl?

He read the poems thoughtfully. One dwelled in great detail on the powerful arms and tender lips of her lover, another described him as Adonis and two others talked about Romeo. Had Shakespeare written any pieces from a woman's point of view? After about fifteen minutes, he realized that the easiest way to make sense of the poems was to go to the source—Lea's English teacher.

Mrs. Lucas proved only too happy to help. Green caught her during her prep time, marking papers in the staff room. She shook her head dolefully when he mentioned Lea.

"These papers are awful," she said, waving a dismissive hand towards the stack at her right elbow. Green saw lots of red ink, which brought back unpleasant memories. "The students just can't concentrate. What a tragedy. Poor Lea."

"Was she a good student?"

"Middling. She was bright enough, but literature wasn't her forte. She loved to write herself, but hadn't the patience to study others."

It was the first criticism anyone had dared to level at Lea, and Green was intrigued. "Her mother says she wrote poetry."

"Reams of it. Mostly snippets of memories from Bosnia. And mostly bad. But you only get better by writing."

"Can you take a look at these poems in her notebook and tell me if any of them were written by her?"

Mrs. Lucas took the notebook and rifled through it. Her eyebrows arched. "Well, these sure aren't Bosnia. She obviously didn't intend any teacher to see this book. Some of this stuff is pretty racy."

"Which ones did she write?"

"All the last two pages. These are bad imitations of Shakespearean sonnets." She gestured to four of the six sonnets Green had noted—the one about the powerful arms, the two about Romeo and the Adonis poem. "We've been studying Romeo and Juliet this term, so it makes sense she'd use that metaphor. I don't know where Adonis came from, although Greek mythology is big in teenage culture."

Green read the first Romeo poem carefully. Unlike Mrs. Lucas, he wasn't interested in artistic merit but in details that might identify the boy.

O what's the future for my love and me?
Our fortunes united or forever torn apart?
The hopes and love of kin a kind of tyranny
That controls the very beating of his heart.
How like a god he towers over me,
Our arms entwined, our eyes in passion locked.
His clouded gaze laments of cares too worldly
While mine of secret love alone doth talk.
O that he could toss all cares and worry aside,
And drink the sweetness of life's most virgin gift.
Forget his warrior duty and others' pride.
And let the demands of morning come not swift.
O Romeo, tonight shall passion meet no earthly bars,
As we chase our dreams across the canopy of stars.

"Pretty uplifting," Mrs. Lucas remarked, reading over his shoulder. "Most teenagers write such profoundly depressing stuff about love."

Green glanced at her wryly. "That's because it's usually going badly. Lea sounds like she's got a more optimistic take."

"That's Lea. Always full of hope."

"Any idea who she was writing about?"

The teacher shrugged. "I doubt the adolescent male in question bears much resemblance to the demi-god described here."

Green smiled. The voice of experience. Too many years, too much teenage angst. No doubt she was right, but there was still much to be gleaned from the poems nonetheless. He left her to her marking and went out to his car where he could think in peace. Taking out a notepad, he jotted down the points.

1. Questionable future together—family pressures and expectations. High achieving family?

2. Towers over her—tall.

3. Less committed than her—distracted by above ambitions?

4. She wanted him to forget all else, put her first.

5. Something special that night—seduction, loss of virginity, something else?

He paused, considering the veiled references of the last six lines. How recently had the poem been written? Was the special night in fact the night she had died? And did the sweetness she was offering refer to something more than her own body?

His cell phone rang, startling him out of his deep thought. It was Gibbs, sounding diffident as always.

"Sorry to disturb you, sir. Staff Sergeant Sullivan s-suggested I give you a call."

"What's up, Bob?"

"I'm at Pleasant Park High School conducting interviews with the victim's friends—you know, trying to ID the boyfriend?"

Gibbs didn't sound as if he'd broken open the case, but nowadays nothing much excited him. Green's hopes rose. "Did you find him?" he interrupted.

"No, sir. So far, no one seems to know. All her girlfriends, even her ex-boyfriend—"

Green perked up. "Who's he?"

"A Grade Twelve acting student named Justin Wakefield. But it doesn't sound like it was very serious. They broke up in April."

Two months was not a long time in the healing of a broken heart, Green thought. "What do we know about this guy?"

"Not much yet, sir. He's very popular in the school and their leading actor. People say he's multi-talented—writes, acts, directs. Kind of like a young Paul Gross. Probably has girls falling all over him since they broke up."

"You'll check him out anyway, right?"

"Oh yessir. I was about to do that when I encountered this other problem."

"What other problem?"

"The one S-Staff Sergeant Sullivan told me to tell you about—"

"Bob!"

"Yessir? I mean, yessir. It's Lea's mother. She's here at the school asking the students all the same questions we are, and she's getting to them before we can."

"Then stop her!" Inwardly Green kicked himself. Marija Kovacev had warned him of her plans, but he had been too rattled about Hannah to forestall her.

"Sullivan says... Well, we were wondering how to handle her."

"I'm near the school," Green said, stretching the truth a little, for he was sitting in the parking lot fifty feet away. "I'll speak to her. Where is she now?"

"That's the thing. She's in the cafeteria, having a long chat with Justin Wakefield."

* * *

Green's first glimpse of Justin Wakefield did not put him in mind of Lea's Romeo. True, even folded into a chair, the young actor was obviously tall, and he had the brooding good looks that seemed to set female hormones flooding. His dark hair was pulled into a wavy ponytail, revealing three silver studs and one long musical note in one ear lobe. He wore a plain black T-shirt stretched over lean shoulders and a silver link choke chain around his aristocratic neck. Vanity oozed from every pore. Green thought that if a man like this killed, it would not be from unrequited love but from outrage that any woman on earth would choose another man over him.

He was seated at a table in the corner facing the room, the better to be on display, Green suspected, and he stopped talking to watch Green's approach. Green had ditched his Bagelshop T-shirt for the standard polyester suit, and although his slight frame, freckles and youthful face didn't look much like a cop, he supposed the attire was enough to give him away. Who else would be wearing a suit and tie on a sweltering day like this?

Green studied Justin's expression carefully but could see no trace of fear, grief or guilt. Merely resignation and a hint of noble sorrow. But the boy was an actor, after all. Marija Kovacev was facing the other way, engrossed in conversation, but now she swung around in surprise. Green could see no sign of guilt in her either at being caught interfering. She was elegantly dressed in a floral summer shift, and her hair was back in its neat bun, but her face was ravaged by grief and lack of sleep. Deep lines furrowed her brow, and purple bruising circled her eyes. She brightened at the sight of him.

"Inspector Green! Some news?"

He shook his head. "But I have plenty of officers interviewing staff and students. We're trying to trace her movements that evening. Mr. Wakefield, my men will be talking to you too."

If Justin was surprised that Green knew his name, he gave no sign. Perhaps fame seemed natural. He arranged a regretful look on his face. "Of course. Although I don't think I can help much, I haven't seen Lea in weeks."

"Justin and Lea dated," Marija said.

"Nothing serious," Justin hastened to add. "For either of us. I was so busy with rehearsals that we hardly saw each other."

Green hesitated. Gibbs needed to conduct an official private interview with Justin, and Marija Kovacev had no business participating in the investigation at all, but this was a rare opportunity to see how the youth answered personal questions about Lea in front of her mother. The interaction of the two might shake loose some secrets as well.

"Did you see her Monday night?" Green asked. "I understand she was getting together with a group of acting friends."

Justin gave no indication he knew it was a lie. He shook his head unhappily. "No. Like I said, we hadn't touched base in a couple of months."

"What were you doing Monday night from nine p.m. to nine a.m.?"

Justin didn't even blink. "I was at home writing a paper. One of those student all-nighters."

"Alone?"

"Well, my parents were in the house." He cocked his head casually. "Why all the investigation? I thought she drowned."

Green shrugged easily. "Because she died in a public place, there will be a coroner's inquest. We're just laying the groundwork. Do you know who she was with that night?"

"Like I said, we sort of lost touch. Mrs. Kovacev just asked me if I knew who she was dating, but I'm so out of her circle now."

"What was her circle?"

"The Newcomer's Club and lately, her Outdoor Ed friends. She was really getting into sports."

"Names?" Green made a show of readying his notebook.

"Oh, I don't know. The school will have the class list."

"I know some names," Marija interrupted. "Larissa, Kaylee, Crystal... Maybe the social worker knows more. She was very interested in all Lea's friends."

Green glanced up from his notes. "What social worker?"

"I don't know her name. She works for the school board. Lea's gym teacher told me that she asked him all kind of questions. He says she has some ideas who Lea's boyfriend is."

Jesus H! thought Green. What the hell is this? Not only do we have the victim's mother running around contaminating the witnesses, but now we've got some school board social worker mucking up the waters even worse.

Nine

The principal of the school looked appalled. Anton Prusec was a tall, gaunt man whose elaborate combover did nothing to conceal his shiny, sunburnt pate. He carried himself in a permanent stoop as if ducking to keep his head out of the line of fire, and in this case he seemed irritated that such an inconvenience as a dead student had placed his school, and himself, in the spotlight.

He immediately ushered Green into his office and paged the social worker. "Jenna Zukowski," he muttered. "She's inexperienced and was probably just trying to help. But I wholeheartedly agree, Inspector. It's inappropriate and unacceptable. Absolutely. I didn't even know she was here today. I only asked for the board's crisis team for two days, and to be quite honest, our own guidance people can do the job perfectly well. But one must be seen to be doing all one can." Irritated, he picked up his phone. "Has Ms Zukowski answered her page yet? Then page her again!"

He hung up and fiddled with his computer. "It's been a very busy few days, and there are so many details to attend to. One expects everyone else to do their part, you know, and to know what that is. The ship must go on. I have over a thousand students and nearly a hundred staff at this school, and each one of them requires my attention. The staff from the school board, well..."

He tapped his pen against his lips as if to shut himself up, then swooped on the phone again to punch in another number. He was obviously calling Jenna Zukowski's boss at the school board, for he explained to her in terse superlatives that her social worker had gone far beyond the bounds of her authority and had interfered with a police investigation. He demanded an immediate reprimand.

"I want to speak to Ms Zukowski myself," Green interjected.

Prusec repeated Green's request with alacrity, as if relieved that his own outrage was being seconded by the senior brass of the police. During the ensuing silence, Prusec covered the mouthpiece and nodded at Green gravely. "The director of professional services is an absolute dragon lady. Ms Zukowski is likely to be filing attendance reports for weeks."

Presumably the social work equivalent to traffic duty, Green decided. The principal returned to the phone for a brief conversation. He jotted down some notes before thanking the dragon lady and hanging up.

"Ms Zukowski is not in her board office. That's not unusual. These people are almost always on the road. But I have her cell phone number..."

"Could you contact her, please?"

Prusec looked nonplussed. Playing secretary to the police, even an inspector, did not appear to be commensurate with his own status, but he paused only briefly before punching in the number. Clearly he'd sized up his options and the possible repercussions of refusing, and he'd elected to safeguard his career. He waited in silence for a few moments before leaving a crisp message asking Jenna Zukowski to contact him urgently regarding a police matter. Even before he'd hung up, he was rising from his chair.

"She's not answering. But as soon as she returns my call, I'll put her in touch with you." He headed for the door and stood aside to encourage Green to pass through.

Green remained in his chair. "I'd like to speak to your gym teacher."

Prusec started as if in alarm. "Ah. Which one? I have five."

"All five then. It will only take a moment of their time." Green smiled expansively. "If you'd be so good as to give me a room where I can conduct interviews."

Seizing the chance to end Green's occupation of his office, Prusec was quick to eject one of the vice-principals from hers so that Green could move in. It was little bigger than a closet, obviously occupied by the most junior VP, but it had a phone and computer. Within three minutes, the first gym teacher was knocking on the door. It took three gym teachers and half an hour before Green got to Ken Taylor.

The young teacher poked his head in the door as if afraid Green would bite it off. His face was flushed, and a sheen of sweat coated his brow. Green gestured the man to a chair and waited in silence until he had settled himself. Taylor was breathing hard, as if he'd been running. Was it fear of Prusec, or something else?

"I've already spoken to three police officers," he said. "I don't know what more I can add. I taught Lea Kovacev Outdoor Education, but I would never have encouraged her to dive in dangerous waters. Outdoor Ed is not an extreme sport; it's about combining fitness with nature."

"Do you know Jenna Zukowski?"

Taylor blinked several times in obvious surprise. "I just met her yesterday."

"Under what circumstances?"

Taylor looked alarmed. "Why? Is something wrong?"

"No, I'm just following up on what she discussed with you. I might add that I'm not happy about her interference in police matters, and I'd appreciate your telling me precisely what you two spoke about."

"Oh. Well." Taylor brushed his palm across his damp forehead. "She seemed to think Lea was murdered, or at least that a boyfriend had encouraged her reckless behaviour. She was asking about my students, trying to figure out who that boyfriend was."

"And did she have any leads?"

"She seemed to have this notion that the boy was a high achiever. A future star. We've got lots of those here."

"Any names?"

Ken Taylor wiped his brow again. Despite the frigid air conditioning in the office, he was still flushed and sweaty. "Really, she had nothing to go on, so I'd rather not repeat gossip and rumour. Innocent boys may be affected."

"An innocent girl is dead."

Taylor's jaw quivered, but still he said nothing. Green chose a softer tack. "We'll be looking at numerous individuals, Mr. Taylor. No boy is going to be accused of anything on your word."

"I did tell her, if she was looking for a boy with star power, she couldn't do any better than Riley O'Shaughnessy. I've been regretting it ever since."

*　　*　　*

"Who's Riley O'Shaughnessy?"

Sullivan glanced up in surprise from his double smoked meat sandwich. Green had called him at the station and asked to meet him at Nate's Deli. "Why?"

"He's a student at Pleasant Park, and his name has come up as a possible boyfriend."

Sullivan had stuffed a fistful of French fries into his mouth, and now his jaw hung open. "Holy Mother of God."

"Okay, so this would be big news?"

"In the hockey world, yeah. He's an idol to my boys. Small town kid makes the big time."

"So he's a hockey star? The kid's only eighteen!"

"Future hockey star. He's a probable first round draft pick that I think the Edmonton Oilers are hoping to pick up."

"What's a first round draft pick?"

Sullivan chuckled. "It always amazes me how a guy born and raised here in Ottawa can know so little about hockey."

Green scowled at him. "So my father didn't *schlep* me to the hockey rink every weekend at six a.m. What did he know about being Canadian?"

"For the uninitiated, eighteen is the youngest age a hockey player can begin playing in the NHL. You know what that is, eh? The National Hockey League?"

Green rolled his eyes. "I think I've heard of it. I'd have to be living under a rock for the past month not to know Ottawa has a team. Didn't it lose something?"

Sullivan bristled, the recent loss in the Stanley Cup final obviously still a sore point. "They made a good run of it. The point is that, just like most other sports leagues, the NHL has this complicated system to allow teams to pick from the pool of promising eighteen-year-olds. Each team gets assigned a number based on their standing that year. For example, the Philadelphia Flyers ended up last of thirty teams this spring, so they get one of the first picks of the pool. The Anaheim Ducks won the Stanley Cup, so they get the thirtieth pick."

"So the weakest teams get to pick the best."

"Ah, the good Canadian boy catches on fast! Yeah, it's supposed to level the playing field. When all the teams have picked their first choice, that's called the first round."

Green smiled as the light dawned. "So there are thirty first round picks. And you don't necessarily get who you want, because the team ahead of you might have grabbed him. How do they keep track?"

"Well, this all takes place with lots of hype in a big open forum at the end of June called the NHL entry draft. This year it's being held in Columbus, Ohio. There's lots of suspense and horse-trading. There is round after round, going on all weekend. It's brutal on the kids waiting to see if they'll be picked, but being a first round pick is a really big deal, pretty much guarantees them an NHL career. They're the top thirty eighteen-year-olds in the world."

Green puzzled over this. "You said Riley O'Shaughnessy's being touted as a first round draft pick already. But the big meeting hasn't even taken place."

"No, the draft is next weekend, but the NHL has scouts who go to all the Major Junior clubs and the European Leagues too, to watch the kids play. All these kids have been ranked and analyzed to death many times before they even get to the draft day."

"And the teams have already put their dibs in?"

"Not officially, but that's part of the guessing game. Sometimes it's pretty obvious. If a team is weak in goaltending, say, you know they're going to be picking up the best goalie prospect available when their turn comes up."

"And Riley O'Shaughnessy?"

"Riley's a skill forward—those are the Wayne Gretzkys of the game. Except he's a right winger and right shooter, which makes it especially hard for a defenceman or goalie to neutralize him. He's a young man with very talented hands and a lot of heart. Any team looking to strengthen their goal scoring would snap him up."

Green licked the smoked meat juice off his fingers as he weighed the implications. "So he's got a lot riding on this upcoming draft?"

Sullivan grinned. "Just his whole future."

"Then I guess he wouldn't be too eager to come forward and admit he was with a girl who died under mysterious circumstances."

* * *

"Mike, we don't even have evidence it was a homicide, let alone that he was the boyfriend!" Sullivan hissed. "But media suspicion at this point could kill this kid's career!"

They were both back in the main office at Pleasant Park High School, where Green was demanding access to Riley O'Shaughnessy's address. Sullivan had dragged him into the corner out of earshot, but curious secretaries were straining their ears.

"If the kid's innocent, nothing will happen to his career," Green retorted. "We're not going to blab to the media."

"Not you and me. But I don't trust some of the guys on the squad. Watts is an asshole, and Wallington is just plain dumb. If they let a word slip over a couple of beers..."

Green remembered his glimpse of Watts cosying up to Frank Corelli of the *Ottawa Sun* yesterday at the crime scene. His gut tightened. Probably nothing, but worth watching. "That's why we're not making it official. Yet. *You* are going to make some discreet inquiries about a number of boys. That's all."

"But I'm already late for the briefing I called at the station. At least let's wait till you hear from this Zukowski woman and see if she has anything concrete instead of rumours and speculation."

Green stalked over to the principal's office and banged on the door. Anton Prusec answered, outrage changing quickly to dismay at the sight of Green. "Ah! Inspector! No, no. Ms

Zukowski has not called me back. I'll try again and get back to you, shall I?"

"You do that, but I also want her cell phone number."

"Ah! Well, I don't think I can give that out—"

"Then give me the dragon lady's. I'll tell her you didn't want to authorize—"

Prusec spun around and pounced on a piece of paper on his desk. Without further comment, he rattled off the social worker's number. When Green dialled it, he listened to six rings followed by a chirpy, apologetic message saying how sorry she was to miss this call but to leave a message because she checked them regularly. Jenna Zukowski sounded about twelve years old.

He left an urgent message, then obtained the dragon lady's number from the secretary, who was eavesdropping nearby. Sullivan grinned as he watched Green turn on the Inspector act.

"One of your staff has seriously overstepped her bounds and has been interfering with a police investigation," he said into the mouthpiece. "Now she has chosen to avoid responsibility for her actions by refusing to return her calls. She may be withholding vital information, and I need to speak to her immediately. If I have not heard from her within half an hour—" Green glanced at his watch. Almost four o'clock! On Friday, no less. No doubt the entire school board would be closing down for the weekend any moment. "I shall be forced to contact your superintendent in charge."

Giving her no time to mount a counteroffence, he dictated his cell phone number, thanked her for her cooperation in the investigation, and signed off. "You bought yourself half an hour," he said, turning back to Sullivan.

Sullivan hesitated and glanced at his watch. "Look, I have to get down to the station and get the reports from the field.

Maybe one of the guys has already found the boyfriend, or some DNA, or an eyewitness to the pair that evening. At least let me check in with my men first."

"But we're out here, probably less than fifteen minutes from his house."

"Mike, I'm not stalling. There are a whole lot of leads we're following, and I'm not going to jump the gun before I'm properly prepared."

Green frowned at him thoughtfully. Sullivan's bristly hair stood in tufts, and his jaw jutted stubbornly. Green was about to argue when Sullivan heaved a sigh. "I've seen this kid on the ice, I've heard him in interviews. He hasn't let all this hype go to his head. He's a genuinely stand-up guy. Believes in honesty and honour on and off the ice. I just can't see him involved in something like this."

"Brian, we're cops." I shouldn't even have to say that, Green thought. How many honest, honourable men have we seen over the years, brought down by a moment of folly?

Smarting, Sullivan hauled himself to his feet. "Exactly, and once we get this Zukowski woman's information, once I know we've got no leads pointing in another direction, I'll go talk to Riley O'Shaughnessy. But it may have to wait till morning." As if to underline his point, he yanked open the glass door to the school office and stalked out.

Green considered the argument as he followed him down the hall. Outside, the heat hit him like a furnace blast, and sweat broke out on his back. Last night's rain had done nothing to break the humidity. He could feel his energy draining away. Sullivan was right. A lot of other evidence may have come to light, and in any case, if they were going to tackle the pride and joy of the local hockey world, they should have more ammunition. With any luck, someone had found the ice cream vendor or the discarded condom, and the luckless boyfriend would have nowhere to hide.

*   *   *

The smell of roast chicken wafted through the front door the moment he opened it. It stirred a strange, long-forgotten longing. His first thought was that Sharon must have come home, but he'd spoken to her only moments earlier to tell her he had to stay in town at least Saturday. Sharon had sounded unexpectedly mellow, as if the week at the lake had worked many of the knots out of her psyche. Her voice was throaty and mischievous, reminding him of the playful, sexy woman of their early years. He had to fight the urge to steer the car directly onto the highway towards the cottage. Instead he dutifully headed home, expecting an empty house without even the dog to talk to.

The smell of cooking took him aback. With slowly dawning amazement, he realized that Hannah was not only still here but cooking dinner.

He walked back to the kitchen to find her bent over a cookbook. Not just any cookbook, but his mother's, which had lain in a box for more than fifteen years before Sharon had unearthed it and given it a proper place on the kitchen shelf. His mother had not read English very well, particularly in the early years, so many of the pages were scrawled with Yiddish translations. This was what Hannah was peering at, so deeply absorbed that she had not heard him arrive. He recognized that absorption as another trait in the genes.

When he walked into the room, she jerked back in surprise and thrust the book away. "That stuff's Greek."

"Yiddish, actually. Your grandmother's."

"How do they read that stuff? It's just a bunch of squiggles." She cast him a quick look from under her long lashes. "Can you read it?"

He glanced at the recipe for herb-roasted *Shabbat* chicken. A lump rose in his throat. "I'm rusty, but I can try."

"It doesn't matter. I made it my way."

Another trait in the genes, he thought with a smile. "It smells good."

She grunted a grudging acknowledgement and turned to the stove. "Well, I thought *Zaydeh* might like it. But you didn't bring him."

He shook his head. "He's got a cold. But I'm glad you visited him the other day, honey. You made his day. And so will this, when we take him the leftovers tomorrow."

He disappeared into the dining room, still fighting the lump in his throat, and took out the silver Sabbath candlesticks. As he was setting the last of the cutlery, he looked up to find her watching him from the doorway.

"Did you really lose brothers and sisters in the Holocaust?"

"Half brother and sister, who would have been much older. *Zaydeh* was married in Poland as a young man. His wife and two children died in the ghetto. The babies always died first."

She pondered that. "They would have been my aunt and uncle. My mother never told me that. She just said your parents never liked her."

Green nodded, remembering his mother's dying plea. He'd been dating Ashley at the time, and his mother had clutched his arm with a strength that belied her wasted body. "Don't let them win, Mishka," she'd said.

He'd rejected her paranoia, which had so stifled his youth, and rushed headlong into the embrace of the forbidden. A mistake, except for one thing.

"Well, at least you did it right the second time," Hannah said.

"Honey—"

She turned and walked back into the kitchen, leaving him no chance to explain. Yet how could he explain to a seventeen-year-old who'd never known hatred or prejudice, how it felt to lose one's whole family, to be hunted down and exterminated by an outside world, simply because of a label?

"My mother would have adored you," he said, following her into the kitchen. "Just the way *Zaydeh* does. And you would have helped her begin to trust again."

"Trust in what?"

"In people. Despite the awful things they do."

Hannah shut the oven door and picked up a pot from the stove. "This girl who died. You said she was murdered?"

Startled by her abrupt shift in topic, Green jumped in hastily. "No, I didn't."

She gave him an impatient glance. "You said so yesterday. I was listening, see?"

He recognized the futility of denial. Tenacity was yet another trait that ran in the genes. "We don't know. We're keeping open all possibilities. Do you know her?"

Hannah shrugged. "I think I've seen her around once or twice. One of those blonde, blue-eyed princesses that gets away with murder."

"What do you mean?"

"Just that looks can be deceiving. While you cops are busy hassling the kids with dreads and mohawks, kids like her pretend to walk on water, when really they're down among the sharks with the rest of us." She cast him an impish smile. "You figure it out from there, Mr. Detective."

"What have you seen her do?"

"Oh, a little weed, a little E."

Ecstasy, Green thought with a twinge of excitement. Ecstasy was a stimulant that under the right circumstances—mixed with strong emotion or exertion—could cause cardiac problems. "Who does she hang out with?"

"Not my crowd, that's for sure. She doesn't even buy direct. She wheedles favours."

"From who?"

"Whom. That's what my English teacher's always saying. From her loyal subjects. That's okay, it's what all the popular girls do. It's how the world goes round."

"Can you give me names, Hannah? This could be really important."

She snorted. "No, I can't give you names. Bad enough you're a cop. If people think I snitch on them..." She peered into the pot, wrinkled her nose and dumped its contents into a bowl. From the smell, Green deduced it was carrots. "Look, you want to eat this stuff now? Because otherwise it will be totally burned."

He took his cue and helped serve dinner onto the plates. As they were carrying the odd-looking concoctions to the table, he tried one more time. "If you do learn something important, will you please slip me a name? Even if you have to write it in invisible ink and pin it under my windshield."

Her lips twitched in a smile as she reached for the matches. He watched her light the candles and recite the blessing for the first time. She was flawless. Afterwards she shot him a quick glance. "Don't hold your breath," she muttered, reaching for the *Kiddush* cup.

Ten

Saturday morning, Green dropped by the station at eight o'clock. The stifling heatwave had finally broken into a tumultuous thunderstorm that battered the street. The temperature had plummeted ten degrees, and a vicious wind ripped through the trees. Anyone with an ounce of sanity would be holed up in their houses enjoying a second cup of coffee, thought Green, but he was not surprised to find Brian Sullivan at his desk, checking the latest developments before he briefed the weekend staff.

Green strode over. "Despite what everyone says, Lea Kovacev was a recreational drug user."

Sullivan looked up. "Says who?"

"My source. Lea used a supplier among her friends. Talk to the drug squad, get them to ask around. Any word from MacPhail in the tox screen?"

Sullivan shook his head.

"Get on it."

Sullivan raised his large, square hands in surrender. "Anything else while you're at it?"

"Yeah, have you done any background check on Riley O'Shaughnessy?"

Sullivan shoved his papers away, looking exasperated. "I did some myself last night so I wouldn't get the rumour mill going."

Belatedly, Green noticed the red-rimmed eyes and the

spikes of unruly hair that betrayed his friend's fatigue. He'd been up half the night. Green softened. "Thanks, Brian. Turn up anything interesting?"

"Mostly what I already told you, about his hockey success. No drugs, no assaults, threats or other hints of trouble. In fact, the kid's a poster boy for the school board's anti-drug campaign. He has only one police contact, as a witness in some minor disturbance."

"What kind of disturbance?"

"A neighbour called the cops about a loud party at two in the morning. It was a residential street in Alta Vista. I live there, so I know you can barely peep after eleven at night."

"Whose house was it?"

"Vic McIntyre. He's a player's agent. Riley's agent, which was probably why he was there. His cousin Ben O'Shaughnessy was there too."

"How old was Riley at the time?"

"Barely seventeen. It was almost two years ago."

"Any other complaints against this agent?"

"Yeah, three earlier ones. Same neighbour. Then I guess McIntyre got fed up and moved, because he now lives in Hunt Club."

"Any more complaints?"

"Not yet, but Vic's a loudmouth. I've seen him interviewed on TV, and one time he even came to my son's hockey game. Scouting the talent early, I guess."

Green absorbed the implications. It was probably all irrelevant, but loud parties usually meant party drugs like ecstasy, so possibly, just possibly, there was a link to the dead girl. "Get someone to interview that neighbour, and let's have a look at who else was at the parties where those complaints were made. We're looking for a possible drug connection."

"What kind of drugs?"

"Ecstasy, cocaine? Something that can cause heart problems. I'm going to bug the RCMP to see if I can get those tox results back any faster."

A few minutes later, he was on the phone to Barbara Devine at her home, giving her an update, discussing the latest press release and prodding her to call her highly placed ex-lover at RCMP headquarters. Devine might not have much police experience on the ground, but she did have a string of judiciously chosen connections throughout the city. Indeed the province. She would need all her charms to obtain any cooperation on a Saturday in June. He had just signed off when his cell phone rang.

"Inspector Green? It's Rita Berens calling."

The voice was brisk and professional, but laced with an undertone of tension. Green took a moment to place the name. The dragon lady from the school board. "I expected a call last night," he said, just to keep her on her toes.

"We've not been able to locate Ms Zukowski, and I waited until we'd exhausted all possible avenues before calling you."

"What have you tried?"

"We've tried her cell phone and her home line numerous times. Yesterday we phoned all her schools, but most of them had closed down for the weekend. She didn't call in Friday afternoon to check messages or report in. I left an urgent message on her home phone, and when she still hadn't called in this morning, I sent one of my staff to her apartment. There was no answer."

"Is this a usual pattern of behaviour for her?"

"No. All my staff know to call in to the secretary at the end of the day, and I expect them to return their calls as soon as they're contacted. Ms Zukowski is generally conscientious about this."

"What's your next step?"

"I don't know. I'm asking you. I'm becoming concerned."

Privately, Green felt the same niggle of concern. There could be any number of innocent explanations, not the least of which was a weekend excursion with family or friends.

"Should we report her missing?" Berens asked.

"You could, but it's not yet forty-eight hours, and there are several steps you can take more easily through unofficial channels than we can. Contact her family, check her apartment, check if her vehicle is in its parking spot."

"It's the weekend, and I have other priorities, Inspector."

"And I have a homicide investigation to run. I can't have precious resources tied up by school board infighting."

"It's not infighting!"

"Until I have evidence to the contrary, that's exactly what it sounds like to me. Fearing disciplinary action from yourself or the principal, Ms Zukowski has chosen to make herself scarce."

"I'll be in touch," she said frostily and hung up. Green allowed her that small measure of defiance. He did plan to assign someone to track down the social worker's whereabouts, but he had no intention of telling the dragon lady that. He knew she would break all speed records trying to locate the missing woman. Control freaks do not tolerate staff who make them look bad. Woe betide Jenna Zukowski if she was in fact just lying low. Green, however, was beginning to fear a more sinister explanation. The woman *had* been poking around in a homicide investigation.

* * *

It took the dragon lady less than two hours to get back to him. He was in his office, poring over witness statements. Second-guessing Sullivan's leadership, but he couldn't help it. A crime was sometimes solved by that little unexpected needle in the haystack of evidence. "We've found her car for you," Berens announced without preamble. "It's parked outside her apartment building. However, she's still not responding to her phone or the buzzer."

"Where are you now?"

"In my car outside her apartment. I'm here with one of my staff."

"Then I suggest you ask the landlord to let you in for a look."

There was a pause, and when Berens resumed, her tone had chilled. "Look, I'm not comfortable with this. I've conferred with our board lawyer, and he's indicated this is a police matter, not one for the school board to be involved in. If you want to talk to her, then it's your responsibility to find her. You have the means to do so, he said."

Fucking lawyers, Green muttered to himself. Especially corporate lawyers, whose first, last and only instinct is to cover the corporate ass. "Well, your lawyer clearly knows very little about criminal law and the notions of obstruction of justice and interference in a police investigation. Ms Zukowski was acting in her capacity as a representative of the school board and is assumed to be operating under your supervision. In any case," he said airily, "we may be the least of your problems. I'm sure you're aware the media is covering every minute development in this case."

She got the point. Sputtering about lodging a formal complaint, she agreed to track down the building super. Once she'd hung up without a word of goodbye, however, Green remained in his chair, gripped by second thoughts. He'd won his battle with her, but it would be a hollow victory—indeed an ultimate loss—if her amateurish search of the apartment contaminated the scene and destroyed valuable evidence.

Grabbing his rain coat, he called her back to ask her and the super to wait outside the apartment until he arrived. As an afterthought, he shoved latex gloves, plastic evidence bags and a magnifying glass into his pocket. Sherlock Holmes would have been proud.

Jenna Zukowski's apartment was in Beacon Hill, one of the hundreds of towering, featureless highrises that had sprouted up all over the city during the 1970s. Its lobby was dingy and sterile, with fake marble floors, cloth panelled walls, and a single rubber plant drooping in the corner. When Green walked in, he stopped short in surprise. Rita Berens didn't look like any dragon lady he'd ever imagined. She was less than five feet tall, with short, curly blonde hair, impeccable make-up and a pert figure Sharon would die for, neatly packaged in a belted white trenchcoat and high black boots.

By contrast, the super was a six-foot, three-hundred-pound bruiser, recently roused from bed, to judge from his bloodshot eyes and sulky scowl. Fortunately his brain seemed too hazy to be concerned with warrants and technicalities. He pulled out his massive key ring without a word.

Green gestured to the bank of apartment buzzers. "Still no answer?"

Berens shook her head. Not a single curl dislodged.

"Let's go look at the car first," Green said, returning outside. The storm had reduced to a drizzle which coated everything in a chilly mist. Berens led the way around the building to the parking lot at the rear. The super frowned, roused slightly from his stupor.

"She's not supposed to park here. This is the visitor parking lot. I tell the tenants all the time, don't park here, we get complaints from visitors there's no room."

"Does Ms Zukowski park here often?"

"No, she's not one of the troublemakers. It's them that's too lazy to walk up the stairs from the underground garage."

Jenna's car was one of the legion of ubiquitous and unremarkable Honda Civics, this one silver in colour and sporting a single dent on its left rear bumper. Green had the same dent on his Subaru, caused by backing up into a lamppost in a moment of distraction.

Otherwise the car was untouched, although spattered with dusty raindrops. Green peered inside. The back seat of the car was buried in papers and fast food containers. Berens had joined him in peering through the window, and her nose wrinkled in distaste.

"What did she carry with her?" Green asked. "Briefcase, file folders, laptop?"

"I have no idea," Berens said, as if such minor housekeeping details were beneath her. "Most of my staff carry briefcases with their files. Some of them have laptops as well and keep their records on them. Perhaps in the trunk?"

Green hesitated. He still had no official investigation, no owner permission, no warrant, yet the car's presence in visitors' parking was out of character. Perhaps a little unobtrusive sleuthing was in order. He sent the super to get a hanger. While he waited, he snapped on latex gloves, extracted his magnifying glass and examined all the door locks and handles for signs of tampering. Nothing. The super arrived with a hanger and a long lock jimmy, which he handed to Green, who refrained from questions. It was many years since Green's skills in car jimmying had been tested, so it took him nearly five minutes to pop the lock on the Civic, and he could feel the super itching to take over. As he opened it, he noted it had an alarm which hadn't been set. A quick search through the debris of the interior and the glove compartment revealed nothing useful. Jenna was a Diet Coke and Tim Hortons addict and was doing serious harm to her arteries, if not her pocketbook, by her choice of food.

He popped the trunk latch, then lifted it with trepidation. Too many memories of bodies stashed in trunks. But the trunk was crammed full of winter tires, ski boots and old winter clothes. There would have been barely room for an emergency kit, let alone a briefcase or a laptop.

He returned to the front of the car. "Do your employees collect mileage records?"

"We reimburse their travel, but how precisely they keep track of mileage is up to them."

Green glanced in the car. If her records were as chaotic as her car, not very precisely at all. Still, it was worth a try. He slipped into the driver's seat to check the odometer and was surprised to find he had to stretch to reach the pedals. How tall was this woman, he wondered, and when he posed the question, Berens looked alarmed. She too had noticed how far back the seat was set.

"She's short and dumpy. No more than five-three, I'd say."

Green kept his expression bland, but recorded the odometer reading and the station the radio was set to. Sometimes criminals gave themselves away by the smallest of details. Climbing out of the car, he turned to the super, who was sitting on the curb looking more annoyed than concerned that trouble had brought the police to his door.

"How do tenants access the underground parking?"

"There's an access code."

Not a key or a magnetic card, which would be available to anyone in possession of Jenna's personal effects, but a memorized code carried inside her head. Whoever had parked this car had not done so with her permission, for otherwise she would have given them the code.

He called the com centre to request a patrol car. Before he impounded the car, he needed to check out Jenna's apartment to make absolutely sure she was not up there, closeted away with her lover, but he didn't want to leave it unguarded while he went upstairs. He had serious doubts she would be there. Twenty years of experience on the force told him quite another story.

Once he had the officer on guard, he nodded to the super, who was looking more sullen by the moment. Berens, on the other hand, looked unnerved to find herself out of her depth.

Inside, the apartment building was as featureless as outside. Its long straight corridors had rows of numbered beige doors along each side. When the super stopped at one of these, Green intervened before he could insert the key in the lock. Feeling like Sherlock Holmes, albeit more foolish, Green bent to examine the lock with his magnifying glass. There were no telltale scratches to suggest forced entry. Just inside the door, however, he could hear a cat meowing frantically. He took out new latex gloves and instructed them all to put them on before giving the super the go-ahead.

The cat rushed to greet them as they entered and began to twine itself between their legs, meowing. The apartment smelled of fermenting fruit and cat urine. Piles of newspapers, mail and dirty dishes cluttered the counters, and a linen suit lay tossed over a chair in the living room.

Jenna, however, was nowhere to be seen. A quick check of the rooms revealed her toothbrush in the bathroom and her pyjamas rumpled on the bed, but no cat food in the dish. She had not planned a trip away. She had intended to return, but judging from the cat's agitation, had not been home in some time.

Without waiting for permission, Berens began hunting through kitchen cupboards, presumably for cat food. Green left her to it and asked the super the last time he'd seen Jenna.

The super shrugged. "I got a hundred units in this building. You think I see everyone that comes and goes?"

"Does she have visitors? Perhaps a boyfriend?"

"I'm not the nanny, just the super. Her tap drips, her toilet leaks, I see her. Else I..." He lifted his massive shoulders again.

"Her car is here. Is it usual for her to go out on foot? Or take the bus?"

This time just a marginal lift of the shoulders. Then "Listen, can I go now? I got work to do."

Green gestured them both back towards the hall and nodded to Berens. "Find someone to take the cat. I'm going to seal this room until I get a warrant to search it. You can go back downstairs, but I'd like the two of you to keep yourselves available."

After some protests about their busy lives and multiple duties, they complied, leaving Green alone in the apartment. He phoned for another uniform back-up, then briefed Sullivan and asked him to start the paperwork for a search warrant. As he waited for the back-up, he began a preliminary, unofficial search for her work files, computer and appointment book, hoping one of them would give him a hint about what she'd been up to and whose paths she might have crossed.

A quick search turned up no briefcase or computer, so he began to look in earnest. It was nearly impossible. Newspapers, junk mail and work files cluttered almost every surface without apparent logic or method. He sifted through the piles carefully so as not to dislodge anything, and worked his way systematically through the kitchen and hall.

In the living room, under Thursday's paper, he found a

laptop. He hesitated. He ought to wait for the warrant and for proper technical back-up before delving into her private world. Yet he was convinced something had happened to her, and time might be running out. He opened the lid and stared at the cluttered desktop. Computer whizzes like Gibbs could find out what files she'd been working on most recently, but to Green the array of icons was a mystery, except for recognizable programs like Word, Internet Explorer and Outlook Express.

He clicked on the latter and was relieved to encounter no password or other barrier between him and her inbox. Thirty-six new messages began pouring in. The usual stock tips, penis enhancers and pleas from Nigerian banks, some digests from message groups and an online social work discussion forum. Surprisingly, no personal emails at all, leading him to think Jenna must not have an extensive social life. He checked the date of the first message to arrive. It was sent Thursday at 10:02 p.m.

Which meant Jenna Zukowski had not been near her email since Thursday evening, the day she had been nosing around at the school.

He checked her Sent box, but she had sent nothing at all on Thursday night. A more thorough search of the laptop could wait for the Hi Tech crew, but for now he just needed to know what she'd been investigating. He clicked on Internet Explorer and then on History, proud that he'd managed to retain something from watching Gibbs at work.

The History button unfolded a long list of sites. The girl had been very busy indeed, prowling all over the web in the last two days. Green's heart began to race as he read the names of the sites. Justin Wakefield, National Theatre School, the NHL Entry Draft, and at least half a dozen pages pertaining to one particular player—Riley O'Shaughnessy. He'd been the last thing she'd researched the night before she disappeared.

Eleven

Mentally, Brian Sullivan could feel his feet dragging as he followed Green across the lawn to the school. The man who greeted them at the door wore a scowl on his thin, weasely face which didn't improve when Green thanked him for his help. The drizzle had stopped, leaving the air fresh and cool, but his bald dome still glistened with sweat. Sullivan suspected he knew the cause—harsh words from the top of the school board food chain, whom Green had called personally to obtain cooperation from the school.

"This is most improper, you know," the guy said. Prusec, Green had called him, and Sullivan thought the name suited him. The priss relocked the doors behind them and led the way down the darkened hall. "That information is confidential, and his parents could have my head."

"A student of yours has died under questionable circumstances, Mr. Prusec. I doubt very much any parent would want to object. Riley O'Shaughnessy has an image to maintain, don't forget."

Sullivan remained quiet, wrestling with mixed feelings. He was curious to meet the young star both his sons aspired to emulate, but unhappy at the prospect of grilling him about his role in Lea Kovacev's death. But with Jenna Zukowski's disappearance and Riley O'Shaughnessy's name on her computer's search history, he knew there was no longer a choice. Green was on a roll, and all

Sullivan could do now was limit the media frenzy. Green's idea of doing that was to do the field interview himself rather then involve more officers. That was his excuse anyway.

Prusec sat down at the computer in the main office and began to type. "This information is on every computer down at the Board, including the director of education's."

Sullivan smiled to himself. Green had said the officious prick was in major cover-your-ass mode, and he was certainly playing true to form.

"Possibly, but this way, if we need anything else like access to his student locker," Green said blandly, "you'll already be here."

Prusec pursed his thin lips as he clicked through screens until he finally arrived at Riley's file. "He lives with his uncle, has for the past two years that he's been playing for the 67's. Even so, he misses a great deal of school, but many elite athletes do." Prusec arched his eye brows. "He manages to maintain a decent average despite that. Of course, he has a reduced timetable, and one of his classes is Outdoor Education, which he should excel at."

Green remembered the cousin mentioned in the McIntyre noise complaint. "Does his uncle have any children at this school?"

Prusec pouted and scrawled something on a message slip. "This address is what I was told to give you, this is what you get. And should you need any further assistance from me, I'd appreciate it if you called me directly."

He let them out the front door with a very audible click of the lock behind them. Green chuckled as he handed the paper to Sullivan. "Saunderson Avenue. You know where that is?"

Sullivan stared at the paper in dismay. Not only did he know the street, he knew the uncle. Darren O'Shaughnessy was a fellow hockey dad like himself, with a teenage son in the sport and a temper that had nearly had him barred from the games. Darren owned Waterworks Plumbing, and he drove a large muscle van with a logo of a smiling toilet on its sides and banners for the Ottawa Senators on every inch of bumper space. Some hockey parents didn't even go in to watch the game when they saw that van in the parking lot, and a couple of young referees refused to officiate the games his son was in.

Sullivan had had only one run-in with the man, when then ten-year-old Sean was on a house team with Darren's boy. Sean had been playing defence and Benny O'Shaughnessy right wing. Benny had been on a rush from behind his own net, but had been tripped into the boards by the other team's forward. He'd been down on the ice only a couple of seconds before Darren had leaped over the boards and charged toward the players, screaming at Sean for not protecting his teammate by intercepting the other team's forward. It had taken Sullivan and two other fathers to keep Darren from flattening Sean into the ice. There had been a lot of games in the years since then, and the boys had gone their separate ways, but Sullivan had never forgotten that raw rage. Why had he never made the connection between that prick and Riley O'Shaughnessy?

Darren's van was visible in the driveway from a block away, and as Green drew his Subaru to a stop at the curb, Darren himself pulled his lumpy, shaven head out from under the hood. He squinted at them a moment then lumbered down the drive, wiping his grease-coated hands on his jeans. The years had not been good to Darren. He'd put on at least forty pounds, all of it in a beer gut, and his face was the colour of raw steak. He grinned when he recognized Sullivan and stuck out his hand.

"Sully! How's it going, man?"

Sullivan sensed Green's surprise as he introduced the two, but Darren pumped his hand cheerfully. "Good to see you, Sully. I see your boys are doing great. Your older one might be a future NHLer yet."

"How is your boy doing?"

Darren shrugged. "Ben's coming along. He could be really good if he put his mind to it, but you know how it is with teenagers. Girls, parties... Now what can I do you for, fellas?"

Sullivan studied him closely. Darren had always been the friendliest, most outgoing guy as long as his son wasn't on the ice. The kind of guy to drive six kids all over hell's half acre to tournaments or lend a hand fixing your deck. Sullivan could see no sign of guardedness or concern on his face, just genuine delight, which in itself was strange. Most people show a bit of both when two cops show up at their door.

"We'd like a word with Riley, Darren," Sullivan said. "Is he here?"

Darren's eyebrows shot up in astonishment. "Riley? No, he went back to Gananoque for the weekend. He and his dad drove down this morning with some of his stuff." Now wariness hooded his eyes. "Why? Something wrong?"

"We just need to talk to him."

Darren's face hardened, giving a glimpse of the old hockey dad. An instant later, the anger was gone and he was all cooperation again. "He'll be back tomorrow night, in time for school Monday. Is that soon enough?"

"That'll be fine," Green interjected before Sullivan could open his mouth. "Brian's been telling me all about your nephew. He has a big day coming up, eh?"

Darren grinned, but not before Sullivan caught the wary flicker in his eyes. He wants to know where the hell we're going with this, he thought.

"The kid's a phenom," he said. "Maybe even the next Great One."

Green leaned casually against the side of the car. "Are you all going down to Ohio for the draft?"

137

"I wish," said Darren, shaking his head. "But I've got a business to run. Too bad it's this year. Next year the draft's in Ottawa. My brother Ted—that's Riley's dad—will be driving him. It's about a twelve hour drive to Columbus. I was thinking of sending Ben. He's playing for the Nepean Raiders now, not in Riley's league, but he's got good potential. I was thinking I'd send him along for the ride, just for inspiration, you know?"

"Don Cherry says it's better for the draft hopefuls not to go," Green said. "Too hard on the nerves."

Sullivan nearly choked on his own laughter. Green might not know the hockey commentator from Wayne Gretzky, but he'd obviously done his homework and was pulling off a pretty good imitation of a guy who knew what he was talking about.

Darren snorted. "Cherry's full of shit. Greatest day in the kids' lives! And Riley will get picked, don't you worry. My brother says both the Flyers and the Oilers are fighting over him."

"I bet it's been pretty exciting for your son to have him around for the past couple of years."

"Yeah, well, you know..." Darren shifted and wiped the sweat off his forehead with the back of his hand. "The kid's been really busy. Practices and games and conditioning and all this personal development stuff. His agent keeps him pretty tied up. This is the first weekend Riley's had off all year. Not that I'm complaining. The man's done wonders with him."

Sullivan stepped in to rescue Green, who was sure to be at the end of his hockey expertise by now. "Vic McIntyre? I've heard stuff about that guy. Wild parties, bully tactics..."

"That's bullshit, man. The hockey establishment hates him because he drives a hard bargain. But the guy gets results. Sure, he rides the kids hard, so he lets them cut loose sometimes too. Whatever he does, it worked for Riley. He always had talent, but this year he's really bulked up, and mentally he's tougher too."

"Is that in an agent's job description?" Green asked casually. "I don't know much about the business, but it seems to me that's a coach's job."

"Just protecting his investment. Vic's been in all aspects of the business, and he knows what's needed." Darren's eyes narrowed as he glanced from one detective to the other. "Look, is this about Riley or Vic McIntyre? Because I know Vic's had a little trouble with you guys before, and I don't want shit rubbing off on Riley. The kid's put his heart and soul into the game."

Sullivan shrugged noncommitally. Let the man think what he wanted. "At this stage, Darren, we're just checking into things." Sullivan flicked his card out of his pocket and handed it to Darren. "Have Riley or his dad give me a call some time when they're back, okay?"

"Yeah, sure. Monday good?"

"Monday's fine." Sullivan climbed into the car with a casual wave.

Darren was still standing at the curb watching them as they pulled away. "Do you think it worked?" Green asked.

Sullivan shook his head. "With everything this family has at stake, I doubt it. I think Darren will be on the phone to his brother before we even round the corner."

Green nodded. He had that faraway look in his eyes that Sullivan recognized all too well. The rest of his Saturday was going to be shot; they were going to Gananoque. He made a last ditch effort to salvage it.

"I don't think he knew Lea Kovacev was Riley's girlfriend, though. He seemed to have no idea what we were there for. And trust me, he's not that good an actor. This guy wears everything on his face."

"Perhaps," Green said. "But the minute he tells Riley the cops were asking after him, Riley's going to know why."

"If he was Lea's boyfriend."

Green inclined his head. "True. If."

*　　*　　*

Before the two detectives were even halfway back to the station, Sullivan's phone rang. Wallington was on the line. The roar and hiss in the background made it hard to hear him.

"I'm at Hog's Back," he shouted. "I've got the girl who sold Lea the ice cream, and she has a story I thought you might like to hear. Do you want me to bring her to the station?"

Sullivan made a quick calculation. He was just approaching Riverside Drive; a quick detour west along the river would bring him to Hog's Back. "Just hang on to her. I'll be there in a jiff."

The "girl" turned out to be a dumpy, middle-aged woman with frizzy orange hair and a pair of missile tits you could impale a moose on. Someone should have told her pointy bras went out with Marilyn Monroe. According to her name tag, she was Phyllis. She was working behind the counter at the Pagoda, where a line-up had begun to form. She ignored the loud protests when she slapped the "closed" sign on the counter and stepped outside to talk to the detectives.

She talked at breakneck speed. "I don't got much time, because I'm not supposed to close like that, but this is important, eh? I thought I recognized that girl when I saw her picture in the paper last week, but people can look so different, eh? And it was dark, and even with the lighting, there's a glare. But when the detective asked me if I sold anyone like her an ice cream, well, then I was sure, eh? It was Monday night, you said?"

"Well, was it?" Green asked drily.

"Nights are all the same to me, eh? So I'll take your word for it. Anyways it was late, I was closing, and there weren't too many people in the park. This girl and her boyfriend came up and asked me for ice cream, and I said I'd already cashed out, and she begged me. They were such a cute couple, they looked so lovey-dovey—hard to believe that still happens to today's kids, or to anybody for that matter. I mean, before my Billy took up with Rufus, he'd hardly ever touch me—well, maybe that was the reason. But these two had their arms around each other's necks and their lips all over the place. I hardly wanted to look. She must have given him fifty kisses while they were waiting. Anyways, she just wouldn't take no for an answer, she was that excited and determined. In the end, I opened up the freezer and gave them two. No charge. It wasn't worth my time to open up the cash again. But if the company ever found out..."

For the first time, she stopped for breath long enough for Sullivan to get a word in. Beside him, Wallington was grinning. Obviously the woman was just as entertaining the second time around.

"Did you get a good look at the boyfriend?"

"Well, he was quieter. It was her did all the talking. But he was a dishy one, tall, dark and handsome like in the fairytales."

"Do you mean dark-skinned?"

"Oh, no, he was white. Just dark-haired. Curly. She kept ruffling it and laughing."

"How long was the hair?"

"Not down in his collar or anything. He was neat looking. The shoulders on him—whew!" Phyllis fanned herself.

Painstakingly, Sullivan extracted a description from her, and with each detail, his heart grew heavier. The picture she painted fit Riley O'Shaughnessy to a T. Green, however, had been oddly silent, and once Sullivan had arranged for her to view a photo line-up later in the day, Green stepped quietly into the breach.

"Did anything about the girl's behaviour strike you as odd?"

Phyllis, who had just turned to go back to her post, looked taken aback. "How do you mean, odd?"

"You said she was excited and laughing. Unusually so?"

"Well, she was in love, like I said. And love can make you goofy. That's what it was, I'm sure."

As Green and Sullivan headed back to the car, Green shook his head. "I'm not so sure."

"You're thinking the marijuana roaches?"

"Possibly. But given the degree of mania that woman described, and the unexplained cardiac arrest, I'm thinking something stronger. This is the first concrete evidence we have that Lea was high the night she died. I want Lyle Cunningham to expedite the analysis of the roaches and also look at every piece of physical evidence collected at the park bench that might have contained drugs"

Sullivan climbed into the car, his spirits lifting marginally. It made sense now to wait until Phyllis had confirmed Riley as the boyfriend before they headed off to interview him. Which meant that the rest of Sullivan's afternoon was not going to be shot on a three-hour round trip to Gananoque. Furthermore, if Lea Kovacev had been high on drugs the night she died, then her death might have been accidental. Perhaps terror and panic had nothing to do with it, and Riley O'Shaughnessy was guilty of no more than being a hapless bystander. If that was the case, the poor kid might not come out of it with his reputation unscathed, but adolescent indiscretion was far less damaging than criminal negligence or homicide.

Except for that damn business of her being thrown over the cliff afterwards.

*　　*　　*

It was no surprise to either detective when Phyllis picked Riley O'Shaughnessy out of a photo line-up later than evening. Reached at home, Lyle Cunningham agreed to expedite the drug analyses, but could promise nothing before Monday. Green protested when Sullivan filled him in. They were sitting in Green's office doing a last minute check of the day's reports. The clock on Green's desk read 20:06.

"I wanted those results when we go to interview Riley in the morning," Green grumbled.

Sullivan tipped his chair back and eyed Green wearily. "You know, Mike, we could just as easily wait till he's back in town Monday. Save ourselves the trip and maybe have the drug testing to back us up."

Green shook his head. "I want the element of surprise. With his uncle tipping him off, he's already had too much time to prepare himself and cover his ass."

"He's a kid, not a hardcore criminal. The longer he waits, the more scared he's going to get." When Green continued to shake his head, Sullivan sighed. "This is our Sunday we're giving up. It's Sean's hockey team picnic tomorrow. I promised him I'd go. I miss way too many of my kids' things as it is, and so do you."

Green fought his own impatience, knowing Sullivan was right. Knowing that there was no substitute for time invested in their children's lives, and that even as he sat reviewing reports, he should be down at the cottage with his own son.

"There is a third alternative," he said, as an idea struck. "Gananoque is not far from the cottage we're renting on Lower Rideau Lake. I can go to the cottage this evening, swing down to Gananoque tomorrow morning, and still have most of the day with the family." He warmed to the prospect. "Who knows, I may even persuade Hannah to join us at the lake."

Sullivan's tense posture relaxed, and a grateful smile spread across his broad, freckled face. "You got an address in Gan?"

"No, but it's not that big a town. I'm sure everyone in town will be able to point me to where the local hockey hero lives. I just wish..."

"What?"

"I wish I had something, a little something more, to use as leverage."

The solution came to him fifteen minutes later just as he was packing up to go home. He'd already phoned Sharon to tell her he was coming out, and he'd left a message for Hannah on her cell. When his own cell phone rang, he thought it was her, and it took him a moment to focus on the clipped French Canadian voice. The man's tone was chilly.

"Dr. Pommainville, toxicology. You want this result right away?"

Green glanced at the time on his watch, astonished. Almost nine o'clock on a Saturday night! He wondered what acrobatics Barbara Devine had performed to accomplish that. "Yes! Thank you very much. Anything?"

"Three substances were present in her blood. A small amount of ephedrine, and large concentrations of THC and amphetamine."

Green was surprised. Ephedrine was a common stimulant found in cold medicines and diet pills, but hardly a drug of choice for kicks. "No ecstasy?"

"No, but methamphetamine is much stronger. Judging by the concentration, injected or smoked."

Both extremely dangerous, potentially addictive ways to get a buzz. Green felt an irrational surge of anger at Lea's blind, youthful quest for thrills. "Enough amphetamine to kill her?"

"That's for the pathologist to determine."

"But can you guess? You must see cases like this all the time."

The scientist paused. "I have seen death from this amount. In a small woman, perhaps, with other factors like exertion. And since ephedrine is a stimulant, maybe together..."

Exertion, Green thought, as in a physical struggle before death? He thanked the man and hung up, his thoughts already planning the next step. He needed to check with Lea's mother whether the girl took cold medicine or diet pills, but regardless of that, the ephedrine was a minor contributor. A meth overdose combined with a struggle had killed Lea. That meant whoever had inflicted those bruises on her arms had contributed to her death. Until Lyle Cunningham got the marijuana roaches and other items analyzed, the exact means of the drug overdose remained unclear, but at least this was leverage he could use with Riley.

He was formulating his line of questioning when his cell phone rang again. This time he recognized the high-pitched, manic voice at the end of the line.

"Mike, old buddy!" crowed Frank Corelli. "How ya doing?"

"I'm not talking to you, Corelli. Not after what you pulled today."

Corelli's voice dropped a notch. "The photo? I know, that was tacky. I tried to get the guys not to run it, but what can I say? We got to sell papers."

"And the Nazi quote? Also not your department?"

"Yeah! You know I don't write the headlines. Come on, the more you work with me, the more you control the story."

Green hesitated, for the reporter had a point. Part of him wanted to slam the phone down in the two-faced whiner's face, but part of him was already considering how to gain an advantage.

Corelli seemed to interpret the silence as acquiescence. "I'm dying here, Mike. We go to print in a couple of hours, and I've got nothing but a black hole. Any post mortem results on the Kovacev case? Any forensic tidbits you can toss my way?"

"There is a whole lot of forensic evidence to process, Frank. Three crime scenes. We're still working on it. You can fill your hole with that."

"Aw, come on. That won't even get me the back page. Anything on her love life? I hear she had a secret lover."

"Oh, yeah? Did you get a name too, Frank? We could really use one."

"So you're saying the police don't know who her secret lover is? Are you appealing to the public?"

Green thought fast. "Yes, that might work. Also..." He hesitated as a crazy idea came to him. He'd used Frank before to plant information that he wanted a suspect to know—information that was not yet official and was sometimes even misleading—in the hopes it would drive the bad guy to action. "There's some suggestion bad drugs were involved. Her blood shows more than safe levels of an illegal substance, so whoever sold it to her is looking at...oh, I don't know, a possible manslaughter charge? You might want to warn people that there are bad drugs on the street."

"I see. So this is a kind of public safety announcement."

"Yeah."

Frank chuckled. "You're a prince! Always looking out for the public, and your friendly neighbourhood scribbler."

"Anonymous police source, remember?"

Corelli sputtered his usual reassurances before slamming the phone down. Green pictured him already hitting the keyboard. The reporter would spin that tidbit into a nice little story that would hit the news stands all over Eastern Ontario well before Green headed down to Gananoque in the morning.

Twelve

Corelli outdid himself. His story hit the front page with a full page picture of Lea and the usual understated *Sun* headline "BAD DRUGS KILL TEEN". When Green picked up a copy of the paper in Portland on his way down to Gananoque the next morning, he was grateful he'd taken the time to warn Lea's mother before he and Hannah headed out to the country.

Gananoque was a small town on the St. Lawrence River in the heart of the Thousand Islands, and although tourism was the lifeblood of its economy these days, it had once done a thriving business in rum running and other forms of smuggling. The rugged, slightly defiant character of the town still remained today. Riley O'Shaughnessy was one of their own, from a family with deep roots and broad tentacles in the region. O'Shaughnessy boys had first tilled the land north of the town in the early 1800s, and their numerous descendants had tried their hand at ship building, milling, blacksmithing and most recently guide fishing. All this Green learned from the Esso gas station owner on the edge of town, who even admitted that a little rum running had probably figured in the mix.

"O'Shaughnessys are resourceful, that's one thing. Not good at keeping money, but they find lots of ways of making it." The gas station owner had mistaken Green for yet another journalist looking for an angle, and Green had not bothered to dissuade him. He listened without interruption until the man spotted another

147

customer ambling towards the cash and cut the conversation short with a vague gesture towards the east end of town.

Green had barely begun his search of the modest Victorian woodframe houses when a big banner stretched across the front porch of one of the houses caught his eye.

"Knock 'em dead, Riley," it read. Green stopped in front of the house. It could just be a fan, or one of the many O'Shaughnessy cousins who lived in the area. It was a simple, two-storey clapboard house with a steeply pitched roof and a covered porch running the length of the front. The white paint was fresh, and the garden boasted splashes of showy pink flowers. An ancient blue Buick sat on blocks in the gravel drive, and a collection of boats under tarps littered the side yard.

Green climbed out of his car, folded the *Sun* article into his pocket and walked up to the front door. A small wreath of dried flowers announced "welcome", but the large black cat on the porch hissed as it scurried away. He rang the doorbell, and after what seemed an eternity, a woman opened the door. She was tall and raw-boned, wearing blue sweatpants stretched over expansive hips and a thin brown sweater several sizes too small for her. Her greying hair flew about her shoulders in frizzy clumps, and her broad face looked apprehensive. The smell of burnt baking drifted from the interior.

"Can I help you?"

"Mrs. O'Shaughnessy?"

Irritation replaced the apprehension, and she made to shut the door. He stuck his foot in the crack. She kicked it with surprising strength. "Go away! Come back at eleven, my husband will be back from church."

Hastily he produced his badge and introduced himself through the crack in the door. The scowl vanished, and her eyes widened in dismay.

"Oh my! I'm so sorry!" She flung back the door. "I thought you were another of those reporters, or someone else come to gawk. It's been getting worse and worse. Come through, please. I'm sorry about the mess, and the smoke." She waved her arms as if to dispel it. "I forgot the meat pies I was making for lunch. Clean forgot. Fell asleep..." She turned to him, reddening. "Well, that's no excuse, and anyway, that's not why you're here, I'm sure. My brother-in-law Darren rang us yesterday and said you wanted a word with Riley. But he said you'd see him when he gets back to Ottawa."

"I'm renting a cottage on Lower Rideau Lake and felt like a Sunday drive. I've never been to Gananoque."

She led him into a small living room overstuffed with furniture and knickknacks, everything from family photos to hockey trophies to stuffed fish. It was a friendly room and, like the message on the door, welcoming. He had the impression the O'Shaughnessys had lived there a long time, possibly generations, and had never thrown anything out.

"Oh no? Well, you must take one of the boat tours of the islands, see where all the millionaires live. But I'm afraid you may have a wait right now, because Riley's not here."

Green groaned inwardly. Talk about the runaround. "Is he at church too?"

"No." She paused, and a faint distaste curled her lip. "His agent called. Said he had something to show him. Picked him up about an hour ago."

Green was intrigued by the hint of distaste. Was it just because Vic McIntyre was an asshole, he wondered, or was it something more specific? "Did Mr. McIntyre take him back to Ottawa with him?"

"I haven't the least idea. He didn't tell him to pack his things or anything, so I don't think so. But you never know with that man."

"Are they very close?"

"Too close, if you ask me. But then, no one ever does. Don't spoil the boys' dreams, everyone says. But this is the first weekend we've had Riley home since last fall, and I've got up a big family dinner with all the cousins, to wish him luck. By next weekend he'll be on the road to Ohio. And now look, I've even burnt the meat pies."

"That's too bad," Green murmured. "I imagine there's a lot of pressure on him right now. A lot of people wanting a piece of him, like the media, hockey fans."

Her skin had a pale, almost translucent quality, and it mottled pink and blue as she flushed. "That's why I was so rude to you, I confess. His agent keeps setting up these interviews. Yesterday it was the *Kingston Whig-Standard* came around, and Riley almost bit their head off. He's always been really good with pressure, but when he hid in his room and told his father to get rid of them, I knew it was getting too much. His father says he doesn't know what Riley's worried about, he's going to the NHL for certain, but having the whole town hanging their hopes on you..."

Belatedly, a thought struck her, for she sucked in her breath. "Has something happened? Riley hasn't been himself this weekend—even the visit here was unexpected, his dad decided he needed a break. But why do the police want to speak with him?"

Green had already decided on the version of the truth he was going to offer. Innocuous but credible. "A girl at his school died this past week, and we're interviewing all her friends to find out what happened. Riley was in one of her classes, and we understand they were friends."

Mrs. O'Shaughnessy looked dismayed. "How awful. How did she die?"

"We're not sure. Her body was pulled from the river near the waterfall where she disappeared." He provided just enough detail to nudge her toward the conclusions he wanted.

"We have the same problem here. Every year kids do reckless things and drown in the St. Lawrence River." She frowned. "I wonder if that's why Riley has been so upset this weekend."

"Upset in what way?"

"He didn't say. Riley works everything out on his bike. Or on the ice. He just goes really quiet, takes out his bike, and disappears for hours. Racing along the river parkway, sometimes all the way to Brockville. If he hadn't gone into hockey, he could have been a competitive bike racer."

"Did he say anything at all?"

She shook her head, looking distressed, as if she'd somehow failed to help him.

"To his father, maybe?"

"That's unlikely. His father is not much of a talker either. Oh, he would do anything for Riley. He's our only son, and Ted used to do everything with him. All those endless hockey practices—I was busy with the girls—and the private skating lessons and the hockey camps."

Green nodded, grateful that all Sullivan's whining over the years was coming in handy. "Yes, I have a friend who's a really dedicated hockey dad. Even on a good salary, it's hard to keep up."

"Ted works hard and makes a decent living for us, but not for all the equipment and the camps Riley needed to keep up with the other kids. And the girls need things too, and it's not really fair..." She checked herself. "That's why Ted was so keen when Vic came along. Someone who knew the business and could look after Riley's interests in all this. He handles all the sponsors and endorsements too. Riley's an extraordinary hockey player, but he's still just a boy."

Through the living room window, Green saw a battered white pick-up truck slow and turn into the drive. A man climbed out, paused to eye Green's Subaru at the curb, and headed up the walk. He had a leathery, sunburned face, a long, reedy body and a full head of curly salt-and-pepper curls, yet Green recognized the resemblance to Darren O'Shaughnessy immediately. This must be Riley's father.

His wife's smile turned to dismay as he walked in the door without a word of greeting. "Where are the girls?" she asked.

He didn't look at her but instead rivetted his tense gaze on Green. "They wanted to play at Brandy's new house. Who's this?"

"This is a detective from Ottawa, waiting to see Riley."

"Mike Green. And you're Ted O'Shaughnessy?"

Ted took a step back like a wary fighter. "What's this about?"

"He wants to talk to Riley about the girl who died. I told him maybe that's the reason Riley's upset."

"He's not upset. He's got a big day coming up. What kid wouldn't be on edge?"

"So you haven't noticed anything?" Green asked.

Ted shrugged as he took off his suit jacket. "Nothing that a bit of peace and quiet won't fix."

"I think Mr. McIntyre's riding him too hard," the mother said.

Ted headed into the kitchen, returning with a can of Coke. "I keep telling you, Noreen. He needs that. He's a big boy, and it's a tough world he's getting into."

"How did he meet Mr. McIntyre?" Green asked casually.

Ted cracked open the Coke and dropped into a chair by the window. "Vic used to be a scout, and before that a minor league trainer and coach in Toronto. He knows his stuff. He saw Riley when he was playing for the Midget team here in Gananoque. He was only fourteen and sprouting up like a beanpole, but even back then he was already being talked about and winning scoring trophies. He was fast, and he could handle the puck."

"That was Ted's doing," Noreen said. "Ted got him in just

152

about every skating class he could find between Brockville and Kingston, and every winter he flooded our backyard..."

"Noreen, I don't think the detective wants a blow-by-blow."

She twisted in her chair with an effort and gestured to the big empty backyard, most of which now lay in weeds. "Ted never let me plant a thing. He made the biggest rink he could, and he and Riley would practice, practice, practice. Ted was a pretty fair goaltender in his day, and he'd challenge Riley to rush him. To this day, Ted insists that's why Riley's so good at scoring."

Her eyes glowed with pride, as if she could talk for hours about her son. Privately, Green was ticking off all the people who had a major stake in Riley's success. His parents, his agent, even Uncle Darren, for whom Riley was an inspiration to his own son.

Ted, however, fiddled with his Coke irritably and glanced outside. "I don't think Riley's coming back any time soon. I don't want to waste your time, detective."

Green shrugged. "A few more minutes is no problem. Did you ever get up to Ottawa to see his games?"

"Oh yes," Noreen said. "Ted hated to miss a game when it was in this area—Belleville, Kingston, Ottawa." She laughed. "We've seen every cheap Super 8 hotel in a five hundred kilometre radius. At least Ted has. It was harder for me, with the girls at home and..." She paused, and a look of sorrow stole over her face. "I tried to get to some of the games."

"You don't mind the driving, Ted?"

"It's not that far. But I'm self-employed, and every hour missed is a dollar lost, so it can be tough."

"At least in Ottawa, Ted has his brother to stay with," his wife countered. "A good excuse for the brothers to get together." Again a faint distaste twisted her smile. So the brother-in-law, like the agent, is not on her list of favourite people, Green thought.

"You don't stay with Riley's agent?"

Ted looked surprised. "Oh, no, McIntyre keeps our relationship strictly professional, pretty much between Riley and himself."

"So you don't discuss Riley's affairs with him at all?"

"Not since he turned eighteen. Like I said, he's a big boy."

Green allowed a little incredulity into his voice. "Maybe, but you don't grow up overnight, no matter what the law says."

Ted's jaw tightened, but he didn't reply. Noreen flushed at the implied rebuke. "That's the way Mr. McIntyre wants it. Besides, Riley's always known exactly what he wants. Some of the media and the other parents used to accuse us of pushing too hard, but it was always Riley doing the pushing. He was always so focussed and organized, no theatrics or hidden agendas. Strong-willed, yes—but that's a good thing in a man. No matter what you asked of him, he could do it and more."

"Still, it's a big complicated world he's stepping into. Full of people who might try to take advantage."

Both of them sat very still for a moment, then Noreen gave him a long, searching look. "Do you have something else on your mind, Inspector? Besides the classmate who died? Is there something we should know?"

"About what?"

"You've asked questions about Mr. McIntyre, and now you're talking about people taking advantage."

Of all the topics he had casually covered, Green found it interesting that she had connected those two. He decided to push it. "I do have concerns, yes, about the possibility of exploitation or manipulation when I hear that McIntyre is working directly with Riley."

She got to her feet, and for the first time he noticed the effort it took. The woman is not well, he realized. She walked to the window and leaned against the frame, peering out into the street as if hoping her son would appear safe and sound.

"It's simple business sense," Ted snapped. "Look at all the endorsements McIntyre's lined up already. He stands to make a whole lot more money if Riley does well, so he's not going to do anything to harm him."

"I know you say that, honey, and it makes sense, but..."

"But money isn't everything, is it," Green added softly. "There's his health and his happiness."

Ted crushed the empty Coke can in his fist. "You know this is what Riley wants, Noreen. Ever since he first stepped on an ice rink. He lives and breathes hockey!"

"But that's the point. He's never known anything but hockey. What other career does he have to compare it to?" she said, gesturing to their dilapidated backyard cluttered with rusty chunks of engines and tools. "There's the folks around here, scraping to make ends meet, and then there's the folks on Millionaires' Row on the St. Lawrence. Waterfront estates so extravagant it would take most of the budget of Gananoque to keep them running. That's what money buys."

As if by uncanny coincidence, a low rumble sounded in the street, and Green glanced through the window to see a flash of red pull into the drive. Noreen gasped and hurried to fling wide the front door. Green followed in her footsteps just in time to see two men climb out of a shiny red Ford Mustang.

One he recognized as Riley O'Shaughnessy, his cheeks ruddy and his dark curls whipped by the wind. The other was a stubby, middle-aged man stuffed into an unflattering green golf shirt and black stovepipe jeans. He had a pugnacious jaw and small, pig-like eyes that sized up the O'Shaughnessys shrewdly.

"Mom! Dad!" Riley shouted. "My graduation present!"

"Jesus, Mary and Joseph," Ted muttered, yanking his tie loose as if it were strangling him. Then he turned his back and disappeared up the stairs.

Anger rather than delight flitted across his mother's face. "But Riley, you can't afford that!"

The stubby man held up his hand. "It's only leased, Mrs. Noreen. We traded in his old Jeep and got a good deal. Plus it's a business expense. It's just a little fun leading up to draft day." He reached up and ruffled the boy's hair. "Handsome devil, isn't he? He'll be fighting off the girls. But the camera will eat it all up too, and that won't hurt his image one bit. When the big endorsements roll in, he'll be able to buy each one of you the car of your dreams. That old pick-up of Ted's? History."

Then the man, whom Green took to be Vic McIntyre, caught sight of him standing in the open doorway, and his slick grin vanished. Does the guy know I'm a cop, Green wondered, despite the cottage jeans and T-shirt?

McIntyre marched towards the door, making no pretense of civility. Staring hard at Green, he addressed the mother. "Is this one of Riley's cousins?"

Noreen said nothing for a moment before her own civility finally won out. "No, this is Inspector Green of the Ottawa Police."

McIntyre's lips tightened, but he showed no surprise. He knows exactly why I'm here, Green thought, and why I want to question Riley about Lea Kovacev. "Aren't you way out of your jurisdiction, Inspector?"

"Police Services cooperate all the time," Green replied breezily. It was true, although the fact that he hadn't mentioned his presence to the Gananoque Police made it misleading. But for this asshole, he suspected loopholes were the essence of the law.

"Have you got some kind of warrant? Otherwise I don't believe we have to tell you shit."

"You don't have to, although at that point I obviously get suspicious, so I call in the OPP and I escort Riley back to Ottawa, where we have a nice, formal taping room for interviews.

Someone from the media is bound to get hold of that."

McIntyre's jaw thrust out further. During this interchange, Green was aware of Riley walking around his car, brushing dirt from its sides. In person, he was an extraordinarily charismatic presence. Taller and more powerfully built than his father, he moved with the grace and agility of a cat. Vitality radiated from every muscle. Now he turned to walk up towards the house, and he caught sight of Green. His jaw dropped, his step faltered. Robbed of energy, he looked as if he hadn't slept in days. His eyes were hollow and shot through with red, and his whole face seemed to sag. He looked at Green not with puzzlement but with fear.

The boy too knows why I'm here, Green thought.

"Don't you fucking threaten me," McIntyre was saying. Not a guy for subtlety.

Green drew out his notepad. He loved the drama of that prop. "What's your name, sir?"

"I'm Victor McIntyre, not that it's any of your fucking business."

Riley's mother stepped in. She had been watching the drama in silence, but flinched at every vulgar word from the man's mouth. "Vic—"

The attempt at caution was futile. McIntyre shot her a look that bordered on contempt. "I hope you two didn't tell him anything, Noreen."

Noreen flushed. "Just general chitchat. Riley's career, ah..."

Green rescued her. "Are you Riley's lawyer?"

"I'm his agent."

"In that case, Mr. McIntyre, you have no standing in this matter. You are neither his lawyer nor his relative, besides which Riley is eighteen, so he speaks for himself." Green manoeuvred himself between McIntyre and the boy, who was hanging back at the bottom of the steps. "How about we grab a coffee somewhere, Riley? My car is right over there."

He nodded towards the Subaru sitting at the curb. Riley had begun to rally some confidence, perhaps from his asshole agent, and his expression had become guarded.

"I don't have anything to say that can't be said in front of them."

"You're probably right. But you never know what topics we'll discuss. In my experience, people always find they're more comfortable in private."

"The boy doesn't want privacy," McIntyre interrupted. "He wants support."

Green ignored him with an effort. "This will only take half an hour, and I'll have you back in plenty of time for your party."

Riley shot McIntyre a glance that Green couldn't interpret. Part questioning, part pleading. But also perhaps, part fear? "I'd like him to be present," he said. "He can stay if I request it, right? If I give permission?"

Green debated how to proceed. He could press the issue, but risked losing Riley's cooperation altogether. But he was damned if this loudmouth bully was going to censor the boy's every answer. "If you want someone present, I suggest your father. We're going to be discussing personal things, Riley. Your father is the most appropriate person."

"He's obviously not interested," McIntyre said.

"He's just gone to change," the mother said. "I'm sure he'll be down in a minute."

"I don't want my father. I want Vic," Riley said, loud enough that Green was sure his father could hear. His lips were beginning to tighten, just like his mentor's. Green wanted to strangle the interfering asshole but kept his face impassive as he rethought his options. He could, of course, insist on a private interview, but that would entail making the interview formal, notifying the local police and probably dragging a lawyer into the fray who would make Vic look like a pussycat. The power game he was playing with Vic almost required him to take that option. Yet he would lose valuable time, Riley would gain time to bolster his defences, and Green would miss the opportunity to observe McIntyre and gauge what he knew about Lea's death. Even going along with Riley's request, at least he could rattle a few nerves.

"This is not a me-against-you situation, Riley," he said, trying to make the best of it. "So you don't have to feel threatened. If at any time you decide you don't want Vic there, you just give me the word." He glanced at Noreen O'Shaughnessy, whose cheeks were blotched pink with anger. "Would it be all right if we used your living room?"

She nodded. "Since you're going to be longer than you thought, perhaps you'd like that drink after all? Coffee? Coke?"

Riley shook his head, but Green accepted a coffee. She shot a defiant look at McIntyre before turning on her heel without offering him the same. Green signalled both men into the living room and invited Riley to sit in one of the armchairs flanking the window. He immediately chose the matching one opposite, effectively splitting Riley off from McIntyre, who was forced to sit on the sofa across the room. With this arrangement, Green and Riley were backlit by the window, making it more difficult for McIntyre to read their expressions. More importantly, he had forced McIntyre out of Riley's line of vision and reduced the chances the agent could control him.

McIntyre didn't see all this until it was too late, when he could do nothing but glower. Green gave Riley what he hoped was a fatherly smile. "Do you know why I'm here, Riley?"

Riley shook his head. He perched forward on the wing chair as if poised to flee, his elbows on his knees and his long, fluid hands dangling restlessly.

"You know a girl in your school, Lea Kovacev, died. We're interviewing all her friends and classmates, trying to figure out how the accident happened. Your name came up."

Riley managed a very small "Oh."

"It's a terrible tragedy. She was a lovely girl by all accounts. There will be a coroner's inquest, probably more rules and higher fences by the falls—" He paused, then lobbed his next question as gently as he could. He'd already decided that with McIntyre playing guard dog, his only hope was to sneak up on the topic. "How did you meet Lea?"

"She is—was—" Riley balled his fists and fixed his eyes on some distant point out the window, "in my Outdoor Education class. I missed a lot of the excursions, but we did go on one or two together. Winter camping in Gatineau Park, and just last month, mountain biking."

"How long have you known her?"

"Just since classes started in September."

"And did you socialize together outside of class?"

"No." The word came out quickly. Too quickly. Then Riley hesitated. He seemed to be scanning his memory for incidents that could contradict his story. One leg jiggled. "Well, she came to a couple of my games. And we probably had drinks together a few times. You know, as part of a group."

"Any personal get-togethers? Just the two of you?"

"Well..." Riley glanced at McIntyre, who nodded almost imperceptibly. They've been rehearsing this, Green thought. "She did help me on a couple of English assignments. She's a good writer, and I...I didn't always have time to read the books we were supposed to."

"You mean she wrote the assignments for you?"

"No! She just told me what the book was about. Mostly Shakespeare, which I don't really get."

Green grinned sympathetically. "Lots of people don't really get him."

"And then she'd read my essays afterwards, just to doublecheck them."

"Whose idea was this?"

"Hers." Riley clamped his jaw tight for a moment, as if he was struggling to keep his feelings at bay. His fists clenched and unclenched. "She was super friendly, always out to help people. She was the type of girl to make everyone feel special."

Green dropped his tone gently. "Sounds as if you liked her a lot."

It had the desired effect, for Riley's eyes reddened. He didn't answer. Green suspected he couldn't. A movement in the shadows caught his eye, and he glanced up to see Ted pause halfway down the stairs. He was watching his son, and in that unguarded moment Green sensed a profound sadness. More, a father's impotence to take away his child's pain.

"Would you say you knew her better than most of her classmates?"

"Riley already answered that, Inspector."

McIntyre's interruption was designed to buy Riley time to compose himself, and it worked. The youth sat back in the chair, feigning calm.

"Like I said," he resumed in a stronger voice, "she was friendly with a lot of people."

"Do you know if she had a boyfriend? Someone special?"

Riley shrugged, well in control now. "I didn't know her well enough for that."

"She seems to have had a special boyfriend whom she loved very much. She wrote beautiful poems about him."

Riley shrugged again, a gesture of defeat this time. "I don't know."

Green sensed McIntyre stirring again. He could have pushed further and told him about the ice cream seller's ID, but decided not to tip his hand. Not with Cerberus running interference. Better to wait for the formal interview. Meanwhile, he would let the kid box himself into a corner with lies. He unfolded the *Ottawa Sun* article in his hand. "Have you seen today's paper?"

The boy blinked in surprise, momentarily relieved until Green handed him the paper. He took it, then let it fall in his lap as if it were hot. "Oh, no!"

McIntyre reached over to snatch the paper from Riley. He scanned it, then tossed it aside with contempt. "It's the *Sun*. What do you expect?"

"It suggests Lea took a drug that might have killed her," Green said, gritting his teeth and turning back to Riley. "Did you know she used drugs?"

The boy was starting to shake his head when McIntyre cut him off again. "Hardly a big deal. Lots of kids take drugs these days. The paper's just trying to stir up shit."

Green stared him down. "Oh, but in this case, with the coroner's inquest coming up, we have to take every contributing factor seriously." He softened and turned back to Riley. "We think she just used them recreationally, to add to the party, but we have to trace who she buys them from. Did you ever sell to her?"

Both Riley and McIntyre shot forward in their seats. Their denials were simultaneous and vigorous.

"Well, we'll be looking at all her friends, to see their drug involvement and to see who might be dealing. You see, whoever sold her these particular drugs could be facing a manslaughter charge."

"I don't know anything!" Green had the sense Riley was beginning to panic and depart from the rehearsed script.

"What she did was her own business."

"Like I said, drugs are everywhere in high school, Mr. Green," said McIntyre coldly. "But Riley never uses them, so he knows fuck-all about the drug scene at Pleasant Park."

"But he knows some of the students she hung around with. A name would be really helpful, Riley. Point us in the right direction. And help balance the tragedy of her unnecessary death." He leaned forward. "After all, she was such a super girl. She shouldn't have died the way she did. Her body trapped on the bottom of the gorge, washed up like a piece of garbage on the rocks down below."

Riley was shaking his head vehemently, looking for a way out. "She might have mentioned there was a girl in our Outdoor Ed class who she used to hang around with."

McIntyre leaped in. "Riley, you don't have to give them shit."

"Name?" Green demanded.

Riley shot McIntyre a confused glance. "I don't know who. It's something she mentioned. But she also mentioned Justin Wakefield, and I think he deals a bit to his friends."

Green made a show of jotting down the names, then spread his hands apologetically. "This is just routine, son, but I have to ask. Where were you last Monday night from nine p.m. to three a.m.?"

McIntyre rose from his chair as if to signal the end of the interview. "Okay, that's enough. He's answered all your questions, but this one, you're way out of line."

Green waited, pen poised. Riley looked about to open his mouth, but McIntyre waved him silent. "He was with me. We were discussing draft offers and it got late, so he crashed at my place. Now I trust this is the last time you'll need to bother us."

You can trust all you want, Green thought, but you don't know the half of what I've got in store for your golden boy. I've set the hook, but I haven't even begun to reel him in.

Thirteen

Green managed to spend most of the rest of the day at the cottage, immersing himself in the warm, sunny June day at the beach and only checking in with the sergeant on duty by cell phone twice. There was still no news on Jenna Zukowski's disappearance, although Ron Leclair had launched all the usual inquiries. Green put his nagging uneasiness out of his mind until he and Hannah headed back to the city early Monday morning. The full force of the investigation hit him again, however, the moment he walked back into the office, an hour late and clutching coffee and a bagel from Vince's Bagelshop.

Gibbs was already at his computer, a rare excitement lighting his face as his fingers flew over the keys. "I-I've been chasing down drug leads all weekend, sir. I've got a great new idea!"

"Did you ever leave that desk, Bob?"

A flush crept up Gibbs' long face, and his Adam's apple bobbed. "I spent yesterday with Sue, sir," he said, sounding almost apologetic. "I took her for a drive up in the Gatineau. We had a picnic and w-went around the Sugar Bush Trail. It's got handicapped access. She tried to walk the whole way, but..." He didn't need to finish the sentence. Sue Peters was in rehab, relearning how to walk, but she fatigued easily. Being Sue, she did not take this failure of her body lightly.

"That's progress, Bob. Don't lose sight of that."

"Yes, sir. But she gets so angry, she ends up in tears. It's—it's hard to watch."

Particularly hard since the old Sue Peters would have hated the tears and would have hated even more that others were witness to them.

"We'll get her back, Bob. Remember what the doctors said. Her brain is still healing, and the more we stimulate it, the better."

"I know," Gibbs said, and his voice grew lighter. "That's why I told her about the case. I thought it might lift her spirits to know what we were up to. And it was her that came up with the idea."

"What idea?"

"Well, you know how you said Lea had a drug source at school? So I got the names of all her friends and the kids in her classes and ran them past our school resource officers to see if they knew who might be dealing in the schools. They checked around, and talked to the vice-principals—they're the ones who really know what's going down in the school. Of course, there was nothing to say it was one of the kids in her classes, but I figured it was a place to start. Anyway, the VPs came up with a bunch of possible matches."

"Was Riley O'Shaughnessy one of them?"

Gibbs looked surprised. "The hockey player?"

Green hesitated, unhappy that he'd let the name slip. But if Bob Gibbs couldn't be trusted to be discreet, no one on the squad could. "It looks like he might have been the secret boyfriend."

A shadow crossed Gibbs's face which Green couldn't interpret. Dismay? Or hurt at being excluded? He covered it with a brisk shake of his head. "No, he wasn't on the list, but it's a pretty long list. I was planning to start interviewing first thing this morning."

"But?"

"Well, then Sue had this great idea. Just a long shot. Remember how we had police contact sheets on all the people at Vic McIntyre's parties when the noise complaints were made?"

"Yes, I remember. Riley was one of those. So was his cousin Ben."

"Sue suggested I cross-reference those to see if any of them went to Pleasant Park and if they were on the list of possible dealers."

Green smiled broadly. Before her injury, what Sue Peters lacked in finesse and subtlety was compensated by her creative mind and talent for thinking the unthinkable. It was a huge relief to know that talent had not been lost when her skull was crushed. "And?"

"That's what I-I'm doing now, sir. I'm almost done."

"Good work, Bob."

Gibbs's Adam's apple bobbed again as he worked up to his reply. "I—I'd like to make sure Sue gets the credit for the idea, sir. A visit from you...to tell her so... That would mean a lot."

Green cringed. He was touched to think how far Gibbs had come to have the courage for such a request. It was a courage not to be dismissed, but Green hated hospitals. He'd visited Sue half a dozen times in the past two months, but each visit took him days to psych himself up for and to recover from. He dreaded the sight of badly damaged bodies struggling to gain back the functions that had once been second nature.

"I will. Soon," he replied, grateful to spot Brian Sullivan coming off the elevator, bearing two Tim Hortons double-doubles. Sullivan jerked his head towards Green's office. Once inside, Sullivan kicked the door shut with his foot, signalling a desire for privacy.

"Okay," he said, propping his huge feet on Green's desk and prying the lid off his cup. "How'd it go yesterday?"

Between mouthfuls of bagel, Green filled him in on the meagre harvest from his Gananoque visit. "It wasn't a total loss," he said. "I learned that Riley is a basket case over Lea's death, that McIntyre is pulling all the strings, and that the mother doesn't like that one bit."

"Did you meet Dad?"

"Yeah, once he got home from church." Green sorted through his impressions. "A bitter man."

Sullivan snorted. "Church? Doesn't sound like any O'Shaughnessys I know. Maybe the good Irish boy's got religion all of a sudden. More likely putting money in the bank with the Big Guy so he'll look kindly on Riley in the draft. Catholics still believe that stuff, you know. We may act all rational, but give us a wish, and we're down on our knees doing Novenas faster than you can say Hail Mary. Dad thinks McIntyre is the Second Coming, by the way. I ran into Darren O'Shaughnessy at the hockey picnic yesterday, and we talked some more. His brother sees Riley as the brass ring that's going to set them all up in a fancy house on the river, with a monster boat to cruise the Great Lakes and winter vacations in Florida instead of running his shitty little snow ploughing business. He's out at five a.m. in the pitch black on a freezing January morning, clearing laneways so the rich can get their Beemers out in time for work. Darren says Ted was always looking for a shortcut, but instead found himself saddled with one son, four daughters and a wife with MS, scrabbling for a buck any way he can."

Green picked sesame seeds off his desk thoughtfully as he recalled Noreen O'Shaughnessy's awkward movements the day before. He felt a twinge of sorrow for the woman and moderated his judgment of Riley's father. The man had a lot on his plate. Green remembered his muttered curse when Riley arrived with the Mustang, his sad expression on the stairs. "I think privately he has his doubts. Or maybe just jealousy. But I don't think we can count on him to pry Riley away from McIntyre."

"There's too much riding on it."

"Or he's afraid of losing Riley altogether. But the kid's eighteen. We can bring him in for formal questioning any time we want."

Sullivan swirled his coffee in slow, pensive circles. "Do we have enough yet? Yeah, we have him with Lea the night she died, but we've got nothing to tie him to her body or even the park bench. We've got gaps between the time she died and the time she got thrown—" His cell phone rang, and he fumbled at his belt to retrieve it. As he listened, his expression grew alert. After a brief conversation, he thanked the caller for the hard work and hung up.

"All right!" he crowed. "That was the lab. The marijuana roaches Cunny found at the scene? They were laced with crystal meth. Enough to give you a real buzz, and if you took too many, to stop your heart cold. Six roaches were found at the scene. More than enough, the lab says."

Green thought about the methamphetamine in her tox results. "So she did die because she bought laced marijuana."

"From someone who obviously didn't know what they were doing."

"Or someone who wanted her dead."

Sullivan stared at him. "That's a stretch. They might just as easily have knocked out Riley too. In fact, they probably would have if he wasn't so anti-drugs."

Green tapped his pen impatiently on his desk. "Anyway, we now know the how of her death, if not the why. And Gibbs is working on the who—the supplier. If this was some amateur who didn't know what the hell they were doing—" He jumped to his feet and flung open his office door. Gibbs was still at his computer, jotting notes on a pad.

"Bob! Any progress?"

"Yessir!" Gibbs snatched up his notepad and loped towards them. "A couple of interesting prospects. One is Ben O'Shaughnessy—with that name, I figure he's related to Riley?"

"His cousin." Green perked up. "He's a dealer?"

"No, he's not on the suspects list for that, but he is in Lea's English class, and he was at one of McIntyre's parties."

Sullivan was leaning forward, his eyes narrowing. "His father mentioned he liked to party."

"Motive?" Green asked.

"In these families, with this much competition, who knows?" Sullivan replied, and Green knew he meant old Irish Valley families. Sullivan was the expert on how twisted the roots could become. "Good, old-fashioned jealousy? Riley was certainly the golden boy, got all the success and attention. And all the girls. Good work, Bob. Keep digging on him."

Gibbs nodded. He looked more excited than Green had seen him in weeks. "But I've got someone even more interesting! I got one hit on all three counts. I've found a kid who was a friend of Lea's from her Outdoor Ed class, who was on the list of possible dealers at the school, and—" his eyes sparkled, "who was present at Vic McIntyre's party."

"And who is this sonofabitch?"

"Daughter of a bitch. Girl by the name of Crystal Adams. Sixteen years old, and not a mark against her except that witness contact. The vice principal wasn't even sure if she's a dealer, but the rumours are there. Small time, friends only, he thinks."

An amateur, thought Green in disgust. A fucking amateur.

They sent Gibbs away, ostensibly to research background on Crystal Adams, but actually so they could argue in private over what to do next. Sullivan wanted to go straight to Crystal, but Green wanted to tackle Riley.

"Until Gibbs gets us more details," Green said, "we've got nothing concrete to tie her to that night. We've got rumours she's dealing and evidence she was at McIntyre's party, but that's it. Until we get the DNA from those roaches, we can't even prove it was the marijuana that killed Lea. Crystal is a minor, and the minute we lean on her, we'll have her parents down our backs. If she's not smart enough to see we've got nothing, they will be."

Sullivan looked skeptical. He propped his big feet on the desk, drained the last of his coffee and lobbed the cup over Green's desk towards the waste basket. It hit the floor and rolled under the desk. Green grinned. "I moved it. I got tired of your perfect record."

Without a word, Sullivan scooped the cup from the floor and lobbed it again, this time directly into the basket. "The same thing could be said about Riley, only Vic McIntyre will have the smartest lawyer in town on our ass. I think we should lean on Crystal. Scare her into telling us who sold her the adulterated marijuana. She's not going to like staring at a possible homicide charge, and I think her parents will be smart enough to figure that out."

"We could always pick them both up," Green said with a grin. "Hedge our bets, play them against each other."

Sullivan laughed and was just drawing breath to respond when his phone rang. All traces of levity vanished as he listened, and after a couple of moments he said three simple words: "Be right there."

When he hung up, he was already shrugging on his jacket. His expression was grim. "We've got another body. No doubt about how this one died."

* * *

170

Bruce Pit had once been a sand quarry on the outskirts of the city but was now surrounded by suburbs and bounded by major city roads and highways. It was an overgrown scrubland officially designated as an off-leash dog park with a network of trails through the fields and the adjacent woodland. There were several official access points, including a large parking lot on the west side, but the first officer on the scene directed Sullivan to a field off Hunt Club Road. It was at the remote southern edge of the park, he said, but closest to the body.

"The murderer sure as hell didn't know anything about dogs," Green observed as Sullivan bumped the car over the uneven grass towards the collection of vehicles in the middle of the field. A brilliant June sun shone in the cloudless sky, baking the ground. "There must be two hundred dogs that pass though Bruce Pit every day. A buried body would be heaven for every one of them."

"Maybe he just didn't know Bruce Pit was an off-leash dog park. Not everybody has dogs, Green. Maybe he just figured, wow, here's a nice, isolated place to ditch this body. Convenient if you don't want to drive too far with a body stashed in your trunk."

Up ahead, Green could make out an ambulance as well as Coroner and Ident vans, and through the trees beyond, flashes of moving white. Alongside one of the cruisers, a uniformed officer was waiting for them.

"We've closed off the entire park, sir," he explained when Sullivan showed his badge. "There are still lots of walkers on the trails, but we're interviewing each one as they come out."

Sullivan nodded his approval. "Where is she?"

The officer led them to the edge of the woods. About a hundred yards in, Green could now distinguish the unruly white hair of Dr. Alexander MacPhail, as well as the bulky outline of Lou Paquette. Under the canopy of trees, the air was hot and moist. A whiff of decay drifted past Green's nostrils, churning his stomach and telling him the body had been there some time.

"A man and his dog found her," the officer was saying. "Mr. Reg Talbot, lives in the neighbourhood. We've got his preliminary statement, but he's over there—" he nodded to one of the police cruisers, "if you want to speak to him. We had the paramedics check him out, on account of his age."

Sullivan glanced at Green. "I want a look at the body first."

"I'll talk to him," Green replied quickly. Hysterical witnesses were infinitely preferable to rotting bodies. He found Reg Talbot in the back of the squad car, clutching a paper cup of vile-smelling coffee and huddled under a blanket despite the heat. Beside him, a small white terrier panted with excitement, steaming up the windows. The man started when Green opened the door, and beneath his leathery, liver-spotted skin, he was paper white. His eyes were huge.

Green led both of them out into the sunshine and urged the man to take deep breaths as they strolled through the tall grass towards the road. The terrier scampered off ahead, pouncing on rocks and leaves in her path. When they were sufficiently far from the crime scene, Green invited Reg to tell his story.

"Maggie was off-leash," he began, his voice surprisingly strong for his frail frame. He watched his dog anxiously as he walked. "I know she's not meant to be in that part of the park, but I could never see the harm in it. There are so few people around, especially at that hour, and she finds all the big dogs in the main area too overwhelming. I love the woods, especially when all the woodland flowers are out. The violets and trilliums were spectacular last month. We take the same route every day, you see." He paused and turned back to gesture towards the far corner of the woods. "We start in the parking lot and we hug the outside trails all the way around, where almost no one else goes. It takes me about an hour, but I'm not very fast any more, and it's an excellent workout for both of us. Maggie runs off chasing chipmunks and digging up sticks."

Knowing the value of letting the recollections flow unimpeded, Green refrained from interruption, but his impatience must have showed, because the man pulled himself erect with determination.

"Today we were about halfway around, when all of a sudden Maggie tore off into the woods out of sight. The next moment she set up this high-pitched barking—the kind she makes to warn me. I called her repeatedly, but to no avail, so I left the trail and followed the sound through the brush. About a hundred yards in, I see her racing in circles, digging. I can smell the decay at this point, so I'm afraid she's going to roll in some dead animal. Terriers are good diggers, and by the time I reached her, she'd dug up the ground all around this pile of dead branches and leaves. I had an uneasy feeling, and then I see she's tugging on something and trying to pull..."

For the first time, Reg's voice faded. Green waited. "It's a foot. It's the first time I've found my cell phone useful since my daughter gave it to me. In case of emergencies, Dad, she said, and I guess this qualifies. I dragged Maggie away and came out into the field here, thinking this would be the best way for the police to access it. The parking lot would be an awfully long trek in, and the paths get very confusing. I know them like the back of my hand, of course, but only the regulars would. After I called 911, well..." He managed a faint smile. Some colour had returned to his papery skin. "I just sat down to wait. There was no strength left in my legs after that."

Green nodded. He'd been studying the grass as they

walked, and besides the tracks made by their own vehicles, he could see no signs of disturbance. It didn't look as if the killer had driven in by this route. "Did you notice anything unusual in the park today? Anything out of the ordinary?"

"Like what?"

"You're here every day. You see the regulars, the patterns. Was anything different? Cars, people, dogs?" Reg was shaking his head. "Did you encounter anyone else on your walk this morning?"

"Oh yes, there were at least half a dozen cars in the parking lot, and I saw walkers on the trails. I gave descriptions to the other officer."

"What about farther out, closer to the body? You said far fewer people go on the outer trails."

"That's because dogs aren't allowed off-leash, you see. So the area is left to kids having drug parties and setting camp fires."

And killers burying bodies, Green thought. "Did you meet anyone at all there today?"

Reg wagged his head back and forth in denial. He whistled sharply as his dog ranged too close to the busy road. Maggie wheeled about and raced back towards them on her stubby legs. "I've been trying to remember," Reg said once he'd slipped on her leash. "But I don't think I saw a soul. Not that that was unusual, at that hour on a weekday."

Green thought about the body, ripe enough to smell. "What about the last three days. You said you walk here every day. Did you notice anything out of the ordinary on...say, Friday or Saturday?"

Reg stopped and stared into the distance, screwing up his craggy face in an effort to remember. Maggie tugged at the end of her leash. "Saturday and Sunday are always much busier around here, with what we call the weekend walkers. You even get kids on mountain bikes going along the path I take. They nearly run Maggie over sometimes, so I usually go earlier in the morning on the weekends. But I don't recall anyone out of the ordinary. Everyone had a dog, it's the ones who don't that you notice. You wonder what they're doing here, and Maggie usually barks at them." His face cleared, and his pallid blue eyes grew wide. "Come to think of it, there was one man on the track without a dog. Saturday? Maybe Sunday. No, Saturday, because it was just before the thunderstorm. Maggie barked at him. But it could mean nothing. You do get joggers really early in the morning, and this man was jogging, dressed in a bulky sweat suit with a hood."

"What colour?"

"Navy? Black? Nondescript."

And hard to see in the woods, Green thought. "Can you describe the individual?"

"Not well. He had his head down and the hood up. I was so busy trying to corral Maggie that I barely noticed. Some of these joggers kick at them, you see."

"But it was a man?"

"Oh, yes. Solidly built, with a powerful stride. A fairly young man, I'd say. At least..." his eyes twinkled, "from my perspective."

"Did he have anything with him? In his hands, on his back?"

"Not that I saw."

"Could you show me where you saw him? Take me there?"

"Yes, but it's quite a ways from here, up near the Cedarview Road portion of the trail. It would be quite a long way to carry a body, I should think, no matter how strong you are."

The two men retraced their route to Green's car, then drove around the outskirts of Bruce Pit to the official parking lot. A flashing police cruiser blocked off the entrance, and the paths had been cordoned off, although a group of curious and disgruntled dog walkers had collected outside the yellow tape. Green noted with satisfaction that the parking lot had a gravel base and a sandy entrance to the trails, both excellent materials to lodge in the treads of tires and shoes. The sand was crisscrossed with shoe and paw prints, however, a forensic investigator's nightmare.

With a warning from Green to stick to the edge of the path, Reg picked up his dog and struck out along the trail that hugged the fence at the edge of a large field, walking with a confident, upright stride that belied his frail appearance. Green kept his eyes to the ground, looking for any clues that suggested a heavy object had been transported along the path. The recent rains had left muddy patches where prints and bicycle tracks stood out in stark relief. The problem was knowing whether any of them were connected to the killing. Lyle Cunningham's and Lou Paquette's teams were already swamped by the physical evidence associated with Lea's death; how would the Ident team even begin to process this scene? He contemplated the unpleasant possibility of asking Barbara Devine to borrow resources from some other police section. In her bid for the Deputy Chief's chair, she would not appreciate the implication that her own department was not up to the job.

Reg stopped at a fork in the trail and gestured to the left one leading into the woods. "I saw him just in there. And truth be told, it's not a very good trail for joggers, too many rocks and roots to twist your ankle on."

"What's up ahead?"

"More of the same. It's a very secondary trail that eventually loops around to connect up with a larger one farther up."

Green stepped forward. "All right. Let's continue your route of this morning to where the body is."

Reg wavered and reached out to grasp a tree trunk. In his arms, Maggie struggled to break free. "I've already shown the police..."

"I know. I just need to know what route was used. We won't go up to the crime scene."

With a far less confident stride, Reg set off again. They walked for about ten minutes, the woods thickening and the path narrowing as it wove around trees and over protruding roots. Suddenly Reg stopped and frowned intently into the dense brush. "This is where Maggie ran off."

The crime scene was too far to be visible through the woods, but Green could hear the distant murmur of voices. He scrutinized the ground. There were fewer prints visible in the mud here, and the dirt looked as if it had been smeared. He was no forensic expert, but beneath the smears, he thought he could make out the deep cut of a tire track slightly thicker than a bicycle tread. His heart quickened. Had someone been trying to erase the track?

After thanking Reg, Green sent him and Maggie back the way they had come, promising to get an officer to drive them home. Green himself went further down the trail and looped in a semi-circle to approach the crime scene obliquely. Lou Paquette's Ident team would have to scout every inch, looking for the entry route through the woods, and there was no point in adding his own contamination to that of previous dogs and walkers over the past three days.

Sullivan spotted him as he approached and broke off his intense conversation with Paquette. His broad face was taut and his eyes flat, as if neutrality was an effort.

Green steeled himself. If Sullivan was shaken, it was bad. "What have we got?"

"Nude body, young adult female, according to MacPhail, quite heavyset—"

Green sucked in his breath. "Jenna Zukowski?"

Sullivan shook his head grimly. "Impossible to tell. The

killer cut her into pieces and stuffed them into garbage bags. The head's missing."

Green felt his stomach rise. "What's MacPhail's estimate on time of death?"

"She's ambient temperature, so probably at least twenty-four hours, but there's still traces of rigor mortis, so three on the outside. MacPhail's gathered bugs, and he says he'll have more for us in a day or two. He did say one other thing. The body was moved several hours after death, according to the lividity on her side."

"That suggests the killer had to wait to dispose of the body. Probably had to wait till cover of darkness. Too many people here during the day." Green was already thinking of the long route in through the woods. "Anything to help identify her?"

"There's no purse or other ID, no clothes, the killer left nothing to help us. But judging from her pubic hair, she might be a brunette."

"Jenna was a brunette."

"At this stage it's all speculation, Green. Pubic hair and head hair are not always the same colour. We could have a sexual predator on our hands who likes to collect heads."

"Other than the dismemberment, are there any signs of violence or sexual assault?"

"Nothing obvious, but MacPhail has to get her cleaned up and onto the table. Right now we don't have any reason to link the two cases, so I'll assign another team to this Jane Doe. Meanwhile, we'll get all the information we can about Jenna—medical history, distinguishing marks, shoe size, fingerprints. The killer thought he was smart cutting off her head, but he didn't realize we can take fingerprints from a corpse."

Green grimaced. "So now there's a severed head lying around somewhere, waiting for some lucky soul to stumble upon it."

"Heads are a lot easier to transport than whole bodies. It could be at the bottom of some lake by now."

Green mulled over the meagre facts. Jenna Zukowski had been missing at least three days, which fell at the outside limit of the estimated time of death of this body, unless she had not been killed for some time after her disappearance. It was possible her disappearance and this body were unrelated, but what were the chances of two heavyset young female victims surfacing at the same time?

He glanced at the white-suited officers working around the makeshift grave. Paquette was setting evidence markers in the soil nearby. Green tiptoed closer with care until Paquette's scowl stopped him.

"Any theories yet on how he transported her here and what route he took?"

Paquette nodded, allowing a grin to sneak through his scowl as he gestured to the ground. Green kept his eyes averted from the bloated white body, but could see little through the leaves and twigs. "At least we're having some luck with that. The body was placed here before the storm, but luckily the thick trees protected the site. Looks like he tried to wipe out his tracks, but we've got one nice clear footprint in the loose dirt he was digging, and some tracks that look like tire marks. Bigger than a bicycle, maybe a cart or wagon. I'll take molds of them. He used a medium-sized spade to try to dig a grave. Dug down only six inches before giving up and piling branches on top. People don't realize how hard it is to dig in the forest, with all the roots and rocks in the way."

So the killer had been equipped with a cart and a shovel when he brought the body here, Green thought. Which meant that, unless he'd hidden them somewhere, the jogger Reg had seen was not their man. Probably just a local resident out for his morning exercise.

Paquette was peering at the ground as he scrabbled through the bush in the direction of the trail Green had used. "Judging from these broken branches and dislodged stones, I'd say he brought her this way." He straightened and surveyed the woods. "Considering how close he is to the field, he took the long way in. Risky too, coming all that way with a body in a cart."

"Which means he must have dumped her in the middle of the night," Green noted. "It also suggests he didn't know the park that well. He was probably playing it by ear looking for an isolated area. All in all, not the best thought-out murder plan."

Paquette grunted. "You guys can speculate all you want, but I'm sticking with my clues here. There's plenty of stuff here to keep me going, and if you bring me the guy's shoe, I can nail him for you."

A distant movement in the field caught Green's eye, and he glanced through the trees to see a cameraman crouching in the long grass just beyond the yellow tape, with his telephoto lens centred on the scene. Parked in the field behind him were half a dozen media vans. Reporters milled around, setting up field shots. Green cursed. Devine had told him to babysit the media, and here they were again, shoving their cameras and microphones into the case before an potential next-of-kin had been warned.

He ploughed towards them, formulating his statement on the fly. Just as he ducked under the yellow tape, three microphones converged on him. The city's on edge, he reminded himself as he tried for patience.

"Is it the missing social worker?"

Green spun around to stare at Frank Corelli, wrestling his surprise under control. How the hell had Corelli found out about that?

"What missing social worker?" the others demanded, but Corelli didn't reply. His eyes remained locked on Green's.

Green turned deliberately away to address the group. "At approximately nine o'clock this morning, police were called to the scene of some remains discovered off one of the trails in Bruce Pit. At this early stage of the investigation, I can confirm that the remains are human and that officials from the coroner's office and our forensic unit are examining the scene. We have no information as to the cause of death nor the identity of the deceased."

"We heard it was a young woman," one of the TV reporters said. Her cameraman was firmly focussed on Green.

"As we learn more, we will be releasing further details, but speculation and rumour are ill-advised. There is no point in creating undue alarm."

"Undue alarm!" the reporter cried. "Two young women found dead in less than a week in our public parks, and the police don't think it's cause for alarm?"

"At this stage, we're treating them as two unrelated incidents." He began to push through them. "I'll have a further statement in two hours down at the station. For now, guys, let us get on with it."

Corelli dogged his footsteps and leaned on the door jamb as Green climbed into his car. "It's the social worker, isn't it? She uncovered the drug connection in the Kovacev case and—"

"Corelli, I don't know where the hell you invent this stuff."

"You told me about the drugs yourself! And I nosed around the school. The social worker was asking questions—"

"Who told you that?"

"Confidential source. Come on."

"Well, don't print it. We don't know anything, there's her family to consider, and—"

"And this is one hell of a juicy story!"

Green locked Corelli's gaze. "Frank, sit on it till I've got something to give you. Don't be a bull in a china shop."

"I get paid to be a bull in a china shop."

"At least wait till the press release in two hours. Then maybe you'll have some facts to write about."

Green drove back downtown with the accelerator almost to the floor, swearing all the way. The reporters were right. Two dead women within a week was cause for alarm, although not for the reasons they believed. He knew in his bones this was no random killing spree, but with the press crawling all over the story, he could barely find the time and concentration needed to put the pieces together.

By the time he reached the station, the discovery of the body was headline news on the radio. In the absence of facts, the airwaves were filled with hastily corralled experts commenting on sexual predators and tips to keep women safe. Back at his office, Green phoned Rita Berens to see whether she had any news on Jenna. The search for the missing social worker had spread, and the dragon lady found herself at the hub of a massive ground search. Jenna was from the close-knit rural community of Barry's Bay that had been Polish for over a hundred and fifty years. Three quarters of them seemed to have descended on Ottawa in vans and pick-up trucks to find their lost kin. They plastered "Missing" posters of her in corner stores and on lampposts all over Alta Vista, and street by street canvasses were being conducted. But so far, all their efforts had failed to turn up a single trace of her.

"The school custodian said he spotted her outside Pleasant Park High School early Friday morning," Rita said, "even though the school wasn't on her itinerary for the day."

"How early?"

"Seven thirty. Before school started. But no one else saw her, and certainly she never reported in to Guidance, which she should have done. I've asked Anton Prusec to continue asking—"

"You've been very helpful, Ms Berens," Green said quickly. "This is an important lead, but we'll take over from here. Sergeant Leclair of Missing Persons is coordinating the case, so if anyone else uncovers further information, please have them pass it on to him. Or me."

There was silence over the phone, followed by a sharp intake of breath. "The body in Bruce Pit. It's Jenna, isn't it?"

"We don't yet know who it is."

"But you can look at it!"

If it had a head, he thought grimly. "It's not that simple. Let's not get ahead of ourselves. We'll be looking into all possibilities, so don't mention anything to her family at this stage."

The platitudes sounded fatuous to his ears, and he doubted he had fooled her for a moment, but the news seemed to deflate her, for she signed off without protest. Next he called Ron Leclair to check his progress in tracking down Jenna. To his relief, the MisPers sergeant seemed really on the ball. He had already requested dental and medical records from her family and had brought a few objects from her apartment that he hoped would yield fingerprints and hair samples.

"I was just beginning to look into banking activity," he said. "Although with the mess this woman makes of her paperwork, it may take us a week in her apartment just to find her bank records. I've put everyone I can spare on it."

Maybe I misjudged the guy, Green thought as he thanked him and told him to stay in touch with Sullivan. After signing off, Green glanced at his watch. Barbara Devine needed to be brought up to date on the headless corpse before she learned it all on the radio, but every moment that ticked by, the trail out at Pleasant Park grew colder. A five-minute executive summary was all he could spare her. He was just reaching for the phone when it rang. He snatched it up, fearing Devine had beaten him to it.

Expecting a shriek to shatter glass, he was taken aback by Bob Gibbs's soft, diffident voice. "S-sorry to disturb you, sir. But I'm not sure who to call. Staff Sergeant Sullivan is still out on a call, and I—I thought it was important."

"What is?"

"I've been trying to track down Crystal Adams, sir. You remember, the one who—"

"Probably sold Lea the drugs." Green cast his mind back to the beginning of their day. It seemed so far away. "What do you mean, trying?"

"Well, that's the thing, sir. There's a problem."

Fourteen

Bob Gibbs had started off his search buoyed by optimism, but his mood was fragile. He'd slept fitfully after falling asleep in front of the television at one o'clock in the morning and had wakened with a crick in his neck and the taste of gin in his mouth. Gibbs was not a drinker, but in recent weeks he'd found that it worked wonders to take the edge off the worry that seemed to plague him constantly. His weakness angered him. It was not him, after all, who had been ambushed by a killer and beaten within an inch of his life. It wasn't him who had struggled first to lift a spoon to his lips and later to move one foot in front of the other at will.

It wasn't him who raged and screamed and wept in frustration when the spoon missed its mark or the foot folded in. It was the woman he loved. Loved. As extraordinary and unbelievable as that idea was. Anyone who knew Detective Sue Peters before her injury would never have imagined the attraction. She had been brash, confident and terrifyingly blunt. He had found her lack of finesse endearing, even alluring, but it was the vulnerability she'd been forced to admit since the attack that had sealed his fate.

He knew he had to be strong for her, but inside he quaked every time he stepped out into the street. Frightening images invaded his mind. Images of hidden assailants lying in wait for him around every corner, in each dark shadow, in the recesses of his dreams. He felt safe at his computer, searching through cyberspace from the safety of his office, but when it came to field work, he started each day much like Sue, forcing one foot in front of another to get himself out of bed and onto the streets.

When the other detectives were called away to the new crime scene, he knew the pursuit of Crystal Adams now fell solely to him. He would crack this part of the case. He would track down Crystal Adams and confront her with the evidence he'd compiled. Sitting at his desk, forcing his reluctant stomach to accept a third cup of coffee, he contemplated adding a splash of Bailey's Irish Cream. In the end, he tossed it down black in a single, angry gulp. He would get through this. He would be strong. And he stomped out the door.

His first setback occurred at the very first step of his plan. He had gone to Pleasant Park High School determined to haul Crystal out of class and demand to know where she bought the drugs she'd supplied to Lea. But she wasn't there. Most of the school was empty as final exams got into full swing. He headed instead to the address the school had on file. It was a dilapidated townhouse in the middle of a low-rent housing project off Russell Road. Not the toughest neighbourhood in the south end, but filled with an uneasy mix of immigrants, hard luck victims and families who'd been at the bottom of the social ladder for generations. He suspected Crystal's family was one of the latter the moment the front door cracked open and two baggy, bloodshot eyes glared out at him.

He tensed, wondering what was lurking behind the half closed door. "Mrs. Adams?" he ventured.

The woman snorted. "Who the fuck are you?"

He showed his badge, and the scowl deepened. "I didn't call youse guys."

"I'd like to speak to Crystal Adams," he said, almost holding his breath. So far, no stutter.

"What for?"

"Is she here, ma'am?"

The woman, whom he took to be Crystal's mother, did not budge. "No one gets in to talk to her unless they tell me what they want with her."

"I'd like to ask her a few questions about the girl who died at her school. They were classmates."

"Well, you're out of luck. She's not here." The door started to close.

Gibbs slipped his foot in the crack. Through the throbbing in his head, he tried to listen for sound from within, but all he could hear was the tinny laughter of a TV sitcom. "Where can I find her?"

"She could be anywhere. She never tells me nothing."

He pulled out his notebook. "Do you know the names of any of her friends?"

The woman heaved an impatient sigh and started to shake her head. Gibbs held up his hand. "This is very important, Mrs. Adams. I wouldn't trouble you for your time if it wasn't."

She yanked the door open and stepped back into a dark hallway cluttered with shoes and boxes. She tugged at her cotton housecoat, trying to pull it across her pregnant belly as she slouched towards the room at the end of the hall. "You better come in. I can't stand on my feet too long."

The house stank of smoke, urine and Kentucky Fried Chicken. Clothes, magazines and dirty dishes littered every surface. *Married with Children* blared from the 52-inch plasma TV that dominated one wall, and Gibbs noticed a brand-new PlayStation 3 still sitting in its box in the corner. The sofa, however, was frayed at the edges and covered with fading stains. Crystal's mother plopped into the middle of it and picked up the cigarette that smouldered in the ashtray on the side table, glaring at Gibbs like she was daring him to comment. He pushed an old *Ottawa Sun* off the chair and perched cautiously on the edge, concentrating on his notebook.

Mrs. Adams bent her head and stubbed out the cigarette. "I don't have much energy these days, so the place gets away from me. Crystal's no help, in case you're wondering. Never has been. Don't like my boyfriend, don't want this baby. So she goes away pretty regular. Staying with friends, she says. She'll be back in a week or two. She always is, once all her friends' moms get sick of feeding her."

"When was the last time you saw her?"

"Yesterday morning?" Mrs. Adams squinted into space, her bleached hair falling in a big hank over her eye. Yesterday's make-up smudged her eyes. "Yeah. She woke me up early, yelling on the phone."

"Who was she talking to?"

She shrugged. "I don't know. All I know is she pays more attention to those friends of hers than she does to me. They say jump, she asks how high. I ask her to pick up a single dish, she says she's busy. Busy! On the phone all day, partying all night. It's not like she's passing school or anything, she's only there half the time."

"Do you remember what the argument was about?"

She looked up through her hair, frowning. "Who said we argued?"

"I meant the argument on the phone."

The suspicion was replaced by indifference. "Youse guys. She was saying you were going to find out." She broke off, her eyes narrowing. "That's what you're here about, isn't it? Not this crap about the dead girl, but you found out she's up to something."

Gibbs sensed the barriers going up, and he tried to think how to stop them. He'd never get this woman's cooperation with threats or confrontation. "Mrs. Adams, your daughter may be in trouble," he said, hoping he sounded more authoritative than he felt. "One girl is already dead, and I don't think your daughter knows who she's dealing with."

"What the fuck are you saying?"

"That your daughter may be in danger, and we need to find her."

"From this guy she was talking to on the phone?"

"So you know it was a man?"

"Don't put words in my mouth. I don't know who she was talking to. But I do want to know what the fuck you're not telling me!"

He felt a rush of nerves. The interview was getting away from him, and any minute now he'd start to stutter. "Ma'am, I'm not a-at liberty to discuss the details of the case, but we do have information that your daughter may know something about the girl's death that puts her at risk."

"It's that stuff in the newspaper, right?" She waved her hand at the *Sun*, now on the floor. "That the girl was given bad drugs? That's what you're saying Crystal did?"

"What makes you think that?"

"Because I'm not stupid, okay? Right after the phone call, Crystal ran out and bought the newspaper. Next thing I know, she calls me a stupid cow and packs her bags."

"So she knew she was in danger?"

"No, she was just mad about what was in the paper. But my daughter don't deal drugs. She's no angel. and she probably smokes a little weed, but she's not going to get into that crap. Her father's been in jail half her life, and she always said she's not going to make the same mistakes he did."

Gibbs tried to think through his nerves and the throbbing in his head. He was getting a very bad feeling about the whole phone call. "It doesn't matter if she sold the drugs or not, the point is maybe the man on the phone thinks she did. If so, that puts her in danger."

Mrs. Adams seemed to absorb that, and some of her defiance faded. "You think he might be after her too?"

Gibbs nodded. "That's why we have to find her."

The woman reached for a cigarette, then caught Gibbs's glance and put it back. She chewed a fingernail. "Well, I mostly know first names."

"First names is a start. Plus the school they go to."

"Oh, she knows friends all over the city. I don't even think half of them are in school."

Gibbs waited, pen poised, and after a moment the woman supplied half a dozen names, all of whom meant nothing to him. None matched the friends Lea had.

"What about Riley? Ever mention a Riley?"

Her face cleared. "Oh, yeah! On the phone, it was always Riley this, Riley that."

"You mean she spoke to him often?"

"Oh, no, it wasn't to him. It was to everyone else. He's that hot hockey player, never gave her the time of day."

Gibbs digested that with interest. "What about Vic? Did she mention a Vic?"

She shot him a quick glance that made Gibbs wonder if she'd recognized the name. But she shook her head. "There were other kids, Vic might have been one of them. Check with the kids at the Alternative School. She seems to know most of them, and a lot of them have been on the street. They have their connections, so when she really wanted to drop out of sight, she'd hook up with them."

"What's the name of the school?"

"I don't know," she whined. "Look it up. Norman something. It's off Bank Street somewhere in Old Ottawa South."

*   *   *

"Norman Bethune," Green said when Gibbs told him. He

dismissed a faint twinge of alarm. There were other kids at Norman Bethune, and Hannah had already admitted to a passing acquaintance with Crystal. Surely that was all it was. Two rebellious teenagers moving in the same crowd.

Green forced his attention back to the information Gibbs had uncovered. The pieces were finally falling into place. It looked as if Frank Corelli's piece on the doctored drugs had worked too well. If Crystal was in fact the supplier, she might have feared the police were about to pin a homicide charge on her, so she had dropped out of sight.

Gibbs' voice broke through the silent phone line. "Should I follow this up, sir?"

Green dragged his thoughts back to the present. "Where are you now?"

"I'm heading to Pleasant Park High School to check out all the names the mother gave me. Then if I have time, I thought I'd head out to this Norman Bethune place."

Green stared at his office ceiling, trying to find perspective. Was Gibbs experienced enough to handle the delicate task, given Hannah's connection to the school, or should he, Green, handle that part of the inquiry himself? "Sounds good, but hold off for now," he said, equivocating. "There's something else I need you to do at Pleasant Park." He told Gibbs about the school custodian who'd spotted Jenna Zukowski outside the school Friday morning. "Find out what she did there, and who was the last person to see her. We've got about forty-eight hours unaccounted for, and we need to trace her movements."

He heard Gibbs's sharp intake of breath. "It's confirmed, sir? The Bruce Pit Jane Doe is Jenna Zukowski?"

"No, it's not confirmed yet, but it's my working assumption, and I don't want the trail to go cold while we wait for forensic tests."

After he'd hung up, Green took a moment to jot down some

crucial notes. With two deaths, two missing women and one unidentified corpse, the case was rapidly spinning out of control. He and the team badly needed a full briefing meeting on the whole case, but with Sullivan and Ident still out at the scene and with Gibbs tracing valuable leads, there was no time for one. The media would not sit on the details of a second woman's death for more than a couple of hours before they flooded the airwaves with hysterical warnings about the perils of Ottawa's city parks. Barbara Devine would be screaming for damage control.

Green, however, did not see these deaths as evidence of a city overrun with random sexual crime, but rather as the determined efforts of a killer trying to cover his tracks. It had all started with Lea's death. No, with the sale of the lethal drugs that had precipitated her death. He jotted down the multiple lines of inquiry being pursued from that point.

1. ID Bruce Pit DOA—autopsy—MacPhail
- medical records—Leclair
- fingerprints—Paquette
- results unlikely till at least tomorrow
2. Forensics on killer—DNA on roach—RCMP lab, long wait
- shoe print at grave site—Paquette. Need shoe
3. Find Crystal Adams—pressure mother?
- friends—Gibbs, drug squad
- phone records—Gibbs
- Alternative school—who?
4. Trace Jenna Zukowski's movements—Gibbs

Staring at this last item, he realized there was a very large piece of the picture that he'd forgotten in the crises of the morning. Riley O'Shaughnessy. The young man who was probably at the centre of the whole story, the young man whom Jenna Zukowski had been researching the Thursday evening before she disappeared.

Suddenly he realized what Jenna was probably doing Friday morning outside Pleasant Park High School, and who she had gone to see. He could call Gibbs and tell him to follow up, but this was an instance when the power and mystique of his own senior rank would come in handy. Grabbing his jacket, he headed out of the office. Barbara Devine would get her report, but it would be via his cell phone en route to the school.

*   *   *

As Green pulled into the high school parking lot, he spotted a solitary figure jogging around the track at the side of the school. The pudgy, balding man looked familiar, and when Green drew nearer, his theory was confirmed. Ken Taylor ran with his head down, his shirt soaked with sweat and his breath exploding in wet gasps. When Green called his name, he started violently and stopped in the middle of the track, his chest heaving. His face was so red that Green feared an imminent coronary. This was not a man who jogged every day. What had precipitated this sudden burst of activity?

"Mr. Taylor," Green said, not wanting to give him time to regroup, "you are aware that Ms Zukowski has been missing for three days?"

Taylor nodded weakly.

"And you're aware the body of a young woman was found this morning?"

Taylor swayed. Green caught his arm and half dragged him to the bleachers, where Taylor sagged onto the bottom bench.

"I...I heard. But I didn't know it was her."

Green let the conclusion stand. "She came to see you out here on Friday morning, didn't she?"

He hung his head and shook it, still gasping for breath.

"I have a witness," Green said. "So unless you killed her yourself, I advise you to talk to me."

Taylor raised a shaky hand to wipe the sweat from his face. "Not me. She came to see Riley O'Shaughnessy."

"And?"

"He wasn't here. He didn't come to school that morning."

"Was that usual for him?"

"He has a big week coming up, what with the draft, so he's been distracted."

"So what did Jenna do?"

"She asked if I knew where he lived."

"And?" Green allowed his impatience to show.

"I don't. I mean, I know he lives with his uncle, but I wasn't about to tell her that."

"Why not?"

"Because it's none of her business."

"What did she do then?"

"She said she could look it up. She can, of course, all the student info is in the system computer."

Green was silent a moment, processing the significance of that, and of Taylor's sudden burst of energy. "And this morning, when you heard about the dead woman, you suddenly realized what might have happened to her."

Taylor sucked breath noisily into his lungs. Almost sobbing. "It's impossible. Riley's a good kid. He's got so much going for him. It makes no sense!"

So much going for him, and so much to lose, Green thought grimly as he headed back towards his car, already dialling Sullivan's cell phone. The big detective picked up on the fourth ring.

"It's time to pick up Riley O'Shaughnessy, but I want all our ducks in a row first. Call all the guys in and meet me at the station."

Fifteen

When Green breezed into the incident room half an hour later, Sullivan was already at the head of the table, an irritated frown on his face. Green wasn't sure whether it was Riley O'Shaughnessy's possible guilt or Green's cavalier assumption of control that had annoyed him the most, although he suspected a little of both. To his credit, however, Sullivan remained calm, jotting down notes while Green filled the detectives in on the Riley O'Shaughnessy connection. Their faces reflected their disbelief and dismay. When Green mentioned laying charges, however, Sullivan raised his head.

"Shouldn't we wait for confirmation on the Jane Doe?" he asked, the epitome of reason.

"The kid is set to drive down to Ohio any moment. He's already panicked once—"

"Wait a minute. We don't know that for sure."

Green saw other heads nod, and he leaned forward to press his case. "It all points that way, Brian, and if everyone wasn't so infected by hockey fever, you'd have seen it ages ago. Look at the facts. The kid's an elite athlete in a competitive sport. That means he's determined, focussed and a man of action. He wouldn't waste time on analysis. When he sees his opportunity, he'll grab it. He's got to be strong, and God knows our killer is strong and not squeamish about using brute force. We know he he was Lea's secret lover, they met that night, smoked some bad weed. We know they struggled, not enough to kill her, but with the drugs in her system, enough to be a contributing factor when she dies, so he sees his future going down the tubes if he's implicated. With a potential criminal record hanging over his head, who's going to sign him at the big draft? So he throws her over the falls, hoping it will look like an accident, and he tries to lie low. But the school social worker starts poking around, and before he knows it, he's backed into a corner. If he doesn't shut her up, he's going to be in even worse trouble, because he covered up the crime. So the social worker has to go."

Silence greeted his analysis, and when Sullivan spoke, he was more subdued. "It's a nice theory, Mike, but what do we have to hang it on? To lay a charge, I mean."

"That's why we need our ducks in a row. I want search warrants for Riley's cell phone records and for his uncle's house." He glanced at the short, squat detective who had already opened his notebook. "Jones, you're the warrant wizard, so you start the ball rolling. We're looking for calls he made last Monday night or early Tuesday morning when Lea died, and again on Friday. The kid's only eighteen. I want to know if he had advice or help. In the uncle's house, we're looking for Lea's cell phone and panties, all Riley's shoes and clothes. Also a shovel and some kind of cart. Cutting up the body would have been messy, so we're looking for an implement like a saw—"

"MacPhail is sure it was an axe," Sullivan interjected. "It wasn't pretty."

Green winced in spite of himself. "And not for the squeamish, that's for sure. There would be lots of blood, probably in the shed or garage. You're hardly going to chop someone up in the backyard in full view of the neighbours." Green's eyes scanned the computer screen where Gibbs was recording the assignments. "We need a team out at the house interviewing the neighbours—did they see or hear anything between Friday and Sunday, etc. etc." He gestured to Wallington and Charbonneau. "You guys take that. The moment the search warrants are signed, we all move. Watts and LeBlanc, you execute the search warrant and Brian, you and I will pick up Riley. I don't want him tipped off beforehand, so we'll hang on to him down here until the results of the search come in." He paused, studying the screen and the postings around the room. "Have we forgotten anything?"

"The vehicle he transported the Jane Doe in?" Gibbs ventured.

Green nodded, grateful for the young detective's meticulous mind. He pictured the brand new Mustang that Riley had been driving on Sunday. There was barely room to squeeze a body in its trunk, let alone a shovel and a cart. But then he remembered the large plumbing van sitting in Darren O'Shaughnessy's drive, with way more room than a Mustang. There would be plenty of room for everything in the van, even for the murder itself.

He nodded at Watts and LeBlanc. "Impound Darren O'Shaughnessy's plumber's van and have Ident go over it with a fine-tooth comb."

Jones had been writing furiously. Now he glanced at the clock on the wall, which read three p.m. "These warrants will take a while. They probably won't be ready before the morning. If I was the kid, I'd be halfway to the U.S. border by then."

Green nodded. "That's why we're going to put him under surveillance. He should be in school writing exams. Watts, you and LeBlanc set that up, for overnight if you have to. As soon as Jones gets the warrants signed, we'll pick him up."

*　　*　　*

The late June sun was still blazing off their living room window when Green pulled into his driveway at six o'clock, having exhausted all possible leads he could follow up that day. He felt restless and out of sorts, and the silence that greeted him when he opened the front door only heightened his mood. No Tony rushing into his arms, no Modo thumping her shy tail on the rug, no cooking smells wafting from the kitchen.

Just the roar of his neighbour's lawnmower and the burned smell of this morning's coffee. Then gradually the pulse of rock music penetrated the roar, and he smiled. To his amazement, Hannah was home. Five nights in a row, previously unheard of. What miraculous transformation had occurred? Not that he dared ask, but he was glad of the result. He picked up the mail and sifted through it as he padded down the hall. Bills, promotional flyers, charity requests—all badges of suburban middle age. He tossed them aside unopened and headed upstairs to shower, the whiff of decay still clinging to his clothes.

He stripped, turned on the hot water full blast and climbed into the tub. An object looped around the showerhead startled him. He picked it up and stepped out of the tub, rubbing it to clear the steamy film.

It was a clear glass pendant in the shape of a tear drop, hanging from a leather cord. He'd never seen it before. It was a new age piece of jewellery quite unlike the beads, chains and silver studs that Hannah wore. Yet who else could have put it there?

After his shower, he dressed and knocked on Hannah's door. The music stopped and after some shuffling, the door opened to frame Hannah's delicate face. To his surprise, she was wearing no make-up, and her hair was wrapped in a towel. She looked almost soft enough to hug, but he contented himself with a smile.

He held up the pendant. "What's this?"

Her eyes flicked over it, betraying nothing. "Looks like a pendant."

"What was it doing in my shower?"

She lifted her shoulders languidly. "Maybe it migrated there. They're supposed to have magical powers, those things."

He played along. "And why would it migrate there?"

"I don't know. Maybe so you'd see it? Maybe it's trying to tell you something."

A faint smile twitched the corners of his mouth. "Tell me what?"

"How should I know, Mike? You're the detective."

His smile faded. Hannah herself was trying to tell him something. Give me a name, he'd told her, write it in invisible ink if you have to. He studied the pendant, watching the light refract as it twisted on its cord. His heart quickened.

"It's a crystal," he said.

"So it is."

"Does it have any other name? A specific kind of crystal, maybe?"

"Gee, Mike, don't ask me. I'm not into all that woo-woo crap."

"Do you suppose if I rubbed it, it could tell me any more?"

"Oh, crystals love to be rubbed." She paused, deadpan. "In the right hands, they'll give you anything you ask."

He remained standing in the doorway, feeling like a fool as he tried blindly to follow her cryptic clues. They were on a delicate footing. Because it was a confidential police investigation, he could not tell her what he knew, and because of loyalty, she would not. He tried a more oblique approach.

"Do you know anything about these crystals?"

She shrugged. "I've heard things. But I gotta go. I'm in the middle of something."

"Can we talk about it over dinner? Hypothetically, of course. Not this particular crystal."

She looked past him into the hall as if sizing up the legion of police lined up behind him. Her eyes, devoid of their usual make-up, looked wide and guileless. Without all the harsh black, he could see his own deceptively innocent hazel eyes.

He cooked hamburgers on the barbeque, a skill he'd been trying to master since becoming a suburban family man, but he could almost hear the laughter of his colleagues on the force, who discussed BTUs and side burners as easily as they discussed cars. The hamburgers were nearly done when Hannah joined him on the back patio, her make-up now complete and her hair freshly spiked. It was, however, now orange instead of blue. Two new silver studs had joined the others on her left eyebrow.

She handed him some unrecognizable brown lumps in a shrink-wrapped package. "Veggie burger. I don't eat red meat any more."

He took the package without protest, for he needed her at her most congenial. "What do you like on these? Onion? Tomatoes?"

"Hot salsa's good."

Kills the taste, he thought but refrained from saying so. A moment later, she sneaked him a smile. "Kills the taste."

He laughed and waved a fork at the wine bottle on the patio table. "Help yourself. A little merlot might help things too."

If she knew he was softening her up, she gave no sign as she poured them both some wine. He waited until all the food was served, and she had doctored her veggie burger to her satisfaction. A soft pink flush glowed through her pale make-up.

He lifted his glass. *"L'Chaim."*

She sipped thoughtfully without replying.

"So," he said, holding up the crystal. "Hypothetically, what can you tell me about this."

She pushed her burger around her plate, and when she spoke, her tone was troubled. Gone were the teasing and the enigmatic allusions. "It's a whole different way of looking at things. Cliques, who's in, who's out, who gets to fuck who and show it off. Everybody's using everybody else. You see it in school all the time, and I hate it." She stole him a glance from under her thick mascara, as if expecting an argument. When he said nothing, she continued.

"At least I'm honest. My sex is honest. If I like a guy, it's because he's interesting or he's hot or maybe just because he's a really good fuck. Not because he's the most popular or richest guy in the school. And I don't go around with my boobs falling out, offering free blow jobs just to get him. All so I can brag."

He clenched his jaw to refrain from commentary. "What kind of crowd would this crystal hang out with?"

She shrugged. "Any crowd that thinks they're cool. But the jocks are the worst, because the guys are all into muscles and power, and who's bigger, faster and stronger than the next guy. The more girls you have hanging off you, the bigger you are."

"And what's in it for the girl? Good old-fashioned status?"

She raised her head to contemplate him thoughtfully. "Good old-fashioned power. Do you know how it feels to have a guy—the hottest guy in town, the biggest man on the hockey rink, the guy in all the headlines—do you know how it feels to have him in the palm of your hand? Begging, promising you anything you ask?"

"That doesn't last, however. Five minutes later, he probably doesn't give the girl another thought."

"He does if she knows how to play it. But that doesn't

matter. The thrill is in catching him and having him under your spell. Hearing those words so you can repeat them over and over."

"But guys will say anything when they're aroused."

"That just adds to the thrill. To get a guy to say anything, to know that this big guy can outscore anyone on the team or outrace anyone on the field, but right now all he wants and all he's thinking about, is you."

"But it's not you. He's just using you."

"Who's using who? Who's in control, Mike?" She locked his gaze. "I used to be like that, when I was about thirteen, and I discovered no matter what else the kids thought of me or said about me, I could get the hottest guy to pay attention to me by giving hand jobs. Sometimes even in the school cafeteria under the table, but that wasn't very satisfying because you couldn't have their full attention. The woods behind Mom's house were better."

He sat in silence, wrestling with dismay and discomfort as he tried to absorb this unwelcome image. He remembered being a teenage boy, and the girls who offered their bodies for free. They'd been disdained and ridiculed, even as their offers were accepted with thrills of delight. In his job, he'd met sexually abused girls who offered sex as a kind of welcoming gift, the only way they knew to please a man. He'd met prostitutes who regarded it as little more than a business deal. But the notion that teenage girls as young as thirteen enjoyed the power and the sense of dominance was unnerving.

While he was working out how to respond, Hannah herself retreated to safer ground. She picked up the crystal. "Girls like this are deep into this sex game. They set their sights on the top guy in the crowd, offer it for free, look for chances. The party scene is the best place, because the guys are on the make too, and everybody's dancing hot and heavy, hopped up on booze and drugs. Even on just weed, a blow job is pure gold." She laughed. "So the guys say."

"So drugs are part of the game for these girls? Using it, maybe even supplying it?"

"Just for fun. Hypothetically, like I told you before, just to help out friends or to add to the party. They're not serious users."

"So where would a girl like this, hypothetically, get these drugs from?"

Hannah hesitated, taking time to lick all the salsa off her fingers. "Drugs are everywhere. But at those parties, sometimes adults have their own agendas. Their own reasons for wanting to see kids drunk or stoned or having a good time."

"What reasons?"

"I don't know, Mike. That's all I heard. I've never been to one of those parties. Like I said, it's not my scene. But nobody opens up a candy store for nothing."

Sixteen

Green's bedside phone blasted him awake at six o'clock the next morning. Barbara Devine's voice over the line was almost as shrill. "Have you seen today's *Sun*?"

Green squinted outside at the steel grey dawn. The stars were nowhere to be seen. Had the woman lost her mind?

"There's a full page close-up of the Bruce Pit crime scene—you can even see the poor woman's naked foot, for God's sake—and the headline is the usual Frank Corelli sensationalism. 'Did school social worker know too much?' Mike, what did you tell the guy?"

Green bolted upright, instantly clear-headed. Goddamn Corelli. Anything to sell a damn paper. "What's in the body of the article?"

"Well, that doesn't matter, does it? People don't read the fine print, the part where he admits the body hasn't been identified and the police are denying a connection between the two deaths. Corelli's got the story the police aren't telling yet."

"Does it name the social worker?"

There was silence as Devine scanned the article. Green pictured her sitting at her kitchen table, still dishevelled from sleep and surrounded by the three local papers she scanned every morning. "No, fortunately not," she said, several decibels lower.

Green breathed a sigh of relief. It was a small reprieve, since

Jenna Zukowski's family and friends would know only too well who Corelli was referring to. Moreover, the killer would know that his attempt to conceal her identity and her connection to the Kovacev case had not worked, making him all the more dangerous and desperate.

But at least Jenna Zukowski's name had not been broadcast across the entire city.

"I want you down at the station ASAP, issuing a clarification, Mike. And you can tell Corelli that his boss will be hearing from me!"

That will make his day, Green thought. The boys in the *Sun* newsroom were probably laying bets on how long it would take the police brass to lodge their complaint. Controversy and conflict sold papers.

"Oh, and Mike!" Devine snapped just as he was about to hang up. "Let's get an ID on this woman so we can put all this speculation to rest."

"Gee, I hadn't thought of that," Green muttered once he'd hung up. Thanks to his early wake-up call, he arrived at the station to find the Major Crimes Squad room still virtually empty. None of the day shift had clocked in yet, and predictably Corelli was nowhere to be found in the *Sun* newsroom. Green used the time to do damage control by issuing a press release and contacting media relations to handle the fallout. Then he called Jenna Zukowski's parents, who, along with half the town of Barry's Bay, had taken over the entire Super 8 Motel in Kanata, but who fortunately had not seen the *Sun.* He reassured them they'd be the first to know of any developments.

Finally he checked in on the surveillance team sitting down the street from Darren O'Shaughnessy's house. LeBlanc sounded groggy but pulled himself together quickly at the sound of Green's voice. No sir, there'd been no activity at the O'Shaughnessy house yet, except an *Ottawa Sun* delivery man around four in the morning. The uncle's van was still in the drive, and the kid had parked his sports car in the garage the night before. In the background, Green heard Watts volunteering that he would too, if he had a set of wheels like that.

Outside Green's office, the squad room had begun to fill up, and he spotted Sullivan coming down the hall from the briefing room. Quickly he told LeBlanc to record everyone who came and went from the house, and if Riley O'Shaughnessy left, they were to call it in and follow him.

Sullivan's bulk filled the doorway, and when Green hung up, he stepped inside and closed the door. A frown carved deeply into his brow. "Fucking Corelli," he said, dropping into the guest chair, which screeched beneath his two hundred and fifty pounds.

Green nodded grimly. "I've tried to put out fires, but the sooner we can ID this Jane Doe, the better. When can MacPhail give us something definite to go on?"

"He's doing the autopsy this morning, but the formal ID is going to be tricky. With no teeth for dental records, it'll be down to fingerprints and DNA. Paquette is going to try to lift the skin from the fingers today, but it's iffy. It'll take a couple of days."

"But there must be some clues—medical records, blood type, height and weight..."

"Yeah, but even that will still take a day or two."

"What about time of death? Can he at least tell us that? We know Jenna's been missing since Friday, so..."

"Yeah. Lots of time to breed flies and maggots, so we shipped the little buggers off to Dr. Narwa. At least we should have some answers on that by the end of the day."

Green had to smile. Dr. Narwa was a wild-eyed entomologist with an unusual enthusiasm for his subject that sent all but his most devoted colleagues fleeing from the room. He would spend all day and night with his magnifying glass, microscope and calculator identifying the species, stage and generation of every bug found in Jane Doe's body.

"But at this point Jenna Zukowski is our best working assumption," Green said. "I mean, we don't have any other likely candidates."

Sullivan shook his head and was about to reply when his cell phone interrupted him. After glancing at the Caller ID, he switched it to speaker phone. "What's up, Bob?"

Gibbs' tinny voice filled the room. "I'm still trying to find Crystal Adams, sir. I haven't had much luck, but I did find out something interesting I thought you'd want to know. I spent most of yesterday afternoon at her high school, tracking down her friends. None of them have seen her since school on Friday. They said she was in a weird mood—"

"Weird how?" Green interjected.

"Oh!" Gibbs sounded startled to hear Green's voice. "Um... uptight. She was s-supposed to meet them Sunday afternoon at the mall, but she never showed."

"Were they worried? Was that unusual?"

"Not worried, sir. More pissed off. She does this, they said. Ditches her friends when something better comes along."

"What would be something better, according to them?"

"Well, it looks like she's a serious puck bunny, sir."

Green raised a questioning eyebrow at Sullivan. "Hockey groupie," Sullivan explained. "Passed from player to player."

"Yessir," Gibbs said. "So I tracked down some members of the Ottawa 67's who are still in town, but they haven't seen her."

"Was she seeing anyone in particular?" Green asked.

"Half the team, it sounds like, but some of the guys said she had her sights set on Riley O'Shaughnessy."

Why wouldn't she, Green thought. Hannah had said these girls liked to shoot for the top. The ultimate power trip. And if that pesky girlfriend was out of the way...

The idea came out of the blue, so obvious that he wondered why he hadn't seen it before. If Crystal had supplied the drugs, she herself was in the best position to doctor them. Getting rid of the girlfriend would give her a clear run at the boy. The only trick was how to keep the boy from taking the bad drugs too.

"Did you talk to Riley O'Shaughnessy himself?" Sullivan was asking.

"N-no, sir. I knew you were working that aspect of the case, and I didn't want to interfere. But this is the thing. I did learn one other thing that might be important. Crystal Adams had an appointment with Jenna Zukowski the day after Lea's death. The secretary in the guidance department remembers her running out of Jenna's office."

Green almost shouted aloud. The pieces were falling into place. It was a safe bet Crystal had told Jenna something about Lea, and rather than report the information to the police, the misguided fool had decided to make inquiries on her own. Did she think she was helping Crystal? Or Lea? Or the killer? "Great work, Bob!" Green exclaimed. "Did any of her friends know what they talked about?"

"No sir, but...I didn't ask." Gibbs' voice fell. "That Norman Bethune School is my next lead. I was planning to go there after... Is that..? D-do you want...?"

Sullivan rescued him. "Go ahead, Bob. We need to find that girl."

Green's mind was racing as the disparate bits of information began to fit together. Gradually an appalling alternative emerged. Crystal Adams had confided something to Jenna, then

Jenna had disappeared. And now, so had Crystal.

Two missing women...

He was so distracted, he barely heard Sullivan's question. The big detective had signed off and was looking at him. "That is okay, isn't it, Mike? I know Bethune is Hannah's school."

Green nodded. "What if it's Crystal Adams?"

"What is?"

"Our Jane Doe."

To his credit, Sullivan digested the idea carefully. "The body'd been in the woods at least a couple of days. When was Crystal last seen?"

"Her mother said she took off early Sunday morning." Sunday morning! A knot of nausea gripped Green's gut. "Jesus Christ. If it is Crystal, this is my fault."

Sullivan stared at him. "How do you figure that?"

"The timing of it. She took off Sunday morning."

"So?"

"Lea died last Monday night, and all week Crystal attended school as normal. She didn't take off. Sure, she was upset, probably from a guilty conscience because she's the one who supplied the drugs. She'd wanted Riley for herself, but I don't think she'd thought through her actions, so when Lea dies, she felt bad—"

"Not bad enough to miss school. Not bad enough that her mother noticed."

Green snorted. "From what Gibbs said, I don't think that mother would notice trouble unless it was happening to *her*. But the point is, Crystal did feel bad enough to go to the social worker for advice, but whatever advice she got, she didn't like it, because she stormed out of the guidance office. But she didn't drop out of sight. She goes on with things, even makes plans with friends. Then suddenly, Sunday morning, she freaks out. What happened Sunday morning?"

"I don't know, Mike. Maybe Riley O'Shaughnessy rejected her, maybe she learned about the social worker's disappearance and thought it was her fault."

Green whipped his head back and forth. "Could be. But there was one thing that happened Sunday morning that very clearly would have freaked her out. Something that was intended to shake the case up. I guess it did."

"Riddles, Mike?"

"The *Ottawa Sun* article. The one I fed Frank Corelli about bad drugs being the real cause of Lea's death. The *Ottawa Sun* hits the stands about six a.m. in the morning. I remember Gibbs told me right after she got a phone call, she went out to get a paper. I'd bet a million dollars that wasn't a usual Sunday morning routine for her."

Sullivan's eyes narrowed, and Green could almost see the connections forming in his brain. But he looked unconvinced. "Yeah, okay, but if she's the one who supplied the marijuana, she already knew about the bad drugs. That's why she was upset all week."

"But when she saw the paper, she knew that we knew, and she realized we'll be looking for the drug supplier. She was probably afraid we'd trace it to her."

"Okay. So she ran away. I still don't see how you get to her being the Jane Doe."

"Because if my theory is correct, someone else was freaked out by the *Sun* article too. Someone who wouldn't want her found, or even identified. I think she was used, Brian. That's the story of this kid's life. Maybe she supplied the marijuana, but maybe someone else gave it to her. When Lea died, Crystal was worried. She didn't know what had caused it, but she was afraid she had a hand in it. When she opens the paper Sunday, there it is. Her fears confirmed. Not only was she tricked into

210

selling bad drugs, but the cops know about them. No wonder she freaked."

The pieces fit, but their conclusion gave him no sense of triumph. In releasing that story to Corelli, he might have signed Crystal's death warrant.

"Find out who she bought the marijuana from," Green said grimly. "If she's the Jane Doe, that's who killed her. Get the drug squad on it and get medical and physical information on her to check against the body."

"Mike, shouldn't we at least wait till we have some results from the entomologist and the autopsy? That's only a day or two. At this point we don't even know whose body it is, let alone what led up to the death."

Green shook his head impatiently. "Something's happened to this girl. We should at least get a warrant for her phone records."

Sullivan checked his watch. "Then I'll put Gibbs to work on it. He's handling the drug angle anyway. Jones is going to be back with the O'Shaughnessy warrants any second, and then I want to move on that house." He reached for his cell phone, but in timing that bordered on prophetic, a knock sounded at the door, and Jones stuck his head in. He waved a sheaf of papers. "I got the search warrants signed and ready to go."

"Excellent! We'll alert the surveillance team we're on our way." Sullivan glanced at Green as he hauled himself to his feet. "You want in on this?"

Green hesitated. He would love to be there when the search was conducted. Nothing in his deskbound life equalled the thrill of seeing a case break wide open. But this latest twist troubled him. Another teenage girl was missing, this one with half a dozen ominous links to the very heart of the case. She was a hockey groupie who had attended parties with both Riley and Vic McIntyre, she had set her sights on Riley, which gave her a good motive for wanting Lea out of the way, and she might have supplied the drugs that led to Lea's death. Most ominous of all, she had received a phone call Sunday morning right after the article in the *Sun* came out.

Then she had disappeared.

Green recalled Hannah's cryptic words the other night about the adults who worked in the background, supplying the drugs and pulling the strings. Nobody opens a candy store for nothing, she'd said.

It might already be too late, but he couldn't wait around for another teenage girl to turn up dead. Much as he hated to miss the fireworks at the O'Shaughnessy house, he was needed elsewhere.

"Take Wallington and Jones," he said. "I'll catch up with you later."

If Sullivan was surprised, he masked it well as he organized his team, coordinated a plan and headed out of the building.

Once the flurry of activity died down, Green stood in the empty squad room, kicking himself for not hanging onto Jones, the warrants wizard. With the raid on the O'Shaughnessy house and the two homicide investigations in full swing, not a single Major Crimes detective was available to follow up on Crystal's cell phone records or her drug connections.

He phoned the heads of the drug squad and the school resource officer program to get them tracking down all all know crystal meth labs and suppliers, then he phoned Gibbs for an update on his search for Crystal.

"Nothing yet, sir."

Green knew it was useless to hound him, useless to add a phone warrant to his list of chores. Even at the top of his game, Gibbs had always been meticulous and thorough, but no one could ever have accused him of excessive speed. In his current state, any pressure would only throw him into a tailspin. Muttering a vague explanation about the urgency of the search, Green hung up and reluctantly turned his attention to the phone warrant.

Green hadn't drafted a search warrant in years. He hated the long, tedious exercise in nitpicky detail and precise legalese. As he was tracking down the latest guidelines in the procedural manual, he remembered the warrant Jones had drawn up to obtain Riley's cell phone records. Moments later he'd printed it off his computer, scribbled out the information on Crystal and handed the task of the new warrant over to a detective in General Assignment who looked eager for brownie points with the inspector.

Belatedly, he realized he hadn't heard any results from Riley's cell phone warrant, even though he was sure Jones had put a rush on it. Maybe it was time to light a fire under the phone company. He headed down to the incident room, where a clerk sat at a computer surrounded by stacks of papers. She was meant to be inputting all the information on the Lea Kovacev case into the Major Case file, but she was actually leaning back in her chair, slowly spinning in circles. She started at the sight of him, nearly tipping her chair. He ignored it.

"Has Bell Mobility faxed the cell phone report on Riley O'Shaughnessy yet?"

As if anxious to redeem herself, she spun around and dived for a stack of papers sitting in the fax machine basket. She rifled through them, squinting at the titles, then pulled one with a flourish. "All these things just arrived this morning, sir."

Green snatched it from her, his eyes scanning the columns. It took a moment to decipher the dates, times and numbers, but two calls leaped out at him, made seconds apart in the early hours of Tuesday morning. The very night Lea had died. The first, logged at 12:01 a.m., had been to 911 and had lasted three seconds. Barely time for the operator to pick up the line before Riley had hung up. The second, logged at 12:02, was to a local Ottawa number. Green felt a rush of excitement. This was the person Riley had chosen to contact from his cell phone as Lea lay dead or dying beside him. Not the 911 operator, not one of his family in Gananoque, but someone right here in the city.

Green grabbed a nearby workstation and entered the phone number into the 411 database. Within seconds, a name and address leaped onto the screen.

V. S. McIntyre
51 Country Club Lane

*   *   *

Darren O'Shaughnessy's house looked quiet in the morning sun. The grass was freshly mowed, the shrubs under the window neatly clipped, and the plumbing van gleamed in the driveway. Darren's been a busy boy since our last visit, Sullivan thought as he drew his Malibu up to the curb behind the plain brown Impala of the surveillance team. Perhaps because of all the media attention his famous nephew had been getting this week. Wouldn't want the place looking like a dump when the photographers arrive.

Now that the euphoria and heartbreak of the Stanley Cup finals was over, the NHL Entry Draft had become the talk of the sports pages. All the sports reporters were feeding the public's hockey addiction by analyzing choices and making predictions. Being a local boy, Riley's photo had been plastered across the sports section several times in recent months, and he'd even popped up on a couple of local television ads, which must have netted him a nice chunk of change. But Sullivan had noticed that recently his agent had done most of the talking, giving the excuse that Riley needed to concentrate on finishing school exams before the end of the week.

School exams my ass, Sullivan thought. The kid is a basket case, and McIntyre is keeping a lid on him. Even a hint of this scandal—of drug use or criminal negligence, especially after his recent slump—and the teams wouldn't touch him, at least in the first few rounds when all the future stars were being snapped up.

Jones and Wallington pulled up behind him in a police panel van. After a brief discussion, the surveillance team headed around the house to cover the back door, while Sullivan and the other two detectives mounted the front steps and rang the doorbell.

No answer. No sound from within. Sullivan rang again, leaning on the bell for a full five seconds. At the end, he heard a muffled volley of curses and some thumping in the distance. He was about to ring a third time when the door cracked open, and a red-eyed youth peered out. He had on nothing but boxers, and muscles bulged on his bare, hairless chest. His straw-coloured hair stuck up in cowlicks around his head. Sullivan barely recognized Ben, whom he'd last seen as a pimply kid with half the muscles. Judging from the blank look on the kid's face, he didn't remember him at all. Sullivan decided to go by the book. Holding up his badge, he introduced himself.

"Is your father at home?"

Ben scratched his stubble, then turned to bellow into the hall. Silence answered him, and after a moment he shrugged. "I guess not."

"But his vehicle is here."

Ben peered out at the plumbing van in the drive. "Must have taken the other car."

"Do you know where he went?"

Ben shrugged again, looking bored. "I just got up."

Sullivan held up the official papers. "No matter. We have a warrant to search these premises."

The bored look evaporated. The youth staggered back, his mouth falling open. "A-a warrant! Why?"

"It's all in here. We also have a warrant for the arrest of Riley O'Shaughnessy. May we come in, please?"

"Riley! No!" Ben shoved forward to block the door. He was a big kid, almost as tall as Sullivan. "I mean, without my dad, you can't come in."

Sullivan pushed past him and signalled the others inside. "It's all quite legal, son. These officers will conduct the search, and I'll ask you to remain in the main room while they're doing that. Where is Riley?"

Ben had backed up into the hall, flexing his fists and breathing hard. He was trying for bluster, but the whites of his eyes betrayed his fear. "You're the one with the search warrant."

"Upstairs?"

Ben snarled but said nothing. Sullivan went to the back door to let the other two detectives in and pointed upstairs. He listened to their footsteps thumping overhead, to doors opening and closing, and a minute later, they came thundering back down the stairs.

"No one there."

Sullivan glanced at Ben and saw no surprise on his face. "Search the rest of the house. I'll check outside."

Sullivan had a bad feeling as he slipped outside into the back yard. The house was surrounded by a tall, overgrown cedar hedge which was easily penetrable if a person was determined to escape. If the surveillance team had been clumsy and Riley had spotted them from his upstairs bedroom window, he could be long gone by now.

The backyard looked like a typical handyman's junkyard. A couple of old doors leaned against the wall, and an old washer and wood stove sat rusting in the corner. A garden shed with peeling paint and a sagging roof filled the back corner of the yard, its door half open. Sullivan moved quickly, checking behind shrubs on his way, and pressed himself against the shed wall.

He knocked cautiously. "Riley, it's the police. Come on out, son. I don't want anyone to get hurt."

Nothing. He shoved the door back hard, causing it to slam against the wall. The whole shed shook. Then stillness. He peered around the door into the interior, which was swept, with tools stowed away against the wall. He spotted a spade and an axe, both gleaming clean. Too clean, he wondered? Who the hell bothers to clean a spade?

Sullivan scanned the yard. There was no sign of a cart, but propped against the back wall of the garage, next to the garbage bins, was a large wheelbarrow.

Wheelbarrow! It was the perfect way to transport a body, lightweight and easy to manoeuvre. Pulling on latex gloves, he eased it away from the wall. It too was scrubbed clean. Not even a speck of rust. He'd never seen a wheelbarrow without at least a few rusty dings in it. Underfoot, the ground was soggy and the grass flattened as if soaked by a strong spray.

He went back inside to find the search team poking around in the bedroom closet. A half dozen pairs of shoes sat in evidence bags on the bed.

"There's a spade and axe in the shed," Sullivan said. "Make sure you bring them, and the wheelbarrow as well."

Wallington nodded. "Do you want us to bag all these clothes?"

Sullivan looked at the closet stuffed with shirts, sweaters and jackets. All high-end, all in camera-friendly colours of rust and green that would look good with Riley's dark hair and eyes. McIntyre's touch. Hardly the kind of stuff you'd wear for chopping up a body. But stranger things have happened.

"Yeah, take it all. But the main thing to look for is old clothes or a raincoat. Easier to rinse blood off."

"He probably threw the stuff out, sir. I would."

Sullivan glanced out the window. "There's a row of garbage cans out back. Check them thoroughly. I don't think he'd be stupid enough to leave the stuff on the premises, but you never know."

Riley's bedroom window looked over the side of the house, with a clear view of both the backyard and the street where the surveillance team had been parked. Sullivan's eyes settled on the garage directly below and he sucked in his breath. From this angle, he could see it was an oversized garage, with plenty of room to skirt around the van in the drive. "You said his car was in there?"

The surveillance detectives nodded like twins. "He drove it in there himself last night."

Sullivan swore as he headed back outside and hauled open the garage door. It glided easily, well oiled and soundless. But when the sunlight finally poured in to illuminate the dank interior, there was nothing but an empty concrete floor.

The kid had flown the coop.

Seventeen

An airplane loomed overhead, so low that it cast a shadow over the street like a massive bird of prey. Its jet engines blotted out all other sound. Green squinted up into the midday sun and tracked its descent over the tall pines. It looked as if it were going to land on nearby golf course, not at the airport more than a mile away. Back in the days before Ottawa's airport was first built, the land around it had been a pleasant, rolling woodland on which the local gentry hunted and played. Now, Hunt Club was a typical labyrinthian tangle of suburban crescents crowded with comfortable four-bedroom homes, tattered basketball nets and SUVs that never saw anything rougher than the soccer field.

But bland, well-mannered suburbia can hide all sorts of secrets behind its decorative glass doors, Green reflected as he stood outside Vic McIntyre's innocuous-looking brick house. McIntyre did not appear to spend much time or imagination on his garden, which was limited to grass and low-maintenance evergreen shrubs. Nor did he have much flair for colour and contrast. The house was entirely coloured in drab shades of brown. The only hint of drama was the red curtains in the living room window. No one would give this house a second glance.

Perhaps that was the intention.

The driveway was empty, but the garage door was closed,

keeping alive Green's slim hope of finding the players' agent at home. However, when ringing the doorbell and pounding on the door failed to bring a response, he had to accept defeat. Casually he strolled around the side of the house down a neat cobblestone path. Halfway down was a side door which probably opened into the garage. Idly, Green tried the knob and was surprised to feel it give beneath his hand. He peeked into the spacious garage, past the empty space where the car would have been and saw a door on the far side which led into the house. Even more surprising, the door was ajar. In the city, few people still left their doors unlocked, and McIntyre did not strike him as the trusting type. Carelessness or haste, Green wondered? He stepped back outside, feeling conspicuous, and continued on towards the back, where he unlatched the gate and slipped into the backyard.

It was like going down the rabbit hole.

Here, hidden from view by a six-foot-high privacy fence, was a playground fit for Hollywood. A huge, kidney-shaped pool glistened in the sun, surrounded by a broad, meandering slate walkway. Reclining lounge chairs, patio umbrellas and a poolside bar were arranged artfully around, and in the corner, an ornate gazebo housed an octagonal marble hot tub. A fake waterfall burbled against the back fence, and wrought iron lamp posts marked every few yards, promising romantic splashes of light on a warm summer night.

Green stood just inside the gate, absorbing the spectacle. This must have cost the high-flying agent well over a hundred thousand dollars. His secret paradise, known only to those privileged to be invited and to the neighbours who looked down on it from their second storey windows.

As if by telepathy, one of them was standing in the McIntyre driveway when Green returned to the front. He was a beefy man in his late fifties by Green's guess, dressed in baggy shorts, a battered Tilley hat and a T-shirt with the Green Party logo. He had a set of keys in his hand and a suspicious scowl on his face.

"You looking for something, buddy?"

Green hesitated, then decided that his police badge might net him more cooperation than some lame cover story. At the sight of it, the man drew himself up and sucked in his gut. Green recorded his name—Eugene Boulder—and his address, then gestured towards McIntyre's house.

"I'm looking for Mr. McIntyre, but he doesn't seem to be home."

"No, he's out most days. You might catch him in the evening, but then again, maybe not."

"He's not here much?"

Boulder shrugged. "Well, he travels all over. He's a sports agent, says he's got to go where the players are."

"Has he been here recently? Say in the past ten days?"

"Oh, yeah. He comes and goes, sometimes at all hours of the night."

"When was the last time you saw him?"

Boulder wiped some sweat from his forehead and squinted at the ground. "This morning. He drives a big, gas-guzzling Lincoln Navigator—black." Boulder sneered. "Hard to miss when it's staring you in the face first thing in the morning."

"So it was here this morning? What time did it leave?"

"Pretty early, for him anyways. Eight thirty, maybe? I was out laying earwig traps over there under my peonies, and he roars off, foot to the floor like always." Boulder shook his head, then sighed as if in resignation and cocked his eyebrow at Green. "What's this all about?"

"Mr. McIntyre is assisting us with some inquiries," he replied drily, then tossed in a diversionary clue. "That's quite a set-up he has around back. Does he have many parties out there?"

Boulder grunted. "Enough. One would be too many for me, but then the wife says I'm a stick-in-the-mud. Pretty noisy affairs, on till all hours. The Stanley Cup playoffs were awful."

"Ever think of complaining?"

Boulder eyed him in silence for a moment as if trying to gauge the impact of his answer. "I thought of it. Told him I was thinking of it, and the next day one of my roses was dug up. I'd been babying it for ten years. I can't prove a thing, but I got the point."

"You should have complained anyway. Otherwise bullies like that win the game."

"Yeah, but you don't live next door to him."

"Tell me about these parties."

Boulder needed no further encouragement to spill forth the frustration and venom he'd stored up in the two years since McIntyre had moved in. Loud music, dancing outside by the pool, a constant parade of girls, each wearing less that the last, cars revving up and down the street at three in the morning, kids barely old enough to drive throwing up in his prize rhododendrons. Other times there were smaller parties, with quieter music, nudes in the hot tub, girls giggling—who knew what was going on?

"The wife says I should get out of the nineteenth century, but this used to be such a peaceful street, and the couple who owned the place before him were such nice people. They had a beautiful maple out back that turned scarlet every fall, you could see it for miles, but he moves in, and within a week he had the backhoe in there and tore the whole place up."

Green made sympathetic noises and prepared to leave. As an afterthought, he pulled out some photos from his car. "Did

222

you ever see this girl here?"

Boulder studied the picture of Crystal and shrugged. "Could be. That's the type you see, and they all look the same, don't they, with all that make-up on and barely enough clothes to cover a baby's bottom."

Green showed him Jenna Zukowski, and he frowned. "He sure likes the ladies, but this one looks too old for him. I'd have to see her with make-up to be sure."

"What about him?"

"That kid, yeah. That's the hockey player, and he's over a lot. Not just at the parties."

"Seen him recently?"

"Well, I don't watch every minute of the day, you know."

Green suspected he did, especially when the half naked girls were on display, but he smiled reassuringly. "Of course not. Just curious if you saw him."

"Well, I did see him this weekend sometime. Can't remember—Friday or Saturday? They had a fight."

"What about?"

"I don't..."

"I know, you don't listen in. But if you heard anything... It might be useful."

"Yeah. The O'Shaughnessy kid came storming out of the house and McIntyre says 'I'm not going to let you ruin your life', and the kid yells back 'you already have'. Then he got in his Jeep and took off."

At that moment Green's cell phone rang, giving him little time to absorb the possible meaning of that outburst. He glanced at the call display with annoyance, but saw that it was Sullivan. He strolled casually over to his car to be out of earshot of the neighbour, who had already exhibited a more than healthy curiosity about other people's business.

"Jesus, Mary and Joseph! The idiots lost him!"

Green took a moment to figure out what he was talking about. "What do you mean—lost him?"

"I mean, the surveillance guys fell asleep, went off for a piss—who the fuck knows?—and Riley drove out from under their noses."

Sullivan sounded taut with anger, and Green could almost picture the dusky red creeping up his neck. Green rolled his eyes. Devine would have a field day with this. Not only had the department dished out hundreds of her precious overtime dollars to keep these guys on the job, but they had bungled it. "When?"

"Who knows? Their best guess? Sometime around five o'clock this morning. He must have seen our surveillance team and realized we were on to him."

Green heard the heaviness in Sullivan's voice. "It looks pretty bad for him, Brian."

"I know. I've already put out an APB, so now the kid's name is going to be broadcast all over the city. Fucking idiots!"

I wouldn't want to be the surveillance team that screwed that up, Green thought. Out of the corner of his eye, he saw the neighbour standing by his car, keys in hand, straining to hear.

"I've set up a briefing in half an hour," Sullivan was saying. "We need to get some teams tracking Riley, and we need to see what Ident and MacPhail have managed to find out about the Jane Doe." A jet roared overhead, blocking out all sound for almost thirty seconds. "Where the hell are you?"

"At Vic McIntyre's house. There's another twist to the story." Green filled him in on Riley's phone call to McIntyre. "The kid barely seems to take a shit without checking with McIntyre, so I'm betting he panicked and called him for advice that night. Maybe McIntyre even helped him cover it up."

Sullivan was silent a moment. "Well, I wouldn't put it past the guy. You'd think he wouldn't jeopardize his career and reputation with something so stupid, but we've both seen smarter men make even dumber choices."

Next door, Eugene Boulder gave up trying to eavesdrop and drove away in his car. Green glanced thoughtfully at McIntyre's deserted house. Boulder had said McIntyre had roared off at top speed at eight thirty this morning. He had been in such a hurry that he had left the inside door to his garage ajar. What was the big rush? Could it be that Riley had asked him for help again? Maybe even to hide him?

"Are you coming down to the briefing?" Sullivan asked.

"You go ahead," Green said. "I just have a small thing to check into."

After he hung up, he got out and glanced up and down the street, studying the front yards and façades of the neighbouring houses. No one was around, no one paying him the slightest heed. He strolled back up to McIntyre's house and ducked out of sight down the side path. At the side door, he hesitated. He had no authorization to do this, no possible justification or defence. Worse, his action could jeopardize future investigation of McIntyre if anyone found out about it. But a dangerous killer was on the loose, possibly two of them working in concert, and if there were any clues in the house as to their whereabouts, what was the harm in a little peek?

I'll be in and out in less than five minutes, he promised himself, slipping on latex gloves. No point in leaving calling cards. Taking a deep breath, he grabbed the knob and ducked inside. The garage echoed emptily. He crossed the concrete in long, rapid strides and entered the house. At the last second, he spotted the alarm panel by the door and felt a quick shot of adrenaline before realizing it had not been turned on.

Another sign of haste? He scoped out the ground floor quickly, but there was no sign of Riley. The decor of the front rooms was lean and masculine. Brushed nickel, smoked glass and burgundy leather. No knickknacks, photos or artwork on the walls, which were starkly painted in reds, chocolates and golds. Highly polished hardwood echoed his footsteps. This was a house out of a designer's set, meant to entertain and to impress. Meant to lure the unsuspecting into believing they were in the company of character and taste.

The family room and kitchen at the back of the house were more lush and sensual. Green's eyes widened at the sight of the cavernous kitchen with its bank of windows overlooking the pool. Granite counters, cherrywood cabinets, Italian tile, stainless steel European appliances. Green had nearly wiped out his bank account on his modest renovations to their own old house, so he could make a fair guess at the cost of this extravagance. On the counter sat an uneaten omelette and a half empty cup of coffee, and spread out beside them was the morning's edition of the *Ottawa Sun*. McIntyre had not even progressed beyond the first page, where Frank Corelli's story about the Bruce Pit death screamed out its outrageous headline.

Conscious of the time, Green moved quickly up the stairs as he registered the implications. McIntyre had begun his breakfast preparations without haste or apparent concern but, much like Riley, he'd been sent into action by the sight of that headline.

Green's speculations were brought to a crashing halt when he reached the door of the first bedroom. A massive circular bed commanded central stage, and mirrored tiles on the ceiling reflected its glossy black sheets. A huge flat screen TV occupied one wall, but the remaining walls were papered in life-sized, pornographic photos of women. Some nude, some dressed only in flimsy lingerie, garters or thongs. None looked over sixteen.

"Holy fuck!" The words were out before he even remembered the need for stealth. He jerked open the door to the closet. Inside was a hidden video camera aimed through a peephole towards the bed. Behind it were shelves upon shelves of boxes. He bent to examine a box sitting open on the closet floor. On close inspection it proved to be packed with DVDs, videotapes and photographs, all cryptically labelled in an alphanumeric code. Curious, Green picked up the TV remote that sat on a shelf in the closet and aimed it at the TV. The screen filled with an overhead shot of the circular bed, this time covered in hot pink sheets. Two naked figures writhed on the bed, and it took Green a moment to recognize McIntyre himself, fondling the tanned, nubile body of a girl probably younger than Hannah. Bottles of wine cluttered the bedside table, and soft, sensual jazz blended with the murmuring from the bed.

Green studied the mirror ceiling tiles over the bed, trying to detect the camera behind them, but it was completely hidden from view. The bastard can videotape whatever he wants, Green thought, without the girls having a clue. He ejected the disk and selected another at random from the box. This one was a shot of the leather sofa downstairs, which sagged beneath the weight of two girls crawling all over a foolishly grinning teenage boy. The girls were wearing nothing but a Senators flag. The boy was stark naked.

Green flicked the TV off in disgust. His thoughts flashed involuntarily to Hannah and Crystal, who thought they understood the world of sex and power. How old were those kids on the sofa? Did they know they were being filmed? Was McIntyre in the room with them, or did he savour the show later in private? Green's mind ticked off all the charges that could be laid against the man, if ever this evidence could be legally seized, but it was small retribution for what he'd done to the kids.

He came back to reality with a start. He'd been in the house far too long. He replaced everything as it had been and hurried down the hall to the next bedroom, wondering what else the man was up to. This one was a huge master bedroom with a balcony overlooking the backyard paradise. It was more tastefully done in dark mahogany furnishings and shiny red and gold striped wallpaper. The king-sized bed had a luxurious red satin duvet and matching sheets. Green sensed this was the man's private abode, his own personal sensual palace. The ensuite bathroom was a massive marble extravagance with two sinks, gold-plated faucets and a Jacuzzi almost large enough for an entire hockey team. A quick search of the cupboards revealed one linen closet full not of towels or sheets but bottles of pills and entire cases of sports drinks. Green picked one up.

"Dr. Rosen's Electro-Boost, the only thirst quencher for the serious athlete" boasted the label. There was no list of ingredients or bar code for commercial sale. He peered at the bottles containing all different sizes and colours of tablets labelled innocuously as Vitamin E, B12, ginseng, garlic. I'd give anything to send all this stuff for analysis, Green thought. I bet I'd find crystal meth, ecstasy, probably all sorts of uppers and downers to relax inhibitions and enhance excitement. Maybe even roofies, so the kids can pleasure him without remembering a thing.

No one opens a candy store for nothing, he thought, and fought back the revulsion that rose in his throat. Reluctantly he replaced the bottles and eased the cupboard shut again. On his way out of the bedroom, he couldn't resist a quick peek in the man's mahogany dresser. He was no longer searching for Riley, but for a fuller view of the man's dark side. Inside the top drawer, instead of the usual array of socks and briefs, he found a jumble of women's lingerie. Panties, bras, camisoles and teddies in black lace, virginal white silk, leather and flimsy chiffon. Green sifted through it curiously. Were these trophies, to remind him of his conquests? The musky scent of sex tickled his nostrils, and he was about to shut the drawer when a fragment of embroidery caught his eye. Part of a name. He pulled the item free and found himself holding a black satin thong with a name hand-embroidered in red across the skimpy triangle of cloth.

For Riley.

*　　*　　*

A minute later, Green was back in his car, starting it up and driving up the block out of sight. His heart was pounding. The panties were the closest they had come so far to nailing the connection between Riley, McIntyre and Lea's death. Physical evidence, straight from the Hog's Back scene, found in the man's personal possessions. McIntyre had probably removed the panties from the scene in order to erase all evidence that tied Riley to Lea, but he had been unable to resist keeping them for his own sick titillation.

If only Green could use it. But since the search had been entirely illegal, he couldn't even let on he knew the panties and the rest of the erotica existed. At least officially. But off the record, Sullivan had to know what the hell they were dealing with, so they could figure out how it all fit together. He turned the car and headed towards the station, his thoughts scrounging for possible ways to justify a search warrant.

He got less than five blocks before his phone rang. He groped for it, expecting it was Sullivan with news from his briefing. But to his surprise, it was a woman's voice, vaguely familiar but distorted by the urgent whisper.

"He's here! He came to see me!"

"Who is this?"

"Marija Kovacev. He is in—"

Green's adrenaline spiked. "Who is there?"

"The boy who was with Lea that night. He came to explain."

Green gripped the wheel with his free hand, all senses alert. "Where are you?"

"In my bathroom. I told him I need to use the toilet, but I phone you—"

"Where is he right now?"

"In my living room."

Green flipped on his flashing lights and slammed the accelerator to the floor. He was only ten minutes from her house, maybe less at full lights and siren. But ten minutes was way too long. As his mind raced over his choices, Marija was still talking.

"He says it was an accident, Lea take some marijuana and she get very sick. I tell him to call you, but he says he can't. So I call."

In a split second, Green had to make a decision. He could ask her to go back and stall Riley until the police arrived, or he could tell her to get away from the house. In the latter case, he risked losing track of his suspect, but in the former, he risked losing Marija herself. He needed to call for back-up, but he had to get her safe first.

"Marija, can you get out the back door without being seen?"

"Yes, but—"

"Then do it. Right now. I'm on my way, and I'll get him."

"But he is not dangerous! He is crying! He is afraid."

"Okay, but let's do it my way," he said as he slewed around the corner from McCarthy Road, tires screaming, and accelerated up Walkley. "Go out the back door."

He listened to the silence over the phone. "Marija? Trust me. Go."

Finally over the roar of his engine, he heard the line click dead. Praying that she had obeyed him, he called the Com Centre for backup. When he raced up her street five minutes later, he saw a cruiser just pulling up to the curb. There was no sign of a red Mustang in the drive, but Marija herself was standing on the lawn. She looked pale and wide-eyed, but unharmed. Green felt a rush of relief. She walked over as he leaped out of the car, and lifted her hands in an elegant gesture of defeat.

"He ran away. He was afraid. I tried to tell you, but you gave me no chances."

He took her elbow. "I'm sorry, but I had to put your safety first."

She stiffened and pulled away. "He is not a criminal."

"I want to hear the whole story, but give me a moment to speak to these officers first."

"So you can hunt him down?"

Green stared at her, puzzled. Why this irrational anger? What kind of twisted loyalty would make her take sides with the man responsible for her daughter's death rather than with those seeking to bring him to account? He tried to sound gentle, belying the urgency he felt. "We need to find him. As you said, he needs to tell us what happened."

That seemed to mollify her, and she went inside while he spoke to the responding officers and relayed the latest information on Riley's whereabouts to the Com Centre. Brian Sullivan was just arriving back at the station and was happy to work with the duty inspector to coordinate the manhunt. Riley could not have had more than a ten-minute head start, and the bright red sports car should be easy to spot.

With the search underway, Green went inside and found Marija in the kitchen, boiling the kettle for tea. She paced, avoiding his probing eyes while she fiddled with the cups and tea bags. He gritted his teeth, willing himself to be patient until the tea was prepared and she had taken her first sip. Only then did she seem to sag with defeat.

He forced a gentle tone. "Okay, tell me what happened."

She cradled her tea, and her eyes filled with sudden tears. "I don't know who to blame. Lea had such a lot of secrets. This boy, the drugs... I never thought she would smoke marijuana, but this boy—"

"Riley?"

She looked startled. "You know?"

"Just his name. Not what happened. I'm sorry I interrupted."

"You didn't tell me." Anger tightened her features again, and he cursed his clumsiness. She sipped her tea in silence for a long moment, as if debating with herself, before she resumed. "Riley said she bought the marijuana, she said it would be fun to try it together. It was very beautiful evening, the first date they have all week, because his sports keeps him so busy. It's always training, training, publicity, meet this person and that person. All he was thinking about was Lea. He tells me he loved her, because she was very different from the other girls—" She shot him a sharp scowl, perhaps anticipating his doubt. "I believe him. He was very upset. Crying, crying. He said he couldn't sleep, and he never wanted this to happen. He didn't want the marijuana. Lea teased him, but he doesn't want drugs in his body. Now he wish he did take the cigarette too. Lea starts to act very wild. They walked a little and sat on a bench together, but Lea couldn't stay still. She started running around, to make him chase her, and they were playing—wrestling, he said—and he tried to stop her. To hold her quiet. Not hard, he said, just her arms, but she was fighting and fighting, then suddenly she was not breathing. He says she panicked. He got scared someone would accuse him, because of the drugs and because he was holding her on the ground when she die."

Her voice faltered on the last word, and she took a shaky sip of her tea. This time Green waited without interruption, although half a dozen questions crowded his thoughts. What about the aborted 911 call, and the call to his agent? What about throwing the body into the river?

"Was Lea taking any medication? For a cold, asthma or dieting?"

She shook her head back and forth vehemently. "Dieting she didn't believe in. She was all the time very healthy. That's why this marijuana, I don't understand it. So many things I don't understand." She lapsed into silence again, nursing her pain.

It doesn't mean anything, Green thought. Parents were the least likely to know anything about their teenager's day-to-day life. Wisely, he kept quiet until she resumed her thread. "He is so ashamed. He thought only of him, not Lea. He didn't call the police, he put the body in the river so it looks like an accident. So maybe people won't discover he was with her. But now, he says something else is going on."

"What do you mean?"

"That's the reason he came to see me. To apologize that he was a coward and now he had to stop. He saw the paper this morning about the social worker who was killed, and he knew it was because of him. Someone is trying to hide what he did by killing again."

Green's eyes narrowed, and he found himself holding his breath. Marija raised her ravaged blue eyes to his. "He was afraid. He was looking all the time out the window like he was looking for something. Like the killer was after him. That's why he ran away. Not so that he can escape from you, but from the killer. And it is the killer that you need to find, not this boy."

"But he knows who the killer is."

She nodded. "I asked who, and he said he couldn't tell, because it was his fault. The killer did this for him."

"Did he explain?"

Her shrug was regretful. "I told him he has to tell you. He can't run forever. I give him your card, but when he said no, I came to the bathroom to phone you. When I came out, he was gone."

"Did you see anything outside in the street? A person? A car?"

"A few cars. Nothing special."

Green gritted his teeth. He didn't want to plant ideas in her head, but he had a very good idea who it might have been. "Do you remember any makes? Colours?"

"Silver one. Another red. And one big black one."

Green gave her hand a quick squeeze, which he hoped was reassuring, and excused himself to relay the information to the Communications Centre. Inwardly, every muscle was taut with fear. It had to be Vic McIntyre. McIntyre drove a black SUV. He was the person Riley had phoned the night Lea died. Moreover, Vic had been a man with a purpose that morning.

What if Marija was right? If McIntyre, not Riley, was the villain behind the deaths? Green thought about all the bits of information he learned about McIntyre. The man had a backyard playground worth perhaps a quarter of a million. He threw noisy, extravagant parties where no doubt the drugs flowed as freely as the booze. He drove a car that cost more than many annual incomes. Where did all the money come from? Granted, there was big money to be made in elite sports, but McIntyre wasn't at the top yet. He was still clawing his way up, pinning all his hopes on the talents of his rising star.

A star who had recently become distracted and fallen down on his training, perhaps wanting some pleasures in his life other than the strict regime McIntyre had ordered. What if McIntyre had supplied Crystal with the lethal drug, knowing full well that Riley, the anti-drug poster boy, would refuse to take it, but that the smaller, more daring Lea Kovacev would not hesitate. Had he intended her to die, or just be so stoned that it would turn Riley against her?

Titrating just the right amount of crystal meth into a bag of marijuana was an inexact science. Perhaps McIntyre hadn't cared whether he killed her or not, as long as it killed the romance.

The second murder was a different story, regardless of which woman the victim proved to be. Both Crystal and Jenna knew too much. Of all the men Green had encountered in the case, McIntyre had the ruthlessness needed to chop a woman into pieces to protect his own interests. What if he was on a deadly campaign to erase all signs that pointed to him? The crucial question was—where would he stop? Riley O'Shaughnessy was his protégé, almost his surrogate son, not to mention his meal ticket to the big time. He had done all this to protect that asset, if not the boy himself. What would he do now that the boy had become a liability?

Green didn't have a moment's doubt. McIntyre had other irons in the fire—other clients, maybe even an exclusive drug business. Riley would be a loss, but some other dream kid would come along. A man who could decapitate a young woman didn't have much room in his heart for sentiment.

Now that man was on the loose, chasing down the boy who could bring it all down.

Eighteen

While the duty inspector snapped out fresh orders over the radio, Brian Sullivan studied the wall map in the Communications Centre, tracing routes with his finger. The Com Centre had all sorts of computer maps and satellite surveillance systems, but despite all the fancy high-tech, the search for Riley O'Shaughnessy had turned up nothing. Sometimes there was nothing like good old-fashioned paper to get the big picture.

"Looks like he slipped the net," Sullivan said when Inspector Ford strode over.

"If he's smart, he's ditched the red Mustang," the inspector replied.

"Green thinks he's not running from us, but from Vic McIntyre."

"The guy in the black Navigator? Well, that'll be easy to spot too."

Sullivan stared at the map. Where would the kid run to? Friends? Hockey mates?

Or home. Gananoque. Sullivan turned to the larger map of Eastern Ontario on the other wall. Gananoque was a straight run down Highway 416 and along the 401. In an opened up Mustang, barely an hour and a half's drive. He tapped the map. "We need to call in the OPP, expand the search south, set up road blocks along 416."

Ford looked unconvinced. He was a sparkplug of a man bulked up by body armour and equipment that made him look twice as wide as he really was. He shook his head slowly. "If I was the kid, I'd take back roads. A red Mustang on the 416 is a sitting duck."

Sullivan's phone rang before he could answer. It was Lyle Cunningham from Ident. "You got an overtime budget for all this new shit your guys just brought in?"

"That's Devine's problem, not mine. Green's okayed it. We've got two murders here, nice young women. If Devine ever wants to make Deputy Chief, she'll know what's good for her."

"If you say so. We're just logging in the stuff from the O'Shaughnessy house, but I thought you'd want to know. We did some preliminary tests before we even took it off the truck, just to see if we could eliminate anything from our investigation."

Sullivan smiled. "You're the best, Lyle. Anything?"

"Good news, bad news. The clothes you brought me? None of them appear to have any blood on them."

Well, that was a long shot, Sullivan thought. The murder clothes would be soaked in blood, so the kid would almost certainly have ditched them. "What about the shoes? Any match to the print?"

"We haven't got to that yet. We can't do everything at once, you know, so I went with the blood first."

"All right, what's the good news?"

Cunningham's voice almost sounded excited. "It's not final yet, you understand. But it looks like the shovel, the axe and the wheelbarrow all have traces of blood on them."

"Even though they'd been cleaned?"

"You know you can never wash all that stuff out of the cracks and pits. That's how we get the bad guys. If there's a molecule left in there, the Luminol will find it. But it could be anyone's blood, or animal blood for that matter. Is your guy a hunter?"

Sullivan pictured the O'Shaughnessys. They'd grown up in a small town in Eastern Ontario, rugged and blue collar. Chances are they all hunted deer. But cutting up deer meat is a very precise science; hunters don't chop up their quarry with an axe.

His heart felt heavy. "Could be, but I'm betting this isn't deer blood."

"We'll need time to see if it's human, even longer to get the DNA back, but at least this gives you a start."

"What about the plumbing van?"

"Jeez, Sully, give me a break. I haven't got to that yet either. The guys just towed it to the lot. There are lots of tools and piping and drop cloths that look pretty clean, but when I know something definitive, you'll be the first to know."

Sullivan thanked him and rang off, deep in thought. The net was closing, and despite what Green believed, things were looking worse and worse for the hockey whiz kid. They now had the tools the woman had been killed with. The body had been stuffed into garbage bags, so it could have been transported in the van without spilling much blood in the interior. But chopping up the body would have produced a mess, even if it was done post mortem. Whoever did this would have needed a concealed location, and even after clean-up, there would be traces of blood left behind.

He remembered the wet, flattened area of grass in Darren O'Shaughnessy's backyard. Was that where the dismemberment had taken place? Did the tall cedar hedge provide enough privacy, or would neighbours have seen and heard something? It was worth making a few inquiries. And with Riley a potential out-of-control killer driving around the city in a panic, it was better than sitting around the Com Centre twiddling his thumbs and waiting for the search to turn up something.

He phoned Cunningham back, fully expecting an earful when he asked for an Ident officer to check out the back yard and the garage, but the man was surprisingly amenable. He couldn't send someone right away, but would put it on the list.

"I saw the body," he said by way of explanation. "Whoever did this to that poor girl deserves to be strung up by his balls."

*　　*　　*

Darren O'Shaughnessy answered the doorbell himself this time, and at the sight of Sullivan, his face darkened in a scowl. He blocked the doorway, six inches shorter than Sullivan but solid as a tank.

"Sully. Now there's a true friend in need."

"It's not a social call, Darren."

"You bet it's not. What's the idea of coming in here when I wasn't home, upsetting my kid and turning the place upside down. With warrants, for Chrissake. I would have given you anything you wanted!"

"Nothing to hide, is that it?"

"You bet. And neither does Riley."

"Then you won't mind answering a few questions?"

"As a matter of fact, yeah, I do mind. I don't owe you a goddamn thing."

"There's a couple of points that have come up in our investigation. You might want to clear them up sooner, rather than later down at the station."

"That a threat?"

"No," said Sullivan, wishing he'd brought someone with him. Given his previous acquaintance with Darren, this was not going to look good if a defence lawyer got hold of it. "But

239

just so you know, we did find blood on the axe, shovel and wheelbarrow in your backyard. That needs an explanation."

"You're bluffing. I keep all my tools clean as a whistle."

"I guess you don't watch enough *CSI*. Blood is impossible to get out of all the cracks and pits."

Darren's jaw fell open. Sullivan pressed on. "We also know that the board social worker, Jenna Zukowski, visited Riley here last Friday morning, asking questions. That's the last time anyone saw her alive. It doesn't take much to build a case once we get forensics."

Darren still blocked the doorway, but now his body swayed. Sullivan stepped forward. "Maybe we should continue this inside."

Darren glowered up at him, then shrugged and turned to lead the way into the living room. Hockey memorabilia was everywhere, including a signed photo of Wayne Gretzky, dozens of trophies and a picture of the Salt Lake City gold medal team. There was not much else in the room except a giant screen TV and a scuffed old lazy-boy chair sitting directly in front of it. A plaid couch with a broken spring was shoved into a corner, covered in newspapers, plumbing pipes, two cases of Labatt Blue, and some bags from the hardware store. Thumbtacked over the mantlepiece was a huge Ottawa Senators flag. A true bachelor's pad. Sullivan's own wife Mary, being a real estate agent, would never stand for the mess, but then Darren's wife had left him in disgust years ago. Sullivan remembered talk about domestic assault, but nothing had ever been proved.

But in spite of the mess, the floor didn't have a speck of dust, and the lazy-boy looked freshly washed. Pretty selective housekeeping, Sullivan thought with interest. He wandered over to the mantlepiece and pretended to study the photos propped along its top. Front and centre was a large photo of Canada's

World Championship Junior Hockey Team, with Riley beaming from the front row. Sullivan was about to comment when he detected some tiny flecks of brown against the white border.

Darren had planted himself by the door with his arms crossed. "I don't know what you're talking about," he was saying. "If that broad came here Friday, I didn't see her."

"Is that what the blood analysis of these specks is going to tell us, Darren?"

Darren turned white. He said nothing, probably a wise move when you don't know what the other guy is holding.

"Where were you Friday morning?"

"Fuck you, Sullivan."

Sullivan strolled around the room, trying to look casual as he inspected the walls and floor. "Darren, we're going to get to the bottom of this. We've got forensics going over everything. Riley's clothes and shoes, your tools, the pressure-washed spot in the back yard. I'll get them to check out this room too. A young woman has been brutally murdered. Do you think the department is going to let this slide? You can answer my questions here and now, man to man, or I can take you down to Elgin Street and do a whole formal interrogation. Your choice. Where were you Friday morning?"

Darren looked like he was turning over Sullivan's words. Finally, he shrugged. "Here. Off and on. I don't always hear the doorbell when I'm in the back. Maybe she rang and no one answered."

"Who else was at home Friday morning?"

"No one."

Too quick, Darren boy, Sullivan thought. "Where was Riley?"

"Out. Training. His agent has been on his case, so he went for a long bike ride."

"From what time to what time?"

"All morning. He went out early, maybe seven o'clock. Didn't come back till noon."

"How do you know that if you were in the back?"

Darren started to speak, then snapped his jaw tight. Sullivan considered his next move. He had evidence that Jenna had planned to come here, evidence that there was blood on the axe and wheelbarrow, and possible traces of blood in this room. But three men lived at the O'Shaughnessy house— Riley, Darren and his son Ben—and there was no way to know for certain which of them was involved. Not to mention how the hell McIntyre figured into the mess.

He should wait for the rest of the evidence, and he should do this interview by the book, down at the station with all the proper procedures and warnings. But Riley was out on the streets in his sports car, running from something but refusing to go to the police. Sullivan thought that if he could lean on Darren, he might be able to get some answers that would help the police know what they were dealing with.

"Here's what I think happened," Sullivan said quietly. "I think Jenna came here to see Riley, and she got kind of pushy. I hear she's like that. You know these social workers, they always think they're right. I bet she accused him of dumping his girlfriend's body, maybe even of killing her. Anyway, Riley's been under a lot of pressure recently, for a small town kid who's just eighteen. His girlfriend just died, his agent is on his case, the media are watching his every move, the scouts are picking apart his recent slump, and the speculators are saying the sky could be the limit if he keeps his shit together. He's been trying to wrap up his exams, he hasn't been sleeping, and Friday, when the social worker got in his face, he just lost it."

"He wasn't here!"

"I've seen Riley play, Darren. He's real aggressive on the ice, trained to go after what he wants, trained to see what he can get away with. He sees his whole future crumbling before his eyes. Maybe he has the O'Shaughnessy men's famous temper, eh? Or maybe it was 'roid rage. He's filled out a lot in the last year. Is he taking steroids?"

Darren snorted. "He would never touch the stuff. Thinks it's cheating."

Sullivan shrugged. "Still, I heard McIntyre's into that. And I know how much Riley listens to him."

Darren tightened his arms defiantly, but his eyes twitched, and Sullivan knew he'd hit a nerve. "Steroids could be enough to push him over the edge," he said. "They could also be a defence, remember, if it comes to that. Whatever happened when Riley and the social worker argued, he just snapped and popped her. Didn't mean to kill her, I'm sure. Freaked out and tried to get rid of the body, forgetting we'd have all kinds of forensics to tie him to the case."

"You don't have shit!"

"But we will. And now Riley is racing around Ottawa in his Mustang. Maybe he's in a panic, maybe he can't think straight. You know what steroids do to the human brain? Irrational rage, paranoia, maybe even hallucinations. There's no telling what he's thinking. We have to get him in, Darren. You need to tell me what happened."

"I don't know what the hell you're talking about. Riley's not on drugs. And you're so far off base with that social worker it's a joke."

"Okay, maybe it was your son, Ben. He's got a temper on him, I can see that."

Darren turned the colour of raw steak. "You leave Ben out of this!"

"Why? Riley's almost like a brother to him. Maybe they even talked about girlfriends. Ben's seen the papers, he knows all about this dead girl and how the cops are trying to figure out what happened to her."

Darren opened his mouth, but Sullivan rolled over his protests. He hadn't primed the pump enough yet. "So when this social worker shows up asking for Riley, Ben puts two and two together. He tells her no way she's seeing Riley, she gets pushy, and before he knows it—pop!" Sullivan slammed his fist into his palm, making Darren jump.

"Your fuse has always been your downfall, right, Darren? No matter how hard you tried, you could only take so much before all of a sudden, before you even know it, someone is on the floor. Almost like you couldn't help yourself. I bet it's like father, like son."

Darren walked over to stare out the window, flexing his fists. Finally he turned to face Sullivan, backlit by the sun. "You fucking bastard. That's dirty, even for you. You know Ben's got nothing to do with this."

"Do I? I saw his temper this morning. And he's bulked up a lot since last year too. I know he hangs out at McIntyre's place. Maybe he's been slipping him some performance enhancers too."

"You said yourself there are three guys live here. How do you know it wasn't me popped that bitch?"

"You said you didn't see her."

"What if I was lying?"

"Are you saying you did see her?"

"I'm not saying anything. I'm saying maybe it was me. Maybe she came like you said. Maybe she pissed me off. Fucking social workers are all the same. It's always the guy's fault. Women are just these poor, helpless innocents that never start anything. Lying? A woman never lies. Conning? A woman never cons. And temper? A woman can tear a strip off you up one side and down the other, but if the guy so much as shows his fist, well, it's jail for him. And sex? Women never heard of sex, it's all some big macho conspiracy to take advantage of them. Sometimes a guy can only take so much shit before he blows."

"So you hit her?"

"Maybe. That's for you to prove."

"Where did this happen?"

"This room looks like a good place."

"So how exactly did it happen?"

"Could have been just like you said, a burst of temper. One pop to the mouth, and she goes down, hits her head, and she's done. There's no intent to kill."

Sullivan sized him up. "Then why didn't you call 911?"

"Like you said, panic is a funny thing. Maybe I thought about what it would do to Riley if the whole mess got in the papers. No way would I want anything to screw up his big chance."

"So what did you do?"

"So I dumped the body in the park."

"How did you transport it?"

Darren paused. "In the wheelbarrow."

"I mean what did you drive it in?"

Abruptly Darren swung around and headed for the door. "You want any more information, you arrest me, you bring me downtown, and I want a lawyer. I'm not giving you another fucking thing for free."

*   *   *

Bob Gibbs approached the Norman Bethune Alternate School with a confidence he hadn't felt in weeks. He had a mission to focus on—to track down a missing teenage girl—and there was slim chance of a homicidal assailant leaping out of the shadows of the school. So far he had struck out with all of Crystal's friends. If they knew anything about her, they weren't talking. He'd spoken to enough sulky Avril Lavigne wannabes to turn him off having children entirely.

Norman Bethune School seemed deserted, with nothing but a single bicycle chained to the fence by the drive. The doorbell brought no response, but when he pounded on the door, he finally heard the shuffling of feet within. A few seconds later, the door cracked open warily, and a middle-aged woman peered out. Frizzy grey hair flew around her head.

"School's out, sir."

He showed her his badge and asked for a word. She led the way down a dark, creaky hallway into a minuscule office stuffed with files and books.

"I'm just working on final report cards," she said, stacking the papers on the floor to clear a space on the chair for him. "Is this about Inspector Green's daughter?"

Gibbs masked his surprise and shook his head, pulling out his notebook. After recording her name and occupation—Eleanor Hicks, guidance counsellor—he produced a picture of Crystal Adams. "Have you seen this girl?"

Ms Hicks arched her thick eyebrows. "Oh, dear!"

"Have you seen her?"

"Is this an official investigation?"

"Yes, this girl is missing."

"Oh dear. Well, I think she was the girl who was here this morning."

So she's still alive, Gibbs thought triumphantly. Finally a lead! "You're positive?"

"Well, she didn't look like this. She had no make-up on, and her hair was all over the place. She looked awful. But I'm pretty sure it's the same girl."

"What did she want?"

"To talk to the girls. They were almost all here this morning, clearing out their things. We had a little goodbye party, because most of them won't be back next year."

"Did she talk to anyone in particular?"

"She came here really upset and demanding to see one of our girls. Normally I wouldn't let anyone in who wasn't one of our students, but we were just having juice and muffins together and a couple of the girls recognized her. And as I said she seemed in trouble, so I decided maybe it would be best. We try to have a supportive, welcoming atmosphere here."

"Who did she talk to?"

"I'm not sure that matters."

The woman's evasion surprised him. "This is important. She may be at risk."

"That's the thing. She came here looking for answers..." She hesitated. "I didn't eavesdrop, you understand, but she wasn't speaking very quietly once she got upset. I could even hear her from this office. She seemed to feel that someone had ratted on her. Her words. She wanted to know who. These kinds of altercations are common enough with the student population we serve, so at the time I didn't think much of it."

"Did she find out who it was?"

"Well, that's the thing. I overheard the girls telling her who it could have been. And now that you're here..."

Gibbs readied his notebook. "Who?"

"Hannah Pollack. Inspector Green's daughter. Hannah wasn't in school, but last I knew, this girl was heading off to find her."

Gibbs sucked in his breath, the flutter of nerves returning to his gut. "Did she have an address?"

"Oh, yes. One of the girls told her. Hannah's been having a hard time since the students found out her father is a police officer."

Nineteen

Green was grateful once again for the flashing lights as he raced down Carling Avenue. He'd barely breathed since Gibbs's call. He didn't dare think about what he might encounter. How dangerous was Crystal? Could she have been the killer all along? First responsible for doctoring the drugs that killed Lea and later killing the social worker who knew too much. Did she have the strength and ruthlessness to sever the woman's head? God only knew. Desperation—or crystal meth—sometimes gives a woman the strength of six men.

When he hurtled the car down his quiet street, dog walkers and mothers with strollers scattered before him. The front of his house looked peaceful, and the door was locked. When he burst inside, he was greeted only by the hum of the air conditioner and the faint smell of coffee. He ran through the house, shouting for Hannah, but to no avail. He forced himself to calm down and inspect the house through the eyes of a detective. There were no signs of a struggle. No overturned tables or broken lamps, no paintings askew. No blood. He breathed a little more easily. In the kitchen, Hannah's empty cereal bowl sat on the counter, just as she always left it. On the kitchen table was an empty plate with crumbs on it, and two cups. He picked one up and sniffed it. Just coffee. Maybe she had gone out before Crystal arrived. Maybe she was safely off on one of her whimsical adventures.

He tried her cell phone, only to hear it ringing from inside her bedroom. A bad sign. Hannah never forgot her phone. Her backpack was also there, but her wallet was missing. He took a deep breath. This case was getting crazier at every turn. How many more people could be on the loose in the city? McIntyre, Riley, Crystal and now Hannah! Who the hell was pursuing whom, and why?

He returned outside and stood in the drive, looking down the street. No sign of Hannah. He drove slowly down to Richmond Road. The bus stop was vacant. He fought an overwhelming frustration. His daughter was an infuriatingly free spirit, inclined to pick up and disappear on a whim. If she had caught a bus, she could be anywhere in the city. There was really no evidence she was in danger. He had a murder case to solve and a search to coordinate. Reluctantly, he turned around and was just heading back towards Carling Avenue to return to the station when his cell phone rang. He wrestled it off his belt, praying it was Hannah. An unfamiliar voice burst through the speaker, deep but youthful and cracking with urgency.

"Inspector Green?"

"Speaking. Who is this?"

"Riley O'Shaughnessy."

Green nearly drove off the road. One handed, he swung his car under the Queensway overpass and accelerated towards the on-ramp. "Where are you, Riley?"

"I didn't kill her. You have to believe me."

"Where are you?"

"In my car."

"Where?"

"It doesn't matter where!" Riley's voice had a manic edge. "I need to know you believe me."

"I do believe you. I'll be at the station in five minutes. Can you meet me there?"

"It wasn't my idea to throw her into the river."

249

Keep him talking, Green reminded himself. In the background, he could hear the rumble of the powerful Mustang. "I know it wasn't. We know all about it. But—"

"How do you know?"

"We've been piecing things together. We know you called Vic McIntyre. But I really want to hear the whole story."

"He's looking for me! He wants to kill me." For the first time, the youth's voice broke, revealing how young he was.

"Then come in." There was a pause. Green barrelled down the Queensway, lights flashing. "Riley? It's the safest thing you can do."

"I thought he was in my corner. I thought he wanted my dreams too. But the bastard doesn't care. I called him for help, and he...he threw her away. Like a piece of garbage! And now that poor social worker. It's not worth it! All the money in the world, all the contacts, are not worth this! Oh, God, I just wanted to play hockey!"

"Riley, where are you?"

"On the 416. I'm going home." The youth's voice broke, and Green could hear him sobbing. He pictured him streaking down the highway, one hand clutching the cell phone, the other locked on the wheel. Tears blurring his view.

Christ.

"Riley! Come back to the station. We'll get McIntyre, but I need to know you're safe."

"No! I want to go home! Shit! There he is!"

Green's pulse leaped. "McIntyre? Where!"

"I just passed his car, sitting behind the pillar. Fuck, he spotted me! He's getting on the highway."

"What's the next exit?"

"I don't know, I don't know! Oh...Bankfield."

Green forced his own voice to be calm. Commanding. "Turn

250

around at Bankfield and come back towards town." He tried to visualize the highway. Bankfield was near the southern extremity of the city. There was nothing but farmland around, and even at highway speeds, it was a good twenty minutes drive from the station. Far too long for an inexperienced driver in a Mustang to run against a Lincoln Navigator. He did some rapid calculations.

"Riley, I'm going to get you some help. Turn around, and get off the 416 at the exit for Hunt Club Road. I'll have a police cruiser waiting for you."

"No, I can outrun him easily in this machine!" The engine's roar increased, almost deafening.

Green shouted over the din. "Riley. Riley! Listen to me. Hunt Club exit. My officers will be waiting for you."

He hung up and immediately called the Com Centre, hooking up with the duty inspector. Without hesitation Ford dispatched a unit to the Hunt Club exit then sent word to the Ontario Provincial Police to watch the highway further south in case Riley continued on toward Gananoque.

Green pulled into the front of the station, leaped out and dashed through the glass doors into the lobby. Just as he was climbing on the elevator, his cell phone rang again. An unknown number. Not Riley, not Hannah. McIntyre himself, perhaps? He punched "talk".

"Mike?"

Relief flooded through him. *Baruch Hashem*. "Hannah? Are you okay?"

She paused. "Are you at the station?"

The elevator hummed upwards. "Sort of. What's up?"

"Just stay put."

"But—"

The line clicked dead. He frowned at his phone but had no time for bewilderment before the elevator door opened onto the tense excitement of the Com Centre. Inspector Ford was pacing behind a row of dispatchers, coordinating the search. "Any news from Hunt Club?" Green asked.

"Not yet, but the unit's just arrived."

"We should call up the Tac Team," Green said. "Just in case things go sour."

The duty inspector ran his hand through his bristly crew cut, frowning. "Where would we send them?"

Green thought fast. "There's no way to know where—or if—the situation might explode. I think we should at least have them mobilized and ready to move."

The inspector shrugged. "I'll see what the team supervisor says," he muttered and flipped on his phone. While he waited, Green glanced around, but there was no sign of Sullivan. He phoned him. When Sullivan picked up, he sounded tense.

"I'm en route. I've got a cruiser bringing Darren O'Shaughnessy in."

Green was astounded. "What for?"

"For questioning in the murder of Jenna Zukowski."

"What!" Riley O'Shaughnessy had been their prime suspect, Vic McIntyre a late alternative, but Darren had never even been on the radar.

"Ident found blood on Darren's axe and wheelbarrow, and I think there's traces of blood in his living room."

"Did he admit it?"

"He's playing coy. It's hard to tell—"

At that moment, the Com Centre dispatcher shouted for attention. "It's the unit at Hunt Club exit," she said, turning up the speaker. A strident female voice penetrated the static. "A red Mustang just blew past us on the highway, going at least a hundred and sixty klics an hour."

Green's relief was short-lived. The boy had turned around,

but he hadn't stopped for help. "He's coming all the way in. Any sign of a black Navigator?"

"Not yet. Oh! Yeah, there he goes! He's about one kilometre behind."

Green glanced at the duty inspector, who was still tied up on the phone with the Tactical Unit. Green thought fast. "Take up pursuit. Try to box in the Navigator. We'll send some other units to help." He studied the wall map. The cruiser was positioned only about four kilometres from where the highway 416 merged with the much busier Queensway that drew local traffic as well as long distance traffic into the city's core. In the middle of the day, all the lanes would be crowded, and a high speed pursuit along the Queensway would put countless lives at risk.

The duty inspector put the Tac supervisor on hold and joined Green at the map. He immediately relayed the information to all available units in the west end, with orders to intercept and contain the Navigator if possible.

"Tell the Tac Team that our boy in the Mustang will probably be coming into the station off the Queensway in about ten minutes," Green said. "We have a unit in pursuit, but have them clear the area and work out a plan to secure him, and the driver of the Navigator in case the unit can't apprehend him en route."

"Mike!" The shout came from Green's cell phone, which he'd forgotten. Sullivan was still on the line. "What's going on?"

Green filled him in with three terse sentences.

"We're coming down Main Street," Sullivan said, "only about a kilometre away."

"Stay clear of the Metcalfe-Queensway area, Brian. We've called the Tac Team to control it, but I'm not sure what the hell is going to happen."

By this time, half a dozen senior brass had piled into the Com Centre, as well as the Tac supervisor, who was conferring urgently with the duty inspector. Both were snapping orders into their radios. Green left the coordination of the take-down in their much more capable hands and snatched up a radio.

"I'm going down to check outside."

The Tac supervisor scowled at him, but Green ducked through the door before the man could order him to stay the hell away from his operation.

When Green exited the large glass front doors of the station, the afternoon sun was baking the asphalt, and a parched wind buffeted the trees. He hurried along the side of the building towards Metcalfe Street, scanning the area. Police cruisers were peeling out of the underground parking lot. Two swung around the front of the building to cut off the entrance, and three raced towards the Queensway. Red lights strobed the pavement, and sirens screamed.

In the background, his radio crackled with continuous conversation as officers took up positions and reported in. The Tac team was still not in sight, but Green suspected they were already suited up and heading for the rooftop and corners of the station.

"3107 to Central," snapped a female voice Green recognized as the Hunt Club unit in pursuit. "I have a visual on the red Mustang up ahead, heading east on 417 just before the Parkdale exit."

"Central to 3107, copy that," came the response, which Green assumed was the duty inspector. "How far back are you?"

"Just past Carling."

Almost half a kilometre behind, Green thought. Too far! The Parkdale exit was less that three minutes' drive from the station at the speed Riley was going. The duty inspector must have read his mind. "What about the Navigator?"

"Right on the Mustang's ass," the unit replied. "Maybe fifty metres back."

"Step on it," Ford said. "But don't put on your lights and

siren till you're a lot closer."

Jesus Christ, Green thought with horror. The bastard's worrying about legal technicalities when we've got two civilians blasting full-tilt down a crowded highway. They're going to come screaming off the Queensway at the Metcalfe exit, straight into the dense, stop-and-go traffic of downtown.

"Get cruisers to hold back regular traffic on Isabella and Catherine Streets," he yelled into the radio, not bothering with call signs or radio procedure. The two roads ran along either side of the Queensway, serving as collector lanes. "And get a cruiser ready to cut off the Navigator on the ramp once the Mustang goes through."

"Already ordered," came the dry reply from upstairs.

By now, Green could hear insistent honking on the elevated expressway and the blast of sirens as cruisers raced into position. He ran along the side street towards Metcalfe Street, which bordered the back of the station. His eyes were glued to the Queensway which ran overhead just beyond Catherine Street on the opposite side of the station. He could see nothing, but the honking drew nearer, and he knew that any second, the Mustang would come racing down the ramp, under the Queensway and up Metcalfe towards him.

A flash of movement caught the corner of his eye. He glanced up the side street that intersected Metcalfe straight ahead. Two figures were approaching from Bank Street on foot. Women. No, girls. One with bedraggled blonde ringlets and the other...

He froze. What the *fuck!* Hannah! She was hurrying with her head bowed, leaning into the wind. Straight into the path of danger.

"Hannah, stop!"

The traffic roared, and the sirens screamed. Hannah didn't even look up. Green began to run, waving his arms. "Stop! Stop!"

He heard the screech of tires as he reached the intersection. Glanced left. Saw a red flash as the Mustang careened around the corner and spun onto Metcalfe, fishtailing. Green sucked in his breath. Why the hell hadn't the kid pulled over!

Hannah and Crystal stepped off the curb, oblivious. Green screamed again, and Hannah raised her head. Her eyes locked his. Widened in recognition. She stopped in the middle of the street.

Green glanced at the Mustang and saw Riley wrestling with the steering wheel. Saw his jaw drop as he spotted the girls in his path. He slammed on his brakes. The car began to spin. Tires shrieked, and smoke billowed into the air.

"Back!" Green screamed.

Hannah grabbed Crystal and turned to run. Fifteen hundred kilograms of red metal hurtled past Green and hit a lamppost with an explosion of metal and glass. The impact sent hubcaps, glass and chunks of fender flying. The car continued to spin, metal tearing and rubber screaming until it skidded to a stop on the green lawn of the Museum of Nature. An eerie hiss descended on the wreck.

Hannah lay flat against the far curb. As Green raced across the street towards her, she lifted her head. Relief coursed through him. By the time he reached her, she was struggling to sit up.

"Lie still!" he said. "Let the paramedics check you." His gaze scanned her body, looking for blood, torn clothing. Nothing. Thank God!

"It didn't hit me, I tripped." Then she sat up, her eyes wide with horror. "Where's Crystal?"

The girl was walking slowly across the street towards the mangled car on the lawn. Her arms hung limply at her sides, and her gaze was rivetted to the car. Smoke and steam swirled from the wreck, and the stink of burnt rubber choked the air. Already officers were rushing toward the scene, thrusting Crystal aside. Two of them were peering inside. People shouted, steam hissed, and in the distance Green heard the harsh blasts of a fire engine.

"No-oo!" A bellow rose above the din. Green swung around to see a man leap out of a black SUV and charge up the street towards the scene. A flashing squad car was right behind. Reflexively, police officers reached for their holsters. Green grabbed Hannah and thrust her into the shelter of a house on the corner, shielding her with his body.

Uniformed officers swarmed Vic McIntyre with their guns drawn and forced him to the ground. Green could see his limbs flailing and hear his shouts of fury.

"What did you do, you fucking idiots!" he screamed. "You killed him!"

Fury rose in Green's throat. He told Hannah to stay put and hurried towards them. "Cuff him and get him the hell away from the scene."

McIntyre struggled for words, gasping. "You—"

"Later," Green snapped, not trusting his temper. He turned his back, and breathing deeply, he walked towards Crystal, who was still in the grip of two female uniforms. Her eyes were fixed on the car, and her body shook with silent sobs.

"Crystal Adams? I'm Inspector Green," he began, trying to make his voice gentle. He reminded himself that despite her role in Lea's death and her endangerment of Hannah, she was only sixteen.

She turned her head to stare at him. Her face was slack with shock and defeat. "I didn't mean it to happen."

Against his orders, Hannah appeared at his elbow. "We were coming in to see you, Mike. That's what I was trying to tell you. She had agreed. She was going to tell you everything."

Crystal's chin quivered. "She promised me you'd go easy on me, since I'm under eighteen."

Green looked at his daughter. At her tiny frame and her innocent pixie face. Never let me underestimate this girl again, he thought. He nodded to Crystal's escorts. "Get them some blankets and make sure the paramedics check them out when they arrive." He swung to address Crystal. "After that, the officers will take you both inside and get you some tea. Then we'll get a chance to talk."

She hung her head, and he turned away towards the accident just as two fire trucks roared onto the scene, closely followed by an ambulance. Fire fighters and paramedics raced over to the car. Green drew as near as he dared, but could see little through the debris except shattered glass and long, drenching streaks of blood.

"Is he alive?" he murmured to an officer near by.

"He's breathing, but I wouldn't bet on his chances."

By this time, the area was flooded with curious passersby and officers from the station. Police set up a cordon, and the crowd watched in tense silence as the firefighters and paramedics worked over the car. Green saw McIntyre standing at the edge of the crowd, handcuffed and firmly gripped by two officers. None of the restraints seemed necessary, as the agent stood unmoving and unblinking as he watched. Green walked over.

"He wants to see if the kid is all right," one of the officers explained anxiously, as if expecting a reprimand. "We figured it would be okay to wait."

McIntyre shifted his emotion to Green. "You did this! You chased him down like a dog!"

"On the contrary, Mr. McIntyre, you did. He was running from you."

"Bullshit! I was just trying to catch him."

"Yes, to kill him."

"No! To stop him going to you. To stop him ruining his life. You don't have a thing on him." Belatedly, confusion clouded his expression. "What the hell do you mean? He thought I was going to kill him?"

"That's what he told me."

"That's bull! I love that kid! I would never..." He backed up, causing the officers to tighten their grip.

"You'd already killed once."

"That girl's death was an accident! Riley knows that. He called me, for fuck's sake."

"I'm talking about Jenna Zukowski."

"The social worker? He thought I...?" Astonishment raced across McIntyre's face. He stared at the car wreck in disbelief, and gradually his face twisted. "Oh my God, Riley!"

Green tried to make sense of McIntyre's disjointed words. Of the stricken look on his face. "You thought Riley had killed the social worker?"

McIntyre tore his eyes from the accident. He began to shake his head in mute horror, but at that instant he spotted Crystal being led across the lawn towards the police station, and his panic turned to fury. "It was that bitch! She gave Lea the bad drugs."

"But I bet you sold them to her."

McIntyre's jaw snapped shut, and his face grew cold. "You better not throw that kind of outrageous crap around unless you want your ass kicked to the next country by my lawyers."

"Let's leave the threats and accusations till we have everyone's statement," Green said. "Then we'll see what's outrageous. Book him on criminal negligence and dangerous operation of a motor vehicle for now," he told the officers. "I'll send word about Riley's condition as soon as we know."

McIntyre tore off the restraining hands and stepped forward. "If he dies, or even a single bone in his body is broken, I'll see you never carry a badge again, Green. The country loves that boy."

Green watched McIntyre being led away, his head high and his gaze defiant. As the small procession passed by the flashing cruisers that cordoned the area, Green saw Darren O'Shaughnessy standing with a uniformed officer outside a police cruiser. O'Shaughnessy was in handcuffs but was offering no resistance. He had been staring at the wreck, but now his gaze shifted to McIntyre. Bewilderment flickered across his tense, florid features. Some other emotion too. What was it?

Shame? Or guilt.

Green studied the scene of chaos before him. The bloodied body of Riley, the defiant agent, the tormented Darren, and Crystal, whose nasty drug deal had started it all.

Something didn't make sense.

* * *

It took the emergency crews almost an hour to extricate Riley from his crushed sports car, and the evening rush hour was in full force when the ambulance finally whisked him towards the Civic Hospital. By that time, Darren O'Shaughnessy had been booked, printed and was in a holding cell awaiting his lawyer, Vic McIntyre had managed an impromptu news conference on his way through the media scrum that pressed around the accident scene, and Bob Gibbs had taken the two teenage girls under his wing.

Green had been busy dealing with the clamour of the media, the Professional Standards department and Barbara Devine. Both the car chase that had jeopardized countless innocent commuters and the spectacular crash that had possibly ended the life of a promising young athlete had everyone screaming for explanations. In retrospect, Green was grateful for the quick thinking of the duty inspector who'd vetoed the use of lights and siren during the pursuit, and equally grateful that he'd kept his own objections to himself. Lights and siren would not have changed the outcome one bit, but would have redefined the incident as a police chase, drawing Professional Standards, the Special Investigations Unit and a host of procedural nitpickers into the fray. This way, the blame for the crash would be laid squarely at McIntyre's feet.

When Green was finally able to escape and track down Hannah and Crystal, Bob Gibbs had managed to get them a warm meal. Green phoned Crystal's mother, who after much swearing and whining, agreed to send her boyfriend JD down to the station to support the girl.

"She don't say a word without a lawyer," Mrs. Adams snapped, almost as an afterthought.

"We can get one of the duty defence counsels—"

"Oh no, she's not getting one of them morons sits in your back pocket. JD knows someone. I'll get him to give the guy a call in the morning."

"Tomorrow is too late, Mrs. Adams. We need her statement."

"That's not my problem, is it? My daughter's had a shock, she's entitled to a good night's sleep, a lawyer, and somebody to watch her back while youse guys go trying to pin something on her."

Green listened to her smoke-gravelled voice as she built up a head of self-righteous steam. He remembered Gibbs's reference to the expensive electronic equipment in her welfare townhouse, and he wondered just who she was really protecting. But through the half-open interview room, he could see Crystal and Hannah slumped in plastic chairs against the wall. Neither seemed to have the energy even to speak. Crystal stared into space, looking very young beneath the skimpy tank top and cascade of curls.

In the end, he agreed to allow her to go home with a firm appointment to return the next morning accompanied by an adult family member and the lawyer of their choice. As he watched her slink out under the dead-eyed stare of a man with a straggly goatee and snakes tattooed all around his biceps, Green hoped he hadn't made a mistake.

He took Hannah's hand when she started to follow them out the door. "I'll get a patrol car to drive you home."

She yanked her hand away. "Mike, pul-lease!"

"Unmarked. Okay? Humour your old man."

"I'm not a baby. I got across the country by myself, I can get across town."

"I know, but you've had a shock, and shock does funny things to the body."

She considered. "Will it be a cute cop?"

He managed a smile. "I'll see what I can do. I'll be home as soon as I can, promise."

She didn't brush it off as unimportant, but instead gave the briefest nod of appreciation. As the cruiser pulled away from the front curb, piloted by the tallest, youngest constable he could spare, she turned in the passenger seat and gave him a big thumbs up.

He wanted to toss all his obligations out the window and rush after her, but at that moment a muddy pick-up slewed into the semi-circular drive and jerked to a stop almost on his toes. Out of the cab piled three men and a woman, all identically dressed in T-shirts, jeans and work boots, with faded ball caps pulled low over their eyes. Green knew instantly that this was Jenna Zukowski's family. They were all built like beer kegs, half as wide as they were tall, with broad, sunburnt Slavic faces and arms like tree trunks.

The three men headed for the glass doors to the lobby without a glance in his direction, but the woman stopped. She peered at him through blue eyes bleak and bruised by pain.

"You're the inspector."

He extended his hand. "Mrs. Zukowski. Yes, we've spoken on the phone."

"When did you plan to tell us about this accident? You got an answer on the dead woman yet? Is this boy the killer?"

Inwardly, Green sagged. He thought of all the tasks clamouring for his attention upstairs in the squad room. Arranging a legal search warrant for McIntyre's house, interviewing Darren O'Shaughnessy, finding out the news on Riley's condition... All of them would have to wait. In the crises of the day, the fate of Jenna Zukowski had inexcusably slipped from his mind. But for her family the nightmare continued.

He took the mother's elbow and opened the door for her. "I don't have those answers yet, but please come in. I'll see what I can track down."

He seated them in a small conference room off the lobby while he went down the hall to the Ident lab to check on Paquette's progress with the fingerprints.

The Ident officer looked harried. "Not ready yet. The skin was pretty damaged. But MacPhail did the post mortem earlier. He might have some news."

Green glanced at his watch. It was nearly eight o'clock, well into MacPhail's serious drinking time. Green steeled himself as he punched in the pathologist's cell phone number. MacPhail must have been at the rosy stage of intoxication, because his manner was ebullient.

"I left you a message centuries ago, laddie. Thought I must have fallen from grace when I didn't hear from you."

"It's been a busy day."

"Oh aye, that's what they all say."

A dull ache flickered behind Green's eyes, and he pinched his fingers to the bridge of his nose. "So have you got confirmation on that ID for me?"

"Possibly, possibly. But that depends on the family. I need the answer to one wee question."

Green jotted it down and returned to the conference room. He dreaded the task. Up to this point, the family had been able to cling to the faint hope that their daughter had not met with a brutal, terrifying end. With this one question, all hope could be dashed.

The elder Zukowskis were slumped in the plastic chairs, looking small and forlorn, but Jenna's two brothers stood at rigid attention against the wall. They all tried to read Green's face as he entered.

"Mr. and Mrs. Zukowski, did Jenna have an accident when she was a girl? A broken bone?"

The mother sucked in her breath. "What kind of bone?"

"Her left forearm. A spiral fracture, as if from twisting."

Even before anyone spoke, Green knew the answer. Shoulders stiffened as if from a physical blow. Glances shot around the table. It was one of her brothers who spoke. Softly. Flatly.

"Jenna was raped when she was fifteen years old. A senior from her high school. Guy pinned her down. The fucking bastard walked away without a charge."

Green heard the implicit accusation but steered clear. "What hospital would have the X-rays?"

"It's why our girl left Barry's Bay, went into social work," the mother said as if Green hadn't spoken. "She wanted to help people."

"And look what she got for her trouble" was the sentence that hung in the air, unspoken. The parents pulled themselves to their feet and headed towards the door.

"The pathologist will be releasing her body in the morning," Green said. "Meanwhile, would you like someone with you? A counsellor..."

"No." The father's voice snapped like a whip in the small room. He reached to take his wife's arm. "We don't need none of that. Once we can take her with us, we'll be going home."

When Green arrived back upstairs, he was still awash in sorrow, futile anger and most of all, a nagging shame. He had resented Jenna's interference, resented her stupidity that had placed her in harm's way. Dismissed her motives as sheer nosiness. After more than twenty years dealing with the tragic choices people make, he should have known better.

Only a few detectives remained in the squad room. Gibbs was on the phone, and Sullivan was preparing the video set-up for Darren O'Shaughnessy's interview. Sullivan jerked his head towards Gibbs.

"He's talking to the ER, waiting for an update. After that, I'm going to ask him to join me in the interview with Darren."

Green chose his words carefully. "You have a history with this guy, Brian. Maybe you shouldn't be involved."

Sullivan's jaw tightened. "A kid is possibly dead, and this bastard knows something. I know the case. I know what to ask him."

"We'll get someone else and give them an earphone. You can supervise from down the hall."

"Who?" Sullivan challenged. "Bob?"

Green glanced at Gibbs, who sat resting his head in his hand. Distress was etched in every line on his forehead. Green had seen him at the accident scene earlier, carefully avoiding even a glimpse of the body on the stretcher. Almost three months had passed since the attack on Sue. Time was not helping. If anything, he was getting worse as Sue's struggle dragged on. Something more drastic needed to be done.

Green shook his head. "I'm not taking the risk. Not with a multiple murder case." He thought of Hannah nursing her fears all alone as she waited for him to come home. Then he thought of Jenna's parents, wondering if justice would be served this time. He heaved a deep sigh. "I'll take the interview myself."

A dull red crept up Sullivan's neck, and Green thought he was about to witness his famous Irish temper. But Sullivan picked up some papers from his desk.

"Here are my notes and questions. Don't forget, the guy has a short fuse."

Green scanned the latest notes from Ident on the blood at Darren's home. "Gibbs can come in with me," he said more gently. "He can wear the earphone and if you think of something that needs asking, feed it to him."

Green's instincts about Gibbs were reinforced when the young detective hung up the phone, looking grim. The detectives all clustered around him. "What's the news?"

"He's in surgery. They said it will be hours. There's internal bleeding, multiple fractures..."

"But he's going to live?"

"Well, you know what they say. The next forty-eight hours..."

"So let's take it one hour at a time," Green said, clapping Gibbs' shoulder. "So far, so good."

Riley was the first word out of Darren O'Shaughnessy's mouth the moment Green and Gibbs walked into the interview room. The man looked exhausted. His shaved head shone with sweat, and his skin had an unhealthy blue tinge. A junior member of the defence bar sat at his side—a young man with a cherubic face and a slight lisp who Green suspected had never seen the inside of a police station before. Darren waved aside the introductions and the charter warning impatiently.

"Riley? Is he alive?"

Green nodded and relayed what little they'd been told. The man's relief was minimal.

"Multiple fractures. To what?"

"I don't know. Let's get the preliminaries over with—"

"Fuck the preliminaries. Is he going to be able to play again?"

Green remembered the crushed and bloody body that the emergency workers had pulled from the car. He remembered the paramedic's off-the-cuff appraisal as he secured the back board. 'The kid will be lucky if he ever walks again, let alone skates.' He relayed none of this. "He's alive, Darren. Let's go with that for now."

"Fat lot of good that does him if he can't play any more. Have you reached his parents?"

Green nodded. "His father's on his way."

Darren's face twisted. "This will kill Ted. He's put so much into that boy."

Green felt a flash of anger that the man seemed more concerned with Riley's playing prospects than with his very life. Or with the life of the innocent young woman he himself had chopped into bits. "Let's get on with the interview, Darren," he said. This time Darren didn't interrupt while Gibbs read the charges and charter warning, and made the introductions for the tape. When Green asked him if he had anything to say in response to the charges, Darren merely snorted.

"You haven't got a thing."

"On the contrary, we have blood on your axe, shovel and wheelbarrow."

"I killed a groundhog this spring that was burrowing under my shed."

Green made a show of consulting Ident's report. "This has been identified as human blood of the same blood type as the victim. Our Ident team has also just confirmed the presence of blood in your living room and back yard. DNA testing will cinch it, Darren."

Darren digested this and grew sullen. "My lawyer says if you can't prove which one of us killed that broad, you can't touch any of us. Reasonable doubt."

"Oh, we'll prove it. There's only you, Ben and Riley in the house. Once we get through going over everyone's clothing with a fine-tooth comb, lifting prints off the body... Did you know we can get fingerprints off a body nowadays?"

"Do you think I give a shit about that with Riley lying in the hospital? All of this would never have happened if that stupid broad hadn't decided to try to ruin his life!"

Green reached for the manila envelope at his side and took out a sheaf of crime scene photographs. Methodically he began laying then out along the table top. Baby-faced lawyer turned green. "This is what was left of that stupid broad by the time the killer was finished with her. When I show them to Ben, do you think he'll be as cool about it as you? Are you telling me Ben's capable of this savagery?"

Darren slammed his chair back against the wall and leaped up, his fists clenched but his face the colour of putty. His eyes bulged and spittle clung to his slack lips. "You bastard! I'm not saying another fucking word, except you touch my son and I'll—"

Baby-face recovered enough to grab his client's arm.

"You'll what, Darren? Punch me out, just the way you did Jenna Zukowski?"

Darren's eyes were riveted to the photos, and gradually his rage transformed to horror. His mouth opened several times, but no sound emerged. He sagged back into his chair, shaking his head. "I got nothing to say. Not while Riley's fighting for his life. If he doesn't recover, it won't matter anyway."

Twenty

Green finally arrived home much later than he'd hoped, only to discover to his dismay that the house was empty. Nothing but a note on the kitchen counter. "Don't sweat, I'm at Jim's." No number, no explanation of who Jim was, no word on when she'd be back. But at least she had left a note. At least she was with someone, not alone reliving her close brush with death while her father the bigshot detective put everyone else first. Again.

As much out of need as guilt, he phoned to touch base with his father, then Sharon. He listened to his son chatter on about Modo and the chipmunk, joked with Sharon about the utter hunting ineptitude of their hundred-pound dog, then hung up to a silence even louder than before. He poured a stiff scotch and spent a long night staring at the ceiling of his bedroom, reliving the case. Wondering if he could have done anything differently, if he could have prevented the tragedy, if they had the right man in custody after all.

Nothing seemed to add up. Riley had believed Vic McIntyre was the killer—or so he claimed—but McIntyre's outrage had seemed genuine when Green accused him of trying to kill Riley to cover it up. They had no forensics, witnesses or blood to tie McIntyre to Jenna on the day she died. Furthermore, McIntyre was still strutting around like a man with nothing to fear, threatening to sue everyone over his incarceration and the car chase that had injured his multimillion-dollar player.

Instead, the forensics pointed to the O'Shaughnessys. The bloody murder weapon, and the probable murder scene, had been at Darren's house. Yet it was difficult to fake the horror on Darren's face when he'd seen the grisly photos. Darren was not a sophisticated man, nor a subtle one. Could he be that good an actor?

To add to all his doubts, there would be fallout from the chase that had led to Riley's accident. Even though neither had been directly the result of police action, Green knew the public would want answers. In the press, the tense, split-second decisions made by himself and Ford would be minutely dissected. With a young man's promising future in ruins, everyone would be looking for someone to blame.

Green's fears were not allayed when he arrived at his desk to find three urgent messages from Barbara Devine and one from the office of the new Chief, who seemed anxious to make his authority felt. Tossing them aside for the moment, he went in search of Sullivan, who was nowhere to be seen. But Gibbs was at his desk on the phone. He looked freshly showered and shaved this morning, but a worrisome aura of gin hung around him.

"Anything on Riley?" Green asked once Gibbs hung up. Others in the squad room drifted close to hear. Riley was a minor celebrity; it seemed he carried the dreams of many on his shoulders.

"Good news, sir. He's out of recovery, and he's conscious this morning. The doctors say he's still not out of the woods yet, but they're amazed at how fast he's come around."

"So the prognosis looks good."

"Better, that's for sure. At least there's no neurological or spinal damage."

The relief in the room was palpable, and Green smiled. He could handle Devine and the media, he could even handle the

Chief himself as long as Riley recovered. He nodded to Gibbs. "You all set up for the Crystal Adams interview? Make sure you find out how she and McIntyre are connected." He slapped his head in dismay. "Speaking of McIntyre, get Jones working on a search warrant of his house. We're looking for drugs. Right now all we have on the *putz* is a couple of driving offences, but he fits into the bigger picture somehow."

He left Gibbs jotting eagerly into his notebook, and he was just returning to his desk to place the call to the Chief when his cell phone rang. To his surprise, it was Marija Kovacev. Her tone crashed him back to earth.

"What did you do!" she shrieked. "Why did you chase him!"

"Marija, I can't discuss the case—"

"Yes, you can! I called you, I tell you where he is, then you trick me—"

"No, I didn't. I was trying to help him."

"But he may die." Her voice rose. "Because of you. Because of me!"

"Marija, listen to me. He's not going to die. He's had surgery, and it's looking very good."

"He was so scared yesterday, and I tell him to trust you. I need to explain to him."

"I'm sure when he's better—"

"No, I am at the hospital now. I bring him his phone."

"His what?" Green asked, startled.

"He forget his phone. Just like Lea's."

The implication did not hit Green until after she'd signed off. "Just like Lea's," she'd said. Lea's phone had never been recovered in any of the searches, whereas Riley had obviously used his own phone to call Green yesterday from his car. What if this was Lea's phone, and Riley had been trying to return it? What if there was crucial evidence on it that would help put all the pieces in place?

Green glanced at his watch. Marija had said she was already at the hospital. If he hoped to intercept her, he had no time to call the Chief's office or fend off Barbara Devine. He was just pocketing his keys and getting ready to sneak out of the station when he spotted Sullivan climbing off the elevator. The big detective looked red-eyed and rumpled, as if he'd slept in his suit.

"Want to grab a coffee?" Sullivan asked.

"I'm trying to get out of here before they catch me," Green said. "Come with me to see Riley O'Shaughnessy."

"The kid will barely be conscious!"

"Maybe. But I'm very curious to hear what he has to say. And to see what's on a cell phone he left at Marija Kovacev's. It might be Lea's."

"The Chief will have your head," Sullivan said as they accelerated out of the parking lot, but he was smiling. Outside, masses of black clouds roiled in the western sky, threatening trouble. Steering with one hand, Green reached for his cell phone and dialled the Chief's office. To Green's relief, the secretary said he was in a meeting.

"I'm returning his call," Green said, the essence of courtesy. "I'll be out of phone range at the hospital for a while, but when would be a good time to call again?"

The secretary wasn't falling for it. "He wants to see you, along with Superintendent Devine, in his office at eleven o'clock."

Green glanced at his watch. That gave him little more than an hour to accomplish what he wanted at the hospital. When it came to this new chief, timing was not negotiable. He flicked on his emergency lights and stepped on the accelerator as he shot onto the Queensway.

"I don't know what the big deal is," he grumbled. "There's no other way we could have handled it."

Sullivan shrugged. "The Chief's just flexing his muscles,

making sure we know who's boss. Probably just an image exercise, so the public doesn't think he's running a bunch of cowboys. McIntyre's lawyer is shooting his mouth off."

"McIntyre's a loose cannon, but I've got Jones working on a warrant, based on what I hope Crystal is going to give us. Once we seize all that stuff in his house, it should shut him up fast."

At the hospital, Green parked right outside the main entrance and slapped a police sticker on the dash. The hospital was bustling with activity, its main corridor more like a shopping mall than a state-of-the-art teaching hospital, but when they stepped off the elevator on the surgical floor, Green instinctively recoiled. Here the beep of machines, the drone of the PA, and the unique smell of disinfectant and disease brought memories crashing back. He'd had too many vigils at hospital bedsides. Sue Peters, numerous assault victims, and his own mother, who'd wasted to nothing during her long, futile fight with cancer. By the end, she'd looked like the concentration camp victim she'd been forty years earlier. That cruel irony still haunted him in the dead of night.

The nursing station on the surgical floor had a broad counter and a wall of TV monitors which beeped and danced. Two nurses sat quietly recording, and one looked up cheerfully as they approached. The sight of their detective shields brought the head nurse running from the back room.

"How is he?" Green asked.

"Conscious and speaking, but still weak. The doctor has ordered visitors restricted to immediate family for the next two days."

"We'd like to ask him a few questions. At least some preliminaries. In cases like this, it's important to get the recollections early."

She looked dubious. "I'll have to check with the doctor, and he's in a consultation right now. If you'd like to take a seat in the waiting room..."

The surgical care waiting room was nothing more than a cluster of plastic chairs shoved into a corner. Marija Kovacev was already there, huddled in a chair. She looked even more gaunt and ravaged than before, her cheekbones protruding and her striking blue eyes sunk deep into their sockets. There was a wildness about her, as if she were hanging on to her sanity by the smallest thread. On the table beside her sat a large vase of roses, which Green suspected she'd picked from her own garden. His heart tightened. She was reaching out to Riley as if he were an extension of her own daughter, as if keeping him alive somehow kept Lea alive.

Her weary eyes lit at the sight of Green, and she pulled herself upright. "They are not letting me visit him—family only—but I talked a long time with his father. I told him Riley visit at my house and that he was afraid. The poor man was very sad about Lea. He has been here all night. He is meeting with the doctor now. I am waiting for Riley's nurse, to give her these flowers and his phone."

"May I see that phone?" Green asked casually.

She shot him a sharp look. "Why?"

"You said it looked just like Lea's. Maybe it *is* hers. We still haven't found it."

She gave a small gasp and immediately plunged her hand into her mammoth purse, rummaging frantically until she found it. She held it in her palm with reverence.

"It has Riley's picture, that's why I think it's his." She flipped it open and stared at the photo on the screen. It showed Riley laughing into the camera against a backdrop Green recognized as Hog's Back Falls. "It looks like a lover's picture," she said in wonderment. "Maybe Lea took this."

On the night she died, he suspected, and he could tell from her quivering lips that she had drawn the same conclusion. She handed the phone to Green. "I don't understand how it is

274

working, but are there more pictures?"

Green pressed buttons with some trepidation. What if these photos were not suitable for parental eyes? Marija had been through enough without unpleasant images to mar her thoughts of her daughter's last night.

The photos were the usual assortment of spontaneous and silly portraits, but their content altered towards the end. Blurry, off-kilter shots of toes and treetops and park signs replaced the staged photos of themselves, and one brief video was a wild, spinning blur of park scenery. Lea high on drugs, losing control and sanity. He closed the photo menu, hoping Marija had not seen the last few.

"She's got messages," he said as text popped up on the screen. He scrolled down. Ten messages. Half were from Marija herself, but four had the caller ID Crystal Adams. "Do you know Lea's password?"

Marija started to shake her head, then her expression cleared. "Try her father's name. Zlatan. She often uses that."

Green punched it in and was immediately connected to the voice mail box. Aware of Marija's tense, expectant gaze upon him, he rose and walked to a quiet corner of the hall. Crystal's first message, logged at five thirty on the day before Lea's fatal outing, was brief and breezy. "Hey Lea, got your stuff! Guaranteed to be some serious weed." The second, logged at noon on the day she died, was decidedly peculiar. "Hey Lea, are you going to party tonight? I got it specially, so don't go giving it away."

The third and fourth were a little more anxious. "Hey, where are you? Have you tried the stuff yet? I really want to know how it went." The final message, logged at 10:57 on Monday evening, was the most telling. "You know what? I think you should throw the stuff away. Call me when you get this. Whatever you do, don't give it to Riley."

The next messages were all from Marija, frantic to know where her daughter was, unaware that by the time of her calls, Lea was already dead. Green disconnected and stood a moment reflecting on the meaning of Crystal's words. Some things were clear. Crystal had indeed supplied the marijuana that had killed Lea, and she knew it was unusual quality, perhaps even laced. Had she known it was lethal? Was that why she warned Lea not to give it to Riley or to anyone else? But she had obviously begun to worry when she did not hear back from Lea. Had she begun to have second thoughts? Or had she begun to fear the drug was more potent than she had intended?

A lot of questions, not the least of which was—was McIntyre her supplier, and had he known the dose was lethal? Key questions that would only be answered when she came in for her interview later that day.

He walked back to join Marija and Sullivan, trying to look nonchalant. "It's definitely Lea's phone. Your messages are on there, plus some from her friends. I'll need to take it in for further analysis."

She looked apprehensive. "Will I get it back? So I can have the photos?"

He reassured her, pocketed the phone in an evidence bag and ushered her onto the elevator with a promise to deliver her flowers personally. He barely had time to fill Sullivan in on Crystal's messages when a door slammed across the hall and a man barrelled towards them. Green caught sight of blazing eyes and purple jowls as the man stormed by towards the stairs. At the last second, he recognized Riley's father.

"Mr. O'Shaughnessy!" he cried, seizing the man's arm. Ted O'Shaughnessy stared right through him and wrenched his arm free without breaking his stride. Good God, Green worried as he looked down the hall towards the patients' rooms. Is it that bad?

The door opened again, and this time a dark, rail-thin man in green surgical scrubs emerged, his black eyes troubled. He stopped short at the sight of Green and Sullivan.

"I'm Dr. Vishnu. Are you the detectives?"

Green made the introductions, hoping that the inspector label would carry some weight, but the doctor seemed unimpressed. He spoke in a clipped, unemotional tone with only the slightest hint of his native India. "I can only allow you five minutes with him, and a nurse must be in the room. Her word goes."

"Is there anything that would affect his statement? Any neurological or memory problems?" Green asked.

"He's been sleeping most of the time, and he's on a fairly strong pain medication. He doesn't remember the accident, which is quite normal, so he may not be able to help you. Don't pressure him or challenge him."

"Any questions we should avoid?"

"Don't discuss whether he'll play hockey again. He may ask you, but don't answer. He'd need a major miracle. His right leg is pinned in three places. I was just telling his father the prognosis. I think that's what upset him so much." Vishnu paused as if debating the wisdom of further disclosure. "I haven't mentioned this to Riley, but I did tell the father as well, and perhaps you should know, since it may have some bearing on the accident. We ran a routine toxicology screen when he was admitted, and it showed two elevated readings—ephedra and creatinine. Ephedrine is a metabolic stimulant found in common over-the-counter medications, but it's often used by athletes as an energy booster. In large doses, it can cause agitation, possibly confusion. Ironically, the ephedrine may actually have been a benefit to him after the accident in keeping his heart stimulated."

"And creatinine?"

"Elevated creatinine can have a variety of etiologies, but based on his muscle bulk and water retention, I would estimate that he was taking creatine." Seeing Green's blank look, he continued. "Creatine is a performance-enhancing supplement athletes use to build muscle mass. It's not nearly as dangerous as steroids, but we don't know much about its side effects with adolescents. Regardless, mixing substances that rev up the metabolism is never good."

Green remembered the manic edge to Riley's behaviour during the car chase. "You're saying it could have a bearing on the accident?"

"Well..." Vishnu paused. "It's not my field, but it might have increased his agitation or interfered with his judgment. Not seriously, but in a stressful situation..." He looked uncomfortable venturing beyond his expertise. "Both these drugs can easily be bought over the counter or on the internet, you understand. Neither one is illegal."

"Not illegal, just unsportsmanlike," muttered Sullivan once they'd thanked the doctor and were following the nurse down the hall in the ward. "So much for being a role model for our kids."

Green was thinking of the cases of bottled sports drink in McIntyre's closet. "Dr. Rosen's Electro-boost". More likely Dr. McIntyre's private concoction, which Riley probably drank almost like water. If he had known it contained ephedrine, would he have let Lea drink it that night? "It's possible he didn't know."

Sullivan shot him an incredulous look. "What kid wouldn't know? Unless he chooses not to know."

Green's reply was cut short by the nurse, who stopped in front of a half open door and placed her finger to her lips. Green steeled himself for the worst, but when the nurse peeked inside, Riley was propped up in bed, a little bleary-eyed but alert. His skin was waxen pale, but except for the sutures that criss-crossed his face and the tubes and wires that snaked all around him, he looked almost normal. His right leg was in a massive, full-length cast suspended from an overhead pulley.

Sullivan, the father of two teenage boys, spoke first. His voice was soft. "Hi, Riley. I'm Brian Sullivan, and this is Mike Green. We're detectives. How are you feeling?"

"Like I've been checked into the boards by Zdeno Chara."

Sullivan laughed, and even Green understood the reference. Zdeno Chara was a six-foot-nine hockey legend who crushed forwards with a single nudge. The kid's on the ball at least, Green thought with relief. He let Sullivan carry on.

Sullivan eased himself casually into the chair by the bed. "You're looking better than yesterday, for sure."

Trailing his IV tubing, Riley raised one hand to stroke his injured leg. "I know I banged up this pretty good, but I'll be back on the ice. If I have to visit every doctor on the planet."

"That's the spirit. Do you remember what happened?"

Riley tried to shake his head, but winced. "Dad told me I totalled my Mustang."

Sullivan nodded. "But there's always another where it came from."

"Probably not where that one came from. Not with Vic in jail."

Green sat down gingerly on the edge of the bed. "Riley, Vic didn't kill the social worker."

Riley's eyes filled. "But...but..."

"I know you think he did, but the evidence doesn't point that way. We found the tools used and the place it happened. It wasn't anywhere near Vic's place."

Riley grew even more pale. "Who?"

"We've arrested your Uncle Darren."

"Uncle Darren!" Riley stared at them, his colour flooding back in. "That's insane! Why would Uncle Darren kill that woman?"

"They got in an argument. She came to his house and confronted him—"

"About what?"

"About Lea. He lost his temper. It's all at his house, Riley. The blood in the living room, the wheelbarrow he moved her in—"

"I can't believe this! I know Uncle Darren's got a temper, but..."

"He's as good as admitted it."

From the corner of his eye, Green saw the nurse step forward, as if preparing to intervene. Riley ignored her. "When did he do this? How could I not know? I live with him!"

"Last Friday morning. The social worker was last seen heading over to his house."

"But that's impossible. Friday morning he was—" Abruptly, Riley's eyes bulged and all traces of colour fled his cheeks. He clamped his mouth shut.

"He was what?"

"Nothing."

"You were going to say something."

"I...I just couldn't believe he would do it." Above his head, the heart monitor began to race.

"I think it's time—" began the nurse.

Green leaned close. "But you said it was impossible. Do you know something?"

"No! No! I didn't mean that!" He squirmed in the bed as if trying to escape. The nurse leaped forward.

"Okay, that's enough, you two. Time to go."

Green hesitated, watching Riley. The youth was ghostly pale, his breathing ragged and his face twisted in panic. Why panic? What was he hiding?

"Out!" the nurse thundered and yanked open the door.

Both detectives were silent as they made their way outside. The black clouds now blanketed the sky, and wind swirled debris across the parking lot. Back in the car, Sullivan turned on his cell and called Gibbs to tell him about Crystal's messages. Gibbs was due to interview Crystal in-depth later that day and the more ammunition he had, the better. Green didn't start the ignition but instead sat drumming his fingers on the steering wheel. He knew the Chief was waiting for him, but something far more important was at stake. His mind raced over and over Riley's reaction, picking apart the nuances of his words.

What exactly had happened back there in Riley's room? What had the boy started to say, and why had he refused to go on? Green sensed that the timing of his reaction was crucial. At first, Riley had been shocked to learn that Darren was the killer. Shocked and incredulous, but ready at least to entertain the possibility. Until…

Until he had learned the time of the murder. Only then had he said it was impossible. He'd blurted it out without thinking, as if he knew Darren couldn't have done it at that time.

"Brian, have we double-checked Darren's whereabouts on the Friday morning? Checked his work log or customers?"

Sullivan had been listening quietly to his phone, and now he cocked his head thoughtfully. "Watts and LeBlanc were on it. I'll check with them. But Gibbs just told me one interesting piece of news from Ident. There is no trace of blood anywhere in the interior of Darren's plumbing van."

"Which means either he used some other vehicle to transport the body, or Riley's right. He didn't do it." Green felt a shiver of excitement. "Riley must know Darren wasn't at the house Friday morning. It's the only explanation for what he said."

"But if he knew Darren wasn't there, why wouldn't he say so? Why clam up?"

Green remembered the boy's panic. "Because he realized that if he gave Darren an alibi for that morning, we'd start looking elsewhere."

"And he didn't want that?"

"No. I bet when he heard the time, he realized who the killer must be, and it was worse than his Uncle Darren."

"Not necessarily," Sullivan said, always the pragmatist. Green made intuitive leaps, but Sullivan knew they had to look at every small step in between. "Maybe he just got scared about incriminating anyone else."

"No, he was horrified. Who would horrify him that much? Who would he want to protect even more than his uncle?"

Sullivan's eyes narrowed, and Green could see him methodically going over the same choices in his head. Weighing the possibilities and discarding them just as Green had done, until only one name remained.

"His father."

"Bingo."

"But we don't even know if he was in Ottawa that morning."

"Not yet we don't, but he always stayed with Darren when he came up. And remember..." Green stabbed the air with a triumphant finger, "remember last Saturday, when we went looking for Riley at his uncle's house. Darren said he and his father had just driven down to Gananoque that morning with some of the stuff. Which means he could have been in Ottawa Friday! We should call down to Gananoque and ask some discreet questions."

The first fat raindrops splattered the windshield. Sullivan pulled out his notebook and began a list. "We'll need his shoes—another search warrant for Jones."

Green nodded. "And his vehicle. I know he drives a pick-up, perfect for transporting a body."

Sullivan paused with his pen poised. His broad face was creased in a frown. "It does explain Darren's behaviour, why he's playing hard to get. Leading us on and then dancing out of reach. He figures if there's enough confusion, maybe both of them can stay in the clear. All the same..."

Green smacked his forehead. "I don't know why I didn't think of the father before. It was staring me in the face last Sunday, when I saw how committed he was to his kid's dream."

"But so were a lot of people."

"But he spent years shaping this kid. Flooding his backyard, teaching him how to score. He even let himself be edged out by McIntyre, all for the sake of the kid's future."

Sullivan shook his head slowly, as if arguing against himself. "I don't buy it. It doesn't sit right. Ted was a good father, he put in a lot of time and yeah, he wanted his kid to go far, but so does every other parent on the competitive minor league circuit. If that was a motive for murder, there'd be a hell of a lot more bodies littering the sport."

"But the man's got the same O'Shaughnessy temper. You saw his face this morning. He looked on a mission to kill." Green froze. "Holy shit, maybe he's not done yet. Maybe he is on a mission to kill."

"Who?"

"Vic McIntyre. Good thing McIntyre is still in lock-up."

"He's not. He got released on his own recognizance this morning."

"Jesus!" Green started the car. "Call dispatch. We need to get over to McIntyre's house right away!"

Twenty-One

Detective Bob Gibbs pressed "Print" and sat back at his desk with a feeling of satisfaction. The list of questions he'd prepared for Crystal's interview was perfect. He didn't expect trouble; the girl had seemed thoroughly shaken by her experience the day before, and he suspected she'd put up very little resistance once she heard her messages on Lea's cell phone. Her own admission of guilt would be nice, but he was more interested in where she had bought the lethal marijuana and who had told her how to mix it. Someone else had to be behind the scheme, someone who had used her naïveté and her friendship with Lea to accomplish his ruthless ends. All signs pointed to the bullying, coercive Vic McIntyre, and Gibbs hoped that Crystal would be able to provide the missing link in the chain that had led to Lea's death so they could nail the slimeball for good.

He took up the printed questions and was just starting down the hall to check the video set-up in the interview room when his phone rang. To his surprise, it was Crystal's mother, sounding more subdued and concerned than he would have thought possible.

"She's gone," the woman said without preamble

Gibbs's heart sank. He'd sworn the girl was ready to talk.

"A man came and picked her up."

"What man?"

"I don't know. Some older guy. He acted real friendly, but

Crystal weren't too happy to see him."

"But she went with him?"

"Yeah. Not sure she had much choice. He whispered something in her ear that I couldn't hear, and then he takes her by the arm and off they go. He was nicely dressed, and he didn't look like a creep, that's why I told Crystal to answer the door. I wasn't dressed yet."

"When was this?"

"About an hour ago. I wasn't sure I should call, or if she was just taking off."

"You did the right thing. Can you describe this man?"

"Short but built, like he works out. Sens baseball cap, red face."

Gibbs's suspicion began to crystallize. He felt sweat break out on his back, and the phone grew slippery in his hand. "Did you see if he had a vehicle?"

"Yeah, he did. Big, pricey SUV, black as the devil."

Please God, Gibbs thought. The familiar finger of dread shot down his spine as he reached for his cell phone.

* * *

When Green rounded the corner into sight of McIntyre's house, he felt a small relief. By then, rain was pelting the street, and the windshield wipers slapped a noisy rhythm through the sheets of rain. McIntyre's house looked deserted. There was no SUV in the driveway.

"Looks like he's not home," he said. "With any luck, Ted O'Shaughnessy won't know where else to look."

"What's that?" Sullivan asked.

Green followed his finger. There were only three vehicles parked on the street, and Sullivan was pointing to a vaguely familiar, rust-riddled white pick-up parked in front of McIntyre's neighbour.

"Doesn't look like it fits," Sullivan added. The few cars in the driveways were late-model minivans or Japanese sedans with barely a speck of rust among them. "It could be a contractor or a gardener."

Green drew up beside it. The cab was empty, but an open box of ammunition sat on the passenger's seat. A chill shot through him. "Run the plate."

Sullivan was just activating the mobile computer when the side door to McIntyre's garage opened, and a man in a yellow rain slicker emerged. He glanced nervously around but didn't notice the unmarked car, which was screened by the truck. He slipped down the path and opened the gate to the backyard. His hood was down, as if he was indifferent to the gusting rain. In that brief glance, Green recognized Ted O'Shaughnessy, carrying what looked like a hunting rifle.

"Jesus H.," Green muttered. "He's armed."

"Winchester 30-30, looks like. A lot of gun."

"Call it in. I'm going to park out of sight until back-up arrives."

While Green parked the car, Sullivan spoke to the Communications Centre, and within minutes, the duty inspector and the Tactical Team supervisor were on the speaker phone.

"Jeez, Sully!" Inspector Ford exclaimed, once Sullivan had filled them in. "You boys are bad for my health. What the hell have you two stepped into this time?"

"Luckily, I don't think the target is at home," Green replied. "The suspect is lying in wait, probably in the backyard or possibly inside if he can gain access."

"Is there an escape route through the back yard?"

"Only to other backyards, if you feel like vaulting a six-foot fence."

"Okay, we've got the property on satellite," said another voice Green recognized as the Tac supervisor. "Sit tight and watch the place till we arrive. If the target arrives, detain him."

No kidding, thought Green, biting back a sarcastic retort. He was distracted by the ringing of his cell phone. He was tempted to ignore it, but saw it was Bob Gibbs.

"Trouble, sir," the young detective burst out as soon as Green answered. "Crystal Adams, you know the—"

"What about her, Bob?"

"McIntyre paid her a visit this morning and took her off in his car."

Green glanced at the house in dismay. "What time was this?"

"A-about an hour ago, sir."

Green did a split second calculation. Crystal lived in a public housing project on the eastern edge of Alta Vista, but very close to Walkley Road. The drive from there to Hunt Club would only take fifteen minutes. Maybe twenty in this pouring rain. Plenty of time for McIntyre to get home, spirit the girl inside, and do god-knows-what before Ted O'Shaughnessy arrived.

He stared at the closed doors of the two-car garage. They had to check inside that garage!

"Bob, I don't have time to explain. I'm going to pass this on to the Com Centre, and I want you to go straight up there and tell the duty inspector everything you know."

When he'd hung up, he immediately relayed the news to the Com Centre. "We need to know if McIntyre's vehicle is in the garage, so I'm going to go—"

"Green!" snapped the Tac supervisor. "Don't be a hero!"

"We need to know! A sixteen-year-old girl is at risk." Far more than you know, Green added silently, remembering the sex dens and the hidden videos. Before the Tac supervisor could object further, he slipped out of the car and turned back to Sullivan. "Use the binoculars and see what you can make out through the windows."

"Be careful! That's one serious firearm he has."

Green nodded and grabbed his body armour and utility belt from the trunk. He started down the street, trying to hug close to shrubs and cars along the way. He felt like a sitting duck, aware that both McIntyre and O'Shaughnessy would recognize him on sight. Sullivan should have done this, he realized belatedly. Sullivan could have walked right up and knocked on the front door, pretending to be a Jehovah's Witness. At the thought, a manic chuckle bubbled up inside. Here he was, wearing a vest that a Winchester 30-30 round would slice right through and carrying a pistol that he'd never fired outside the practice range in all his years on the force. When all along, a Jehovah's Witness could do the trick.

By the time he reached McIntyre's house, his clothing and hair were drenched, and water blurred his eyes. He crept along the foundation so that he was not visible through the windows, crossed the driveway and peeked around the corner of the garage to the side path. No sign of O'Shaughnessy. He listened but could hear nothing above the rain hammering against the house. With a wary eye on the gate ahead, he sneaked along the stone path to the side door. As before, he slipped it open and peered inside the garage. Fear gripped his throat. The black Navigator was there.

Which meant that McIntyre and Crystal were already inside.

He scurried back down the path, across the front yard, and around the hedge into the neighbour's side yard. When he was sufficiently out of earshot, he huddled under a tall tee and radioed in to report the bad news. As he spoke, he caught a glimpse of a police cruiser slipping quietly into place at the end of the street, barricading the block.

"Any signs of a confrontation?" the Tac supervisor wanted to know.

Green squinted at the house through the rain. "It's hard to hear above the weather, but it seems quiet. The curtains are drawn."

"Then go back to your vehicle and wait for us. We're ten minutes away."

"We don't have ten minutes," Green said. "There's a killer wandering around with a Winchester 30-30, and a minor who may already be harmed."

"If he spots you, it may set him off."

Green stared back at the house. It looked so serene, but what the hell was going on inside? That's what he needed to find out. He muttered a hasty reassurance to the Tac supervisor, signed off and phoned Sullivan.

"Grab your gear and meet me at the neighbour's side yard." He didn't give Sullivan time to protest before hanging up. Then he hunched down under the neighbour's tree and counted the agonizing seconds until Sullivan appeared.

"We're not going in," Green said as they checked their Glocks, "but we need to get close enough to hear. So we're going to scout the house and if possible, get a peek inside."

Sullivan's face tightened. "Does Tactical know this?"

"They'd just tell me not to. But procedure does tell us to go in if we suspect imminent risk to others. I do." He hunched over, ducked around the hedge and retraced his steps along the front of McIntyre's house, conscious of Sullivan's steps squishing through the grass behind him. They rounded the side of the house and headed down the path to the back gate. Cautiously, Green eased the latch up and cracked the gate open two inches. He peered through the gap. The pool glistened undisturbed, its surface pebbled by rain. In his line of vision, he could see no sign of O'Shaughnessy. He pushed the gate open enough to squeeze through and pressed himself against the back wall of the house.

The backyard was empty. Ted O'Shaughnessy had disappeared, almost certainly inside the house. Green beckoned to Sullivan and the two of them inched along the back of the house. Up ahead was a large window, further on a set of French doors, and at the far end, a smaller bay window. Ted must have entered by the French doors.

Green signalled Sullivan to check in the first window while he ducked along to the French doors. He pressed himself against the wall, feeling the rough brick against his cheek as he edged forward to peer through the door. He could make out the leather sofas and floor-to-ceiling fieldstone fireplace of the family room. Sullivan came up behind him.

"Nothing," he whispered, barely audible above the driving rain and howling wind.

Green reached to lay his hand on the door handle, and Sullivan grabbed it. He shook his head vigorously.

"We need to hear," Green whispered. He pressed down on the handle and felt the door give. It creaked as it drifted open, and both detectives ducked back out of the line of fire. Nothing. Gripping their guns, they stepped through the door onto the polished hardwood floor and eased the door shut, closing the wind and rain behind them. Now Green could hear the faint strains of music. He recognized the sound. Soft, seductive jazz. He held his breath and cocked his head. No voices, just the occasional groan. It could have been a moan of pleasure or a whimper of fear. Beside the family room, the kitchen was also empty, its counters clear except for a collection of empty wine bottles near the sink. He tried to recall the layout of the house. Ahead lay the hall and to the right the closed door leading to the home office. But the jazz wafted through the house from a distant room.

Were McIntyre and Crystal in one of the bedrooms, he wondered? Even more important, where the hell was Ted O'Shaughnessy?

His questions were answered by the ear-splitting crack of a rifle shot, followed by a girl's scream and a man's hoarse shout. The detectives hit the floor and rolled behind the couch, fumbling to aim their guns at the doorway.

"Jumpin' Jesus," a man bellowed from some far recess of the house. "Ted! You could have fucking killed me!"

"If I wanted to kill you, you'd be dead. I want answers!"

In the background, a girl wailed.

"Ted, take it easy, before somebody gets hurt."

"Get up and get away from the girl."

"Ted, you don't want to—"

"Get away from the girl!"

"Now listen to me, you ungrateful prick—"

Another shot rang out. The girl's shriek rose higher.

"You gonna shoot the girl, huh? Is that what you want?"

"This is all your fault!" O'Shaughnessy roared, and Green could hear an edge of hysteria in his voice. He and Sullivan were racing across the house and up the stairs. No need for stealth, just speed. "Riley may never play again! You fed him drugs—"

"He never touched drugs—"

"Performance enhancers! You made him crash. All because you didn't want him to see that girl!"

"That was this little lady's idea," McIntyre replied. "She came up with the plan. You want to kill her too?"

"She's a kid, McIntyre."

"Some kid. Look at these melons. Want a piece of her too?"

The girl's only response was a whimper.

"You're sick!" Ted snapped. "Why did you do it, huh? You

291

couldn't control him any more? He wouldn't listen to you?"

"Come on, Ted, don't play innocent," McIntyre snapped. "He was off his game. The most important playoffs of his career, and his focus was shot, all because he was thinking with his dick. Everybody said do something!"

From the top of the stairs, Green could now see Ted looming in the doorway of the bedroom at the end of the hall. He was facing into the room, brandishing his rifle.

"Riley would never take drugs! You tricked him, you freaked him out, and now it's all over. His life, my life..."

As he crept down the hall, Green steadied his gun with both hands. Mentally rehearsed procedure. Aim weapon. *Police! Don't move!* He prayed for calm. Over the barrel, he glimpsed the massive bed with its red silk duvet tossed on the floor. McIntyre was crouched on the bed in a tangle of sheets, his doughy skin glistening in the reddish glow of a dozen romantic sconces. In his arms, her naked body pressed against his as a shield, was a wide-eyed, sobbing girl. She was rigidly still, but as Green reached the door, her eyes locked on his. For a split-second, they widened.

O'Shaughnessy lifted his rifle and started to swing towards the door. Adrenaline shot through Green, and he was just aiming his Glock and preparing to shout when Sullivan barrelled past him and slammed his footballer's shoulder into O'Shaughnessy's side. The rifle flew up in the air, hit the ceiling and clattered harmlessly to the floor. Green dived to retrieve it, keeping his eye fixed on McIntyre and his gun trained on O'Shaughnessy. The man flailed briefly beneath Sullivan's weight, but within ten seconds, Sullivan had him pinned and cuffed.

Crystal had scrambled to the corner, where she cowered, shivering and weeping. Green grabbed the red duvet from the floor and threw it over her.

At that moment, the Tactical Unit burst through the door.

Twenty-Two

McIntyre's house was in chaos for most of the afternoon. Two CID teams arrived to handle the arrests of both McIntyre and O'Shaughnessy. Lou Paquette and his partner showed up with the official search warrant, grumbling about the mountain of physical evidence already collected in the Lea Kovacev case.

"Tell the bad guys not to do another major crime for at least six months," he warned the CID teams in his gravelly, whiskey-soaked voice.

Paramedics swept in to examine Crystal and ultimately take her to the hospital. The girl had been virtually mute since her rescue and huddled in the corner, refusing to answer questions.

"She's in shock," the senior paramedic told Green. "Plus she's stoned. She's lethargic and doesn't seem to remember how she got here."

"Did he rape her?"

The paramedic shrugged. "I'll leave that for the ER team to determine. There are no visible signs of assault, but I'm betting he fed her something."

Once he'd recovered his dignity and his clothes, McIntyre began to scream about lawsuits and criminal charges. He protested his innocence all the way into the back of the cruiser, demanding to speak to his lawyer, Green's superior and "whoever really wears the pants in your chicken-shit organization." He said Crystal and he had a special relationship, and that he'd never realized she was only sixteen. If she was on drugs, she had taken them herself.

Ted O'Shaughnessy said very little, but watched in resigned silence as McIntyre was driven away. A tow truck arrived to take Ted's pick-up truck to the impound yard. Even from a cursory glance, Green could tell Ted had washed the truck bed clean with a pressure washer, but there were plenty of cracks and crevices where blood could still cling. Lyle Cunningham promised he'd examine it as soon as he could climb over the bags of evidence already piled up in his lab.

On Sullivan's advice, Ted didn't say a word about Jenna's murder, but he showed no surprise when the charge was read out, nor did he proclaim his outraged innocence. Green stood on the front lawn and watched him as he was bundled into the back of the cruiser. He looked like a man shell-shocked by the unravelling of his life, as much in disbelief about his own actions as others were.

Sullivan appeared at Green's side, car keys in hand. "You coming with me?"

Green hesitated. He was still flying high on adrenaline, and he knew what awaited him back at the station. Not the thrill of interviewing the witnesses and wrapping up the case, but hours of debriefing, media clamour and damage control. Guns had been drawn, Tac orders ignored, civilians placed in harm's way. It didn't matter that no one had been killed, no shots had been fired, at least by police, and two suspects were now in custody with promising cases against them. The minutia of police protocol would come before all else.

Meanwhile here at McIntyre's house, Lou Paquette and his partner were just starting a thorough search of the premises. Green wanted to hang around to ensure that they uncovered all the sleazy secrets he knew lay within.

By the time he arrived back at the station three hours later, the adrenaline had worn off, but he felt the triumph of a case well solved. Paquette had been able to seize all the photographs, videos, bottles and pills. If even a few of the seizures contained something illegal—underage girls, crystal meth or designer drugs—they should have enough to put the bastard out of circulation for a few years.

Lea's panties were just the crowning touch. Paquette ordered DNA testing right away, and maybe in the end, it would be through those panties that Lea would be able to extract her final revenge.

After enduring a remarkably painless preliminary debriefing with Devine, who was just happy that the whole fiasco looked like a success on the six o'clock news, Green arrived down in the squad room to find Sullivan at his computer, preparing his interview notes for Ted O'Shaughnessy. Sullivan glanced up. "You want to be in on this, Mike?"

Green shook his head. "And I don't think you should be either."

Sullivan frowned. "There's no history between me and Ted."

"We're both too close, after what went down today. We can coach from the video room, but let's give it to Gibbs. It's time we gave him something to shoot for."

Sullivan gave him a long, searching stare but put up no resistance. Neither did Ted O'Shaughnessy when Gibbs completed the preliminaries and invited him to talk. Ted had met with a lawyer, but had ignored his pleas to remain silent. He sat rigidly in the interview chair, staring down at the table. Grey stubble darkened his chin, and his eyes were hollow.

"I don't care about me," he said. "What the fuck does it matter any more? McIntyre's ruined everything, but you'll never get him, you know. He'll weasel out of everything. That girl... I overheard him talking to her in the bedroom, saying he could really help her get ahead, promising her invites to his special parties and dates with his hottest prospects, if she kept quiet about him supplying her the drugs. She was so high, she would have agreed to anything. I couldn't stand to think of him manipulating yet another naïve young kid. I didn't know what I was going to do when I actually found the asshole— probably just scare the shit out of him—but when I heard him smooth-talking her, I wanted to kill the bastard."

Watching from the video room, Sullivan groaned. "Ted," he muttered to himself, "you don't want to say that till you've talked to your lawyer again."

Green glanced at him questioningly, but Sullivan didn't meet his eye.

Gibbs's voice came through the speakers. "Why don't you start at the beginning?"

Ted seemed caught up in his own memories. "This is my fault. From the very beginning. Not noticing the signs, what the guy was really like. Riley's coach tried to warn me, but being down in Gan, with him being up here... But that's no excuse." He clenched his large fists on the table and thrust himself back in the chair, as if to retreat from the truth. "My wife tried to warn me too, but I kept pushing it. I pushed my son right into the asshole's clutches."

No one in the video room dared move. Green leaned forward intently. "Let him run," he breathed into the earphone. "Wait him out."

Gibbs didn't move. Didn't speak.

Ted bowed his head and pressed his fingers to his temples. "This past week has been sheer hell. I love my son, and I'd do anything for him, but I could tell he'd been on edge, even before his girlfriend died. Like he was wired. Temper flare-ups, refusing to follow his training. I thought it was the pressure, but it was the fucking drugs McIntyre had been slipping him.

So when his girlfriend turned up dead, thrown in the river, I thought Riley did it." He pressed his eyes shut, his chin quivering. "God help me, I didn't trust my own son."

Sullivan slapped the video room wall, sending a shock wave through the tiny room. "Jesus, Mary and Joseph! That's the missing motive! That's the father I can understand."

Green hushed him sharply. He was watching Ted. Watching the proud, defiant man disintegrate before their eyes.

"Tell me about Jenna Zukowski," Gibbs said quietly. Unprompted. Good boy, thought Green. Subtle, supportive, a rock solid delivery. Not a single stutter.

O'Shaughnessy wagged his head slowly back and forth. Began to weep. "Knowing what I do now—that Riley didn't do it, that he called that fucking snake for advice—I'd give anything to have that moment back. To take back that punch. She was demanding to see Riley to ask him about his relationship with Lea. I panicked. One punch. That's all it was." He flexed his fist and stared at it through streaming eyes, as if it were an alien affront. "It sent her flying back against the fireplace. Everyone was out of the house, and once I realized I'd killed her, I knew I had to get rid of the body. Cutting her up, hiding her in garbage bags in the back of my truck, waiting till dark... That was the longest wait of my life. And then having to go back in the morning, to make sure I hadn't left any traces. I just kept thinking, I have to get rid of all the evidence, I have to erase that this happened." He dragged a deep, sobbing breath into his lungs. "God, if I only could."

An hour later, Gibbs emerged from the interview room with the entire confession neatly on disk. For the first time in weeks, he wore a broad smile, but he was reluctant to hang around for congratulations.

"I want to go see Sue, tell her the good news. Keeping up with the cases..." He flushed and gave a shy smile. "It kind of makes her day."

Green knew there was no rebuke in his words, but he felt the sting anyway. It had been on the tip of his tongue to tell Gibbs to say hello to her for him, but he stopped himself. That was not something that could be done by proxy any longer.

Gradually, the squad room emptied as detectives headed off shift for a celebratory drink together. Green spotted Sullivan shrugging on his coat and shoving his keys in his pocket, ready to head out alone. At the end of the session, he had not joined in the general cheer, but had left the video room without a word and had busied himself with follow-up notes.

Green stopped him with a firm hand on his arm. "We need to talk."

Sullivan ran his broad hand through his hair, making it stand in erratic spikes. "Mike, can it wait till tomorrow? I'm bushed."

"Let's go grab a quick beer by ourselves at the Mayflower. My tab."

The Mayflower Pub had been a fixture on Elgin Street for decades, long before trendier pubs and restaurants had gentrified the neighbourhood. A noisy cluster of patrons ringed the bar watching a baseball game, but the two detectives found a quiet booth at the rear and ordered draughts. Green waited while Sullivan took a deep slug of Kilkenny. The big detective had been avoiding his eyes, but now he looked him square on.

"Okay, Mike. What's on your mind?"

"You should have shot him when we got to the doorway. It turned out okay, but that rifle could have killed any one of us if it had gone off. Not to mention I could have shot you myself. If the brass ever found out..."

Sullivan's eyes probed his. "They're not going to hear it from me, Mike."

"Nor me, you dope. But don't put it past McIntyre to use

anything he can to discredit our actions."

Sullivan shrugged. "McIntyre is pond scum. I wasn't going to shoot Ted just to save his despicable ass." His expression grew sombre. "I've never shot a man, Mike. It's not as easy as our training tries to make it. I looked at Ted in the doorway, and I saw a father of a teenage boy, a father who spent most of his free time driving that kid around the province in pursuit of his dream. A dream that's just been shattered in the blink of an eye, because he'd put his trust in that snake. I could feel his rage. There but for the grace of God..."

Green set down his beer, untouched. "But don't forget the other side of that rage. That same dream drove the father to strike an innocent woman and then chop her body into pieces."

"I know. I wasn't thinking of that when my finger refused to squeeze the trigger. Maybe if I had..." He tossed back half his beer, and Green saw the faint tremor in his hand.

* * *

It was almost nine o'clock when Green arrived back home. The sky had cleared, and the June sun had just set. Long spears of orange shot across the darkening sky. He had stopped on his way home to visit Sue Peters and had walked with her and Gibbs out onto the grounds of the rehab centre to enjoy the last warm rays of the sinking sun. Sue had leaned on Gibbs as they walked, but Green sensed that perhaps that was more by choice than by necessity. Her face still bore the scars of her beating, and her speech was more measured, as if each word now required conscious thought. But she had stood unsupported while he told her he was looking for a way to get her back into the squad room, even if only a couple of hours a week for now, and he pretended not to see the tears that sprang to her eyes.

Afterwards, he had longed to drive straight down to the cottage, but when he drove through a red light and missed the turn to his own street, he realized the roller coaster day had finally caught up with him. Besides, there were still far too many loose ends to tie up on the case before he could even consider escaping to the country. Furthermore, he'd not had a chance to connect with Hannah since her close call the day before, and he was grateful to hear the television blaring through the house when he opened the door.

He found Hannah sitting on the living room floor, chatting on her cell phone as if nothing had happened. He felt an overwhelming desire to hug her, but contented himself with a quick kiss on her head. To his surprise, she hung up her phone and shut off the TV.

"I've been watching the news. That unidentified female minor they're talking about at the agent's house? Was that Crystal?"

Green hesitated, then threw the rule book out the window. After what she'd done for Crystal yesterday, Hannah deserved to know. He sat down beside her on the couch. "Yes. She's all right. Physically, that is. McIntyre claimed he wasn't going to hurt her, just persuade her not to implicate him in the drugs Lea took." Seeing her roll her eyes in disbelief, he shrugged. "I know. Hard to disprove, though. He claimed the bad drugs were all Crystal's doing, to get Riley away from Lea."

"That's bullshit."

"Is it?"

She raised her head, startled. She was without her trademark pale make-up and black eyes, which had served so well to camouflage her, and without them she looked ten years old. Her pixie expression grew thoughtful.

"When we were talking yesterday," she said, "she didn't seem upset about Lea—like, dying and stuff. I mean, not as upset as you'd expect. She was more worried about herself, about getting caught and going to jail. She never said that McIntyre tricked her or that she didn't know about the laced drugs, just that no one was supposed to die."

Green thought about her increasingly worried cell phone messages to Lea that night. Yes, the girl had known the drugs were dangerous. Potentially deadly. "Do you think she could be that conniving and cold-blooded to not care if Lea died?"

"She always was a stupid, selfish girl. Beyond that..." Hannah lifted her palms in a gesture of defeat. "They were probably in it together. Who knows which one had the original idea."

We'll probably never know for sure, thought Green, reviewing the fleeting glimpses he'd had of the girl. First, standing at the accident scene, slack with horror and grief at the carnage she had unleashed. Then slouching defiantly out of the interview room under the dead-eyed stare of her stepfather. And finally, cowering in the corner of McIntyre's lair, her raw fear already giving way to defeat.

The fight for survival, the primacy of self, was all she'd ever known.

Crystal had no priors, and she was only sixteen years old. She came from a wretched, loveless home and had been lured into dubious company. She'd get a slap on the wrist, maybe six months' probation, then she'd be free again, back in the same wretched home with the same sleazy friends. Until life dangled another temptation in front of her eyes.

As if she were reading his mind, Hannah leaned over and picked a long dog hair off her grungy jeans. "I've been thinking... Next fall I want to go to regular high school. The kids at Norman Bethune... I don't really fit in any more."

Next fall, he thought, and his chest tightened. He'd won a reprieve, and maybe—just maybe—he was starting to be a father to this girl.

Barbara Fradkin was born in Montreal and obtained her PhD in psychology. Her work as a child psychologist has provided ample inspiration and insight for plotting murders.

Her novels featuring Ottawa Police Inspector Michael Green are *Do or Die* (2000), *Once Upon a Time* (2002), *Mist Walker* (2003), *Fifth Son* (2004), *Honour Among Men* (2006), and *Dream Chasers*. *Fifth Son* won Best Novel at the 2005 Arthur Ellis Awards, and *Honour Among Men* repeated the honour in 2007.

Fradkin lives in Ottawa, Ontario.

Acknowledgements

Dream Chasers is a work of fiction, and although all the locales in Ottawa and Eastern Ontario do exist, the people and events are the invention of the author, and any resemblance to actual people is purely coincidental.

As always, I am grateful to all the people who contributed to the accuracy or polish of this manuscript. First of all, to my terrific friends in the Ladies Killing Circle, Joan Boswell, Vicki Cameron, Mary Jane Maffini, Sue Pike and Linda Wiken, who scoured the earliest draft with an eye to logic flaws and bad writing. Secondly, to my agent, Leona Trainer, editor Allister Thompson and publisher Sylvia McConnell at Napoleon for all their support. Thanks also to Dr. Doug Lyle for his input on issues related to drowning.

Lastly, a very special thanks to Mark Cartwright of the Ottawa Police for his continued generosity and support in reviewing my work to ensure that I don't bend police procedure beyond all recognition.

Do or Die

An Inspector Green Mystery

Barbara Fradkin

In the first novel of the series, Inspector Michael Green is obsessed with his job, a condition which has almost ruined his marriage several times. When the biggest case of his career comes up, his relationships and many people's lives are put into grave danger. A student is found expertly stabbed in the stacks of a university library. As Green probes into the circumstances of the man's life, a web of jealousy and intrigue is revealed. He finds himself emboiled in a rivalry in the delicate arena of university politics, where gigantic egos collide.

"Do or Die *is a wonderfully entertaining first novel.*"
-Peter Robinson, author of the Inspector Banks mysteries

ISBN 978-0-929141-78-7, $12.95 CDN, $10.95 U.S.,
264 pages, 5 1/8" x 7 1/2", trade paper

Once Upon a Time

An Inspector Green Mystery

Barbara Fradkin

Shortlisted for an Arthur Ellis Award for Best Novel

When an old man dies a seemingly natural death in a parking lot, only Green finds it suspicious. Why did the victim have a mysterious gash on his head? The family secrecy only increases Green's curiosity. A search of his house turns up an old tool box containing a German ID card from World War II. Was the victim a Jewish camp survivor or a collaborator who had sold out his own people? Could someone have tracked him down for revenge? This tightly plotted police mystery is a compelling tale of unhealed emotional wounds from a time of unspeakable atrocity.

"An entertaining, darkly comedic tale worth the price of admission..."
-The Ottawa Citizen

ISBN 978-0-929141-84-8, $12.95 CDN, $10.95 U.S.,
264 pages, 5 1/8" x 7 1/2", trade paper

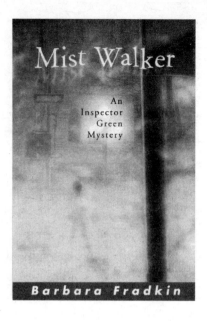

Matthew Fraser was an idealistic young teacher accused of sexually assaulting a schoolgirl and acquitted in a sensational case that left the truth hidden and his life in tatters. Ten years later, his distraught confidante walks into Inspector Green's office insisting that Fraser has vanished. Green's curiosity is piqued when he discovers that Fraser left behind his beloved dog and an apartment crammed with research on his case. Has Fraser fled to escape the wrath of his victims, new or old? Or was he innocent all along and spent the last few years trying to clear his name?

"...leads us through an unsettlingly realistic investigative maze that lays bare the mine fields surrounding pedophilia...
Mist Walker *is the gold standard for the series."*
-The Ottawa Citizen

ISBN 978-0-929141-78-7, $12.95 CDN, $10.95 U.S.,
264 pages, 5 1/8" x 7 1/2", trade paper

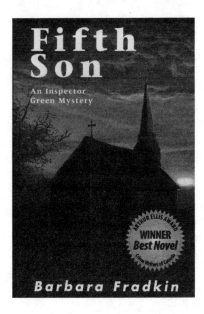

Winner of the Arthur Ellis Award for Best Novel

Accident or suicide? That's the simple question put to Inspector Green when a derelict stranger falls to his death from an abandoned church tower in a quiet river village at the edge of his jurisdiction. But when the victim turns out be a long lost son of a local farm family cursed in recent years by tragedy, madness and death, Green begins to suspect something far more sinister is at work. Probing the family's past, he uncovers a toxic mix of rigid fundamentalism, teenage rebellion and a family secret so horrific that twenty years later, someone is still desperate to prevent the truth from coming to light.

"Barbara Fradkin's Inspector Michael Green series gets better with every book...it all works beautifully right up the twist at the end."
-The Globe and Mail

*ISBN 978-1-894917-13-1, $13.95 CDN, $11.95 U.S.,
304 pages, 5 1/8" x 7 1/2", trade paper*

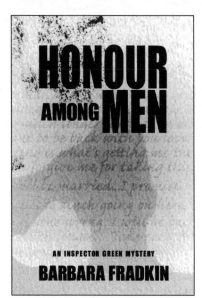

Winner of
the Arthur
Ellis Award
for Best Novel

AN INSPECTOR GREEN MYSTERY

BARBARA FRADKIN

Inspector Green is coping with an office job, still eager to get back into the day-to-day fray of policing. His chance comes when an unidentified woman is drowned in the Ottawa River. In her possession is a Medal for Bravery from a Canadian peacekeeping mission. As Green and his team dig deeper into the military past, Green finds himself sucked not only into the murky past of a peacekeeping unit but into the high-stakes present of a federal election race. What crime was committed in Yugoslavia more than a decade ago? And does the diary of a dead soldier hold the key?

*"Fradkin...gets better with each outing...
the story seems eerily prescient."*
-The Globe and Mail

*"Canadian crime fiction is having a banner year...
with the publication of Barbara Fradkin's*
Honour Among Men, *it just got even better."*
-Halifax Chronicle-Herald

*ISBN 978-1-894917-36-0, $15.95 CDN, $13.95 U.S.,
352 pages, 5 1/8" x 7 1/2", trade paper*